Ruthless...
Three Latin
what –
Nothing and ... ...
their way; but even the best-laid plans
don't turn out quite as expected...

BEDDED
by
BLACKMAIL

Three intense, exciting romances –
seduction and glamour guaranteed! –
from bestselling authors **Lynne Graham**,
Jacqueline Baird and **Trish Morey**.

BEDDED BY BLACKMAIL
Lynne Graham
Jacqueline Baird
Trish Morey

Available in April 2010

BEDDED FOR REVENGE
Julia James
Carole Mortimer
Trish Morey

Available in May 2010

BEDDED *by* BLACKMAIL

LYNNE GRAHAM

JACQUELINE BAIRD

TRISH MOREY

All the characters in this book have no existence outside the imagination of the author, and have no relation whatsoever to anyone bearing the same name or names. They are not even distantly inspired by any individual known or unknown to the author, and all the incidents are pure invention.

All Rights Reserved including the right of reproduction in whole or in part in any form. This edition is published by arrangement with Harlequin Enterprises II B.V./S.à.r.l. The text of this publication or any part thereof may not be reproduced or transmitted in any form or by any means, electronic or mechanical, including photocopying, recording, storage in an information retrieval system, or otherwise, without the written permission of the publisher.

This book is sold subject to the condition that it shall not, by way of trade or otherwise, be lent, resold, hired out or otherwise circulated without the prior consent of the publisher in any form of binding or cover other than that in which it is published and without a similar condition including this condition being imposed on the subsequent purchaser.

M&B™ and M&B™ with the Rose Device
are trademarks of the publisher.
Harlequin Mills & Boon Limited, Eton House,
18-24 Paradise Road, Richmond, Surrey TW9 1SR

BEDDED BY BLACKMAIL
© Harlequin Enterprises II B.V./S.à.r.l. 2010

Reluctant Mistress, Blackmailed Wife © Lynne Graham 2006
The Italian's Blackmailed Mistress © Jacqueline Baird 2006
The Spaniard's Blackmailed Bride © Trish Morey 2007

ISBN: 978 0 263 88024 3

012-0410

Harlequin Mills & Boon policy is to use papers that are natural, renewable and recyclable products and made from wood grown in sustainable forests. The logging and manufacturing processes conform to the legal environmental regulations of the country of origin.

Printed and bound in Spain
by Litografia Rosés S.A., Barcelona

RELUCTANT MISTRESS, BLACKMAILED WIFE

LYNNE GRAHAM

Lynne Graham was born in Northern Ireland, and has been a keen Mills & Boon® reader since her teens. She is very happily married, with an understanding husband who has learned to cook since she started to write! Her five children keep her on her toes. She has a very large dog, which knocks everything over, a very small terrier, which barks a lot, and two cats. When time allows, Lynne is a keen gardener.

Look out for Lynne Graham's latest exciting novel, *Virgin on Her Wedding Night*, available in May 2010 from Mills & Boon® Modern™.

CHAPTER ONE

As wry amusement lit his eyes, which could be as dark and deep as an underground river, Alexandros Christakis watched his grandfather walk round the sleek silver Ascari KZ1 he had just had delivered. A supercar, it was the ultimate boy-toy, for only fifty would ever be built. The older man's excitement at being that close to such a rare and powerful vehicle was palpable.

'A car that costs almost a quarter of a million.' Pelias, tall and straight in spite of his seventy-five years, shook his grizzled head and smiled with almost boyish approval. 'It is sheer madness, but it does my heart good to see you taking an interest in such things again!'

Alexandros said nothing in response to that leading comment, his expression unrevealing, his legendary reserve impenetrable. Gossip columnists regularly referred to the billionaire head of the CTK Bank as beautiful. Alexandros loathed the press, and had little time for such frivolity. His lean, bronzed features might have a breath-taking symmetry that turned female heads wherever he went, but the forceful angle of his jawline, the tough slant of his cheekbones and the obdurate set of his wide, sensual mouth suggested a fierce strength of character that was more of a warning to the unwary.

'You're still a young man—only thirty-one years old.' Pelias Christakis spoke with caution, for he had long been in awe of his brilliant grandson and rarely dared breach his reticence. 'Naturally I understand that you will never forget your grief, but it is time for you to take up your life once more.'

Marvelling at the old man's essential innocence, Alexandros murmured flatly, 'I took my life back a long time ago.'

'But all you have done since Ianthe passed away is work, and make more and more money from bigger and bigger deals! How much money can one man need in a lifetime? How many homes can one man use?' Pelias Christakis flung up his hands in an extrovert gesture that encompassed the superb Regency country house in front of him. And Dove Hall was only one item in his grandson's vast property portfolio. 'You are already rich beyond most men's dreams.'

'I thought onwards and upwards was the Christakis motto.' Alexandros brooded on the unhappy truth that people were never satisfied. He had been raised to be an Alpha-male high-achiever, with the merciless killer instincts of a shark. He was competitive, ambitious, and aggressive when challenged. Every aspect of his upbringing had been carefully tailored to ensure that he grew up as the exact opposite of his late father, who had been a lifelong layabout and an embarrassment to his family.

'I'm proud of you—immensely proud,' his grandfather hastened to assert in an apologetic undertone. 'But the world can offer you so much more than the next takeover or merger. Companionship may seem an old-fashioned concept—'

'Of course there have been women.' Alexandros compressed his handsome mouth, only his respect for the older man's good intentions restraining him from the delivery of a more caustic response. 'Is that what you want to hear?'

Pelias raised a beetling brow in rueful emphasis. 'I'll be more interested to hear that you've been with the same woman for longer than a week!'

Exasperated by that censorious response, Alexandros immediately grasped what his grandfather was driving at, and cold annoyance overpowered tolerance. 'But I'm not in the market for anything serious. I have no intention of getting married again.'

His companion treated him to a look of surprise. 'Did I mention marriage?'

Unimpressed by that air of virtuous naivety—for Pelias was not a good dissembler—Alexandros said nothing. He was grimly aware that the very fact that he was an only child put an extra weight of expectation and responsibility on him. Traditional Greek culture set great store on the carrying on of the family name. Understandably, his grandparents held the convictions of their age group. But Alexandros felt equally entitled to his own views, and believed that only honesty would suffice. As he had not the slightest desire to be a father, he had no plans to remarry. Becoming a parent had been his late wife's dream, if not her obsession. Now that Ianthe was gone, he saw no reason to pretend otherwise.

'I don't want another wife…or children, for that matter,' Alexandros admitted in a flat, unapologetic undertone, his lean dark face aloof. 'I appreciate that this must disappoint you, but that's how it is and I'm not going to change.'

Pelias Christakis had lost colour. Stripped of all the natural exuberance of his warm, engaging personality, he suddenly looked old, troubled, and very much at a loss. Feeling like the guy who had not only killed but also tortured Santa Claus, Alexandros suppressed any urge to soften the blow and raise false hopes. It had had to be said.

* * *

Now a veteran at jumble sales, Katie leapt straight into the competitive fray, rummaging through the pile of baby clothes. Emerging victorious with an incredibly smart little jacket and trouser set, she asked the lady on the stall, 'How much for this?'

It was more than she could afford, and she put it back with a regret that was only fleeting—because she had long since learned that her real priorities were shelter, food and warmth. Clothes came fourth on her survival list of necessities, so newness and smartness were almost always out of reach. She found a sweater and a pair of jeans at a price within her means. Though both garments were shabby they had plenty of life left in them. The twins were growing so fast that keeping them clothed was a constant challenge. As she paid, the lady offered to reduce the price on the trouser set, but Katie flushed and said no thanks, for she had now spent what she had to spare. The pity she saw in the woman's eyes embarrassed her.

'They're lovely boys,' the stallholder said reluctantly. She had noticed that Katie's hands were bare of rings, and although she hoped she was a charitable woman she very much disapproved of young unwed mothers.

Katie glanced at her sons, seated side by side in the worn twin buggy, and a rueful smile of maternal pride crept across the weary line of her mouth. Toby and Connor were gorgeous babies, and very well advanced for their age of nine months. The combination of black curly hair, pale golden skin and big brown eyes gave them an angelic air that was rather deceptive. The twins thrived on attention and activity, screeched the place down when disappointed, whinged at length when bored, and required very little sleep. But Katie absolutely adored them, and often studied them with the dazed feeling that she could not possibly have given birth to two such clever and beautiful children. Not only did they not look like her, they did not act like her either. Only in low moments, when she was fighting total exhaustion, was she willing to admit that she was finding it a real struggle to cope with their constant demands.

On the walk home, she found herself looking at other young women. It bothered her when she caught herself thinking that the ones without kids seemed more youthful, light-hearted and attractive. She saw her reflection in a shop window and stared, her heart sinking. Suddenly she wanted to cry. There had been a time when, had she made the required effort, she would have been called pretty. Now that was just a memory, and she was a small thin girl with a pinched face and red hair caught back in a ponytail. She looked nondescript and plain. She swallowed hard, knowing that Toby and Connor's father would never look at her now.

Once she had marvelled that he had ever deigned to notice her. She had thought it was so romantic that a dazzlingly attractive male who could have had literally any woman should instead have chosen her. But the passage of time and cruel experience had destroyed her fanciful illusions one by one and forced her to face less palatable truths. Now Katie accepted that he had only noticed her because she had been the sole female in his vicinity when he'd felt like sex. She had given him what he wanted without making a single demand. He had never at any stage regarded her as anything other than a social inferior—for he had never even taken her out on a date. When her breathless adoration had palled, he had dumped her so hard and fast she still shivered thinking about it. Nothing had ever hurt her as much as that cold, harsh descent from fantasy to reality.

Only a few minutes after she'd got back to her bedsit, her landlord appeared at her door. 'You'll have to go,' he told her bluntly. 'I've had another complaint about the noise your kids make at night.'

Katie stared at him in horror. 'But all babies cry—'

'And two babies make twice as much of a din.'

'I swear I'll try to keep them quieter—'

'You said that the last time I spoke to you, and nothing's changed,' the older man cut in, unimpressed. 'You've had your warning and I'm giving you two weeks' notice. If you don't move out willingly, I'll have you evicted. So let's keep it simple. Get yourself down to Social Services and they'll soon sort you out with another place!'

Appalled at his belligerent attitude, Katie tried in vain to reason with him. Long after he had gone, she sat with her arms wrapped round herself while she fought the awful feeling of despair stealing over her. She was painfully aware that she had virtually no hope of fighting such a decree when complaints had been lodged against her. Her tenancy was only of the unassured variety, and she did not even feel she could blame the other tenants for kicking up a fuss. The walls were paper-thin and the twins did regularly cry at night.

The bedsit needed decorating, the furniture was battered and the shared facilities were dismal. But the room had still come to feel like home to Katie. Furthermore, the building was in good repair and the area was reasonably respectable and safe. She was not afraid to walk down the street. Unlike during her pregnancy, when she had spent a couple of months in a flat on an inner city estate. Drug dealing and gang warfare had been a way of life there, and she had been terrified every time she'd had to go out.

Although she had been about to put Toby and Connor

down for a nap, she realised that she would have to go straight back out again. In two short weeks she would be homeless, and she needed to give the housing authorities as much time as possible to locate alternative accommodation for them. Just when had she sunk so low that she no longer had the power to help herself? She blinked back a sudden rush of tears. She was twenty-three years old. She had always been a doer—independent, energetic and industrious. But she had not realised how difficult it would be to raise two children alone. She had not realised how poor she would be either. Indeed, in the latter stages of pregnancy she had made enthusiastic plans about getting her career back on track. She had expected to return to full-time employment, not end up dependent on welfare handouts for survival. Ill-health, accommodation problems, transport costs and sleepless nights had slowly but surely destroyed her hopes.

A week crawled past, during which Katie did everything she could to find somewhere else to live. But the few leads she had got turned into dead ends. Midway through the second week she began to panic, and a social worker informed her that she would have to go into emergency bed and breakfast accommodation.

'You'll hate it,' her friend Leanne Carson declared. 'The room won't be yours to do what you want with, and there probably won't be any cooking facilities.'

'I know,' Katie muttered heavily.

'Crying babies won't be flavour of the month there either.' The pretty blue-eyed brunette whom Katie had met in hospital sighed, 'You'll be moved on again in no time. Why are you being such a doormat?'

'What do you mean?'

'You told me that the twins' dad had money. Why don't

you spread a little of that cash in your own direction? If the stingy creep is newsworthy and wealthy enough, you could sell your story to the press.'

'Don't be daft.' Katie pressed pale fingers to her pounding temples.

'Of course you'd have to spice the story up. Ten-times-a-night sex, how insatiable or kinky his demands were— you know the sort of thing…'

Katie reddened to the roots of her hair. 'No, I don't—'

'The sordid details are what make tittle-tattle like that entertaining and worth oodles of cash. Don't be such a prude! The guy's a total bastard. He deserves to be embarrassed!'

'Maybe he does, but I couldn't do it. That's not what I'm about. I appreciate that you're only trying to help, but—'

'You're never going to get up out of the gutter with that bad attitude.' Leanne rolled scornful eyes heavy with mascara and glittering blue shadow. 'Are you just going to lie down and die? Let the bloke get away with it? If you really love your little boys, you'll be ready to do whatever it takes to give them a better life!'

Katie flinched as though she had been slapped.

Leanne dealt her a defiant look. 'It's true, and you know it is. You're letting the kids' father…this Alexandros whatever…you're letting him escape his responsibilities.'

'I contacted the Child Support Agency—'

'Yeah, like they've got the time and resources to try and pin your kids on some foreign business tycoon! He's rich. He'd refuse to take DNA tests, or he'd stay out of the country, or pretend he'd lost all his money. If you insist on playing it by the book, you'll never see a penny from him,' the other woman forecast with cynical conviction. 'No, if you ask me, you're only going to escape your current problems if you do a kiss-and-tell for the tabloids!'

Katie couldn't sleep that night. She thought of the sacrifices her own mother had had to make to bring her up.
Widowed when her daughter was only six, Maura had had
to work as a cleaner, a caretaker and a cook to make ends
meet. In the darkness, Katie lay still and taut with discomfiture. Alexandros had dumped her, ignored her appeal for
help and broken her stupid heart. She had decided she
would sooner starve than appeal to him again. But had she
let false pride get in the way of her duty towards her infant
sons? Was Leanne right? Could she have done more to
press her case with Alexandros?

Two days later, Katie moved out of her bedsit with
Leanne's help. Luckily her friend was able to store some
stuff for her. The surplus had to be dumped or passed on
to be sold on a market stall, because Katie could not afford
storage costs. The bed and breakfast hotel was crowded and
her room was small, drab and depressing.

After spending her first night there, Katie rose heavy-
eyed, but driven by a new and fierce determination. She had
decided that she was willing to do whatever it took to give
Toby and Connor a secure roof over their heads. The
prospect of public embarrassment and humiliation and
further rejection should not deter her. Right now she was
letting her kids down by acting like a wimp, she told herself
squarely. Leanne had been right to speak up. More
vigorous action was definitely required.

With that in mind, Katie went to the library to use the
internet and see if she could discover any new information
about Alexandros. She had tried and failed several times
before, and quite a few months had passed since her last
effort. But this time the search offered her the option of
trying an alternative name, and when she tried that link she
stared in shock as the screen filled with potential sites. A

recognisable photo of Alexandros folded down on the very first she visited.

It only then dawned on Katie that her previous searches had been unsuccessful because she had spelled his name as Crestakis, *not* Christakis. She had got his name wrong. She was stunned. That crucial yet simple mistake had ensured that she hadn't found out that Alexandros was the chief executive of CTK Bank, which had a substantial office in London. All the time that she had been engaged in a desperate struggle for survival, Alexandros had been making regular trips to the UK!

For a while she just surfed, seeing him variously described as brilliant, beautiful, arctic-cool, impassive. This was the guy she had fallen crazily in love with, all right, although she had refused to accept back then that she was on a highway to nowhere. The nape of her neck prickled when she read a newspaper report about a merger announcement expected from CTK the next morning. If something big was in the air, Alexandros was almost certain to be putting in an appearance. If she got up early, she could go to the City, wait outside the bank, and try to intercept him when he arrived.

Of course she could also go the more normal route and ask for an appointment with him, couldn't she? Her soft mouth down-curved at that idea. She was convinced that he wouldn't agree to see her. After all, he had given her a useless phone number on which to contact him at their final meeting, and had also ignored her letter asking for his help. No, perhaps it would be wiser not to forewarn Alexandros. An element of surprise might just give her the edge she badly needed; she was no longer naive enough to believe that she could easily hold her own with someone that clever and callous.

Katie left the twins with Leanne at a very early hour the next day.

'Now, don't you take any nonsense off this guy,' her friend warned her anxiously. 'He's got more to lose than you have.'

'How do you make that out?' Katie lowered Toby and then Connor into the playpen already occupied by Leanne's daughter, Sugar. As always, she was looking around herself and wishing she was in a position to afford similar accommodation. Although her friend's home was tiny, the rainbow pastels she favoured made the rooms feel bright and welcoming even on a dull day. Helped by a family support network that Katie lacked, Leanne worked as a hairdresser. Her mother often looked after her grandchild in the evenings, and her ex-boyfriend paid maintenance.

'I bet you anything he won't want a scandal,' Leanne declared. 'According to what I've read, bankers are supposed to be a very conservative bunch…anything else makes the punters nervous!'

Conservative? That adjective danced around in the back of Katie's mind when she was on the bus. On first acquaintance, Alexandros *had* struck her as conservative—indeed, icily reserved and austere. She hadn't liked him, hadn't liked being treated like a servant, and had hated the innate habit of command that was so much a part of his bred-in-the-bone arrogant assurance. But not one of those facts had snuffed out the wicked longing he had stirred up inside her. Her response to him had shocked her, and shattered all her neat, bloodless little assumptions about her own nature. His sizzling passion had shocked her even more. He had just grabbed her up and kissed her, and then carried her off to bed without hesitation or discussion. She cringed at that recollection, which she rarely let out of her memory-bank. She had acted like a slut and—not surprisingly, in her opinion—he had treated her like one.

CTK Bank was situated in the heart of the City of London, an impressive contemporary edifice with a logo hip enough to front a top fashion brand. She stared up at the light-reflecting gleam of ranks of windows, marvelling at the sheer size and splendour of the office block. Anger flared through her nervous tension, making her restless. Alexandros Christakis was, she finally appreciated, a very wealthy and powerful man. She positioned herself at the corner of the building so that she could watch both the front and the side entrances. Employees were starting to arrive. Rain came on steadily, quickly penetrating the light jacket she wore and drenching her. With her head bent to avoid the downpour, she almost missed the big car purring to a discreet halt in the quiet side street.

Straightening with a jerk, she began to walk very fast towards the limo—if the VIP passenger was Alexandros she didn't want to miss him. Two other cars had also pulled up—one to the front of the luxury vehicle, the second to the rear. Several men emerged and fanned out across the street. Katie's scrutiny, however, was glued to the tall dark male descending from the limousine. The breeze ruffled his luxuriant ebony hair. Without warning, a painful sense of familiarity, sharp as a knife-blade, pierced Katie. She would have known him anywhere just by the angle of his imperious head and the economic grace with which he moved. The chill of sudden shocked recognition engulfed her. Her attention locked to his lean, powerful face, marking the straight slash of his black brows, the dark, deep-set allure of his brilliant gaze. Her tummy flipped and she was dazzled.

'Alexandros…' She tried to speak but her voice failed her.

Because even though he could not have heard her, for she was still too far away, he did seem to be looking her way.

Alexandros had picked up on the alert stance of his security team and zeroed in on the source. But the instant he saw the small slender figure approaching him he knew her, and he was so surprised he stopped dead in his tracks. The wet gleam of her wine-red hair and her pale heart-shaped face struck a haunting chord that plunged him into an instant flashback. He remembered sunshine streaming through a rain-washed window over that amazing hair, lighting up eyes of an almost iridescent green. It had been a stark moment of truth in an interlude that he was reluctant to recall. One of his bodyguards blocked her path with practised ease, just as a posse of paparazzi came charging down the street behind her, waving cameras.

'Inside, boss,' Cyrus, his head of security urged as Alexandros hesitated. 'Paparazzi and a homeless kid... could be a set-up!'

In one long stride, Alexandros mounted the steps and vanished into the building. A set-up? A homeless kid? Cyrus could only have been referring to Katie. Why was she still dressing like a scruffy student? And *why* had she come to see him? He could not believe that her sudden appearance after so long would be a coincidence. What did she want from him? Why would she try to approach him in a public place? Had the paparazzi been waiting and watching to see if he acknowledged her, ready to spring some kind of a trap in which he was the target? Hard suspicion flaring in his shrewd gaze, he told Cyrus to watch Katie's every move.

It took a lot to surprise Cyrus, but that instruction achieved it.

'The female you assumed was a homeless kid? Her name is Katie Fletcher. Don't let your team lose her!' Alexandros warned in rapid Greek. 'Follow her. I want to know where she lives.'

As his efficient security chief hurried back outside to carry out his orders, Alexandros switched back into working mode. Stepping into the executive lift held in readiness for him, he was immediately immersed in a quote of the latest share prices and the final adjustments to the press release to be made about the merger. When another memory tried to surface from his usually disciplined subconscious, he rooted it out with ruthless exactitude. He was not introspective. He did not relive past mistakes. In fact he had long since accepted that on the emotional front he was as cold as his reputation.

At the end of his first meeting he discovered that he had printed a K and encircled it, and the knowledge of that brief loss of concentration, that subliminal weakness that had defied his control, infuriated him.

Taken aback by the blocking technique of the security man, who had got in her way, and then rudely crowded off the pavement by the heaving, shouting and disgruntled members of the press, who had surged past her in an effort to get at Alexandros, Katie was momentarily at a loss. Alexandros had seen her. But had he recognised her? Had he sent that beefy security guy to ward her off? Would he have spoken to her if the journalists had not been present?

She thought not. He hadn't smiled, hadn't shown the smallest sign that a friendly welcome might be in the offing. He was such a bastard, she thought painfully, a horrible sense of failure seeping through her. But even as her shoulders drooped, a defiant spirit of rebellion was powering her up again. She marched back round the corner and through the front doors of the bank, and right up to the reception desk.

'I'd like to speak to Mr Christakis,' she announced.

The receptionist who came to attend to her studied Katie fixedly, as if trying to decide whether or not she was pulling her leg. In that intervening moment of assessment Katie became uncomfortably aware of her sodden hair and shabby jacket and jeans.

'I'll take your name.' The elegant young woman behind the desk switched on her professional cool. 'But I should warn you that Mr Christakis is exceptionally busy and his appointments are usually booked months in advance. Perhaps you could see someone else?'

'I want to see Alexandros. Someone else won't do. Please just see that he gets my name. He knows me.' Aware of the silent disbelief which greeted that declaration, Katie retreated with as much dignity as she could manage to a seat. She watched the receptionist commune with her two colleagues. Someone stifled a giggle, and her anxious face burned as she affected an interest she did not feel in the heavy-duty financial publications laid out for perusal on a coffee table. She was getting paranoid, she scolded herself. In all probability nobody was talking about her—just as the most likely explanation for what had happened outside was that Alexandros simply hadn't recognised her.

She lifted an uncertain hand to her wet hair and suddenly reached round to undo her ponytail. She dug a comb out of her bag and surreptitiously began to tease out the limp damp curls, praying for her natural ringlets to emerge, rather than the pure frizz that had made her scrape her hair back so tightly when she was a teenager that her eyes had used to water. She wondered why she was bothering. He wouldn't agree to see her.

While she sat there she finally registered a fact that should have occurred to her sooner. She had got his name totally wrong. Had Alexandros ever even received her letter telling him that she was pregnant? She had sent one to his Irish residence, and when there had been no answer she had sent a second one care of the rental company that had leased the house to him. But would a letter with the wrong name on it have been forwarded? What if Alexandros hadn't got either?

'Miss Fletcher?' the receptionist murmured.

Katie stood up hurriedly. 'Yes?'

'I have a call for you.'

Surprise marking her delicate triangular features, Katie accepted the cordless phone extended to her.

'Katie?'

It was Alexandros, and she was so taken aback by the sound of that dark melodic drawl of his that she almost dropped the phone. 'Alexandros?'

'I'm waiting for a fix on a satellite link and I'm afraid that I only have a few minutes. You've picked a bad day to call…'

'The merger,' she filled in, the receiver crammed tight to her ear as she wandered away in a preoccupied daze. His voice had an aching familiarity that tugged cruelly at her heartstrings and threatened to take her back in time. 'But that's why I came. I knew you'd be here, and I have to see you.'

'Why?' Alexandros enquired with the most studious casualness. Everything she had so far said was setting off warning bells of caution. 'Do you need some sort of help? Is that why you asked to see me?'

'Yes…but it's not something I can discuss on the phone or without privacy,' Katie told him tautly. 'Just out of interest…er…did you ever receive a letter from me?'

'No.'

'Oh…' Katie was stumped by that unhesitating negative, for if he didn't even know that she had been pregnant he was in for a huge shock.

'Why can't you just tell me in brief what this is about?' Alexandros enquired drily.

'Because I *have* to see you to talk about it,' she reminded him, feeling under unfair pressure and not knowing how to deal with it in the circumstances.

'That may not be possible—'

Katie lowered her voice to say, almost pleadingly, 'I wouldn't have come here if I wasn't desperate—'

'Then cut to the chase,' he cut in with cold clarity. 'I'm not into mysteries.'

A surge of angry tears burned the back of Katie's eyes. 'Okay, so you won't see me,' she gasped. 'But don't say I didn't give you the chance!'

With that ringing declaration, Katie cut the connection and marched back to the desk to return the phone. Before she could even set it down it started ringing again, and as she walked away the receptionist called her name a second time. She spun round. The handset was being offered to her. She shook her head in urgent refusal. She was uneasily conscious that quite a few people seemed to be staring in her direction, particularly a thin fair man with sharp eyes that made her colour. Without further ado she turned on her heel and headed hurriedly out of the bank.

She was furious that she had been so impulsive and naive. It had been downright stupid to try and speak to Alexandros again! He didn't want to speak to her or hear from her, and the news that he was the father of twins would be even less welcome. She reckoned that the only way she was likely to get financial help from Alexandros now would be by approaching a solicitor to make a paternity claim. But she also knew that legal wheels turned very slowly, and would not provide an answer in the short term. So she needed to think about overcoming her scruples and approaching a newspaper, she conceded unhappily.

Alexandros would be very angry with her. A shard of all too vivid memory was assailing her. She remembered throwing a breakfast tray at him and screaming. His expression of shock would live with her to her dying day. It had dawned on her then that nobody had ever spoken to Alexandros like that before, or told him that he was absolute hell to work for and impossible to please. Her disrespect had affronted him. Only when he had been persuaded to see her side of things had he been willing to forgive the offence, and he had still ended up getting his own way. *My way or the highway* was a punchline that might have coined for Alexandros Christakis.

It took Katie an hour to get back to Leanne's flat, but nobody was in when she got there. Her friend had warned her that she might go shopping with her mother, she recalled ruefully. As she walked back along the street, a limousine nudged into the kerb just ahead of her, and a big middle-aged man in a suit leapt out to jerk open the passenger door.

'Mr Christakis would like to give you a lift,' he announced.

Taken by surprise, she froze, studying the tinted black windows of the long glossy silver vehicle with frowning intensity before moving forward in abrupt acceptance of the invitation. Whether she liked it or not, she knew that it was the best offer she was likely to get. Her heartbeat racing so fast that she felt dizzy, she climbed into the limo.

CHAPTER TWO

ALEXANDROS dealt Katie a grim nod of acknowledgement that would have made her shiver, had not less cautious responses already been running rampant within her.

Lounging back in a black designer suit teamed with a striped shirt and smooth silk tie, he was the very image of the billionaire banker she had read about on the internet. Handsome, incredibly sophisticated, and intimidating to the nth degree though that sleek image was, there was also something impossibly sexy about him. She went hot pink with shame at that perverse thought. He had not lost the power to reduce her principles and her common sense to rubble round her feet.

'If you wanted my attention, you've got it,' Alexandros delivered with lethal cool, while he appraised her, his keen scrutiny highly critical. She had the heart-shaped face of a cat, big eyes above slanted cheekbones and a generous mouth. Unusual, rather exotic, but ultimately nothing special, with a tangle of bright copper hair that cruelly accentuated the hollows and shadows in her pale features. She was tiny and fine-boned—too thin for his tastes. By no stretch of the imagination was she beautiful—and some of the most beautiful women in the world had adorned his bed. He could not imagine why she had once made him seethe with lust.

Her lashes lifted on languorous eyes as rich and deep a green as moss. His gaze instantly narrowed, increasing in intensity almost without his volition. She shifted position with an indescribably feline movement of slender limbs that made his big powerful frame tense.

The silence stretched and stretched.

'So...?' Alexandros prompted, his dark drawl rough-edged as he fought the raw tide of sensual memory afflicting him. She had always smelt of soap and fresh air. The most expensive perfume in the world made her sneeze uncontrollably. He cleared his mind of that frivolous imagery with the rigorous restraint that had been second nature to him from his early twenties. He had learned then how to shut down and shut out unwelcome emotions and reactions. He thought it significant that he had got involved with Katie Fletcher when he had been emotionally off balance. Presumably, and ironically, that had added an extra edge which his encounters had lacked since then.

'What's this about?' he asked with level austerity.

Just watching him, Katie felt her mouth run dry—because he was *so* incredibly handsome. She found herself tracing the image of her sons in his lean bronzed features, noting the straight dark brows, the definite chin and nose, and the ebony hair that gleamed with vitality. Her little boys were like mini-clones of their father. She lowered her lashes, discomfiture taking over, for what she had to tell him loomed over her like a mountain that shut out the sun. He would soon be wishing that he had never laid eyes on her, she thought painfully. 'I wish you'd got that letter I sent you...'

To Alexandros she looked so young at that moment that

guilt penetrated even his polished armour of self-containment. What lustful madness had overcome his scruples eighteen months ago? He might as well have seduced a schoolgirl. Every word she spoke underlined the reality that she had been defenceless. The other women he had known wouldn't write him letters after he dumped them.

'Let's move on from the letter.' Alexandros was now taking further note of her shabby clothes, and the fact that the sole was peeling off one of her trainers. Her poverty was obvious and his distrust increased. He could not forget the potential threat with which she had concluded their exchange on the phone. 'What's happened to you?'

Wretchedly aware of his visual inspection, and inwardly cringing from it, Katie muttered tightly, apologetically, 'I know…I don't look the same, do I? Life's been tough over the past year—'

'If you need money, I'll give it to you. Drama and sob stories are not required,' Alexandros imparted.

Her pointed chin came up in a defiant motion, her green eyes full of strain and hurt pride. 'My goodness, did you think I was about to make you sit through some sob story? Well, then, I won't try to wrap up the bad news. I'll just get to the point. You got me pregnant…'

Astonished by that claim, Alexandros went straight into defensive mode, not a muscle moving on his darkly handsome face.

Katie was as pale as milk. 'I wasn't very pleased either. Well, to be honest, I was just terrified—'

'Is this some kind of sting? It's a very clumsy one.'

Her white brow indented. 'A *sting*?' she repeated blankly.

'I don't believe that I made you pregnant. Why would I only be hearing about it now?' Alexandros demanded in a smooth, derisive undertone that suggested that what she had said was too stupid for words. 'How can you expect me to believe this nonsense?'

'The reason that you're only hearing about it now is that you didn't give me your address.'

'But I left you a phone number.'

'And I rang it more than a dozen times, and every time I was told you were unavailable or in a meeting!' Her voice rose as she recalled how her sense of humiliation had grown with every fruitless phone call.

Alexandros continued to look stonily unimpressed. 'I don't accept that. My staff are very efficient—'

'Eventually one of your employees got so tired of my calls that she took pity on me. She explained that I wasn't on the special list she had. And, as she said, "If your name isn't on my boss's list, you won't get to speak to him this side of eternity!"' Katie completed rawly.

Alexandros was frowning. 'Your name must have been on the list—'

'No, it wasn't. Why pretend? We both know why my name wasn't on your fancy VIP list,' Katie condemned, with a bitterness she could not hide. 'You didn't want to hear from me. You had no wish for further contact. That's fine, that's okay, but don't try and criticise me for not telling you I was pregnant when I had no way of contacting you!'

'You're hysterical…I'm not continuing this conversation with you,' Alexandros asserted with cold clarity, outrage turning his dark eyes into chips of gold ice because she had raised her voice.

Katie snatched in a deep, shuddering breath even as she wondered if he remembered her once serving him coffee on her knees to make him laugh. 'I'm not hysterical. I'm sorry I'm so angry, but I can't help it. I should've known this wasn't going to work. I shouldn't have come to your precious bank and I shouldn't have got into this car—'

'Calm down,' Alexandros interposed with chilling cool, while he tried to work out her motivation for the tale she was telling so badly. He could not credit that what she was telling him was true. He was willing to admit that with her he had not been one hundred per cent careful when it had come to contraception. There was a very slight possibility that conception could have taken place. He thought it highly unlikely, though, and his usually alert and versatile mind was curiously reluctant to move on from that concrete conviction. He did not recognise his own unresponsiveness as simple shock at the announcement she had made.

Katie put trembling hands up to her face and covered it. *Calm down?* Her brow was pounding hard with tension; her tummy was in twisting knots. As he watched her, his lean hands clenched but he remained otherwise motionless.

On the other side of the glass partition, Cyrus was trying to catch his employer's eye in the mirror, to work out where to go next. In a sudden decision, Alexandros touched a button to seal the passenger area into privacy. If she cried, he did not want her tears to be witnessed. 'It's all right,' he told her grittily, for gentleness did not come naturally to him and he would not let himself reach across the space separating them to make physical contact with her. 'You'll be fine.'

'Nothing's all right…' Katie felt as if she was banging her head up against a brick wall. He wasn't listening. He didn't believe her. She was wasting her breath. He would probably look at Toby and Connor and find it equally easy to say that they weren't his. Then what? She bowed her head, exhaustion overwhelming the nervous energy that had powered her into confronting him.

Alexandros recognised her fragile emotional state. She

was desperate and broke. Presumably that was why she had come to him with a foolish story that she had hoped would engage his sympathy. It must not have occurred to her that a fictional tale about a pregnancy that had come to nothing was pointless. But his anger had already ebbed, to be replaced by an effort to understand her predicament that would have disconcerted anyone who knew him well. While he gave freely to a host of worthy charitable causes, he had always avoided situations where anything more personal was required.

'Are you unemployed?' he asked, deciding to concentrate on practicalities in the hope that those issues would ground her.

Katie darted a surprised glance at him above her fingers and slowly, carefully, lowered her hands back down on to her lap. 'Yes.'

'So you decided to approach me for…help. That's okay.' Alexandros resolved to offer assistance in every way he could. 'Where are you living at present?'

Unsure where this dialogue could be heading, Katie blinked. 'In a bed and breakfast hotel…I had to leave the bedsit I was in.'

Alexandros had not a clue what a bed and breakfast hotel was. But he knew a bedsit was one room, which he found shocking enough in the accommodation stakes. He surveyed her, wondering if she had lost weight because she wasn't getting enough to eat. He was sincerely shaken by that thought. 'Are you hungry?'

Slowly, she nodded, for it was hours since she had eaten, but his questions were bewildering her. 'Aren't you going to ask me about the baby?'

The repetition of that unfortunate word 'baby' had the same effect on Alexandros as a bucket of cold water. His lean, strong face hardened. 'I thought we had moved on from that improbable tale. It's not winning you any points with me.'

Katie flushed a deep painful pink. 'Why are you so convinced that I'm lying? Do I have to go through a solicitor for you to take me seriously?'

Almost imperceptibly Alexandros tensed; that reference to legal counsel did not fit the conclusions he had reached.

'You just don't want to know, do you?' Katie shook her head in pained and angry embarrassment. 'But I'm bringing up your children!'

'My...*children*?' Alexandros repeated in blunt disbelief. 'Are you out of your mind?'

'I had twins... Have you any idea how hard this is for me?' Katie demanded chokily. 'How do you think it feels for me to have to ask you for a hand-out?'

Twins! That single word hit Alexandros harder than any other. It was a fact known to few that he was a twin, whose sibling had been stillborn. 'You're telling me that you have given birth to twins?'

'What do you care?' she gasped. 'Look, stop the car and let me out...I've had enough of this!'

'Give me your address.'

While Alexandros opened the shutter between them and the chauffeur and communicated in Greek, she clasped her hands tightly together to conceal the fact that she couldn't hold them steady.

Alexandros focussed bleak dark golden eyes on her. 'What age are the twins?'

It dawned on her that he was finally listening to her. 'Nearly ten months old.'

The improbable began to look ever more possible to Alexandros. Yet on another level he could not believe that he could find himself in such a situation. On every instinctive level he resisted that belief. 'And you are saying that your children are mine?'

There was no mistaking how appalled Alexandros Christakis was by the idea that she might just be telling him the truth after all, Katie registered with a sinking heart. His vibrant skin tone had paled, and the stunned light in his gorgeous dark eyes spoke for him. 'What else do you think I'm doing here? Oh, right—you're still hoping it's a sting. Sorry, I'm not a con-artist. The twins are yours and there's no mistake about that.'

'I will insist on DNA tests,' Alexandros asserted.

Katie veiled her eyes, angrily reeling from that further insult as though he had struck her. How dared he? He was the only lover she had ever had, even if he had chosen not to acknowledge the fact. The harsh bite of hurt and rejection lurked behind her annoyance, but she stubbornly refused to acknowledge it. Never once since he'd walked away from her had she allowed herself to wallow in the pain of that loss.

Yet what more had she expected from Alexandros Christakis today? she asked herself unhappily. Had she dreamt of a welcome mat and immediate acceptance of her announcement? From a guy who had ditched her while carefully retaining his anonymity? A guy who had patently never thought about her again since then? Of course he wasn't pleased, and he would never be pleased. Of course he was still hoping that there was some mistake or that she was a lying schemer.

After all, Alexandros Christakis had no feelings for her. She had been a casual sexual amusement when he'd been bored and at a loose end. Turning up again now as she had, looking scruffy and down on her luck, she was nothing but a source of embarrassment to a male of his sophistication and wealth. Add in her announcement about the twins, and she became the stuff of most single guys' nightmares, she reflected painfully. He didn't love her and he didn't want to be with her, so what could fatherhood mean to him? Men only wanted a family with women they cared about. Alexandros wouldn't want her children. Well, that was all right, she told herself doggedly. All she wanted and needed from him was financial help.

The limo came to a halt. In an abrupt movement that revealed his stress level, Alexandros broke free of his shield of reserve and closed a lean brown hand over hers. 'If they are my children, I swear that I will support you in every way possible,' he breathed in a driven undertone. 'Give me your mobile number.'

'I don't have a phone.'

He dug a card out of his pocket, printed a number on it and extended it to her. 'It's my personal number.'

His *personal* number. Her eyes prickled and stung like mad. She wanted to scrunch the card up and throw it at him, because he had been so careful not to give her that number eighteen months earlier. Her throat was so thick with tears that she could hardly breathe, much less hurl the tart comment she wanted to fling. She had loved him so much. It had been a savage hurt when he'd rejected her, and to be forced back into his radius and made to feel as undesirable as the plague was salt in that wound.

Alexandros watched her cross the busy pavement. She moved with the sinuous grace and light step of a dancer. He tore his attention from her, refusing to acknowledge that reflection, and the door closed, leaving him alone with his bleak thoughts. If a man could be said to have ditched a woman with good intentions, he was that man. Now it seemed that although he owned the race in the cut-throat world of high finance, his private life was destined to be a disaster area. Once again he had screwed up. Once again he would have to pay the price. As she had paid it. Just what he needed, he reflected with a bitterness he could not suppress: a guilt trip that would last the rest of his life.

How likely was it that her children were his? He remembered Katie's indiscreet, straight-from-the heart forthrightness. He had found her honesty such a novelty. There had been no half-truths and no evasions. Very refreshing—until she'd said those fatal words he could not stand to hear on another woman's lips. *I love you*—that little phrase that Ianthe had made so much her own.

Why had he let Katie get out of the limo? Chances were she was telling the truth and he *was* the father of her twins. He suppressed a shudder. He knew exactly what was required of him. He knew he had absolutely no business thinking about himself or about how he felt. He had dug his own grave. He recalled that Katie didn't even have a phone. He swore long and low under his breath. Perhaps she needed food more.

'You have appointments, boss,' Cyrus remarked in an apologetic tone.

Alexandros ignored that reminder. Acting purely on impulse, he went to Harrods and bought an enormous hamper, and the latest mobile phone in Katie's favourite colour. His own out-of-character behaviour seriously spooked him. He called his lawyer. His lawyer called for legal reinforcements and urged crisis talks, DNA specialists and extreme prudence. Alexandros might still have acted on his gut instincts, had it not been for the timely reminder of the potential for a huge scandal. Personal visits and gifts, it was pointed out, would only reinforce any claims made against him, and add to the risk of sordid publicity.

'Your grandparents…'

The reminder was sufficient to halt Alexandros in his tracks. Pelias and Calliope Christakis would be very distressed if an unsavoury scandal engulfed their grandson. The older couple were not of an age where their continuing good health could be taken for granted either. In the short term, Alexandros grudgingly accepted that a discreet and cautious course would be wisest.

Katie was intercepted before she could climb the stairs to her room.

'Miss Fletcher?'

It was the same thin fair man she had seen watching her in the foyer of CTK bank. 'Yes?'

He handed her his card as an introduction. 'I'm Trev. I work for the *Daily Globe*. Mind me asking what your connection to Alexandros Christakis is?'

Taken aback, Katie muttered, 'I don't know what you're talking about—'

'But you do. You just got out of the bloke's limo!'

'You saw me? Did you follow me all the way from the bank? And to my friend's as well?' Katie was unnerved by that awareness, and turned towards the stairs again.

The reporter was in her way. 'I hear you have a couple of kids…'

'What's that got to do with you?'

'Christakis is a very interesting guy. If you have anything to tell us about him it could be well worth your while,' he told her with a meaningful look. 'People don't talk about him. He lives in a world most of us can only envy. So anything of an exciting personal nature would have a very high cash value.'

Katie hesitated, distaste filling her. She wanted to tell

him to get lost and leave her alone. If only Alexandros had given her a more concrete promise of support than a phone number! Leanne had said that she should be prepared to do anything to give Toby and Connor a better start in life. But talking to a newspaper in return for money struck her as sleazy, and she wanted to think that she was above doing that sort of thing. And yet she was also painfully aware that it was her job to provide her children with a decent home, and achieving that would require cold hard cash.

'We're on your trail now, so if there's any dirt to dig we'll find it anyway.' Threat and warning were linked in Trev's hopeful appraisal. 'So why don't you make it easier for us and turn a profit too?'

'I'm not interested.' Even as she spoke, Katie did not know whether or not she was making the right decision.

An hour later she went back to Leanne's, to pick up Toby and Connor. While her friend saw her mother out of the flat, Katie scooped up her sons, one at a time out of the buggy, and hugged them tight. After a busy morning of occupation, Toby gave her a huge sunny smile, and Connor laughed.

'So, *tell*…' Leanne urged impatiently. 'What happened? Did you get to see Alexandros?'

Katie explained, while her friend listened with avid interest and made her describe the limo in detail.

'Alexandros is obviously stinking rich.' A calculating expression formed on Leanne's pretty face. 'And the best offer he can make you is a DNA test?' she sneered. 'He'll need to do a lot better than that!'

'He was shocked… I'll give him a couple of days and see what happens.' Katie displayed the card she had been given by the journalist to the brunette.

'Whoopy-do!' Leanne snatched the card to study it, more impressed by the interest of the *Daily Globe* than by anything else. 'This Trev took the trouble to follow you? Hey, Alexandros must be a real celebrity! And you turned the reporter's offer *down*? Are you out of your tiny mind?'

'I have to give Alexandros a chance to help us first.'

'But if the press find out whose kids Toby and Connor are without your input, you won't make any money at all!'

Katie was beginning to feel uncomfortable. 'I know, but I don't think anyone will work out what my relationship was with Alexandros any time soon. I mean, nobody knows about us—'

'You could make pots of money out of this, Katie. Haven't you got the guts to go for it?' her friend demanded

'Alexandros would hate that kind of publicity, and he'd never forgive me for it.'

'So what? What's he to you?'

'He'll always be the twins' father. I don't want to make an enemy of him. Flogging our story to the newspapers has to be a last resort for me.'

Leanne gave her a scornful look. 'You're being really stupid about this. There's money to be made. Your problem is that you've still got feelings for that bastard—'

Katie was affronted by that suggestion. 'No, I haven't!'

'Much good it'll do you. He doesn't want to know now, does he?' Leanne sniped, and soon after that Katie thought it wisest to thank the brunette for looking after the twins and go.

Mid-morning the following day, a young man in casual clothing came to her door. 'Are you Katie Fletcher?'

At her nod of confirmation, he extended a mobile phone to her.

'I'm a solicitor, engaged to represent a certain person's interests, Miss Fletcher,' the brisk voice on the phone informed her. 'I'm sure you'll understand the need for discretion in this case. Are you willing to undergo DNA testing?'

Katie was taken by surprise, but recognised that such speed of action was essentially an Alexandros Christakis trait. 'Yes...'

'Then sign the consent form and the matter will be taken care of immediately, with the minimum of disruption.'

An envelope and a pen were passed to her, the phone returned. Her caller departed. She drew out a brief document, scanned it with strained eyes and then scrawled her signature. Alexandros was doing what came naturally to him. It was insulting and humiliating, but also a necessary evil if she was to prove her claim. Within half an hour a doctor arrived with a medical bag. He explained that the test consisted of painless mouth swabs being taken from her and the twins. In a matter of minutes he had carried out the procedure and smoothly taken his leave again.

She walked the floor that evening, trying to soothe Toby. Although it was barely nine o'clock, someone banged on the wall to complain, and a man knocked at the door and asked her to keep her kids quiet because he was a shift worker trying to get some sleep. Tears were tracking down Katie's weary face while she struggled to quieten Toby, who seemed to have no more notion of sleeping at night than an owl. It was impossible for her not to look back and wonder how her life had drifted so far off the course she had assumed it would follow...

After Katie's English father had died, her mother had taken her daughter back to Ireland to live. Katie had enjoyed a happy childhood in a small town where everyone had known everyone else. Armed with an honours degree in Economics, she had been ecstatic when she'd got her first job as a PA in London. But when her mother had fallen ill she had had to resign and return home.

In spite of her ill health, Maura Fletcher had insisted on keeping up a couple of part-time jobs. Fearful of losing her livelihood, the older woman had only been persuaded to take the doctor's advice and rest when Katie had agreed to stand in for her until she regained her strength.

Maura had acted as caretaker and occasional house-keeper at a superb contemporary house which overlooked a sea inlet a few miles from their home. Owned by a German industrialist and rarely occupied, the property lay down a long gated track and enjoyed an incredibly private and beautiful setting. Katie had one day prepared the house for the occupation of a single mystery guest. A car accident had put the two domestic staff travelling with Alexandros out of commission and the rental agency, unaware that Katie was doing her mother's job for her, had recommended her parent as temporary cook and cleaner.

A fax had followed, detailing more exact requirements, and Katie had been staggered by the number of rules she was expected to observe, ranging from meals to be served at rigid hours and a duty on her part to being both invisible and silent. On the other hand, the salary offered had been generous enough to bring a delighted smile to her mother's anxious face, and the cutting-edge equipment being installed in the office with a sea view and a balcony had suggested that the guest would be much too busy to pay heed to the amateur level of the household help. Of course, accustomed as Alexandros was to perfection in every field, he had refused to settle for less, and Katie, secretly resenting the role of servant, had refused to be suitably humble. That they should clash had been inevitable.

No passage of time could eradicate Katie's memory of

her first glimpse of Alexandros. After he had arrived by helicopter, he had gone straight down to the seashore. From about twenty yards away she had watched him, dumbstruck by his sleek, dark, masculine magnificence. Clad in jeans and a husky grey cashmere sweater, and even with his black hair tousled by the breeze and designer stubble obscuring his stubborn jawline, he had bewitched her. She had never known a man could be that physically beautiful, or seem so alone and isolated. Wanton desire and longing had leapt up in her that very first moment, and she had never been able to overcome it…

Someone rapped at the door and she studied it in dismay, fearing another complaint just when Toby had mercifully subsided to the occasional long-drawn-out whimper of dissatisfaction. Tiptoeing over, she eased the door open a crack, for she was dressed in her pyjamas, and then fell back in complete confusion.

'May I come in?' Alexandros asked grimly, his dignity having been severely ruffled by Cyrus's insistence that it was necessary for his employer to enter the building in a clandestine manner and via an alley full of dustbins. An instant later Alexandros' irritation had vanished into the ether—a triviality when set next to the cold shock of his surroundings…

CHAPTER THREE

ALEXANDROS was a man of action, and playing a waiting game when Katie had asked for help ran contrary to his masculine code of ethics. Ignoring legal advice and doing what *he* felt had to be done came much more naturally to his dominant nature.

But Alexandros had never before come into personal contact with the kind of poverty that now confronted him. The room was tiny, cramped and shabby. A clothes airer stacked with damp washing, a pram and a bed were crammed up against a cot from which he swiftly averted his attention. In the single patch of space between the battered wardrobe and a sink stacked with baby bottles stood Katie. His golden gaze arrowed in on her like a laser. Against the riot of copper curls tumbling round her startled face her eyes shimmered green as emeralds, and, that fast, his body responded with a testosterone-charged surge of sexual hunger.

Even as the unreasoning shock of that lust hit, the darker side of him revelled in its resurgence. Instantly memories he had buried so deep he only dreamt about them surfaced. Katie up against the kitchen wall, tumbled in a pile of white linen, in a bubble bath with a ring of candles round her. The candles had been snuffed out by the overflowing water when he had hauled her up into his arms. Time after time he had discovered that he could never get enough of her, and that lack of control so foreign to his temperament had gone very much against the grain.

'I wasn't expecting you...' Katie could feel the tension in the air leaping and crackling round her like mini-lightning bolts, and she could not dredge her attention from him. He had always had that effect on her. He walked into room and owned it and the occupants until he chose to release them from the power of his potent presence and forceful personality.

'If I hadn't had a dinner engagement I would have called earlier.' Belatedly registering the brief camisole and shorts she wore, Alexandros was striving not to notice the milky pale swell of her round breasts above and below the worn fabric. His even white teeth gritted while he tried to work out why she should have such a dramatic effect on his libido.

'I'm glad you're here,' Katie admitted, feeling that her faith in him had been justified. She was pleased and proud that he had not lived down to Leanne's low expectations.

A little snuffling whimper drifted from the cot. Alexandros went rigid. A tiny hand curled round a bar in the cot and a small face appeared behind the bars. Gripped by the most excruciating curiosity, in spite of his resistance to the very idea of parenthood, Alexandros slowly moved closer. Katie's acquiescence to the demand for DNA testing without a single objection had convinced him that she was very probably telling him the truth.

'Boys?' Alexandros almost whispered, looking down at the two curly dark heads.

'Yes.'

'But not identical.' The cynosure of two pairs of curious

dark brown eyes, Alexandros was frozen to the spot. They were his. One observant glance was sufficient to persuade him of that reality. For both small faces bore compelling evidence of their Christakis lineage: straight brows that were a light baby version of his own, an early hint of the family cleft chin that even his grandfather carried, skin and eyes a little paler than his, but hair as blue-black. The curls were their mother's, and the only proof that he could see of her input into their gene pool. His level regard was being returned by the babies without fear. He was a father, he registered in shock, whether he liked it or not.

'No,' she agreed in a taut rush, for she was desperate to know what he was thinking. 'But well-spotted! At first glance most people do think the twins are identical.'

Unaffected by that hint of a compliment, Alexandros continued to survey the two little boys with brooding force. There they were, sharing the same cot, like orphans in some squalid children's home. His sons, his responsibility. Life as he knew it was over, he conceded bleakly. His freedom had just been imprisoned and was awaiting sentence to be hung drawn and quartered. There would be no escape from the agonies ahead. He would have to offer her marriage. It was his own fault. He had brought this punishment on himself. What a mess. What a bloody mess!

One of the babies cried, and she bent over the side of the cot to lift the child, treating Alexandros to a provocative view of her apple-shaped derrière. Tiny and slight she might be, but she was still one hundred per cent woman in the places that mattered, he found himself thinking—until he cracked down on that inappropriate reflection.

'I think you should get some clothes on,' Alexandros told her, with the censorious air of a Puritan being tempted by a loose woman.

Only then registering that she was hardly dressed for visitors, Katie straightened, clutching Connor, her face pink with embarrassment. 'For goodness' sake, I'm wearing my pyjamas.'

'It's barely nine-thirty in the evening—'

'So? I sleep whenever I get the chance!' She stuffed her son into Alexandros's arms without even thinking about what she was doing, and turned away in a hurry to snatch up her dressing gown. Her cheeks were burning. Had he told her to cover up because he believed she was trying to tempt him with her body? Did she look that desperate? Perhaps she did, she thought painfully.

As Katie thrust Connor into his arms, Alexandros turned to stone. Connor also froze. The little boy then reacted to his father's extreme tension by opening his mouth and howling like a burglar alarm. Aghast, Alexandros studied the screaming child and put him straight down on the carpet. 'No more,' he told his son in reproving Greek, as if he was a misbehaving seven-year-old.

As Connor's ear-splitting cry mounted to a shriek, Katie scooped him up and hugged his squirming little body protectively close. 'How could you just put him down like that? Don't you think he has feelings?'

Alexandros winced as Toby loosed a first warning squeal from the cot. 'I'm a stranger to him. I thought I had frightened him. I have never held a child before.'

'Neither had I when the twins were born. But I had no choice but to learn!'

'I don't need to learn,' Alexandros drawled, sardonic in tone and equally dry. 'I can afford a nanny.'

'I'm thrilled for you.'

Backing off to the door, Alexandros watched her efforts to placate the babies. With two little screeching horrors to look after, it was little wonder that she looked exhausted. He held at bay the knowledge that he had helped to create those screeching horrors now dogging her daily existence, and imposed a strict mental block on the noise of their cries while he watched Katie. He was still fiercely determined to penetrate the mystery of her attraction, since she bore not the smallest resemblance to the women he normally went for. She wasn't tall, she wasn't blonde, and she wasn't ravishingly beautiful.

Tiny and slender though she was, however, there was something about the arrangement of her delicate features and the unexpectedly lush curve of breast and hip that raised her to a seriously appetising level of desirability, Alexandros acknowledged abstractedly. He considered the reality that she had conceived and given birth to his children. All of a sudden that seemed an extraordinarily sexy achievement to him. He imagined sliding his hands under the thin camisole she wore, and the exquisite feel of the silky skin on her narrow ribcage beneath his palms before he curved his fingers up and round...

'Just what is the matter with you?' Katie launched at Alexandros in almost sobbing frustration. She could not cope when both the twins cried at once, and was enraged by his supreme detachment from the rising decibel level in the room. 'Haven't you got any interest in your own children?'

Unwillingly forced from the realms of erotic fantasy, Alexandros dealt her an enquiring glance from below his luxuriant black lashes, the faintest hint of colour scoring his stunning high cheekbones. 'I'm here,' he fielded without expression. 'That should tell you something.'

'That you don't *want* to be here!' Katie condemned helplessly, devastated by his failure even to ask the twins' names. 'That's what your attitude is telling me!'

'How may I help?' Alexandros ground out, his accent very thick.

'Lift Toby…'

Alexandros approached the cot, squared his shoulders, reached in and closed his hands round the wriggling baby. He performed that feat with the same enthusiasm with which he might have stuck his hands in a blazing fire. *Toby.* Alexandros sounded the name under his breath, reading the look of anxious surprise in the child's brown eyes as he lifted him. He drew Toby awkwardly closer. More able to rate the experience the second time around, he was amazed at how light in weight Toby was—and then transfixed by the big smile that transformed the little boy's face. That open happy grin reminded Alexandros very much of Pelias, and made Toby feel familiar.

Engaged in soothing Connor, it was a moment or two before Katie registered that peace had fallen again. She glanced up and saw Alexandros smiling at her eldest son. That smile stopped her heart in its tracks, made her chest go all tight, rousing memories so painful that hot tears burned the back of her eyes. Once, and for a very brief period, Alexandros had looked at her like that, and she had wanted to turn somersaults and sing with the sheer joy of living. It had not occurred to her then that losing him would hurt like hell, that the world he had made seem so bright and full of promise could just as swiftly turn grey and threatening. But now, she reminded herself doggedly, she was no longer so naive and trusting. Expecting more from Alexandros Christakis than help with the rent would be asking for trouble.

'What is his brother called?' Alexandros enquired.

'Connor.'

'We will have to discuss the requirements of this situation.' Alexandros utilised the business terminology that he was most at ease with.

'I'm not looking for much from you. I only want us to have somewhere decent to live,' Katie muttered with low-pitched urgency, as she settled Connor carefully back into the cot and held her arms out for his brother.

Alexandros surrendered Toby. He straightened his broad shoulders, his wide, sensual mouth compressing. Could she really be so clueless? Or was he supposed to be impressed by her pretence of innocence? She could hardly be ignorant of the fact that the simple act of having had his children would turn out to be a highly profitable enterprise.

'I'll move you out of here as soon as possible,' Alexandros responded. 'Tomorrow, I should think.'

Katie spun back to study him in wide-eyed astonishment. 'Tomorrow? Are you serious?'

'I would take you home with me now...' Dark golden eyes rested on her for a heartbeat, with an intensity that made her mouth run dry and the skin at the nape of her neck prickle. 'But it would be too unsettling to move the children at this hour.'

An uneasy laugh fell from her lips, for she assumed that that reference to taking her home was a joke—and not one in the best of taste. 'Luckily for you, I'm not expecting to go home with you. I'll be more than happy to be placed in a position to afford a small flat for the three of us.' Her colour heightened, she avoided his gaze and jerked a narrow shoulder in an awkward gesture. 'My goodness, why is anything involving money so embarrassing to talk about?'

Alexandros, who had never found money a source of embarrassment, and could not imagine ever doing so, was unmoved. 'Naturally I have no intention of leaving you to raise the twins alone.'

Katie tied the sash on her dressing gown with nervous hands and said nothing. So he was planning to take on some sort of paternal role? A visit once a month? Sandwiched in between business trips and dirty weekends with gorgeous women?

'I'm not a total bastard,' Alexandros breathed.

With care, Katie averted her gaze from his. She deemed it wisest not to comment, for she had, after all, spent eighteen months thinking of him in exactly those terms. He had taken her virginity, got her pregnant, dumped her and left her with a dud phone number for emergencies. In addition, the one website she had lingered on after she'd found out about his connection to CTK Bank had described him as a notoriously successful womaniser with a taste for supermodels. In comparison she was nothing and nobody, and she was determined not to let herself forget that demeaning truth. This time around she intended to keep her silly feet on the ground in his radius.

Alexandros, who was as much a stranger to criticism as to female disapprobation, was annoyed by her unresponsive silence. 'Katie…I have honour.'

She lifted her head, collided with the scorching gold challenge of his potent gaze, and felt the burn of his anger. It had the most disturbing effect on her, for she could not help recalling that he could go from anger to passion in the space of a moment. That icy façade concealed a molten core. Her mind a hopeless blank, she snatched in a stark lungful of air, suddenly maddeningly aware of the little knot of awareness forming in the pit of her stomach. Her breasts felt heavy, the tender peaks pinching taut below her clothing. Heat was pulsing through her. She let her head angle back and slightly to one side, copper curls trailing, lashes lowering over softened green eyes.

'Alexandros…' she framed shakily, in the grip of something that had very swiftly got stronger than she was.

As alert to her every signal as a natural-born predator, Alexandros had switched to the same channel of communication without even being aware of it. He was studying the moist pink softness of her generous mouth with strictly dishonourable intentions. If he kissed her, she would stop talking at him, voicing stupid sentiments that could only offend. He was already so hot for her he ached, and he was savouring that fast, fierce arousal, acknowledging how long it had been since he had wanted any woman to such a degree. He closed a hand over her shoulder and tugged her to him, curving strong hands below her hips to lift her up to him.

Katie shut her eyes tight shut at the first intoxicating taste of him, let her head fall back in invitation, her lips open. He took advantage of her offer with the devastating sensuality that had always been her downfall. He did not ask, he demanded, and that raw, unapologetically masculine urgency turned her bones to water below her skin. It was like hitching a ride on a rocket. Her head was in a whirl. She could hardly breathe as her body reacted to the overwhelming surge of excitement with excruciating enthusiasm. On all systems go, she quivered and clung to his broad shoulders, moaning beneath the erotic plunge of his tongue.

It was an unfamiliar sound that stopped Alexandros in the very act of bringing her down on the bed behind her. Stepping back from her with a hoarse exclamation, he focussed on the baby watching them with pronounced interest through the cot bars. He was appalled that he had let control slip that far. He had forgotten about the children. His mind could not encompass how he could possibly have forgotten the presence of the twins he had only just learned were his.

'I shouldn't have done that. It was inappropriate,' he breathed icily.

Katie reeled back from him on weak legs. She was seeing mental stars, and sweet sensation was still shimmying in seductive waves through her newly awakened body. She knew she ought to hate herself for succumbing to that passionate kiss, but in reality she just wanted Alexandros to flatten her to the bed and have his wicked way with her. Shame infiltrated at that mortifying awareness, but even so there was just one question that she needed to ask.

'Is there someone else…?' She had to know. Indeed, she tried and failed to stifle that overpowering need to know.

The silence lay there like a giant chasm, yawning suddenly below her feet. She could feel herself falling from a terrifying height and drowning in that horrendous silence. She always said the wrong thing with him. Like *I love you*—and he had left the country, never mind her, behind. Her fingernails scored crescents that hurt into her palms. She wanted to wring her own throat, tie a knot in her tongue, for she didn't have to look at him to work out the answer. The atmospheric vibes were full of warning flares. He was such a player, such a diplomat. She could feel him wincing at her lack of cool. This was a guy who could barely cross a room without getting a female come-on…

'This is not the moment to get into that.' Alexandros was sincerely appalled by such reckless in-your-face candour. He surveyed her downbent copper head. She looked so vulnerable. Why did she always make him feel such a bastard?

'You shouldn't have touched me—'

'You wanted to be touched.' He tossed a slim package down on the bed. 'This is for you. I'll be in touch tomorrow.'

It was the latest phone—very thin, very small, and in

her favourite colour. The door shut fast on his exit. Dazed, she blinked. Maybe he was scared she still fancied herself in love with him. She swallowed the great fat lump in her throat. He was gone. The room felt emptier than empty, sucked bare of life. She wanted to throw herself up against the door and sob like a baby. She didn't like him, and she knew he was bad for her. But that didn't mean that she had learned how to stop loving him, or craving what was bad for her...

Alexandros got back in the limo and received a call from a close friend—the titled owner of a well-known tabloid newspaper. 'I thought I should warn you that there's a rumour the *Globe* may run with a big story on you this week...very hush-hush stuff.'

Alexandros tensed. The paparazzi were always on his trail. They could not get enough photos of him, the women he entertained, the lifestyle he enjoyed. He refused to credit that word about Katie and the twins could already have leaked into the public domain. But he contacted his press officer to check whether or not he had been asked for comment. There had been no such approach. An uneasy feeling persisted when he recalled Katie angrily telling him after he'd spoken to her on the phone at the bank that he would not be able to say that she hadn't given him a chance.

He called her on the mobile he had given her.

It took Katie a second or two to identify the source of the ringing, and she snatched the phone up, fearful that the twins would be disturbed. 'Er...hello?'

'Have you talked to any journalists about us?' Alexandros enquired, in the most casual of tones.

Katie reddened with instantaneous guilt. 'No...'

'Are you certain?' Alexandros murmured, with a lethal cool that trickled down her spine like an executioner's warning. 'If I was to find out that you had lied about this, I would be seriously ticked-off.'

'I'm not lying...but I *was* approached by a reporter,' she confided, and hastily furnished the details of that encounter.

'But you told him nothing?' Alexandros checked.

'Absolutely nothing,' she confirmed.

'I don't tolerate press intrusion into my life.'

'I don't know why you're telling me this—'

'You're now a part of that life, and I would be very displeased if any revelations of even the most innocent kind involving either myself or the children were to appear in print. As far as the Christakis family is concerned, *all* publicity is bad publicity.'

'Right—I'll consider myself duly warned...okay?' But, feisty though that response was, Katie was secretly cherishing the assurance that he already considered her a part of his life.

'Okay.' Alexandros ended the call.

His grandparents would have to be carefully prepared for what he had to tell them about Katie and the twins. He was not in a hurry to tackle that challenge, so he would await the official DNA results. He would have to fly out to Greece to break the news personally, and in as gentle a manner as possible. But, even so, the old couple would be distressed. His lean, strong face clenched hard. He sincerely hoped there would be no reference to old history, no reminder of his own less then satisfactory start in life. He had every intention of doing what he knew to be his duty. Hadn't he done so all his life to date? Since when had he put his own needs first?

Alexandros was wakened soon after dawn by an urgent call from Pelias Christakis.

'Is it true? Is it true that you are the father of a pair of baby boys?' his grandfather demanded in a quavering voice of disbelief. 'Or is it a shocking calumny?'

Alexandros thrust back the duvet and vaulted out of bed, stark naked.

'I have friends in the publishing world,' Pelias shared. 'But if this startling story is genuine, I would have preferred to have heard it from your lips.'

While volcanic fury was taking hold of Alexandros, Katie was suffering an equally rude awakening to events. Someone was hammering on the door, and when she opened it a man stuck a microphone in her face.

'Katie? Would you like to comment on today's spread in the *Daily Globe*? Is Alexandros Christakis the father of your kids?'

'What spread?' she gasped.

With a cheerful grin, she was passed a newspaper. Thrusting the door shut, she bolted it and unfolded the paper.

Billionaire's Secret Babies of Shame ran the headline on the front page. Below was a photo of Alexandros giving a speech under a world trade banner, juxtaposed with a photo of a drab jean-clad young girl wheeling a buggy. Her mouth fell inelegantly wide when she realised that the girl was herself, and that the picture had been taken on the street outside without her knowledge.

Someone was banging on the door again and shouting her name, and the mobile phone beside the bed was ringing. Her tummy in apprehensive knots, Katie ignored those demands for her attention to tear open the paper and find the rest of the story. *The Banker and the Maid* shouted the sub-heading. She shuddered. She had *not* been the maid! But hadn't Alexandros once awarded her that lowly label? In disbelief she saw a recent picture of herself and her children in a local park, with Toby and Connor's faces carefully obscured. Leanne had taken that picture. How had the *Globe* got hold of that? And the one precious stolen photo she had of Alexandros? There he was, working at a laptop, black hair flopping over his brow, lashes so long they were silhouetted against the light along with his classic profile. That had been kept in a box she had left to be stored at Leanne's apartment. Had she been burgled?

Her mind shied away from the possibility that her closest friend could have betrayed her.

Stretching out a reluctant hand, Katie answered the phone. 'Please don't blame me for this....'

Alexandros was much too clever to risk frightening her into flight. 'I believe your accommodation is under siege by the press?'

'There's even people at my door,' she confided nervously.

'Don't worry about packing anything, and don't open that door to speak to anyone. My security team will get you and the children out of there within the hour. When my security chief is ready, you'll be alerted on this number.'

It had now gone silent in the corridor outside. She surmised that her neighbours had complained about the noise and the hotel manager had made her unwanted callers leave the premises. She washed and dressed in a frantic panic, and did the same for Toby and Connor. Having given them a drink and some baby rice, she filled a bag. Alexandros could not be expected to understand how impossible it was to go anywhere with young children without certain necessities. That done, she made herself lift the *Daily Globe* again, and read the inside story.

In actuality she only read the first line and got no further.

Alexandros Christakis, who married shipping heiress Ianthe Kalakos at the age of twenty, may have a secret family...

Married? He was married? Alexandros was a married man? He had a wife? He had had a wife when he'd slept with her? When he'd got her pregnant with the twins? Devastated by that new knowledge, Katie collapsed down on the bed. She pushed the newspaper away from her in anguish and disgust. Tears lashed her eyes. What a total clown she was! So besotted that she had refused to face what should have been obvious eighteen months ago! No wonder Alexandros had such a thing about publicity and discretion. No wonder he hadn't given her a proper phone number! When she had told Leanne about Alexandros, the brunette's very first question had been, 'Is he married?' She had fallen in love with another woman's husband.

Now he was offering to come to her rescue, no doubt determined to swiftly spirit her away from any contact with the press. Ought she to allow him to do that? She drew in a quivering breath. Even if he *was* married, she still needed his help to give the boys a decent upbringing, and the twins were entitled to that support. But what a louse she had picked to get involved with!

Her phone rang again. She lifted it. A man who introduced himself as Cyrus announced that he was waiting in the corridor to escort her out of the building. She recognised the big thickset chauffeur from her first trip in Alexandros's limo. He shook his head at the buggy and lifted Toby out of his seat. She hooked her baby bag on her shoulder and grabbed Connor. In silence they descended the back stairs and left by the fire exit. A limo was waiting at the end of the alley.

Alexandros had a wife. That awful awareness slunk up on Katie afresh, and she bit the soft underside of her lower lip hard in punishment. Desperate to give her thoughts another direction, she dug out her mobile phone and punched in Leanne's number. Her friend answered almost immediately.

'It's Katie—'

The brunette burst straight into speech. 'What do you want me to say? The money was there for the asking and I went for it. I've got debts...all right? I needed the cash. I'm sorry, but survival of the fittest and all that...'

'You went through my personal belongings to get those photos. They were private and they were mine—'

'Your personal belongings are cluttering up *my* bedroom! Maybe Christakis will pay his dues for the twins now. Maybe you'll find out that I've done you a favour!'

'I'll pick up my stuff as soon as I can.' Hurt, because she had been very fond of Leanne, Katie finished the call. She had trusted the other girl one hundred per cent. But how close had their friendship really been? She had not known that Leanne was in debt. Survival of the fittest?

A married man. Alexandros belonged to another woman, who was probably gutted by the tale that that newspaper had printed. Katie's conscience went into convulsions. A further apprehension assailed her. What if that sordid story somehow stretched as far as New Zealand, where her mother now lived in happy ignorance of the fact that she was the grandmother of two illegitimate kids? Katie paled at that prospect. Maura would be distraught at the secret that her daughter had kept from her. As the ramifications of the *Daily Globe*'s revelations began to sink in, angry bitterness began to gain the edge over the guilt Katie felt at Leanne's role in her plight.

Toby and Connor were sound asleep in their car seats when the limousine finally pulled up outside a vast country house. Katie climbed out very slowly, for she had not been prepared for such an imposing destination.

'There are staff here at Dove Hall to take care of the little boys,' Cyrus told her when she hovered, her green eyes huge as she studied the great sandstone historic pile in front of her. 'Mr Christakis is waiting to see you.'

Rosy colour warmed Katie's triangular face. She straightened her slender back and lifted her chin. 'Good...'

A housekeeper was waiting in the wide elegant hall, and Katie was shown straight into a pale blue drawing room with a spectacular painted ceiling. The grandeur of her surroundings made her feel more nervous than ever.

A door at the other end of the big room swung back on its hinges beneath an impatient hand. Katie spun round. Alexandros was framed in the ornate doorway. He looked exceptionally tall and austere, and his darkly handsome features were set like granite in a blizzard.

'So...' Green eyes raw with angry pain, Katie was determined to get what she had to say in first. 'Exactly when were you planning to tell me that you have a wife?'

CHAPTER FOUR

'As a red herring, that won't cut it,' Alexandros told her forbiddingly.

'Evading the question won't win you any points with me either,' Katie fielded, squaring up to him, equally set on confrontation. 'You know very well that you didn't tell me that you were married, and that's inexcusable—'

'I'm not married,' Alexandros cut in.

'You're divorced?' Involuntarily Katie hesitated as she made that deduction. Some of her anger dissipated, curiosity sparking, so that it was an effort to fire the next phase of attack. 'But you must still have been married when you came over to Ireland!'

'No.'

Katie waited for him to add some form of explanation, but that one bald word seemed to be all that was coming her way. 'I don't think I can believe you…'

Alexandros shrugged a broad shoulder.

'I have a right to know—'

'You don't have a right to know *anything* about my marriage,' Alexandros delivered, regarding her with a punishing degree of disdain.

Katie went very pale.

'You don't have good reason to doubt my word either.'

Katie found her voice again. 'Oh, yes, I do!'

Alexandros shifted a lean brown hand in a silencing motion. 'I have no time for this. If you did not have those little boys, you would not be here in this house now.'

'Did you imagine I might think otherwise?' Katie was rigid with tension. 'You didn't exactly overwhelm me with a welcome at the bank, did you?'

'You know what I'm saying to you. Last night you listened to my warning and you swore that you hadn't talked to the press. I find it hard to credit that you had the nerve, but you *lied* to me—'

'I didn't!'

'Keep quiet,' Alexandros countered with icy emphasis. 'I didn't trust you fully last night, but I was willing to give you the benefit of the doubt. I will not make that mistake again. How could you be so stupid as to alienate me when you're dependent on me?'

Off-balanced by that attack, and with her pride smarting beyond belief, Katie sucked in a stark breath. 'I am not and I never will be dependent on you! I'm a lot more independent than that—'

'Is that how you describe selling tacky stories about me to a tabloid? Independence?' Alexandros derided.

Her heart-shaped face flamed and her hands balled into fists.

'Don't you dare even think about throwing something at me,' Alexandros told her softly.

Angry embarrassment consumed Katie, for she considered that taunt to be a very low blow. 'I wasn't going to.'

A level ebony brow climbed. 'No? I was under the impression that you always throw things when you're losing an argument.'

'You're not arguing with me, you're sneering at me, and I can rise above it—'

'You'll need a hell of a long ladder to rise above the vulgarity of your current status,' he slotted in with offensive cool.

Katie lifted a hand in a furious motion. 'Of course it doesn't occur to you that I might not have been the one to sell that story to the *Globe*!'

Alexandros vented a sardonic laugh. 'Hey…is that a unicorn outside the window?'

'Right now, you're just reminding me of all the things I really hate about you!' Katie launched.

Alexandros dealt her a look of burning contempt, and rage rose inside her with explosive ease. His bone-deep arrogance, his inbred conviction of his superiority, and that quality of insolence he exuded literally made her feel light-headed with temper. But she struggled to control her annoyance, because she knew how much he cherished his privacy and it *had* been violated by the *Globe*. Furthermore, she might not have been the one to profit, but she did feel responsible for what her friend had done.

'When I spoke to you last night I was telling the truth when I said I hadn't talked to that newspaper guy. I can understand that you are angry—'

'Why would I be angry?' Alexandros drawled silkily.

'And I'm sorry about what's happened—'

'Sorry is a waste of your breath. It will be a very long time before I forget this episode.'

'It wasn't me who sold that story…it was my friend, Leanne,' Katie told him heavily.

'There's a *herd* of unicorns out on the lawn,' Alexandros murmured with biting clarity. 'Why are you feeding me this nonsense?'

Katie gritted her teeth together. 'I will say it just one more time. It wasn't *me*.'

'You took photos of me in Ireland without my knowledge,' Alexandros condemned. 'Their appearance today in the *Globe* confirms your guilt.'

'Cameraphone…stupid.' Her nose wrinkled, her throat muscles tightening as she thought of how desperately she had once wanted a picture of him.

'Stolen photos—'

'Oh, shut up!' Rage and pain coalesced and mushroomed up inside Katie like a pressure cooker, venting steam without warning. 'You're the most incredible control freak! So I was infatuated with you, and I went sneaking around like a silly kid, so that I could snatch some idiotic photos of you with my phone…get over it!'

A faint hint of colour now scored his fabulous cheekbones. 'And those photos appeared in that filthy article—'

'Aren't you lucky that I didn't take any revealing ones? Your problem is that you don't know what a *real* problem is, so you make a fuss over trivial things—'

'Trivial?' Alexandros dealt her a searing look of charged disbelief. 'According to that tabloid rag, I pour vintage champagne over my women and then I shag them in hot tubs…that's when I'm not making them dress up as French maids for a dirty thrill!'

'You're joking…' For a moment, Katie studied him aghast, because she had not read the article in the *Globe* beyond that enervating first line relating to his marital status. But her horror was entirely on her own behalf as she imagined rumours of such shocking shenanigans reaching her mother and her stepfather in New Zealand. 'What are you complaining about?' she asked fiercely. 'So all the guys think you're a heck of a lad? But I get labelled as a slut who plays sex games for your benefit! That is just so typical of the world we live in—'

Totally disconcerted though he was by her attitude, Alexandros gave not an inch, and breathed with icy restraint. 'Whose fault is that? You concocted the grossest lies to sell that tripe.'

Katie felt something snap inside her. Her angry despair at his refusal to believe her claims rose to such a choking peak of emotion that she couldn't trust herself to speak. Instead she shifted her hands in a clumsy gesture of dismissal.

'Katie…'

Ignoring him, Katie turned on her heel to walk towards the door.

'What are you doing?'

'I'm leaving.'

'Where do you think you're going to go?' Alexandros demanded with rampant incredulity.

Katie opened the door. 'Back where I came from!'

In a move that took her entirely by surprise, Alexandros reached over her head with infuriating ease to flip shut the door again.

'What do you think you're playing at?' Katie whirled back to face him in a fury. 'I'm not staying here!'

'At present, there isn't a better option.'

Her green eyes shone with defiance. 'You can't make me stay—and do you want to know something? I really do wish I *had* sold that story! It's what you deserved, but I was too nicely brought up to do it. I didn't have the guts.'

'If that is true, then I would owe you an apology. But the devil is in the detail. Where did your friend get the photos?'

'Leanne is storing a lot of my stuff in her flat right now. That included those photos.'

'But there were certain facts that only you knew—'

'She was my friend...so I talked to her,' Katie said defensively.

A level ebony brow climbed. 'Yackety-yack...what happened to discretion?'

'So I'm not as inhibited as you are!'

'Who are you calling inhibited?' Alexandros planted his lean powerful frame so close that she could not turn round to reopen the door. 'You only make love in a blackout...lights off, curtains closed, sheet to throat!'

Her face aflame with furious chagrin, Katie backed up against the door. 'Get out of my way, Alexandros!'

'No. I'm thinking for both of us right now.'

Outrage shone in her flushed face. 'Tell me I didn't hear you say that—'

Alexandros rested lean brown hands either side of her head, so that she could not escape his circle of entrapment. 'I remember this like it happened yesterday,' he breathed soft and low. 'You get so mad you don't think about what you're doing—'

'And you're the insulting, scornful voice of all-knowing logic, are you?' Katie hissed, standing up on tiptoe, the better to fire back those disdainful words at him.

Alexandros gazed down at her with shimmering dark golden eyes full of molten appreciation. Her tummy flipped, and a little frisson of heat curled low in her pelvis. 'I know what you want *now*...'

Her mouth ran dry, and she felt her heart thumping a little too fast for comfort behind her breastbone. 'You just think you do. You always think you are one step ahead.'

'If I wasn't one step ahead, you'd be on the other side of that door right now.' Alexandros let his hands slowly slide down to her shoulders. It was a caressing move, and wholly confident. She quivered, green eyes welded to his with an electric anticipation that she couldn't hide. Only with her had he ever experienced that kind of non-verbal communication. It gave him the most incomparable sense of power and heightened arousal.

'Please don't…' Katie whispered shakily, stealing a quick shallow breath and fighting what she was feeling with every weapon in her armoury. She knew that she should lift her hands to push him away, but she didn't trust herself to make physical contact. Even as she held her slim body still she was extraordinarily conscious of the taut swell of her breasts and the ache of almost unbearable tension at the heart of her.

'Don't what?' Alexandros murmured, soft and low as a purring tiger, his entire concentration bent on her. 'If you want me to back off, tell me.'

His dark golden eyes were as hot and bright as strong sunlight. He knew she wasn't going to tell him to back off. Rage rose in her, but she knew it too. Her palms tingled, for she would dearly have loved to slap him for his audacity. But when she focussed on those lean, darkly handsome features, more primitive responses took precedence and made nonsense of all thought and restraint.

Alexandros smiled and her heart danced. Long brown fingers tilted up her chin and she shifted almost infinitesimally closer, her pupils dilated. He let his wide, sensual mouth graze the merest corner of hers, his breath fanning her cheek, and a faint gasp of disappointment was wrenched from her. He bent down, dropping his hands to her waist and lifting her to him with an easy strength that sent a burning river of desire snaked through her.

'*Theos mou*…I want you.'

'We can't…we mustn't,' Katie gasped as he brought her down on a sofa and leant over her.

But a hot-wire sensation that almost hurt tightened in her pelvis, and her fingers spread and speared into his black luxuriant hair. She drew him down to her, controlled by a helpless hunger that paid no heed to more sensible promptings.

He tasted her generous pink mouth with the provocative sensuality that was so much a part of him.

'I hate jeans, *pedhi mou*,' Alexandros reminded her hoarsely, skimming a censorious hand down over a slender thigh sheathed in denim.

His second kiss was slow and deep, and she shivered violently, breathing in shallow bursts. Pulling back from her with the predatory grace and assurance of a hunter who enjoyed the kill, he pushed the T-shirt she wore up out of his path and bared her narrow ribcage.

'Alexandros,' she breathed shakily, on the edge of an exhilaration so intense she was terrified.

'Your skin is very white...' Scorching golden eyes fiercely focussed, Alexandros inched up the garment that still concealed her from him. When he finally exposed the pert, rounded swell of her breasts, his attention lingered on her taut rosy nipples and a gruff little sound of masculine appreciation was drawn from him. He bent his head and employed his mouth on a single throbbing peak, and a low keening moan of pleasure was wrenched from her.

Across the room, a phone rang. 'Ignore it,' he told her thickly.

But the phone rang and rang and rang, and it had no sooner fallen silent when a few moments later a knock sounded on the door. With a splintering Greek curse on his lips, Alexandros vaulted off the sofa and raked his hand through his hair in a gesture of fierce frustration. 'Whatever you do, don't move—and don't start thinking, *pedhi mou*.'

For several seconds she lay there obediently, still ensnared by the flood of excitement he had released inside her. And then the low murmur of voices from the door at the other end of the room, allied to that suspicious injunction against thought, combined and exploded her out of her waking sensual dream with a vengeance. Hauling her clothing back into place with clumsy hands, Katie sat up and scrambled upright. She was shaking like a leaf inside and out. How could she have forgotten herself to that extent? Her heart-shaped face turned a slow painful pink. How could she have lain there, revelling in what he was making her feel, as if the past had not happened?

Lean, powerful face clenched taut, Alexandros closed the door again. 'Apparently the nanny I engaged is having trouble with Toby and Connor. I can't believe that the children can't do without you for five minutes. It may well be that my staff have hired some over-zealous nurse—'

Katie's guilt went into mega-drive. 'Where are they?'

'The housekeeper will take you to them.'

As Katie surged past him to yank open the door again, Alexandros caught her hand unexpectedly in his and wound her back to him as easily as if she had been a toy. 'Don't keep me waiting too long...'

Katie stiffened, and refused to meet his smouldering gaze. She was at the mercy of a seething discomfiture that told her she could be justly accused of blowing hot and then cold. 'I don't want anything to happen between us...okay? Been there, done that—'

'And can't wait to do it again?' Alexandros slotted in, impervious as a brick wall to that suggestion of caution and moderation.

'No, I'm serious. I don't like being in your house,' Katie

admitted tightly. 'It feels wrong. I'll feel much more comfortable somewhere on my own—'

'On your own?' Alexandros repeated drily.

'I don't belong here. I don't like being around you—'

'Correction…you like it too much.'

Katie flinched as though she had been slapped, and half turned her head away. 'The twins and I do need your help to get somewhere decent to live—'

Alexandros swore under his breath. 'If the DNA tests confirm what I already expect, do you think that finding you an apartment will be enough to satisfy me?'

'If you want to see the kids, of course you can visit… whatever…' Katie muttered, desperate to conclude the conversation. 'But that's the only contact we need to have.'

He released her hand with exaggerated immediacy. 'And that's what you want?'

'Yes.' Even as she spoke she knew she was lying. She wanted him, feared that she would always want him, that there would never be a time that she could look on his lean, dark, devastating face without feeling almost more than she could bear in silence.

Angrier than he had been in a very long time, Alexandros watched her leave. He had always appreciated the fact that she didn't play female games with him. What she said she always meant; what she promised had always been delivered. He loathed pretence. That she should deny him when he could feel her hunger in every fibre of his being infuriated him. She had to have an ulterior motive for her behaviour, he reflected grimly.

The housekeeper, a trim middle-aged woman, was waiting for Katie at the foot of the magnificent staircase. Katie felt as though she had gone ten rounds with a boxer and had staggered up after being knocked out cold. She knew how narrow her escape had been in the drawing room. Alexandros would not have hesitated to take her on the sofa, and she would never have recovered from letting herself down like that, she thought in an agony of self-reproach.

Glancing up as she climbed the stairs, she focussed on the huge oil painting of a woman on the wall above. It stirred a vague memory of a photo she had seen in Ireland and her blood ran cold. 'Who's that?' she asked abruptly.

'The late Mrs Christakis, madam.'

A stunningly beautiful ice-blonde, garbed in a magnificent blue evening gown. Mrs Christakis? Late? As in…dead? Alexandros was a widower? Having denied that he was either married or divorced, what else could he be? Her face tight and pale, Katie stared up at the portrait which now exercised the most fatal fascination over her. 'When did she die?'

'October, the year before last…a car crash in the South of France. A terrible tragedy,' her companion replied.

Katie had to literally drag her eyes from the painting and force her paralysed limbs to move her on and up the stairs. As the housekeeper spoke, her heart had sunk to her toes, and her tummy had responded with a sick lurch. Her skin felt clammy, and she realised that she had gone into shock. Perhaps her reaction was not that surprising now that she knew that she had had a passionate affair with a guy who had buried his wife only weeks before he'd met her. And he hadn't told her. In fact he had deliberately denied her that painful truth.

'Who's that?' she had asked, when she had picked up the tiny photo from the floor in his office.

'Nobody important,' he had asserted.

No, just his wife. Whom he had married when he was barely out of his teens, according to the *Globe*. Of course he hadn't wanted to talk about her, and when she had looked again later there had been no sign of the photo. She hadn't thought anything of the fact. Incredibly, innocently happy as she had been with Alexandros that winter, she had not been at all suspicious of anything he said or did.

But in retrospect it was as if she had suddenly been handed the missing piece of a jigsaw that she had somehow previously believed complete when it was not. Alexandros had come to Ireland and locked himself away in that remote and beautiful house because he had been grieving. Hadn't she seen that brooding sadness and anger in him? She had simply assumed that he was some high-flying business executive suffering from burn-out after working excessive hours. The actual truth was far less welcome.

Toby and Connor's wails provided only the briefest respite from her unhappy thoughts. The anxious nanny looked on with relief when the babies calmed down as soon as their youthful mother reappeared. Katie sat on the carpet with a twin settled on either thigh and held them close. As she breathed in her sons' warm familiar scent, and kissed first one dark head and then the other, she was hiding the reality that her own face was wet with tears.

Her affair with Alexandros and its abrupt and cruel conclusion now made much more sense to her. She had offered comfort of the most basic variety. He was a very physical, very passionate guy. He hadn't wanted to tell her about his wife or talk about his loss, and that said so much, didn't it? That loss would have gone very deep; he had married young and shared his life for a good decade with Ianthe.

Had he felt guilty about sleeping with Katie within weeks of that tragedy? No doubt that was why Alexandros had been so keen to eradicate her from his life again. She had been the living, breathing adult equivalent of a hot water bottle or a soothing teddy bear. Just a source of physical relief. Acknowledging that hurt Katie a great deal, and made her all the more aware that living in the radius of Alexandros Christakis was very bad for her self-esteem.

When she had started working for him in Ireland she had found him impossible to please. From the first day he had made her feel as though her very presence below the same roof during the hours of daylight was an irritant. At first he had barely spoken, but his impatience, exacting standards and exasperation had soon cleared that barrier. Everything she'd done had seemed to annoy him. He had requested dishes she didn't know how to cook and had rejected her best efforts. By the end of the first week he had rebuked her for being too talkative, for being late, noisy and disorganised, and had also contrived to imply that she was guilty of chatting up the delivery men. She had gone from fancying the socks off Alexandros and standing breathless in his presence to hating him with such roaring virulence that she had positively boiled with her sense of injustice

'What an achievement… That tastes even more poisonous than it looks,' he had commented silkily on the sixth day, thrusting away the meal she had presented him with.

And as Katie had loaded the rejected dish back onto the tray and turned away, she'd suddenly totally lost the rag with him and had spun back to pitch the entire tray down at his feet. 'You are the most obnoxious guy I've ever met!' she'd launched at him. 'Nothing I do is good enough for you!'

'So you try to assault me?'

'If I assaulted you, you'd know about it!'

Alexandros had surveyed her with icy dark affront and censure, and told her that she was sacked.

She had stalked out of the house, and as she'd cycled down that endless lane, dismounting to get through every successive gate, her anger had soon ebbed, to be replaced by growing dismay and regret. After all, the job she'd sacrificed was actually her mother's, and it was her mother's reputation and references that would suffer, not her own. Appalled that she had let anger overpower all judgement, she had returned to the house.

'No…' Alexandros had delivered, the instant she'd attempted to apologise. 'You have no discipline, and you're not up to the duties involved.'

'I could learn—'

'You've got the wrong attitude.'

'I'm willing to grovel.'

A level dark brow had elevated. 'I will not tolerate or forgive impertinence or incompetence.'

'Please don't report this to the agency.' Seeing no point in continuing the pretence that she was her mother, Katie had made a full confession on that score and had had to admit that her only previous experience lay in an office environment.

'You amaze me…you confess to barefaced lying and expect to be re-employed?'

'I'll change my attitude and cook stuff you like…any time you like,' Katie had proffered in desperation, green eyes connecting with burnished gold, her heart starting to race without any warning. 'Give me another chance and I'll do whatever you ask me.'

'Bring me breakfast in bed? Wear skirts instead of jeans?'

Her eyes had opened very wide in surprise.

'I didn't say that,' Alexandros had asserted in hasty retraction, his stunning gaze narrowed, very bright and almost defensive. 'But certain offers are open to misinterpretation.'

And that was when it had finally dawned on her that the aggression in the air between her and the aloof Greek might well stem from an attraction that they were both determined to suppress.

'I should not have said that.'

'But you did...' Suddenly maddeningly aware of the way his intent gaze was welded to hers, Katie had laughed, feeling dizzy with a wanton sense of achievement that was new to her.

'Don't flirt with me,' Alexandros had told her.

Compressing her lips, she'd nodded, bowed her head and regarded him from below her lashes.

'Even the way you look at me is provocative.'

Face flaming, Katie had closed her eyes tight.

'Try to act normally,' Alexandros had urged gently.

Eyes opening a chink, she'd nodded vigorously.

The helicopter, which made regular deliveries, had come the next day, and, solemn as a judge, Alexandros had presented her with a Greek recipe book. She'd had to ask him to translate the recipe she chose. He'd stayed to watch her cook, and had invited her to eat with him. Barrier after barrier had come down at breathtaking speed. He'd no longer ignored her. He'd begun to smile and respond a tad stiffly to her conversational sallies. Within forty-eight hours she'd been walking on air and had abandoned all caution. It was that same week that a male childhood friend of her mother's had flown in from New Zealand for a long vacation. Blossoming beneath daily visits that had soon evolved into a determined courtship, Maura Fletcher had been too preoccupied to notice the increasing irregularity of her daughter's working hours.

The third week Katie had started wearing skirts, and Alexandros had accused her of flirting with the gardener, who had been old enough to be her father. In the ensuing argument, during which Katie had threatened to resign,

Alexandros had called her a tease and hauled her into his arms and kissed her. He'd kept on kissing her all the way upstairs to his bed. That reckless conflagration of passion had plunged them into an affair without any boundaries whatsoever. Nothing they had shared had been discussed or decided in the weeks that followed.

Lying sleepless in her beautiful bedroom in Alexandros's fabulous country house, Katie came back to the present with an even stronger conviction that she had to protect herself from being hurt a second time. She had lunched with the twins, taken them out for a long walk that afternoon, and dined alone. She could not forget how she had once sunk without trace in the intensity of her feelings for Alexandros. Holding nothing back, she had closed her eyes to every warning sign and just revelled in adoring him. She had never loved like that before, had in truth never even grasped what temptation was until she had succumbed to it without the smallest struggle. Although a healthy number of young men had shown interest in Katie at university, they had almost all left her physically cold. The only one who hadn't had bruised her heart and her ego by swiftly bedding someone else when she'd proved to be too much of a challenge. Now she wondered fearfully if she was the sort of misguided female who only really fell for the guys who wanted her least…

The next morning, Alexandros surveyed the single sheet of paper. He was not surprised by the DNA test results. The 99.9999% result tallied exactly with his gloomiest expectations. He was the father of the two little boys currently occupying the nursery on the top floor.

His private line buzzed. He swept up the receiver, his lean dark face clenching hard when he recognised his grandfather's unusually low-pitched voice. He breathed in deep. 'The children are mine,' he confirmed.

'How do you feel?' Pelias Christakis enquired, in an upbeat encouraging tone that disconcerted Alexandros—until he worked out that the older man had to be masking his true reactions out of affection for him.

'How I feel doesn't come into it,' Alexandros responded flatly.

'It must be fate,' his grandfather informed him without hesitation. 'You said you would have no children but… here they are.'

Alexandros gritted his teeth at that untimely reminder, and offered to fly out so that he could break the news to his grandmother. The older man said that he would prefer to perform that task himself. Alexandros salved his guilty conscience with the assurance that he would marry the twins' mother as soon as it could be arranged.

In answer, Pelias released a heavy sigh.

Katie had just finished bathing Toby and Connor when she received the message that Alexandros was waiting for her in the library. In the act of returning to her bedroom to tidy herself, she froze. Her face was pink, her hair was tumbled and she was clad in jeans and a T-shirt—but did that matter? she asked herself staunchly. She needed to learn to look on Alexandros as simply Toby and Connor's father, and suppress any more personal sense of connection. In any case, she could fuss the rest of the morning and it would make precious little difference when she had no make-up, no smart clothes and her hair badly needed a trim.

On the way downstairs, her sons left in the care of the nanny, Katie did wonder why Alexandros kept on hauling her into a clinch? Was he just oversexed? At a loss as to how else to relate to her? She focussed on the portrait of the exquisite Ianthe and glanced hurriedly away again, stifling a pang of envy that made her feel ashamed. But there was no comparison between them. Ianthe had been Greek, rich and classically beautiful, *and* the love of her husband's life. Katie discovered that she did not even want to look in the direction of that painting, which seemed to stand for everything that she herself was not and made her feel very small, cheap and forgettable.

Alexandros swung round from the window when she entered. Immaculate in a charcoal-grey business suit and a snazzy red and grey striped silk tie, the impact of his lithe bronzed male beauty punched a hole through her defensive shell.

'You have to be the most invisible guest I believe I've ever had,' he murmured, his attention nailed to her triangular face while he tried to work out how she could look so good without the artifice of cosmetics. 'I have not laid eyes on you since yesterday.'

Katie shot him a winging glance and swiftly veiled her gaze. But she still saw his image in her mind's eye, and he took her breath away. The armoured indifference she longed to achieve was still a long way from fruition. 'It's a big house.'

'Before I forget, I want you to authorise the removal of your possessions from the place where you were staying. The items you had stored at your former friend's apartment should also be collected.'

'Of course.' Hurt by that inadvertent reminder of Leanne's betrayal, Katie paled.

'Would you like coffee?' Alexandros enquired, coolly polite once the details of those arrangements had been spelled out.

'No, thanks.'

'Take a seat. What I have to say will take some time.'

Katie folded obediently down on to the edge of an antique armchair and studied his desk rather than him.

'The DNA tests confirm that the boys are mine.'

Her cheeks reddened.

'No comment?'

'What do you want me to say? The tests were offensive, but pretty much what I expected from you.'

Alexandros tensed. 'How…offensive?'

'You know when Toby and Connor were born, and you know you were the first guy I slept with. I fell pregnant the first week we were together,' Katie reminded him tightly as she stared into space. 'Another contender in the paternity corner wasn't very likely.'

Almost imperceptible colour demarcated his superb cheekbones. 'I had to be sure. I take nothing at face value.'

'Especially bad news.'

'Katie…that kind of comment is counter-productive at this stage. Naturally this development has come as a surprise, but I will adjust to it.' Alexandros contemplated the rounded swell of her small breasts below the cotton top, and wondered if it was a flesh-coloured bra or skin that he could see beneath.

'But you don't need to adjust to anything.' Uneasily conscious of his masculinity, Katie raked a restive hand through her tousled copper tresses and jerked a thin shoulder in dismissive emphasis. 'Nothing has to change in your life. I'm not looking for a father for the twins.'

It was a bra, not skin, Alexandros registered in some disappointment when she moved. He emitted a sardonic laugh that struck her as distinctly unamused. 'Very funny…'

Her green eyes gleamed. 'I wasn't trying to be funny. Just fair and honest—'

'How very considerate of you,' Alexandros breathed with scarcely leashed impatience, forcing his attention to a level above her head while he questioned the juvenile fascination he had with her skinny little body. 'But I should not need to state that I fully intend to be a father to my own sons. That is a duty I will not take lightly.'

His unemotional choice of words stung Katie's pride and stirred her into anger. She was tempted to tell him that as long as Toby and Connor had her love they would all manage very well without his dutiful input. 'I'm not sure I want you to act as a role model for the twins.'

Alexandros dealt her an icy glance. 'What reason have you to insult me?'

A mutinous expression on her heart-shaped face, Katie tore her gaze from the shimmering golden challenge of his and dropped her head. She bit back further hasty words, regretting her lack of control over her own tongue. It would be madness to make their relationship a hostile one, she reminded herself ruefully. 'I'm sorry…I didn't mean to offend you.'

'Evidently it has not yet occurred to you that I'm prepared to *marry* you and provide the perfect role-model for my sons!' Alexandros spoke with a harsh emphasis that clarified his attitude towards that prospect better than any words could have done.

Shock reverberating through her slight taut figure, Katie blinked and stared fixedly at him. 'You're prepared to marry me? At this moment you're *asking* me to marry you?'

Alexandros released his breath in an exasperated hiss. 'What else did you expect from me?'

All of a sudden the reason for his bleak and sardonic mood became clear to Katie. Even though the angry flush in her cheeks had receded, she was if anything more furious with him than ever. A hollow sense of pain settled like a stone inside her. She imagined that when he had proposed to Ianthe, the late lost love of his life, the scenario, the atmosphere and the emotions involved would all have been very different. 'Well, I didn't expect your grudging proposal, and I'm not grateful for it either!' she countered, with a defiant rise in volume. 'Thankfully, there's no need for either of us to make such a horrible sacrifice of ourselves.'

'There is every need. The twins should have two parents.'

Humiliation writhed inside Katie like a wild thing. She wanted to sob with rage and hurt. 'I don't even like you…and I certainly wouldn't want to marry you purely for my children's sake!'

Alexandros surveyed her with scorching eyes of gold, his stubborn jawline squaring. There she sat, all five-foot-nothing of her, being bloody cheeky, feminine and infuriating. Of course she would marry him! For her to pretend otherwise was nonsense. 'You don't feel like that.'

'Don't tell me how I feel—'

'I probably have a better grasp of how you feel than you do. Why are you so angry with me? Here I am, ready and willing to do the decent thing and make you my wife!' Alexandros threw up lean brown hands in a gesture that encompassed his opinion of the sheer magnificence of that offer.

Loathing leapt up like a core of steel within Katie's anger. *The decent thing?* She shook her copper head in vehement refusal. 'Luckily for both of us, I'm not that desperate, greedy or stupid. We have nothing in common but the twins—'

'Sex,' Alexandros slotted in, without a shade of discomfiture. If he was doomed to live with an adolescent preoccupation with her body, marriage would at least provide an ample outlet for it.

Katie was mortified by that bold and earthy reminder of her weakness. 'We'd need something rather more than that to make a marriage.'

Alexandros dealt her a sincerely enquiring glance. 'Such as what?'

Katie was momentarily stunned by the obvious fact that Alexandros appeared to rate sex as the most important element of marriage. Acknowledging that she was out of her depth, she decided not to pursue that controversial angle. 'Look, feeling as I do right now, nothing would persuade me to marry you.'

Alexandros contrived to look exceedingly unimpressed by that declaration. 'I could persuade you to share my bed again in the space of a minute.'

Katie leapt upright, her fair complexion aflame with chagrined colour, for she really could have done without that mortifying reminder. 'So…what does that prove?' she challenged, in defiance of her own embarrassment. 'That it's been a long time since there was a man in my life?'

Alexandros frowned. 'Don't talk like that…it cheapens you. I don't like it.'

Katie twisted her head away, fighting for control. He had been the only man, and that awareness rankled. While he had entertained himself with a succession of supermodels her life had fallen apart, destroyed first by pregnancy, then by motherhood and lack of cash. All of a sudden she could no longer silence her strong sense of injustice. 'I really don't care what you like. I'm only twenty-three years old. You are so precious about your privacy, your reputation, *your* life! What about mine?' she demanded wrathfully.

'Meaning?' Alexandros queried, with the weary aspect of a guy forced to humour a hysteric.

'Do you think this is the life that I wanted or would have

chosen? I didn't want to become a mother at my age. And I don't feel like getting married either,' she confessed shakily. 'I want to go out clubbing again. I want to date. I want my single life back!'

CHAPTER FIVE

HUGELY taken aback by Katie's startling confession of intent, Alexandros discovered that he had to call on every atom of self-discipline to keep his temper. He was astonished that his proposal had met with a negative response.

Surely she recognised that the twins' future security and their rights of inheritance could only be safeguarded by their marriage? It was the practical solution, and he was a practical guy. He knew what he owed his children, even if she did not. His family were very conservative, and took certain conventions for granted. His irresponsible father might have flouted those principles, but Alexandros had made it his mission to live within them.

He regarded Katie with smouldering force, an aggressive current that was unfamiliar to him blurring his usually ice-cool thoughts. She wanted her single life back? What the hell was that supposed to mean? Running about with other guys? Sleeping around? If she had hoped to pack in that kind of experience, she should have taken care of it before she'd met him, because now it was out of the question. Of course it was out of the question, when the only male she had ever slept with was him. His level ebony brows pleated while he tried to work out why the suggestion that she might get into another man's bed should outrage him to such an extent.

Theos mou, she was the mother of his children, and that was reason enough! That put her into a very special, indeed unique category, he reasoned fiercely. She wasn't entitled to a single life. But perhaps now was not the moment to spell out that inescapable truth, for his legal counsel had already warned him that unmarried fathers had very few rights within the law. For the first time he appreciated that marriage would bring advantages other than sexual. He would gain control over her *and* his sons.

Registering that she was trembling, and that her eyes were full of stinging tears, Katie walked jerkily over to the window and turned a defensive back on him. She wrapped her arms round herself and fought to get a grip on her flailing emotions. How dared he look so shocked! Did he think no other man would ever look at her? How dared he think that she would marry a guy who was only asking her out of a sense of obligation? Catch her accepting the role of a poor second best to the love of his life! Catch her saddling a reluctant father with children he had no interest in!

'I don't feel right staying here. Please find me somewhere else to go as soon as possible,' Katie muttered uncomfortably, her delicate profile taut. 'Then we can both get on with our lives.'

Alexandros stilled, anger cooled by an instant warning jab of disquiet. He realised that it was time for the creative thinking at which he excelled in finance. Her hostility and her desire for independence disconcerted him, because he knew it was essential that he keep her on board and engage in dialogue. Perhaps what was required was a breathing spell in a more relaxed environment. 'I think we can do better than that,' he asserted smoothly. 'I have a speech to give in Rome tonight. Why don't you fly out the day after tomorrow and join me at my home in Italy for a few days?'

Taken utterly by surprise at that suggestion, Katie could not conceal her confusion. 'I…well—'

'We need time and space to talk our options over…as friends, if nothing else.'

A faint flush of discomfiture warmed Katie's cheeks when she discovered that her immediate reaction to that suggestion of friendship was one of recoil. She did not want Alexandros as a friend, yet she knew that she ought to be relieved by that sensible offer. Her every instinct was now at war. She was even irked by the speed with which he had abandoned his talk of marrying her, and could not credit how contrary she was being.

'You'd love the sunshine,' Alexandros remarked casually. 'The twins would enjoy it too.'

'Yes…all right.' Katie was reluctantly impressed by that angle, immediately gripped by the fear that only a cruel mother would deny Toby and Connor such a treat.

'Would you mind if I spent some time with the children now?' Alexandros knew to quit while he was ahead. But he was remembering again: Katie rushing outdoors in Ireland to rejoice in a pitiful patch of wintry sunlight, telling him cheerfully about the excitement of her one and only trip abroad. He had been touched by her happy recollection of a childhood which had struck him as wretchedly impoverished.

'Of course not…'

His formality set her at a distance. As she accompanied him upstairs, he asked if the provisions made for the twins were acceptable.

'More than acceptable.' Katie raised a speaking brow, because the nanny was experienced and the nursery was full of designer baby equipment and toys.

'The nanny is, of course, only temporary. My staff are already drawing up a shortlist of more permanent options. You may make the final selection,' he advised. 'I've also made financial arrangements to cover your needs and that of the children in the short term—'

Katie stiffened. '*My* needs? But you only have to worry about Toby and Connor's.'

'If my sons are to live in comfort, so must you. To do so, you will require adequate funding,' Alexandros countered. 'You'll have to accept a personal allowance from me above and beyond the children's expenses.'

'I couldn't possibly—'

'I can't see that you have a choice. Obviously you've gone without many things, but there is no longer any need for such self-sacrifice. You need clothes.'

That blunt comment silenced Katie, because she was embarrassed by the fact that he'd noticed that all she owned was jeans and casual tops.

'I'll see that you're taken out shopping tomorrow. The children require clothing as well.'

When Alexandros entered the nursery, Toby and Connor displayed instant interest at his appearance. Indeed, Toby hauled himself up to stand on wobbling legs using the cot bars, his little face lighting up with a huge smile as he raised his arms to be lifted. When, without the support of the cot rail, he then fell over on his bottom the affront to his expectations was too great, and he burst into angry tears of frustration.

Katie was disconcerted when Alexandros strode straight over and scooped Toby up into his arms, voicing what sounded like a sympathetic phrase of Greek. In the space of a minute Toby went from tears to delighted chortles. Equally confused by his own behaviour, Alexandros gazed down at his son, marvelling that some hitherto unknown instinct should have prompted him to immediately offer comfort to the distressed child.

In search of an equal share of the attention, Connor loosed a plaintive yell. Katie lifted him, but Connor was much more interested in Alexandros. The twins were used to women, and a man was an infinitely greater source of fascination. Her face tightened and she stifled an ignoble spark of hurt when Connor stretched out eager hands in his father's direction.

'They're very friendly babies.' Alexandros, gloriously unaware of the compliment he was being paid, was amused. 'But I'll have to sit down to handle the two of them.'

When Alexandros sank down with lithe grace on to the carpet, Katie set Connor down beside him. The little boy hauled himself upright on a hard male thigh and chuckled with satisfaction. Katie watched in wonderment while the twins swarmed over their father with increasing confidence and pleasure. They tried to use his tie as a climbing rope. They clutched at his hair, explored his face with highly familiar fingers, and were overjoyed when he responded with more excitingly physical and challenging moves than their mother ever did.

For the first time since the twins' birth Katie was ignored by her children. As Toby and Connor crawled round, staging frantic sneak attacks on Alexandros, and the minutes ticked past while the audible sounds of their enjoyment rang round the room, Katie felt that she might as well have been the invisible woman. It had never occurred to her that Alexandros would or even *could* unbend from his reserve and his dignity to such an extent.

Cyrus came to remind Alexandros that he would soon have to leave for the airport. His craggy features betrayed his surprise at finding his sophisticated employer engaging in a baby wrestling match, and his beaming approval of the scene was equally obvious.

'Your suit is going to look like you slept in it,' Katie told Alexandros waspishly.

He raked long brown fingers through his tousled black hair and shot her a sudden charismatic grin, his amusement unhidden. 'I don't think I've had this much fun since I left my own nursery…all boys together, rough and tumble.'

Striving to remain impervious to that lethally attractive smile, Katie folded her arms. 'Toby and Connor can be quite difficult to handle.'

Alexandros vaulted easily upright and shrugged, dismissing her negative comment. 'They like me. That's a good beginning.'

'Yes.' Feeling small and mean and jealous, she tried to inject more enthusiasm into her voice.

The twins cried bitterly when the games stopped and their father departed. Settling them again took time.

That afternoon, Katie was invited to sit in on the nanny interviews. Invited to give her opinion afterwards, she gave her vote to a French girl called Maribel, who was the youngest applicant and whom Katie had found the least intimidating.

The next day, Cyrus and another security man accompanied Katie to Harrods. Assisted by a personal shopper, she bought new clothes for her sons. Not having to worry about the price tags was a wonderfully liberating experience. Then she tried on a variety of outfits for herself, and chose the accessories that went with them. By the time she reached the stage of selecting underwear and nightwear, she felt like an overexcited child let loose in a toy shop.

When the chauffeur went to stow the bags and boxes in the vast boot of the limo, she asked if they could be placed in the back seat with her. She spent the entire drive home carefully examining every purchase and soaking up every last possible thrill from the experience. It was only fair that Alexandros should contribute to the cost of keeping the twins clothed, but she was determined that this would be the only time when she allowed him to include her in that responsibility. In the future she planned to be working and earning and fully self-sufficient.

Walking back into the house, Katie glimpsed her reflection in a mirror and fingered her undisciplined mop of curls in dismay. 'I should've got my hair done...I forgot about it.'

'I'll organise it,' Cyrus told her.

That evening she visited a beauty salon, where her hair was styled and her nails were manicured. She chose some cosmetics as well, and at midnight she was still experimenting with the eye make-up. In bed, she lay as still as a corpse, her mane of ringlets carefully spread in separate lengths across the pillow, her hands, with fuchsia-pink-tinted perfect nails, spread like starfish on top of the duvet. There was nothing wrong with taking pride in her appearance, she told herself, in conflict with the puritanical inner voice that suggested that she was being foolish. Just because Alexandros had been married to a woman with the face and body of a goddess did not mean that she herself had to give up entirely. In any case, she and Alexandros would meet as friends in Italy. It would be a new chapter in their relationship, a more mature and civilised phase, she reminded herself drowsily, wondering why being sensible should make her feel so unbearably sad...

As the car wended a slow path, first through an enchant-ingly pretty medieval village and then down a steep hill into a valley with a meandering river that glinted in the sunlight like a silver ribbon, Katie was delighted with her first impressions of Italy. It was hot and sunny, and the Umbrian countryside was glorious.

Beside her, Toby and Connor were mercifully quiet. The twins were teething, and after a restless night had been in no mood to embrace foreign travel. The disruption to their usual routine had been unwelcome, and the boys had complained vociferously during the flight. Katie hoped that an uninterrupted nap when they arrived at their destination would help her sons catch up on the sleep they had missed out on.

The limo purred up a formal avenue towards a vast villa that looked as if it had been around for centuries, and Katie could not resist a rueful grin. Alexandros had never seemed quite comfortable in the ultra-modern house in Ireland. Classical grandeur, however, provided him with a perfect backdrop. As she entered the villa, she was handed a phone.

'Will you join me for lunch?' Alexandros enquired.

An instant smile curved her generous mouth, for she had been disappointed that he wasn't on the spot to greet them. 'I'd love to…but I do have to get the twins settled first—'

Overhearing that declaration, the new nanny, Maribel, made frantic signs to indicate that there was no need whatsoever for Katie to join her in that endeavour.

'Oh—no…no, it's okay. I can come now.' Katie returned her attention to the phone. 'Where are you?'

'The car will bring you to me.'

The limo moved off again, and turned slowly down a cobbled lane overhung by trees. Katie smoothed damp palms down over her summer dress, a simple but madly fashionable item composed of fine lilac-sprigged organza and shaped with ribbon below the bust. A few minutes later the car came to a halt, and she slid out.

Alexandros strolled out from below an ivy-clad arched gateway. He wore a slate-grey designer suit, casually cut and teamed with a striped black shirt. He exuded cool cutting-edge style. Katie tried not to be dazzled, and struggled to suppress her usual response to his sleek, dark goodlooks. Friends, she repeated inwardly. Even so, her mouth still ran dry, and it was as steep a challenge as ever to dredge her attention from his lean bronzed features.

'Today will mark a new beginning for us…'

Katie moistened her lower lip in a nervous gesture 'Yes…'

Coal-black lashes low over his stunning golden eyes, Alexandros studied her luscious pink mouth with ferocious intensity. He could not understand how she should look so wildly sexy in a dress that concealed her slender curves and showed only a modest length of leg. He could not understand either how he had dismissed her attractions just a few days earlier and yet now burned to get her back into bed again by whatever stratagems necessary. Perhaps, he acknowledged, his strong reaction was magnified by the simple fact that he had never been so focussed on a woman before.

From the moment when it had occurred to Alexandros that his staying single meant Katie stayed single too—with all the freedom and all the choices that status entailed—he had seen the need for aggressive action. Unlike with most of the young women Alexandros met, the acquisition of a rich husband was definitely not the summit of Katie's ambition. Katie didn't *want* to marry him. That revelation had challenged him as never before, rousing hunting instincts that had stayed dormant because he had never had to chase a woman. So he had plotted Katie's downfall with the same ruthless and resolute precision with which he made financial deals. Romance? Success came easily to Alexandros in every field, and he saw no reason why he should not be able to do romance as well as he did everything else. And he had baited the trap with care.

Katie was captivated by her first glimpse of the turreted stone folly through the trees. The winding woodland path petered out into a lush green glade. A glorious rose-entwined loggia rimmed the lower floor of the tower. She fell still under the shade of a chestnut tree, to better appreciate the sheer quality of the scene before her. On the terrace below the climbing roses sat elegant ironwork chairs, festooned with colourful floral quilts and silk cushions, and a white marble table which was a work of art: glittering crystal glasses, delicate silver and glass dishes, offering a mouthwatering selection of finger foods.

Kicking off her shoes, Katie let her toes flex in the springy grass and kept on staring. For perhaps the very first time she was truly appreciating how very rich Alexandros was. An *al fresco* lunch was being offered in an exquisite theatrical display worthy of a glossy magazine spread.

'This is out of this world...' Katie whispered. 'But you don't like eating outdoors—'

'And you do.'

'Since when did you put what *I* liked ahead of what *you* liked?' Katie asked, genuinely not trying to score a point, just saying it as it was.

'I try to do something thoughtful and kind and you want to argue about it?' Alexandros chided in his rich dark drawl.

Guilty pink mantled Katie's cheeks

'Naturally I knew that you would enjoy this sort of thing.' The gesture of a lean brown hand encompassed the superb picnic scene. 'My sole objective was to please.'

'It's just beautiful.' Embarrassed by the tactlessness that had made her sound more critical than appreciative, Katie got very busy spreading a couple of quilts on the grass and dropping cushions in rather pointless heaps here and there.

Alexandros shed his jacket, lounged back against the table and poured the wine. Katie drank with more thirst than delicacy, for even below the wide canopy of the chestnut tree she was warm. She sat down on a quilt and contemplated the ancient tower. 'Was it built just to embellish the woods, or did someone actually live in it once?'

Alexandros spun out an ironwork chair for her occupation. 'The *palazzo* was built by a nobleman in the sixteenth century. He kept his mistress in the tower.'

Relaxed on the quilt, Katie ignored the invitation to eat at the table. 'Was he married?'

Releasing the chair with an acknowledgement that the informality of the quilt would work to his advantage, Alexandros sent her an amused glance. Sometimes her innocence made him want to laugh out loud, but he did not want to hurt her feelings. He offered her a plate of canapés and refreshed her wine glass. 'I've never thought about it, but I expect so…'

'A wife and a mistress within walking distance…' Katie veiled her gaze, his gorgeous image imprinted on her senses like a brand. She was tempted to quip that she was sure that he would behave no better were he to marry purely out of a sense of duty. She wanted so badly to ask him about Ianthe, but resisted the urge as he had made it plain that that was a conversational no-go area. That exclusion hurt, reminding her when she did not need reminding that she had no proper status in his world.

Alexandros settled down beside her with the predatory grace of movement that had always attracted her attention. She made herself look away while he asked her about the twins and the flight. As she talked, her nervous tension ebbed and she relaxed, basking in the dappled sunshine piercing the leaves above her. The heat had stolen her appetite, and she felt a little light-headed from the wine.

'It's so beautiful here—but I suppose you take it for granted because you were born to all this '

'But I *wasn't* born to it,' Alexandros murmured flatly. 'My grandparents took me in when I was six years old, and adopted me two years later.'

Thunderstruck by that admission, Katie stared at him.

'My parents weren't married. I was the result of a one-night stand,' Alexandros extended wryly. 'My mother was a flight attendant on the family jet at the time. She got into drugs when I was a toddler, and died when I was five. I was in foster care when my grandfather, Pelias, learned of my existence.'

Katie was aghast at what she was hearing. 'Didn't your father do anything?'

Alexandros shrugged. 'He never acknowledged me or helped my mother. He was a waste of space. My grandparents spent their lives clearing up after him. He died in a skiing accident when I was ten.'

'I'm sorry…' Her eyes were stinging with tears. She felt so guilty for the false assumptions she had made about his privileged beginnings. Her heart was wrenched by the reality that in his earliest years he had been denied the love and security that every young child deserved.

Alexandros watched her fighting back her tears in silent wonderment at the depth of her sympathy for the child he had long since left behind. He had found her weeping over a children's cartoon fairytale once, and had been fascinated by the tender-hearted emotionalism that went hand in hand with her hot temper. Fascinated—and then appalled—he acknowledged, swiftly burying the memory again. 'I survived,' he said lightly. 'You look delectable in that dress, *pedhi mou.*'

That change of subject and mood totally threw Katie off balance. She blinked. Belatedly aware of Alexandros's gleaming golden appraisal with every fibre in her slender body, she felt her face warm and her heart-rate speed up. Her fingers tightened round her glass, as if it was a lifebelt and she was in danger of drowning. 'I think I'd like another drink…'

Alexandros removed the goblet from her grasp. 'Sorry— when you haven't eaten much, two glasses is your limit.'

'I beg your pardon?' Katie gasped.

'Three glasses make you giggle and crack chicken-crossing-the-road jokes,' Alexandros reminded her without hesitation. 'Four make you wiggle your booty and get on my lap. And that much encouragement could be dangerous.'

That mocking recollection of her behaviour at a certain lunch back in Ireland made Katie flush to her hair-roots. Her defences were blown wide open by that mortifying reminder. 'I really acted the idiot!'

Laughing softly, Alexandros ran a light fingertip along her collarbone in a soothing gesture. 'You always go for the bait. I was only teasing you.'

Casual and brief though his touch had been, it left Katie phenomenally short of breath. 'I wasn't used to drinking wine.'

'I thought you were very natural and sexy. But I suppose I shouldn't be telling you that now.'

Starved of such compliments, Katie was hanging on his every word, disbelieving what he was saying but still revelling in it. The entire dialogue had suddenly taken on the tantalising tones of the forbidden, and she tried hard not to succumb to that lure. 'No, you shouldn't…isn't there someone else in your life?'

'There would've been, but I wanted you more,' Alexandros admitted without hesitation.

In the act of admiring the stunning symmetry of his lean bronzed features, her green eyes collided with the smouldering gold of his. Framed by black spiky lashes, his gaze was a potent weapon. Her heart was already beating so rapidly that she was scared she might be on the brink of a panic attack, and his honesty touched something deep inside her.

Alexandros had almost stopped breathing as well, and the discovery shook him. Almost as quickly, however, the fierce surge of sexual arousal took precedence over the soul-searching that was anathema to him. With unhurried cool and single-minded purpose he laced his fingers into the tumbling mass of ringlets trailing over one slight shoulder and tilted her face up to his.

'I want to kiss you, *thespinis mou*,' he told her huskily.

Say no, a little voice urged inside her head. *Say no*. She was rigid with tension and yet astonishingly aware of the tingling sensitivity of her breasts, the warm sense of melted honey pooling in the pit of her stomach. She felt insanely alive and reckless at one and the same time.

'One kiss,' Alexandros murmured, soft and low, his earthy appraisal full of masculine power and energy.

Katie trembled, knowing it would not stop at one kiss, knowing she would want it to go further. She hated herself, but his aura of sizzling sensuality held her tighter than any chains and tormented her with her weakness. 'But we—'

'Burn for one other.' Alexandros bent his darkly handsome head slowly, as if he had all the time in the world. Even then he did not do what she expected. Tugging her head back, his hand firm in her coppery mane of hair, he let his firm sensuous mouth forge a delicate trail across her collarbone, skim up the length of her satin-smooth throat and nip at the tender skin below one small ear.

By the time he went for the parted invitation of her soft pink lips she was shivering and clinging to his broad shoulders for support...

CHAPTER SIX

'THEOS MOU...this feels good.' Alexandros savoured, then dipped his tongue into Katie's mouth, with a provocative slide-and-thrust motion that sent shivers through her slight frame and reduced her to mental rubble.

Breathless and weak from the devastating expertise of his kisses, Katie made a feverish stab at recovery. 'We should be talking...'

Convinced that that kind of conversation would come between him and the sating of a lust which felt ungovernably strong, Alexandros tumbled her back amongst the cushions and pinned her beneath his long, powerful length. His entire concentration was welded to the concept of giving her so much pleasure that serious discussion would be the last thing on her mind, and he subjected her pouting pink mouth to the sensual exploration of his lips, teeth and tongue.

A seductive tide of pure eroticism engulfed Katie, like a flame-thrower aimed at a sheet of paper. She crackled, burned, blazed white-hot. Her hands moved in restive circles over his broad shoulders and back as the twist of restive heat in her pelvis flamed higher. Frustrated by the barrier of his shirt, she began to tug at the fabric. Levering himself back from her, Alexandros flipped loose the buttons, exposing a muscular segment of bronzed, hair-roughened chest.

Katie sucked in an unsteady breath. He was gorgeous, absolutely gorgeous, and even more perfect than she remembered. Without thought, driven by a desire she had believed she would never feel again, she came up on her knees and let her hands skim with splayed fingers over the strong wall of his rippling pectoral muscles, down to the lean hard slab of his belly. As his big powerful frame was racked by a shudder of very physical response, she was shaken by her own boldness. He peeled off the shirt and tossed it aside.

'Why would we want to talk when we can do this?' Alexandros growled, his Greek accent so thick that she could hardly distinguish the individual words. He brought both her hands back to his sleek bronzed body with the uninhibited sexuality that was the flipside of his cool, controlled nature.

'Alexandros…' Touching his warm tawny skin, she felt weak and hot with longing. He shifted against her so that her fingers trailed through the fine silky furrow of hair that arrowed down beneath his belt.

'Touch me,' he urged, closing his hands to the soft swell of her hips to crush her against him, letting her feel the blatant hardness of his arousal beneath the confining cloth at his groin.

'We shouldn't…we mustn't,' she framed dizzily, fighting the reckless swirl of reckless desire he had ignited.

But even as she spoke her slender body was already acting in direct betrayal of that bemused protest. She was locked to him, revelling in his virile heat, rejoicing in his strength and masculinity. When he crushed her reddened mouth hungrily beneath his, she moaned helplessly and let her head fall back, achingly conscious of the wanton throb at the hidden centre of her body.

Her dress dropped into a silky heap round her knees, and she surfaced from the fevered oblivion that had engulfed her with a gasp of surprise.

'We must…' His lean strong face taut, Alexandros was wholly absorbed in the fetching picture she made with her delicate curves enhanced by lace-trimmed lingerie.

Katie was entrapped by the unhidden appreciation in his glittering golden gaze. Although shy colour blossomed in her cheeks, she could not help but be thrilled that he should think her worthy of such admiration.

With a single finger he unclipped the front fastener on her bra, and the cups parted to reveal the delicate pink pouting peaks of her breasts.

'I don't know what it is about your body,' Alexandros confided thickly, as he hauled her to him with more haste than ceremony, 'but it blows me away, *glikia mou*.'

The erotic caress of his mouth on her sensitive breasts brought down any remaining barriers. As he vaulted up and lifted her into his arms she was quivering with the intensity of her response. He strode through the arched doorway behind the rose-entwined loggia and took her up the short twisting stairs beyond it. She blinked at the unexpected sight of a beautiful turreted room. Filmy draperies festooned a four-poster bed that had a fairytale presence which was enhanced by the gothic windows.

'Wow…' Katie felt rather as though she was in a dream from which she did not want to wake up.

'I know what you like,' Alexandros declared with roughened assurance, laying her down on the bed with an exquisite care that made her shiver with anticipation. 'I know exactly what you like.'

'Yes…' In the course of a split second her memory, un-leashed from all self-discipline, doubled back eighteen months, to recall some of the wildly romantic things Alexandros had once done for her. Candles all round the bath and real rose petals floating on the surface of the water. Little unexpected gifts of perfume and cards and flowers. There had been a copy of a favourite book bound in leather, and a recording of a film she had not seen since childhood, which she had marvelled that he had found for her. He had seemed to have an astonishing understanding of what would make her happy. Her recollection began to move towards the tough conclusion of their affair, which had come as such a shock she had never really got over it, but she shut down and suppressed that dangerous slide back into the past.

'Katie…' Alexandros lowered his proud dark head to extract an exceedingly passionate kiss, and her hold on the past evaporated like a scary shadow she was afraid to ac-knowledge. 'I want you…'

When she looked up at his lean dark face, fierce longing flooded her, leaving no room for rational thought. Every inch of her felt tight, tense, restive. He ran his hands up over her breasts, grazing the prominent rosy tips in a skilful caress, and her back arched as the pleasure thrummed through her in an unstoppable tide. He bent his head there, and used his mouth to toy with the tender crests while he disposed of her last remaining garment.

As he parted her thighs she could feel herself melt deep down inside, and the level of her longing surged afresh. He traced the warm damp flesh at her feminine core, and the first quivering shock of delight claimed her passion-starved body. Abandoning herself to sensation, she was all slick wet heat and desire. He worked his skilful passage down over her writhing body, and before she could even guess what he intended, he subjected her to an intimacy that shocked her. His attentions were an exquisite torture. She went out of control as never before, with breathy little cries and shaken whimpers dragged from her parted lips. The feverish knot of hunger inside her tightened and tightened, until she reached an impossible height of craving and then went spinning wildly off into wave on wave of ecstatic release.

'Good...?'

Struggling for breath, Katie floated back to Planet Earth again, shattered at the intensity of what she had just experienced. She surveyed him with stunned eyes. 'More than...'

An unholy grin of satisfaction slashed his strong, sensual mouth. 'Good. I didn't give you the chance to surrender to your inhibitions...'

In a lithe movement, he settled between her slender thighs, his hands firm on her hips as he pushed her back and moved over her. She was full of languor, her body boneless and wondrously sensitised. He drove into her with a slow deep force that made her gasp and awakened her hunger again. Her lethargy vanished as he filled her to the hilt with the hot hard glide of his flesh, and the first jolt of renewed excitement rocked her.

'Please...' she whispered tightly, the inner rise of need gathering into pleasure-pain.

Alexandros gripped her hands in his and spread them wide, dominating her with his raw energy and passion. 'You feel so good,' he confided with ragged satisfaction, and a shade of disconcertion in his gaze. 'And I feel amazing...'

Her body had a life of its own, arching up in answer to his, while the wild excitement rose and rose until she reached yet another peak and lost herself in the drowningly sweet spasms of pleasure.

In the aftermath she was relaxed, so out of touch with reality that she felt as though she was floating in another world. The dizzy joy of release had spilled over into a fierce surge of emotion. She wrapped her arms round him and strung a drowsy line of kisses across his shoulder.

A husky laugh of appreciation vibrated through his lean hard frame, and he responded by tightening his hold on her slim body. 'I've missed you...you're so affectionate, *pedhi mou.*'

'I'm so sleepy,' she mumbled.

Alexandros eased her back against him and smoothed her tumbled hair back from her brow in a soothing motion. 'Then sleep.'

'Hmmm...' she muttered some timeless period later, when her body, languorous from slumber, was gently wakened to the erotic warmth and insistence of his. Every sense humming with response, she whispered his name in instant acceptance.

It was the most piercingly sweet experience of her life. A slow, deeply sensual joining of extreme pleasure that went on and on, until once again the ripples of release took hold of her. A powerful surge of profound joy and fulfilment washed over her. In that moment, with every defence lowered, words of love formed on her lips—and might have been spoken had not some sixth sense pulled her back from that dangerous brink and silenced her. It was the cruellest recall to the real world that she could have suffered.

'That was sublime, *pedhi mou...*' Alexandros told her lazily.

Her eyes opened, blank with shock and fear, a dark sense of *déjà-vu* tormenting her. She had slept with him again, fallen asleep in his arms like a trusting fool, and very nearly told him she loved him a second time. There,

deep down inside her, below all the anger and the defen-
siveness, was the love she had thought she had overcome.
Panic and confusion at the feelings she had concealed
even from herself were swiftly followed by a flood of
angry shame. This was the guy who had dumped her
without regret. Had he really missed her? Yeah—so much
so that he had never got in touch again! What had
happened to that new beginning and the friendship he had
suggested? Had he deliberately lulled her into a false sense
of security? Those stray thoughts sparked more, one after
the other.

Through wide, questioning eyes Katie stole a glance at
the room. The décor was very feminine, a perfect match to
her personal preferences, she conceded, with a frown
starting to build between her feathery brows. Not only
were pastels her favourite colours, but she also adored fresh
flowers. Had she ever seen more roses and lilies gathered
more prettily and less naturally in one place? What did it
take to rouse her suspicions and put her on her guard? A
fire alarm? A full-frontal attack with a military tank?

The picnic scenario had been equally calculated to
provide special appeal, she reflected tautly. Cue for the ex-
clusive magazine-spread approach to outdoor dining? A
faint chill formed in her tummy and began to grow. She
studied the beribboned silk knots embellishing the bedpost
nearest her and almost choked on the conviction that it was
all brand-new, that in fact she had been hooked like a fish
by an expert angler. And, worse still, how many hours was
it since she had seen or thought about her children? The
lash of guilt that reflection induced was horrendous.

'You're very quiet.' Alexandros sighed. 'I hate to surrender our idyll, but I haven't eaten since breakfast, and it's
now time for dinner.'

Thrusting herself away from him in an abrupt movement, Katie sat up. 'You've made a real fool of me...'

Lazily engaged in admiring the elfin quality her fragile
features possessed, even with her hair all tousled and her
make-up kissed off, Alexandros tensed and came up on one
elbow to say, 'I don't think I quite follow.'

Katie leapt out of the bed as though she had had a sharp
pin stuck into her shrinking flesh. The sun was sinking, but
there was still more daylight than her modesty could stand
coming through the tower windows. Nudity had never felt
more damning or humiliating to her. Espying her panties
on the rug, she swooped on them with shaking hands and
clumsily climbed back into them.

Alexandros thrust back the tumbled sheet and sprang
upright, a vision of lithe, bronzed masculinity. 'What's
wrong?'

'I can't believe you can ask that question!' Katie raged.
'I made it so easy too, didn't I? Just give me a bit of
sunlight, a cartload of roses and beautiful surroundings,
and I fall for the whole seduction routine—'

'What seduction routine?' Alexandros hauled on his
boxers and reached for his well-cut trousers. 'I have never
had to seduce a woman in my life.'

'Don't you think for one moment that I will *ever* forget
you doing this to me!' Katie launched at him, wrenching
the sheet violently off the mattress and wrapping it round
her in a series of jerky defensive movements. What
remained of her underwear and her dress were still lying
outdoors. Her cringing embarrassment felt like a fitting
punishment for such wanton behaviour.

With tears of pain and anger burning the back of her
green eyes, Katie raced down the spiral staircase. The incredible charm of the creased quilts, tumbled cushions and

abandoned wine glasses in the beautiful leafy glade struck her afresh. She went rooting around for her bra and failed to find it.

'Have you gone crazy?' Alexandros enquired from the terrace, where he stood pulling on his shirt. 'One minute we're making love, the next you're screaming at me?'

'What happened to friendship?' she bawled at him.

Alexandros stilled, his shirt hanging loose and unbuttoned. Evening stubble made a sexy blue shadow round his wide, beautifully moulded mouth. Slumberous golden eyes full of immense power rested on her levelly. 'The option was there…you didn't go for it.'

Trembling with disbelief at that calm response, Katie stared back at him.

Alexandros extended a lean brown hand. 'Come back to bed, *thespinis mou*. I'll order food.'

She snatched up her dress, carefully unwound the sheet, and fought her way back into the garment in furious haste. 'You've just got to be joking! I came to Italy because I trusted you. Because I wanted to be fair to you and the children.'

Alexandros lifted expansive arms in a very Greek gesture and dropped them again. 'And you *have* been—for which I honour you. Today we moved on from the past…an important step—'

'The only place I moved on to was your bed, and I regard that as very much a retrograde step!'

'But you had a good time there,' Alexandros countered without hesitation. 'I heard no complaints.'

'That's not the point—'

Alexandros slung her a hard, shimmering smile that tensed her tummy muscles with a mixture of resentment and nerves. 'Perhaps your point is too illogical for me to follow. You wanted me.'

Furious tears in her eyes, Katie bent to lift and shake a quilt to locate her missing shoes. 'So it was okay to set me up, then, was it? Because I still find you attractive, you thought it would be fun to lure me out here with false talk of friendship?'

Watching her dig her dainty feet into her tiny shoes, Alexandros realised how much he liked that physical delicacy of hers. He groaned with impatience. 'I assure you that I am not finding this ridiculous scene fun. I still don't understand what the problem is.'

'Is that a fact?' Katie shot him a gleaming green glance full of bitterness. 'You don't see anything wrong with what you did?'

Lean, powerful face unyielding, Alexandros shrugged, a battle-hardened veteran when it came to avoiding direct and damning questions. 'What did I do?'

'Something that should've been beneath your precious honour after what you've already done to me. I should've smelt a rat the minute I saw this gorgeous picnic scene. It was too good to be true.'

Increasing frustration was starting to rise inside Alexandros. He was a very practical man. She liked fairy stories, floaty things, four-posters and flowers. He had ensured she got the lot and she *had* been enchanted. As far as he was concerned, everything had gone fantastically well: she'd been happy; he'd been happy. What was her problem? She was the only woman in his life who had ever shouted at him.

'Since when was giving you what you like and enjoy an *offence*?'

'It was all a sham—a nasty, manipulative, cheating sham.'

'*Theos mou*…I want to marry you!' Alexandros growled with incredulity. 'How was it a sham?'

Katie was so upset that it was a relief to espy her missing bra in the grass and have the excuse to stoop down to reclaim it. She closed a shaking hand over the small cotton garment. She hurt so much she wanted to scream. Because she knew she had wanted it all to be real, had wanted it so badly that she could still taste it.

'I asked you to marry me and you said no. I don't quit when I want something.' Alexandros dealt her a challenging look. 'That's who I am. That's what I'm about. I employed no deception.'

Outraged by his refusal to acknowledge fault, Katie straightened to her full height. 'Didn't you? You did all that romantic stuff for me before and it meant nothing! You encouraged me to care about you and then ditched me,' she condemned between clenched teeth, filled with hurt and mortification. Terrified that she would break down, she started back down the path through the woodland. 'Well, I'm not going to fall for the same empty charade again. You can't manipulate me like some business deal.'

'Define "romantic stuff".'

'The rose petals in the bath...the flowers...the cards... my favourite film...book,' she recited fiercely over one slight shoulder, enraged by his obtuseness.

Alexandros looked grim. 'I see no reason why so much significance should be awarded to several thoughtful treats and gifts,' he confided curtly. 'There was no intent to encourage or mislead you. I had not been in a relationship of that type before—'

'Yeah...I know. Is that why you referred to me as "just the maid" when you friend flew in for a visit?' Katie squeezed out a humourless laugh as she stalked back through the archway and down the cobbled lane.

Alexandros winced. She had overheard that?

'The friend was a gossip. I was protecting our privacy.'

Katie grimaced through the tears threatening her. 'No, you were telling the truth. That's all I ever was, all I was ever meant to be…the maid warming your bed.'

'You make it sound cheap and sordid, but it wasn't!' Alexandros thundered at her. 'The first day I allowed you to shout at me without fear of retribution you were no longer the maid. You were my equal!'

Taken aback by that explosion of temper, Katie shot him a startled glance and walked on faster than ever. 'Well, today was cheap… What did you do? Bring in decorators and stylists to set the scene for my seduction?'

'*Theos mou*…' Alexandros grated. 'As long as I live I will never try to please you again…you are the most contrary woman!'

'I don't trust you as far as I could throw you. Do you blame me?' Catching sight of the vast villa ahead, Katie spun round, hands planted on her slim hips to confront him again. 'Where were your security guards this afternoon? Their absence is proof that you planned to get me into bed!'

Alexandros spread lean brown hands in a graceful gesture. 'No comment…'

His obvious lack of shame outraged Katie to the brink of screaming. 'May you rot in hell for this, Alexandros Christakis!'

'It's not a crime for me to want to marry you—'

'Look, when I'm so desperate for a husband that I have to take one who just feels guilty that he got me pregnant, I'll let you know!'

Below the pillared portico of the giant villa, Alexandros brought her to a halt by the simple method of closing a lean brown hand over hers and holding fast until she was forced to turn back to him. 'Maybe I appreciate the existence of those little boys much more than you give me credit for,' he bit out in a raw undertone. 'Ianthe pursued every fertility treatment known to the human race and still failed to conceive!'

Dumbfounded by that information, Katie stared at him with wide, unblinking green eyes. Hurt and regret twisted through her, and only caused more pain. Her very first thought was that her own fertility must have struck him as a bitterly ironic blow when his late wife had had to endure repeated disappointment in her desire to bear his child.

'And maybe I'm also aware of how much I owe to my grandparents for taking me into their home and raising me as their son,' Alexandros completed.

'If I ever marry, I want a more personal connection with my husband than my children,' she told him stiltedly.

As Katie spun on her heel and hurried into the villa, Alexandros felt as if a detonator was going off inside him, and he strode through the inner doors to the marble hall like a tornado blowing in. 'What could be more *personal* than what we have now?' he roared in her wake.

Astonished by his dark fury, scorched by the blaze of his fierce golden stare, Katie stilled. 'That's just physical,' she mumbled, in a tight dismissive tone.

'And what's wrong with that?' Alexandros grated in a tone of naked aggression. 'I'd fly round the globe just to spend one hour in your bed! It's the best sex I've ever had. I'm happy with that—more than happy. Why can't you be?'

A floodtide of embarrassed colour flushed her face. She could not initially credit that he had said that to her. 'Alexandros…'

Somewhere behind her she heard a cough. It sounded very much like the sort of warning cough people employed when they were keen to draw attention to their presence. Before her very eyes Alexandros froze, his lean, darkly handsome face shuttering, his lush lashes semi-screening his stunning eyes to wary glimmers of piercing gold.

'Alexandros…'

Slowly, reluctantly, her face very pink at the awareness that someone might have overheard a line or two of that ferocious and very private argument, Katie spun round. A white-haired older man, with her eldest son, Toby, comfortably clutched in one arm, was smiling widely at them both from the foot of the long hall.

'Pelias Christakis,' the old man acknowledged, in the most cheerful, friendly way. 'And you have to be—'

'Katie,' Alexandros sliced in flatly, closing his hand briefly over hers to palm the bra she held and dispose of it she knew not where—for his hand was empty when she dared to glance down again. 'Allow me to introduce you to my grandfather.'

Banding his free arm round Katie's taut spine, Pelias urged her to precede him into the drawing room. 'Katie…this is my wife—Calliope.'

A plump older lady, with shining silver hair and Connor cosily ensconced on her lap, greeted her in accented English.

Alexandros dismissed the nanny hovering in attendance while Katie felt that she was doing well not to succumb to an attack of hysterics. Her cheeks were certainly hot enough to fry eggs on. How long had Alexandros's grandparents been waiting for them to put in an appearance? Did they suspect the cause of their absence? They could hardly fail to have noticed that her hair was a tangled mop and her mascara smudged, and that Alexandros, mysteriously shorn of his usual sartorial elegance, lacked a jacket and socks. Nor could Pelias and Calliope have missed out on the fact that their grandson and the mother of their great-grandchildren had just been engaged in a ghastly argument. But neither of Alexandros's wonderfully charming grandparents betrayed the slightest hint of discomfort or disapproval.

Pelias beamed when Toby held out his arms to be reunited with Katie, and passed him back. 'Of course he wants his mother. Calliope and I were very excited when we heard about the children. I hope you will understand that we could not wait one day longer to meet them. Time is precious at our stage in life.'

Alexandros, who realised that he had been very wrong to assume that his grandparents were devastated by the scandal of his illegitimate sons, gritted his even white teeth. To his jaundiced gaze, the older couple looked as if all their Christmases had rolled in at once. He bent down to press a kiss to his grandmother's soft powdered cheek.

'Your grandfather wanted to warn you of our intended visit, but you know how much I love surprises,' she informed him chirpily.

'It's a wonderful surprise,' Alexandros responded without hesitation.

Explaining that arthritis made her a little stiff, Calliope invited Katie to come and sit beside her.

'They are wonderful little boys. Strong, healthy, full of life. You must be very proud of them,' Calliope remarked, petting Connor, who was lying back and enjoying every minute of such keen attention.

Equally misty-eyed, Pelias patted Toby's black curls before Katie lowered her son to the rug so that he could crawl. 'We are overjoyed by their existence.' He gave Katie a level look. 'I want you to know that, no matter what happens between you and Alexandros, we will always consider you and the children as a part of our family and you will be welcome in our home.'

Katie was touched to the heart by that sweeping declaration. She watched Toby making a beeline for his father. *The best sex I've ever had.* Her face heating at the inopportune recollection, she was wildly aware of the ache between her thighs. Their renewed intimacy had taken her by storm—to such an extent that even meeting Alexandros's eyes was a challenge.

'You'll stay for a few days, of course?' Alexandros was saying quietly to his grandparents. 'Unfortunately I have an early meeting in Brussels tomorrow, and will have to leave later this evening. But Katie would welcome your company.'

Extreme guilt assailed Katie. Was he making work an excuse because of the row they had had? She watched him scoop up Toby with an easy confidence that she could see surprised and impressed the older couple. Doubt and confusion engulfed her. The twins were already learning to love their father. Had she made the right decision? Or the wrong one? All her emotions were at sixes and sevens; all her reactions seemed to be on a razor's edge.

Half an hour later, Alexandros insisted on helping Katie take the twins upstairs. Once they had been settled for the night—the little boys had already eaten and been bathed— he strolled back down the corridor with her and came to a halt outside the bedroom that was to be hers for the duration of her stay. 'I have one question I've been meaning to ask you…it dates back to when you were carrying the twins.'

Katie glanced at him in surprise.

'When exactly did you make those calls to that phone number I left with you?'

Katie compressed her generous pink mouth. 'It was the summer…late June into July.'

Alexandros surveyed her with arrested dark golden eyes. 'And the letter you mentioned? When was it sent?'

'About the same time.'

'But that would have been six or seven months after we broke up. By then you must have known you were pregnant for a long time. Why did you wait until then before trying to contact me?' he demanded incredulously.

Katie almost winced, for it was a question she had hoped he would never ask. But now that he *had* asked she felt she had to give him an honest reply. 'I was waiting to see if you would phone me first.'

His ebony brows pleated. 'I don't get it.'

Katie lifted her chin, denying the raw sense of rejection she still felt. 'I wanted to know if you would get in touch with me again off your own bat. You didn't, which told me all I needed to know.'

'I'd have phoned if I'd known you were pregnant!' Alexandros launched back at her in disbelieving frustration. 'By the time you made the effort to call me, your name had been removed from the list—and that's why you didn't get to speak to me!'

'Some of us don't operate a datelined filing cabinet approach to our love-lives,' Katie murmured sourly.

At that crack, which was full of a defiant feminine logic utterly at war with the unemotional reserve, practicality and self-discipline that Alexandros prized, he drew in a slow, steadying breath of restraint. He was shocked to appreciate that he was a hair's breadth from losing his temper with her again. His scorching golden eyes veiled and cooled. Not with his grandparents still under the same roof. He had witnessed his grandfather's dismay that his grandson should even have raised his voice in Katie's vicinity. He had been dourly relieved that the older man's hearing loss would have prevented him from distinguishing words at such a distance. Unhappily, Pelias thought all women were like his wife—fragile flowers, with eternal smiles, adoring yielding natures and no temper whatsoever.

The only place Katie yielded was bed, Alexandros reflected grimly, reckoning that it was a great shame that he had ever allowed her out of the tower. Never again would he put food before sex. It was a time to think out of the box and come up with a fresh creative approach. But in the short term he felt he should step back and let her work out for herself what she was missing.

'Stay on here at the villa for a while,' Alexandros advised Katie equably, rising magnificently above that last comment of hers. 'It'll give me more time to sort out a suitable apartment for you in London.'

Katie was disconcerted at that change of subject, and at the calm agreement that she should have a home of her own. She looked up at him uncertainly. 'Alexandros…I understand if you're still annoyed with me, but I really feel we've taken a wrong turn and—'

'A couple of hours ago you were in my bed…don't please ask me to be friends now,' Alexandros incised with slashing derision. 'It's too late for that.'

'Maybe that was never a possibility,' Katie conceded, responding to a barely understood desire to soothe and placate that embarrassed her. She found it easy to argue with him, but the instant he started to pull back from her something perilously like panic took hold of her.

'Don't expect me to stand by and watch you bedding other men either.' Alexandros was determined to spell out her boundaries before he departed.

Dismayed that he could think that she would lurch straight out of his arms into another man's, Katie reached down to touch a lean brown hand in an intimate gesture that she did not even think about. 'I'm not like that. Don't you know that yet? I'm not planning—'

'You are pushing your luck.' Hard golden eyes glittering with warning, Alexandros backed her up against the wall and braced his hands on either side of her head, effectively imprisoning her. 'Don't touch if you don't want to be touched back, *pedhi mou*.'

Her breath snarled up in her throat and her mouth ran dry. The fire in his gaze set up a shameful tingle in her body. He was so close that she shivered, and she was shamed by the awareness that it was not apprehension that powered her. A helpless anticipation was making her heart-rate pick up speed

'You need to work on your resistance level, because I haven't given up,' Alexandros spelt out, soft and low like a purring tiger. 'When I want something, I go all out to get it. The next round, I may well fight dirty, *thespinis mou*.'

With a sardonic smile, he dropped his hands, straightened, and stepped back with exaggerated courtesy to allow her free passage.

CHAPTER SEVEN

FOUR weeks later, Katie attended the opening of an art gallery in the company of a handsome young Greek businessman and his sister.

When she had returned from Italy Alexandros had been in New York, and she had spent more than a week as a guest in Pelias and Calliope Christakis's comfortable London home. There she had met a lot of people, because the sociable older couple had made a special effort to draw her into their social circle. Damon and Eugena Bourikas, who had initially visited Pelias and Calliope in the company of their elderly father, had been welcome new acquaintances as they were in Katie's own age group.

For the first time in a long time Katie was in a position to enjoy a social life, and she was trying to push herself out and about to do exactly that. She was also planning to look for a part-time office job, to ease her back into the swing of working life. The breathtaking speed of change over the past weeks, however, had challenged her more than she had expected.

She had finally picked up the courage to phone her mother in New Zealand and tell her about the twins. The news that she was a grandmother had come as a shock to

Maura. Although she had been hurt that her daughter had not confided in her, she had phoned Katie back a day later to ask a flood of questions about the little boys and request some photos of them.

Although Katie was now free of any immediate financial or accommodation woes, she was suffering from shamefully low spirits—which she did her best to conceal behind a cheerful smile. She felt that a job would give her a fresh focus. If she got back into the employment market she would start earning some independence again. Was she planning to live as some sort of kept woman on Christakis largesse for ever? No way. And perhaps a return to the workplace would give her something better to think about than the fact that she missed seeing Alexandros. That intense sting of loss wasn't getting any easier to bear with the passage of time. He had been abroad a great deal on business. He had also contrived to visit the twins on three separate occasions when she was out; what contact they *had* enjoyed had been bereft of privacy and distinctly edgy in tone.

Only a week had passed since Katie had moved in to the stunning fully furnished apartment which Alexandros had organised for her. It was infinitely larger, fancier and more centrally located than she could ever have envisaged. Alexandros, however, had dismissed her protests with the declaration that his sons had a right to benefit from every possible advantage and comfort.

'I guess the rumours about you and Alexandros Christakis must be true.' Damon Bourikas allowed that provocative statement to trail in the air while they wandered round the gallery exhibits.

Wishing his sister had not drifted off, leaving them alone, Katie tensed. 'I never talk about Alexandros...'

'Did the tabloids say it all for you?' the young Greek riposted.

Katie went scarlet. 'My goodness, that was *all* rubbish! What are the rumours you mentioned?'

'That you're not together in any way with him. I made the comment because I saw your nanny when she brought the children to visit Pelias and Calliope.'

Katie studied him in bewilderment. 'I don't understand…'

'Your nanny, Maribel, is a seriously tasty package,' Damon explained. 'Only a woman unafraid of competition would employ a nanny who resembles a supermodel in her home. Particularly one who is an exact match of the female profile preferred by the Christakis males: a leggy blonde with heavenly curves…'

As his meaning sank in, Katie turned bone-white. Until that moment Katie had never thought about the fact that Maribel was a beauty, but now her thoughts went into overdrive. Did the nanny's undeniable charms explain Alexandros's recent visits to the twins when she herself was elsewhere and unavailable? Was Damon trying to give her a warning? Was Alexandros chasing her nanny and was she, Katie, the very last to know?

'Yes, she is lovely, isn't she?' Katie managed to say through teeth that were almost chattering from the sudden chill that was creeping through her taut body. 'I suppose she might remind him of his late wife.'

'She would be a hard act to follow, I would think.'

'Who are you talking about?' His sister Eugena, a talk-ative brunette, rejoined them at that point.

'Ianthe Christakis,' Damon supplied.

'My mother used to hold her up to me as a role model,' Eugena confided with a rueful expression. 'Of course Ianthe was much older than me. She was gorgeous, though, and always doing charity work. She was also totally devoted to Alexandros—'

'He married her and turned into a workaholic,' Damon remarked.

'Everybody knows that they had the perfect marriage!' Eugena shot her brother a look of reproof.

Thrown off-balance by Eugena's generous litany of praise, Katie swallowed hard. 'Pelias and Calliope never mention Ianthe.'

'They were all devastated when she died. It was so tragic that she never had a child.' Then, as if realising what she was saying, Eugena reddened with discomfiture. 'I'm sorry, Katie. I hope you don't think I meant—'

'No, of course not.' Katie smiled with all her might, but there was a hollow sensation inside her.

Well, she had asked and she had been told, she thought numbly, wandering round the exhibits in Damon and Eugena's wake and scarcely knowing what she said when pressed for an opinion on the various works of art. All Katie could think about was that Ianthe had been a genuinely wonderful wife, and Alexandros had been very happy with her. For the first time Katie was forced to confront the demon of her own jealousy. She was desperately ashamed of those feelings, but she still could not shake free of them. She was horribly jealous of what Alexandros had had with Ianthe, and knowing that she had no right to feel that way made little difference. Even so, she was disturbed by the awareness that bitter jealousy and injured pride had prevented her from giving serious consideration to his marriage proposal. On the other hand, was she really so desperate that she had to consider marrying a guy who had openly said that sex was all she had to offer him?

Alexandros had loved his wife. He had been grieving for

Ianthe when he'd met Katie, and he had used Katie like a
sticking plaster on the wound—easily discarded once he
was on the road to recovery. In comparison to Ianthe she
had been a casual fling, a temporary deviation from his sophisticated norm, and only the birth of Toby and Connor
had given Katie a passport back into Alexandros's life. She
saw that those painful truths had savaged her self-esteem
and made her deny the fact that she was still hopelessly in
love with the twins' father. But she also saw that she really
did need to get over her less than presentable emotions
about his late wife and his perfect marriage. The very fact
that Alexandros regarded the subject of Ianthe as too private
and personal ever to be discussed only reminded Katie that
she was still very much on the outside looking in.

When the gallery opening was drawing to a close, Katie
faked a yawn and turned down an invite to travel on to a
party. Damon offered to take her home.

'There's a car waiting for me...'

Damon raised a brow. 'I'll see you out. So, you're not
free after all?'

'I don't know what you mean.'

'Your children aren't here, but you're still running about
in a chauffeur-driven limo. It's an ownership statement.
Christakis is posting very large "Keep off the Grass" signs
all round you,' the young Greek quipped.

'Not necessarily,' Katie muttered uncomfortably as they
emerged onto the dark street. 'I usually take the boys everywhere with me, and Alexandros insists that I use the car.'

'Anyway, don't worry about your nanny's fatal attraction,' Damon told her smugly. 'If she's available, I intend
to keep her fully occupied!'

As that expression of interest in Maribel sank in, a flash
of light from a camera almost blinded Katie, and she

blinked in surprise like a myopic owl. The photographer sped off, and Damon urged her into the limo. 'I'm surprised Christakis didn't give you a bodyguard as well.'

'He did… I told him I didn't need him tonight,' Katie sighed.

After a night spent pretty much tossing and turning, she got up to feed and dress Toby and Connor the next morning and went back to bed when Maribel arrived. It felt like only five minutes later when an urgent knock woke her again, and the door opened a crack.

'Mr Christakis is here, asking for you…'

Katie threw herself out of bed, glanced in the mirror, and almost loosed a shriek of anguish. Her hair was an explosive tangle of ringlets. Why did he have to come calling on her without warning at this unearthly hour of the day? A belated glance at the alarm clock informed her that it was actually mid-morning, for she had slept longer than she'd appreciated. In a frantic rush, she cleaned her teeth, splashed her face and hurriedly pulled on some clothes, emerging from her room breathless, to hurry into the sitting room.

But Alexandros wasn't there. He was in the nursery, with the twins and Maribel. Katie hovered unnoticed in the doorway, finger-combing her copper ringlets to make them flatter and smoothing down her black T-shirt and denim skirt. She wished she had taken the time to put on make-up and shoes. Alexandros was asking questions and Maribel was answering, her pink-cheeked smiles and flickering upward glances the response of a susceptible woman in the presence of a very fanciable and smoulderingly sexy guy.

'Alexandros…'

He swung round and focussed incisive golden eyes on her. There was no smile on his lean, extravagantly handsome face. As he accompanied her to the sitting room, she found herself wondering if her interruption had been an unwelcome one.

'Do you find Maribel attractive?' Suddenly what Katie was worrying about, what she was trying not to think about, spilled from her lips in an unstoppable rush.

The most ghastly silence fell. It seemed to eddy out round her, as if she was trapped in the centre of a whirlpool. In the long stretch of quiet that followed she did feel as if she was drowning, as intense mortification crawled through her. Nothing would have persuaded her to look at him.

'Let me get this straight…' Alexandros was framing English words with the greatest difficulty because he was outraged by the question. 'You're asking me if I want to shag the nanny?'

Hot colour spread across her cheeks. 'That's not what I meant—'

'Of course it is. The answer is no. I don't ever hit on my staff, and I sack them if they try it on with me. You're the single exception—the only employee who has ever ended up in my bed—'

'And taking the fallout of that into consideration, I'm sure it's not a risk you'd choose to take again.'

Alexandros surveyed her with brooding force. With the sexual pull she exerted over him, he was wondering what choice had to do with it. He hadn't liked the way she made him feel then, and he really liked it little better now. But he knew that given the same situation he would repeat the exact same behaviour pattern. In the outfit she was wearing, with her little pink unpainted toes curling into the rug, she looked absurdly young and naive—until she glanced up from below those feathery lashes with witch-green irides-cent eyes that had the most sinful effect on his libido.

'You were with Damon Bourikas last night…explain,'

Alexandros invited coolly, the lust on his mind steadily spreading to even more responsive areas.

Her head came up, chin angling. 'Excuse me…?'

'He's not fit company for you.'

'I'm an adult. I can't believe you're saying that to me—'

'I don't want you associating with him.'

'Nobody tells me who I socialise with—'

Disturbingly calm golden eyes assailed hers. 'I do…and if you don't listen Bourikas certainly will. Because I'm too influential for him to ignore.'

'You wouldn't dare,' Katie told him shakily, her temper sparking with incredulity at that threat.

'Oh, I think we both know that I would, and with pleasure, *yineka mou*,' Alexandros responded with provocative silkiness. He had been incensed when he saw that photo in the morning paper. Damon bloody Bourikas! Rumour linked Bourikas to some very wild parties—but Alexandros had no intention of telling Katie that, in case a bad-boy image increased Damon's sleazy appeal. He was already grimly conscious that, at barely twenty-five years old, the other man was much closer to her age than he was.

Of course the sensible thing to do would be to tell Alexandros that Damon was interested in their gorgeous French nanny, Katie reflected grudgingly. But her pride revolted against that course. And if Alexandros should think that another man was interested in her, it might make her seem more exciting and desirable in his eyes. Alexandros was very competitive in business. Mightn't he prove equally competitive when it came to a woman? It was not the moment to tell him that Damon was too flash and smugly assured of his own charms to attract her.

'You seem to be forgetting that I met Damon in your grandparents' home,' she reminded him.

'They keep an open house. You are not in a position to be careless of appearances,' Alexandros delivered.

Katie breathed in so deep she was afraid that her lungs would burst. Being told that by the guy responsible for turning her into an unmarried mother galled her. 'And why would that be?'

Brilliant dark golden eyes enhanced by inky black lashes rested on her. 'One Greek tycoon...?' He shifted a graceful lean brown hand in an accepting motion. 'But being seen around town with a *second* rich Greek could suggest that you're making a lucrative lifestyle choice.'

Katie went bright pink with bristling fury at that insult. 'How...dare...you?'

'I dare because your reputation matters to me, and to our children.'

Her hands knotted into fists, but that very first reference to the twins as something they shared did not pass her by. 'I make my friends where I choose!'

'No,' Alexandros murmured with lethal finality, strolling closer and taking her hands in his to slowly, intently, unwind her angrily knotted fingers and curl them into his own. 'You're not on your own any more.'

'Hands off! You're the one who warned me not to touch!' Katie reminded him breathlessly.

Lush black lashes screened his gaze to a sliver of gold as hot as sunlight on the animated triangle of her flushed and furious face. He could feel the passion vibrating in her tiny frame, and it drew him like a starving man to life-giving food. 'I like an element of risk. It adds an edge,' he murmured thickly.

The silence hummed with energy, and she snatched in a breath, holding her slight body very taut. But the stirring heaviness of her breasts and the little twist of heat at the heart of her were too pressing to ignore, and bewilderment flashed through her eyes. 'But we're having a fight...'

'I don't want to fight with you,' Alexandros imparted very softly, deciding then and there that when playing it cool sentenced him to celibacy, he had played it cool for long enough.

'I have to take Toby and Connor out for a walk,' she told him hurriedly, struggling to suppress and sidestep the physical awareness that was threatening her self-control.

Releasing her hands, Alexandros startled her by walking out to the hall. He reappeared barely a minute and a half later.

'What were you doing?' Katie almost whispered.

'I was telling your nanny that the boys need some fresh air.'

Katie blinked. 'But...but why did you do that? For goodness' sake, it makes it look as if—'

'It's not her job to think about how anything looks. You have such touchingly naive concerns, *pedhi mou*.' Stunning dark golden eyes rested on her with a measured power that fired colour into her fair skin. 'Come here...'

'No way...absolutely no way!' Katie asserted with feverish intensity.

Alexandros jerked loose his tie and, unbuttoning his jacket, shrugged his shoulders out of it and tossed it on an armchair.

Green eyes huge, Katie stared at him. 'What are you doing?'

'What does it look like I'm doing?'

His mobile phone buzzed like an angry wasp. He pulled out, gave it a regretful look, sighed, and switched it off without ceremony.

'But that's probably the bank and terribly important!' Katie protested, as he cast his tie alongside his jacket and her sense of panic and confusion rose to suffocating proportions.

'*Theos mou*…do you think I always do what people expect me to do? Sometimes obeying one's natural instincts feels more right than following the rules. This is one of those times.' Loosening his collar, he embarked on his shirt buttons.

'Stop!' Katie gasped, hot-faced.

'If I stop, I leave…and I start looking for someone else.' Brilliant dark golden eyes watched her absorb that statement and turn as ashen pale as though some vital life force was being leeched from her.

The very thought of Alexandros with another woman tore Katie to shreds. Just that one little mention of that option and she was living her worst nightmare. Dry-mouthed and trembling, Katie watched a bronzed segment of muscular torso appear between the parted edges of his fine cotton shirt. Her heart was beating very, very fast. 'You're threatening me—'

'No, I'm being brutally honest, *glikia mou*. Did you think I would wait for ever? Either you want me or you don't…'

'Getting married is—'

'No.' Alexandros spread lean brown hands. 'This is much more basic. I'm not talking about marriage. Leave that out of it. You don't know what you want, and it's time you did. I want to go to bed with you, but I don't want a four-act tragedy after it.'

Her chin tilted, green eyes sparkling, cheeks pink. 'I don't like the idea of you with someone else!' she flung back at him chokily, anger and pain coalescing in that forced admission.

Alexandros strolled closer. There was so much all-conquering hero in the blaze of primal satisfaction in his gaze that she was tempted to release her tension by slapping him for an opportunism that smacked of piracy. Furious tears glistening in her eyes, she hissed shakily, 'Sometimes I hate you so much I could scream!'

Alexandros tugged her to him with strong, determined hands. 'I know…and it's refreshing to be with a woman who occasionally finds fault with me,' he conceded, without a shade of irony.

Feeling like a feather fluttering up against a solid steel wall of assurance, she rested her brow against his chest. The rich, awesomely familiar scent of his skin assailed her and she trembled. She loved him; she hated herself. He had forced her into a tight corner and emerged triumphant with a truth she would never have willingly given him: all her proud independence and defiance was destroyed by the very thought of him slaking that high-voltage sex drive of his in the arms of another woman.

He smoothed her hair almost clumsily, and expelled his breath on a slow, measured hiss. 'A month is a long time for me…too many cold showers, endless lonely nights.'

Against her stomach she could feel the hard male heat of him, and her tummy flipped in response. Long fingers knotting in her ringlets, he claimed her generous pink lips with a voracious hunger that made her knees give way under her. Bundling her up into his arms with easy strength, he tumbled her down on the sofa and let his tongue delve with erotic precision into her mouth, while he eased her slender thighs apart to explore the taut stretch of fabric that concealed her most secret place from him. He stifled her helpless whimper of need with his lips when she jack-knifed beneath the tormenting stroke of his lean fingers, every sensual nerve jangling with urgency.

He pushed up her T-shirt, let his teeth graze a stiff pink crest, dallied there while she arched her hips and gasped, insanely conscious of his every move and her terrifying response. All sensation was centred at the damp hot core at the heart of her. He drew up her knees, tugged down her panties, and told her hungrily that lace-edged white cotton was a real turn-on. The tightness low in her pelvis made it impossible for her to stay still. She dug her hands into his shoulders and pulled him back to her, driven by a need so powerful it was a consuming instinct.

'Don't stop...' she pleaded frantically when he lifted his arrogant dark head.

Passionate dark golden eyes slammed into hers. 'We need to get a couple of things straight—'

'Not now!'

'No more nonsense about friendship,' Alexandros decreed raggedly, hauling her to the edge of the sofa with strong hands. 'No more references to duty or love. Let this be pure, perfect enjoyment for both of us.'

Katie wouldn't let herself think about what he was saying. Her body was on fire for him, singing a pagan song of shameless craving. She knew conscience was going to kill her, but she was prepared to pay the piper. He plunged into the hot satin heat of her receptive depths and she almost passed out with pleasure. What followed was the wildest, hottest excitement she had ever dreamt she might experience, and at the summit an incredibly intense climax.

Afterwards she clung to him, dimly wondering if she was in heaven, trying not to be shocked by the fact that they were both still wearing most of their clothes.

'I needed that,' Alexandros confessed hoarsely, seeking and demanding a passionate kiss that demonstrated a renewed hunger that took her aback. He laughed huskily when she looked up at him in bemusement. 'I really, really needed that, *pedhi mou*...and I need so much more.'

He lifted her up into his arms, clamped her legs round his waist, and carried her out of the room.

'No...what about—?'

'Our children were safely off the premises *before* you started screaming with pleasure.' Alexandros pressed his mouth hotly to the sensitive skin below her ear and began doing something so impossibly erotic she moaned out loud.

'I didn't scream,' she mumbled belatedly as he brought her down on her bed.

'You will this time.' With single-minded efficiency Alexandros was stripping off her T-shirt and her skirt, yanking the duvet out of her grasp before she could scramble out of sight below it. 'No...I'm a big boy. I get to look all I like.'

'Alexandros!' she wailed, jerking up to hug her knees. 'I can't—'

'Please...' he said, for the first time, burnished golden eyes smouldering over her.

'It would make me feel shameless—'

'Shameless in the bedroom works well for me.' Meeting her strained gaze, Alexandros hastened to add, 'But only if it's you...'

She shut her eyes tight and lowered her knees, lay down like a sacrifice on a slab.

'You can blush in places that I didn't know could blush,' Alexandros breathed not quite steadily, rearranging her slender body into a slightly more daring pose. 'But if you don't look back at me I'll feel like a voyeur...'

Katie went rigid, and then lifted her lashes.

'That's perfect.' Alexandros spoke very quietly, tugging her hands very gently back down to her sides when they made a sudden sneaking attempt to cover up her most in-teresting areas. 'You're so beautiful...'

She frowned. 'No, I'm not—'

'You are to me,' he told her truthfully, admiring her delicate porcelain-pale curves with immense appreciation, and only vaguely wondering why it was the most intensely erotic moment of his life.

'I'm really not.'

'There may not be much of you, but what you have is in great proportion. Your hair is an amazing colour, and though your nose may turn up like an elf's it suits your face. I like your eyes, and your mouth, a hell of a lot,' Alexandros breathed, pitching his shirt off and disposing of what remained of his clothing with a haste that was possibly more flattering than his honest appraisal of her looks.

'Anything else?' Katie was not too chuffed about the elf crack, but his enthusiasm was undeniable.

'You're so natural…' His slumberous gaze devoured her with earthy boldness. He drew her back to his hotly aroused length, curved long fingers to her pouting breast with distinct satisfaction. 'There's nothing false, nothing surgically enhanced. Half the time you don't even wear make-up.'

'Everything's so physical with you,' Katie muttered shakily.

'You'll get used to it, and learn to like it that way.' Alexandros tugged gently on a swollen pink nipple and wrenched a responsive gasp from her. She quivered like a vibrating piano wire against him. He smiled with approval and let his carnal mouth nuzzle the tender skin of her throat, while he continued to caress her wildly sensitive flesh.

'But there could be so much—'

'No…' Alexandros leant over her, all domineering male, reproof in every powerful line of his lean, gorgeous face. 'This time we do it my way. Simple, straight, nothing messy…'

Moisture prickled at the back of her eyes. She refused to believe that his relationship with Ianthe had been based on straightforward sex. He had loved his wife. He would never, ever love her in the same way. How many times did he have to spell that out to her? When she had told him she loved him in Ireland he had ditched her faster than the speed of light, because her confession had filled him with distaste.

Alexandros could feel her tensing, trying to impose some space between them, and he didn't like that. He kissed her and held her fast, employing every erotic skill in his considerable repertoire to keep her close.

He made love to her again, and then again, until she was so drowsy that she could hardly keep her eyes open. It was as if he couldn't get enough of her. In spite of the ache of hurt at the back of her mind, she couldn't help but be thrilled by the sheer strength of his desire.

She was half asleep when she realised that he was no longer beside her. Black hair still gleaming from the shower, Alexandros was fixing his silk tie and fully dressed.

'You're leaving?' she whispered in surprise.

'A rescheduled meeting to replace the one I skipped earlier. I have to be in Rome tomorrow, and I go from there to Hong Kong,' he admitted, watching her sexily tousled reflection in the mirror like a hawk.

Consternation filled Katie and she sat up, feeling horrendously forsaken and forlorn. 'When will you be back?'

Alexandros breathed in deep, questioning why her obvious disquiet at his departure from the country should act on him like a shot of adrenalin. She didn't want him to leave and she couldn't hide it. Clingy, needy behaviour usually repelled him, left him cold as ice. But when Katie looked stricken at the prospect of having to get by without him it lit a blazing fire of burning satisfaction inside him.

In fact it made him feel happy. He wondered why that was, then acknowledged how fortunate it was for the stability of their children that he *did* feel that way.

Not an atom of that rare instance of self-examination showed on his lean, bronzed face. 'I'm not sure. I'll call…'

Katie nodded like a marionette.

'Doesn't this feel good?' Alexandros gave her a brilliant bracing smile, mentally willing her to follow his lead and act more upbeat. 'No stress, no strain. This is how I always wanted it to be between us, *thespinis mou.*'

Katie listened to the thud of the front door on his exit. He was gone and the apartment was silent. Her throat thickened. *How he'd always wanted it to be:* loads of sex, without love, ties or demands. He was much happier than he had been when he was proposing marriage. And why was that? She had agreed to his terms and, without quite realising how it had come about, it registered that she appeared to have fallen into the role of his mistress. Her eyes watered. She willed the stupid tears back and strove to work out how the heck that had happened, and what on earth she was planning to do about it…

CHAPTER EIGHT

A RARE smile on his wide, passionate mouth, a laden gift box clutched below one powerful arm, Alexandros stepped into the lift in Katie's apartment block. Although he loathed surprises, he knew that she loved them—and he couldn't wait to see her face when she realised that he was back in London thirty-six hours sooner than he had forecast. He had worked impossibly long hours to manage that feat.

During his eight days abroad he had spent an entire evening shopping—and he hated shopping. He had enjoyed the toy stores, though, he conceded, wishing that Katie was as easy to please in the gift stakes as their sons. His level ebony brows pleating, he wondered tautly if he had got it right this time. It was ironic that he knew exactly what Katie liked. Long after he had parted from her he had often found himself seeing something and thinking that Katie would have loved it, whether it was a view, a piece of music, an item of clothing or a joke. He had no idea why he had always understood her tastes so well. Perhaps he listened better than most men, and he had a very retentive memory. Or perhaps it was down to the fact that he was highly observant. But when he had been with Katie in Ireland he had really enjoyed buying her presents, and watching a look of wonder and delight blossom in her hugely expressive eyes.

Before he'd met her, his staff had bought the gifts he gave to women, and they had always been very expensive and impersonal. This time around he had been very careful about what he bought for Katie. He had walked right past a half-dozen items that he had known she would adore. He had purchased no cute cards, no flowers, no favourite any-things that might risk giving her that fatal romantic message and lead to further accusations of deception. So he'd opted for Chantilly lace lingerie with a top designer label. After all, there was nothing wrong with selfishness. He was also hoping that the platinum and diamond pendant carrying the initial 'K' that he had bought from the world's most expensive jeweller would magically exorcise his current infuriating and spooky habit of doodling that same letter every time he got a pen in his hand.

Unlocking the door of the apartment with his key, he was surprised by the noisy thump of music, playing loud enough to shake the rafters. He hadn't realised that Katie was a rock fan, but he was pleased that she was evidently at home. He went straight into the sitting room. She wasn't there, but evidence in the shape of the empty bottle of champagne lying on its side suggested that she was enter-taining. Where?

A garment lay on the limestone floor of the corridor that led to the rest of the apartment. His brows descending over frowning dark golden eyes, Alexandros bent and hooked a finger into the item. It was a man's purple shirt, and it was *not* one of his. In the same second he made that de-duction, it was as if the entire world went into a crazy time-warp. He broke into a sweat, every muscle in his big powerful frame locking into rigidity. The incessant driving beat of the music seemed to swell like the roaring riptide of emotion surging through him. Through the door to the left he could hear a wailing sound that went beyond the level of the music. It was Toby and Connor, crying...

Although instinct urged him to check on them, his savage, glittering gaze was locked to the door ahead, which stood wide open on Katie's bedroom. He strode on to the threshold and saw the naked couple on the mattress. He recognised Damon Bourikas first, and he was about to haul him off the bed and kill him when he registered that the woman in Katie's bed was definitely not Katie. It was Maribel the nanny, an over-endowed blonde, engaged in an act that Katie was still not sophisticated enough to know about. Disgust and relief combined with such force inside Alexandros that he felt momentarily light-headed. When he hit the off button on the entertainment centre to silence the thundering rock chorus, he noticed the scattering of fine white powder and the rolled-up note on the dressing table. He went white with rage and repugnance.

'The party's over. Get out before I call my security team up to throw you out the way you are!'

Damon attempted to make a laughing apology in a flood of Greek.

Alexandros cut in to tell him that it if they weren't gone in minutes he would be calling the police. He strode into the nursery, where one glance at Toby and Connor's red and swollen faces was sufficient to tell him that his sons must have been crying for attention for a good deal longer than a few minutes. His hands clenched into furious fists. Shorn of their usual bouncy confidence, the babies looked pathetic, and pitifully grateful to see him. The sight of their helplessness kicked his heart wide open.

In truth he felt distinctly weird, he conceded, raking

long fingers through his cropped black hair and registering in astonishment that his hand was trembling. For some
inexplicable reason he could not stop reliving that sick
instant when he had actually believed that Katie might be
in bed with another guy. Having sex with someone else,
betraying him, cheating on him. Perspiration dampened his
skin, and it was but a prelude to the startling rolling tide
of nausea that took sudden hold of him. He made it into
the *en suite* bathroom in the nick of time. *Theos mou*, what
was the matter with him? He was never ill. Had he picked
up an infection?

Only ten minutes ago he had been riding high, after a
phenomenally successful trip and the awed approbation of
all his staff. He had travelled straight from the airport to
see Katie and the children. The whole sordid scene he had
interrupted had outraged his every principle: drug abuse in
a property he owned, a sleazeball like Bourikas daring to
desecrate Katie's fluffy girlie bedroom, the nanny neglect-
ing their children. But would that have made him physically sick? Made him feel as though a brick wall had
suddenly fallen on him?

One of the twins sobbed, shooting him back out of his
bemused introspection. Katie hadn't been in bed with
anyone, he reminded himself with fierce exasperation.
Later she would be very much in bed with *him*, in his bed
at Dove Hall. That was not negotiable. He had been too
patient. But now he would take charge of the situation the
way he should have done from the start.

Having washed, he contemplated his sons. He was down
a nanny. Where was Katie? He could phone her, or call in
reinforcements. Or he could look after them himself for a
while. He lifted the little boys out of their cots. They were
damp and needed to be changed. When had they last eaten?

He thought about reinforcements again, but conscience won out: it would be cruel to let strangers handle them straight after what they had suffered. After removing his suit jacket, tie, and his diamond cufflinks, he found clean clothes for the twins and got down to work. Two hours later he called Cyrus to come and give him a hand to get the children down to the limo.

'Don't ask,' Alexandros warned his head of security when the older man was presented with Toby, clad only in a nappy and a chocolate-smeared blanket. His brother was in a similar state. But it was Alexandros who had fared worst of all: bathwater, chocolate stains, biscuit crumbs, spilt milk and juice had destroyed his usual elegance. His black hair sat up in little clumps where it had been clutched by sticky fingers.

When the children were secure in their car seats he took a deep breath and relaxed for the first time in two hours. He fell asleep. The limo was well on the way to Dove Hall before he lifted the phone to call the twins' mother.

'You're a kind girl.' Calliope Christakis gave Katie's hand an affectionate squeeze. 'I hope you get that job.'

'Even though Alexandros will go mad?' That morning Katie had had an interview for a receptionist's position with an upmarket property agency. After it she had met up with Calliope and accompanied the older woman to a dental appointment that she had been dreading. Lunch and a shopping trip had followed.

'A little of what he doesn't like does him good,' his grandmother told her cheerfully. 'Imagine him telling you that it is his *duty* to marry you! All that education and he says that. Of course you said no. He's a Christakis and a banker. He'll come up with a better offer.'

'We'll see...' Katie wished that she had managed to hold firm against Calliope's gentle interrogation technique of questions and seemingly casual comments. When Calliope had hinted that she thought less of her grandson for not offering Katie a more stable relationship, Katie had just had to speak up on Alexandros's behalf. Now, kissing his grandmother's cheek, she promised to come for lunch soon with Toby and Connor, and took her leave.

When Alexandros phoned her she was letting herself back into her apartment. Frowning, she murmured, 'What do you mean...the twins aren't here?'

In a few graphic sentences, Alexandros outlined the scene he had interrupted. Her heart sank like a stone. She was horrified, for she had been out all day. 'Maribel seemed so nice...' she mumbled in a daze.

'Sadly, that doesn't mean she was also a responsible person. With hindsight, perhaps she was too young.'

Having assured Katie that Toby and Connor were fine, Alexandros suggested that she pack whatever she and the children would require for a weekend at Dove Hall.

'Are you blaming me for this?' she whispered.

'No. But I won't let it happen again, *yineka mou*.'

While she packed, Katie wondered what he had meant by that closing comment. Hadn't *she* chosen Maribel for the job? As she was about to leave the apartment she found the bag he had discarded in the hall and unwrapped his gifts. Tears sparkled in her eyes as she attached the diamond pendant round her throat. She studied the lingerie with hot cheeks and stuffed it surreptitiously into her weekend bag, next to the toys he had bought for the boys.

Desperate to be reunited with her sons, Katie raced into the country house and straight up to the nursery. Toby and Connor were fast asleep in their cots, and she breathed again, feeling a little foolish for her concerns. Even so, she was painfully aware that something much more serious might have happened to her children.

Alexandros was in the library, on the phone. Lounging back against his desk, he indicated that she wait, and she wandered over to the huge windows that overlooked the lush green grassy slopes which ran all the way down to the edge of the classic lake. While Alexandros talked in Greek her eyes ate him up, in a series of avid stolen glances that were too nervous to linger.

He was so beautiful, she thought painfully. When he had been abroad she had told herself that she had gained control of her feelings for him. She had thought that her love was at a reasonable rather than obsessional level. And now one glimpse of him had exploded that foolish illusion. There he was, his classic bronzed profile silhouetted against the daylight, turning back towards her, black hair gleaming, inky spiky lashes long enough to cast a shadow on his superb high cheekbones, tawny eyes with that stunning golden impact. He still made her feel as giddy and breathless as a teenager.

'Toby and Connor look quite untouched by all the excitement,' she confided.

'That's not what you'd have said if you'd seen them when we arrived here,' Alexandros admitted wryly. 'I took care of them for a couple of hours at the apartment and I got them in a mess.'

'Why didn't you ring me? I would have come straight home.'

'For some reason I assumed you'd be back soon, and…I am their father.' Alexandros shrugged a broad shoulder. 'I thought I should be capable of looking after them on my own for an hour or so. Pride comes before a fall. I'm *not* capable.'

Katie was amazed and touched that he had even made the attempt. 'What happened?'

After the nightmare ordeal of bathing the twins, he had found it impossible to get clothes on to their squirming and uncooperative little bodies. When he had tried to feed them, everything he had offered had been rejected in favour of the chocolate biscuits he had been eating himself. Unable to get the biscuits back again, he had surrendered to the screams and thrown in the towel.

'At least you tried,' Katie pointed out bracingly, lifting a hand to touch the glittering pendant at her throat, her green eyes warm with appreciation. 'And I love this…it's beautiful. I wish I'd been at home when you arrived.'

Studying her, Alexandros savoured her pleasure and her appearance. He liked the way she was dressed. In a grey pencil skirt, teamed with a white slash-necked top, her feet adorned with strappy high heels, she looked enchantingly small and feminine and ravishingly pretty. He thought it a shame that he was about to spoil the ambience.

'Right now we have something more imperative to consider,' Alexandros drawled levelly. 'I have tried to deal with this relationship on your terms and it's not working.'

'You *are* blaming me! Don't you think I feel bad enough on my own account? You warned me about Damon and I didn't listen…and he had already told me that he was after Maribel—'

'You *knew* that? I thought that it was you he was interested in.'

Saving face on that score was no longer an option, Katie registered painfully, and she went pink with discomfiture. 'No.'

That small point cleared up, Alexandros looked grave. 'I'll be frank. I want my children living with me where there are adequate staff to ensure that what happened today never happens again.'

'But that's not possible,' Katie protested ruefully.

'It is if you marry me. And I'm not asking this time. I'm telling you. Either you marry me or I fight you for custody.'

Shock reverberated through Katie and she stared back at him. She could not immediately credit that he was serious. The last time she had been with Alexandros he had treated her like a lover, and now that warmth, trust and intimacy were gone, as though they had never been. 'I can't believe that you're threatening me.'

'Toby and Connor deserve better than what we're giving them. If I can give up my freedom, so can you.'

Her small hands curled into fierce fists. 'But what if I don't want to be your sacrifice?'

His golden gaze chilled. 'There's no scope for negotiation on this. I've already started making the wedding arrangements.'

Her green eyes flashed in angry disbelief. 'Well, then, you can just unmake them again.'

'Why would I do that? And why the big drama?' Alexandros delivered with derisive force. 'You're sleeping with me anyway, *glikia mou*!'

Katie turned scarlet. 'Don't you dare throw that in my face!'

Alexandros always went ice-cold in situations of conflict. But out of nowhere came a rage that could have lifted the roof off his vast Regency house. 'Throw what? The truth? If you'd been at home when I arrived today, you'd have gone to bed with me. Deny it if you can, but I don't think we need a line of expert witnesses to prove my point!'

The colour seeped back out of her cheeks to be replaced by pallor. She felt utterly humiliated. It was true. She had never been much good at saying no to him sexually, and she *would* have slept with him again. Being confronted by that mortifying fact cut her pride to ribbons. She refused to look at him and compressed her lips. 'Do you know where I was this morning? I had an interview for a job.'

'Do you spend *every* minute of your waking day figuring out how to wind me up?' Alexandros enquired in a raw, incredulous undertone, still struggling to suppress that disturbing surge of black fury that had taken hold of him. 'A job? Why is it your mission to reject everything I try to do for you?'

'All I'm trying to do is be independent—'

'Forget it. I never thought I'd say it, but we need to go back to old-fashioned basics. I don't want a caring, sharing partnership or an occasional lover. I want a wife. There are good reasons why we should marry, not the least being that we have two children and we very much like having sex,' Alexandros spelt out with sardonic bite. 'But the next time we share a bed, I'll be your husband.'

Katie lifted her chin. 'Would you really fight me for the twins in court?'

'If that's what it takes to bring you to your senses, *ne*…yes,' Alexandros declared without remorse. 'I think you're acting irresponsibly.'

'No, I'm not.'

'Maybe you're not mature enough yet to see what I see. Toby and Connor need stability and two parents. I know the worth of those advantages. I believe that I can make a difference in their lives, and that it is right that I should.'

Katie swallowed the thickness in her throat. She was furious with him. His threats outraged her sense of justice. Would he really try to separate her from the twins? Or was he just making a point? Did she appreciate or care what he was doing to her in the process? He wanted equal rights over his sons and a bigger say in what went on in their lives. If he was no longer prepared to compromise, only marriage would grant him those requirements.

Ironically, his refusal to continue taking a back seat role as a parent was not a total surprise to Katie. In recent months she had watched from the sidelines while Alexandros steadily grew from a reluctant father into a committed one. He had made a lot of effort to spend time with Toby and Connor, and as he got to know them he had learned to care for them. In fact, Alexandros had managed to form ties with his sons which were in no way dependent on her.

A sense of foreboding assailed Katie then. No longer could she view herself and her children as an indivisible threesome. Suddenly she was feeling very scared and insecure. Much more uncertainty hung over her own position in Alexandros's life. His sons would always be his sons, but she had no such safety of tenure. It was no consolation to acknowledge that she had last ended up in bed with him because she hadn't been able to contemplate the possibility that he might have an affair with someone else. In fact he had manipulated her into doing exactly what he wanted with shameless cold-blooded efficiency. He was very good at that. Achieving his objectives was what he did best. But what if he had now decided that it might make better sense to walk away and take the children with him? How much of a hold would sex give her when the novelty was beginning to wear off?

A trained observer, Alexandros could feel the tension emanating from Katie's slight, taut figure. He would say nothing that might lessen the pressure on her. Having reached a decision, he was convinced that he had to be cruel to be kind.

'I'm shocked that you should use threats to try and make me do what you want.' As Katie made that ringing condemnation her triangular face was very pale and her green eyes very bright.

Alexandros surveyed her steadily. 'No comment.'

'I won't forget this.' Swallowing the lump in her dry throat, Katie spun on her heel. 'I'll give you an answer tomorrow.'

The door flipped shut on her exit. Alexandros discovered that he wanted to smash something. She was so stubborn. She was the only woman he had ever met who was as stubborn as he was. What did she need to think about? He had laid it out plain and simple and with no avenue for escape. What was wrong with making an instant decision? Was she deliberately making him wait for an answer?

He poured a brandy. A job? Why was she applying for jobs? He raked an impatient hand through his cropped black hair and drank, wondering why she would never, ever do what he wanted—except in bed. He pictured her in an office environment. Someone as full of life and energy as Katie would be popular. She had a quick mind and an even quicker tongue. She worked hard, learned fast. She was very sexy....

He compressed his wide well-shaped mouth into a fierce and puritanical line. Just because *he* never hit on his staff—well, just that once, with her—it didn't mean other men were so scrupulous. More than one guy was likely to find her attractive, and would maybe think she was really up for it when they found out that she was already the mother of two children. In fact some men might even target her because of that background. He imagined the sexual wolves circling her when he was out of the country on business. His even white teeth gritted. He knocked back the brandy. He did not want that situation to develop.

Before he had realised that the woman in the bed in Katie's apartment wasn't actually Katie, he had come within inches of killing Damon Bourikas in cold blood. Bourikas was very lucky that he had kept his grimy paws off Katie Fletcher, for had it been otherwise Alexandros knew that he would not have let the younger man live to tell the tale. Alexandros had accepted that when it came to Katie he was possessive. He wanted to know that she was exclusively his, and that was why marriage was the only option he was now prepared to consider.

Katie ate a snack supper in her beautiful bedroom. She had little appetite for it, though. She was furious with Damon and her former nanny Maribel for what they had done, and deeply shaken that, in spite of all her care and caution on their behalf, her children had still been put at risk. She was hugely grateful that providence had brought Alexandros back to London early, and that he had caught the guilty couple out. How long might such behaviour have gone on behind her back without her finding out?

When she went to bed, she lay awake, torn by uncertainty and worry. But she had no doubts about the answer she had to give. For two very good reasons she *would* marry Alexandros. First and foremost, she could not afford to risk losing custody of her children. Alexandros would be a frighteningly rich and powerful opponent in the parenting stakes. If she fell out with him, made him an enemy, it could turn into a disaster. Suppose he simply took the children back to Greece and fought a court battle from his home turf? What rights would she have then? The fact that she loved Alexandros only got second billing in the reason corner, because just then she felt ashamed that she loved him. But he would soon learn that she had no intention of condoning his use of duress by acting like a proper wife. Oh, no, indeed, Katie reflected bitterly. He might win the contest, but that did not mean he'd win all the usual spoils.

When Katie got up the next morning and discovered that Alexandros had already left for London and the bank, as though nothing had happened and it was another ordinary working day, she was fit to be tied. Once she had dealt with Toby and Connor's needs, she dialled his private number.

Alexandros dismissed the staff gathered round his desk and mentally switched off from the major stockmarket crisis that had forced him into the office at the crack of dawn. '*Kalimera, pedhi mou,*' he greeted her lazily. 'I was making plans for my stag night.'

Up until that point Katie had felt cool as a cucumber, but the instant he said that, emphasising that he had never doubted what her answer would be, she wanted to lunge down the phone line and slap him. 'Not funny, Alexandros!'

Alexandros printed a K on the pad in front of him, enclosed the letter in the jaws of a giant C, and circled it for good measure. Temper as a response from Katie was good, and it told him that he had her cornered. Success was within reach. 'As busy as I am at present, a stag night looks most unlikely. I thought a joke would lighten the mood.'

'Don't joke about what you said last night,' Katie told him thinly. 'You didn't give me a choice, and that's the only reason I'm going to marry you.'

'That's fantastic news,' Alexandros fielded, his intonation as confident and positive as though she had told him she couldn't wait to see him at the altar. 'We'll go for a special licence and get married in two weeks' time. The wedding organiser will work with my staff, so that you can concentrate your energies on choosing your dress.'

'No ideas to offer on that score?' Katie prompted,

tongue-in-cheek, since all the other arrangements and decisions already appeared to have been made.

'I would love to see you in white, *thespinis mou*. White from head to toe, no style statements. It'll be a very traditional wedding.' Alexandros jerked his head in frowning acknowledgement of the frantic pleading signals that two of his executives were giving him from the doorway. 'Look, I'm sorry, the helicopter is here to take me to the airport. I may not make it back much before the wedding, but I promise that I'll call you every day.'

The airport? Where was he going? She wanted to ask, but instead she was left with a dead phone humming and an attack of raging, screaming frustration. A few minutes later she switched on the business news and she found out about the stockmarket crisis.

CHAPTER NINE

TEARS of pride glimmering in her eyes, Maura Sullivan surveyed her daughter with a contented smile. An attractive woman with short copper hair, she looked a good deal younger than her fifty years. 'You look like a princess in a fairytale.'

'Honestly…? You're not just saying that?' Unconvinced, Katie studied her reflection in the elegant fitted gown, which clung with loving fidelity to her slender curves and made the most of her slim figure. The hand-embroidered fabric was gorgeous, but the design was plain, as she had decided that she did not have the height to carry anything more elaborate. A short, flirty crystal-beaded veil, attached to the exquisite diamond tiara which Calliope had insisted she borrow, added the final note.

'I know you're nervous because it's such a big fancy wedding, but Alexandros will only have eyes for you,' Maura declared with warm conviction. 'Dermot and I might only have met him last night, but we were very impressed with him. We weren't expecting someone so rich and important to be as friendly and welcoming.'

'Alexandros has buckets of charisma, and he was in top form yesterday,' Katie conceded, with the keen smile she wore every time she mentioned her bridegroom's name in her mother's presence; she didn't want the older woman worrying about her.

Maura had been thrilled at the news that her daughter was getting married, and Alexandros had phoned her in New Zealand to insist that she and Dermot, her second husband, make the trip to the UK at his expense. For Maura, one of the most enjoyable aspects of the entire affair had been the chance to meet her grandchildren and get to know them.

'It's an awful shame that business has kept you apart for the past fortnight, and then last night—when you must both have been gasping to be left alone—you had to entertain all your relatives and his.' Maura sighed with sympathy. 'But I must say, I do like his grandparents. They're just lovely people.'

'Yes,' Katie agreed fondly. Calliope and Pelias had provided her with sterling on-the-spot support, and the older couple's sincere delight in the wedding about to take place had touched her. At their insistence, Katie and her family had stayed in their spacious home in the run-up to the wedding.

Even so, nothing had so far managed to ease the tight, hard knot of angry hurt and insecurity that Katie was keeping hidden inside her. Thoughts that did nothing to lift her confidence continued to attack her. Ianthe's giant portrait, which still dominated the main staircase at Dove Hall, was a continual reminder of how uniquely impressive true physical beauty was. Either you were born with that blessing or you were born short with a nose like an elf's, Katie reflected bleakly. Whether she liked it or not, Alexandros was bound to be looking back today to his first wedding, and recalling how very different his feelings had been on that occasion. Ianthe had been loved and appreciated and grieved over, while Katie felt her children were of more importance to her bridegroom than she could ever be. Hers was to be a marriage of convenience, rather than love, and because he had already rejected her love once she would not offer it again.

'But I have to admit that I really don't know what you were doing when you decided to invite that Leanne Carson to your wedding,' Maura confided with a slight grimace. 'Did you get around to telling Alexandros about that yet?'

'No, I haven't. But Leanne was my friend, and if I want to forgive her for selling that trashy story to the newspaper, it's my business and nothing to do with him.'

'Well, you've always been very loyal to your friends, and I think that's great, but…' Maura hesitated uncomfortably. 'I wouldn't let Leanne cause trouble between you and Alexandros.'

'I'm giving her a second chance because she was always there for me when I was having a hard time.' Katie saw no reason to tell her mother that she wasn't actually planning to draw Alexandros's attention to Leanne's presence in the midst of several hundred guests. What he didn't know wasn't going to hurt him.

Katie had gone to visit Leanne on impulse. In truth, she had felt a great need to talk over the episode that had ruined their friendship. Leanne had been overjoyed to see her, and had apologised wholeheartedly for what she had done. When the other girl had admitted that she had only approached the journalist because she had been in fear of eviction after she'd fallen behind with her rent, Katie had understood, and had felt even more sympathetic.

At that point in her conversation with Maura, Katie's stepfather, Dermot Sullivan, came to tell them that it was time to leave for the church. A well-built man of medium height, he managed a car showroom in New Zealand. Maura's health and spirits had blossomed tremendously since her second marriage, and Katie liked the older man.

In less than two hours she would be Alexandros's second wife, Katie registered in a daze.

Toby and Connor and their new nanny, a sensible young woman in her thirties, with impeccable references, had already accompanied Alexandros's grandparents to the church. Getting into the white limousine, Katie was careful to keep her short train clear of the ground. The wedding didn't seem quite real to her, since Alexandros had been out of the country while everything was being organised, and her sole contact with him had been via the phone. Their conversations had been so stilted his grandparents could have listened to them and fallen asleep while Katie painstakingly described every minute of the twins' day and ignored enquiries that were the slightest bit more personal.

The night before, however, seeing Alexandros again after a break of two weeks had jolted her equilibrium, and she had been grateful that they were surrounded by other people. When Alexandros had attempted to speak to her alone, she had utilised every evasive tactic she knew and then vanished upstairs. From the landing above she had sneakily watched as Pelias intercepted his grandson before he could follow her.

Of one point Katie was certain: she was not letting Alexandros off the hook for what he had done. While she would act like a bride in public, she had no intention of carrying on the act in private. He had blackmailed her into marriage and he had had no business doing that. No way was she about to share a bed with a husband who had used the threat of a court custody battle to force her to the altar!

Alexandros needed to learn respect, and sleeping with him was clearly not the way to go about achieving that objective. The guy who had sworn he would fly round the world to spend an hour in bed with her was about to hear the word *no* for what might well be the first time in his life. Though she wasn't really looking forward to the moment when Alexandros finally realised how she intended to stand up for herself…

When she arrived at the Greek Orthodox church, Katie was totally disconcerted to find Alexandros waiting to greet her. Sheathed in a grey striped morning coat that was a superb fit, he looked devastatingly handsome. His dark golden eyes arrowed over her in intent appraisal as he presented her with an exquisite bouquet of flowers. 'It's a Greek tradition. You look very beautiful, *yineka mou.*'

'You're actually here to stay…no flight to catch?' Katie prompted sweetly, marvelling at the way in which he simply glossed over the blackmail he had employed to get her to the church. 'Nothing serious going down at the bank?'

Alexandros gave her an appreciative grin that proved the toughness of his hide and still made her heartbeat race. 'From today I'm all yours, and we're having a very long and very private honeymoon.'

The church interior had been beautifully decorated with flowers. Both she and Alexandros were handed a beribboned candle, and the service began. She knew exactly what was happening, because she had had the benefit of two separate meetings with the elderly priest, as well as a wedding rehearsal in which Pelias had stood in for his grandson with much humour. She and Alexandros exchanged rings. Symbolic matching crowns of silver and pearls joined by a ribbon were placed on their heads. They drank from the same cup of wine and circled three times the ceremonial table on which a bible sat. The guests showered them with rose petals. After the blessing the crowns were removed, and the priest joined their hands. It was a solemn and moving ceremony, and Katie discovered that even her anger with Alexandros could not detract from her awareness that they were now man and wife.

They left the church by a rear entrance, their arrival and their departure having gone unremarked by anyone other than the official photographer, a film crew and the security team. A huge number of precautions had been taken to preserve the privacy of the day. The invitations had requested that the guests take no photographs. Every detail of the arrangements had been kept hush-hush, and the reception was being staged at Dove Hall, where security was very tight to keep all members of the press outside the boundaries of the park.

In the wedding car, Alexandros settled an elaborate box on her lap. 'My wedding gift to you.'

Her green eyes sparked. 'What is it? A set of platinum handcuffs?'

Impervious to the possible existence of a sting in that comment, Alexandros lifted her hand and planted a kiss on her palm. Brilliant dark golden eyes set beneath sleek ebony lashes flicked over her with a sexual heat that took her by surprise. 'Would you like that, *thespinis mou*? But you're very small, and your skin would bruise easily,' he murmured huskily, lean brown fingers enclosing her slender wrist to emphasise the point. 'Silk would be kinder to such fragile bones.'

She felt a beetroot blush wash over her fair complexion and snatched her hand free, her skin tingling from his caressing touch. 'It was a joke…okay?'

'We'll see… Over the next eight weeks we will have time to explore a lot of uncharted territory.'

'*Eight* weeks?' Katie gasped, shock making her drop her

cool, frosty front. 'You're planning to take two months away from the bank?'

'It's a special occasion.' Alexandros tugged gently at a copper ringlet and let several more spill across his hand.

Suddenly she was feeling very much like an animated toy, being examined by a new owner, and her nervous tension raced up the scale at speed. When he found out that sex was not on the newly married menu, eight weeks would soon start feeling like seven weeks and six days too long. Now, however, was definitely not the time to make that announcement, for the very last thing she wanted to risk was the eruption of a row while they were surrounded by dozens of guests.

'How much time did you take off when you married Ianthe?' Katie heard herself ask with sudden curiosity.

A sharp silence fell and she held her breath.

'A week. There was no element of choice. I was about to sit my final exams at university.' His intonation was constrained, as if even talking about his first marriage was a painful challenge.

As well it might be to a male so reserved he hid all his emotions, Katie conceded unhappily. Wishing she hadn't asked, she addressed her attention to the still unopened box on her lap and flipped up the lid with an unsteady hand. 'Oh…my word…' she whispered, blinded by the radiance of an emerald and diamond ring.

'We didn't have an engagement…I want to make up for the fact,' Alexandros breathed gruffly.

Katie studied the ring, her hot gritty eyes glazing over with tears. Her heart felt as if it was cracking in two. In a sharp movement she closed the lid down again and stuffed the box back in his hand. 'I don't need a ring to remind me that you dumped me in Ireland!'

Alexandros almost groaned out loud. *'Theos mou*…that has nothing to do with this ring. Am I to live with these recriminations for ever?'

Katie stared woodenly out of the window.

'I thought it was the wisest solution…I put what was best for you first.'

Katie slung him a withering glance. 'Don't kid yourself!'

'After Ianthe…I wasn't ready to make a commitment. I met you too soon. I felt guilty. You were very young and inexperienced—'

'Since when did that influence you?'

'You're the one and only virgin I've ever slept with!' Alexandros ground out furiously. 'If I'd taken you out of Ireland with me, what would I have been supposed to *do* with you?'

Katie elevated a delicate coppery brow in unashamed challenge. 'Oh, I'm sure you'd have thought of something.'

'The only future I was likely to have offered you then was as my mistress…that's why I ended it.'

'It is a far, far better thing that I do than I have ever done before?' Katie misquoted with lofty sarcasm. 'Why don't you just admit the truth? I told you I loved you, and the truth was such a turn-off that you left the country!'

Alexandros found it disturbing that she should have that much insight into the way he operated—particularly when he had not understood his own reactions half so well at the time.

While he was making that acknowledgement, Katie was struck by the level of her own bitterness, and mortified by what she had just said. What on earth was she playing at? The past was dead and gone. Some things—and unwelcome declarations of devotion fell very much into the category— were more sensibly left buried and forgotten. Alexandros had had an affair with her while he had still been grieving for Ianthe and she ought to have come to terms with that by now.

Regret swept over her. In a movement that was as abrupt as her former rejection of the gift, Katie swiped back the ring box from him. Thirty seconds later, she slid the gorgeous jewel onto the appropriate finger. 'Thank you… it's gorgeous,' she said, a tad flatly.

Alexandros was about to comment on that change of heart, and then decided not to look a gift horse in the mouth. It was a very big day for her, and she had had virtually no time to prepare for it. Possibly she was just feeling emotional, he reasoned, resolving to be supportive and understanding. He offered her a drink, asked her if her mother and stepfather were enjoying their trip, and then stuck so rigorously to making polite conversation that they travelled all the way to Dove Hall without a single opportunity arising for her to voice one more controversial word.

The wedding party took up position in the hall and greeted the guests as they filed past into the ballroom. Katie finally espied Leanne, a highly visible figure in her rather brief cerise satin dress, and tensed, hoping that her friend would manage to avoid attracting the bridegroom's notice. Sadly, it was not to be. Leanne, never one to hide her light or indeed anything else under a bushel, was determined to meet Alexandros. Stopping dead in front of him, she left Katie with no choice other than to make an introduction that she would have done just about anything to avoid.

'Leanne Carson…' Alexandros murmured, without any expression at all.

'I played cupid for the two of you,' the blue-eyed brunette proclaimed shamelessly. 'I mean, if it hadn't been for me, you and Katie might never have got together again! She was always very backward about coming forward.'

As Leanne passed on down the line, Katie could not bring herself to look at Alexandros. He inclined his proud dark head in a signal that brought Cyrus to his side, and a low-pitched exchange took place between the two men.

'You can't ask Leanne to leave when I invited her,' Katie whispered fiercely under her breath, fearing that that was his intent. 'I was going to tell you that she was here—'

'No, you weren't,' Alexandros shot back, cool as ice water dropping on a sizzling hotplate. 'You were hoping I wouldn't notice her in the crowd, but vulgarity of that magnitude is hard to miss!'

'What were you telling Cyrus?'

'To watch her…and the silver.'

'Thank you very much!'

Only when the last guests had arrived and they were about to enter the ballroom did Katie have the leisure to finally notice what she felt should have struck her the instant she entered the house. The huge portrait of Ianthe had been removed from above the main staircase and a pair of beautiful landscapes now hung in its place.

Thoroughly disconcerted by that development, she whispered, 'What did you do with Ianthe's portrait?'

The question made Alexandros glance at her in surprise. 'I had it moved.'

Katie almost thanked him, but when it occurred to her that doing so would be tantamount to confessing how sensitive she had been to the presence of that portrait, she embraced an awkward silence instead. Conscience told her that Ianthe had had every right to that place on the wall, and guilt writhed through her. How could she be so petty? Even so, she could not help but be impressed by her bridegroom's forethought and consideration on her behalf.

Reunited with Toby and Connor, she played with her sons for a few minutes, until it was time for her to join the bridal party at the high table.

She enjoyed a couple of glasses of champagne before Alexandros took her on to the dance floor. When he drew her close to his lean, hard body, she shivered a little. Suddenly she was overwhelmingly aware of his potent masculinity and how long it had been since they had last been that close. The faint familiar aroma of his skin enveloped her, and she tensed in dismay at the flicker of sensual heat curling low in her pelvis.

'Aren't you going to say anything more about Leanne?' she queried, happy to offer that potential bone of contention in an effort to distract herself from a response that she knew she had to suppress.

'Why did you invite her?'

'She's very sorry, and she was a friend for a long time.' Her words muffled against his shoulder, Katie linked her arms round his neck until she realised what she was doing.

'I hope you don't live to regret it. You're very trusting. Some will take advantage of that trait and make it a weakness,' Alexandros warned her wryly. 'When someone lets me down, I don't give them the chance to do it again.'

The movement of the dance brought him up against her, ensuring that she was fully acquainted with the lithe strength and power of his hard, muscular frame. Her mouth ran dry. Her body seemed to have a series of triggers, which responded without her mental output and made concentration an outrageous challenge.

As the music segued into another song, Alexandros tugged her head back and gazed down at her with slumberous golden eyes. 'I can't wait to be alone with you. My grandfather wouldn't even let me come up and talk to you last night,' he confided hoarsely. 'Admittedly talking wasn't much on my mind...'

Colour stung her cheekbones. She didn't know what to

say, and was entirely disconcerted when he lowered his proud dark head and tasted her generous pink lips with an intoxicating sensuality that left her head swimming and her knees weak.

Laughing appreciatively at the applause that had broken out from their audience, Alexandros brushed her flushed cheekbone with a long forefinger. 'Later…a wedding night to remember for a lifetime, *thespinis mou*.'

Katie veiled her eyes, feathery lashes concealing her troubled expression. Why was she feeling guilty? For goodness' sake, was loving Alexandros so deeply rooted in her psyche that she could deny him nothing? Even when he was very much in the wrong? She had been weak too often with Alexandros, and this was the reckoning time, she thought apprehensively. It was not a matter of trying to level the score. How could it be? Alexandros was her husband, and naturally she wanted a future with him. But it had to be a future in which she was more than the twins' mother and the woman in his marital bed. He might never love her, but she was determined that he should learn to treat her as an equal, a wife worthy of his respect.

As the afternoon wore on, however, it started to dawn on her that, in public at least, Alexandros did treat her very much as an equal. He had never been so attentive. He never once left her side while they worked their way round their guests. On more than one occasion he reminded those who wanted to talk business with him that it was his wedding day.

When the bride and groom had satisfied the conventions, they sat down with Toby, Connor, Maura and Dermot for a while. That was the moment when their younger son, Connor, chose to haul himself up on the edge of a sofa and take his first wobbling steps towards his mother. His little face lit up with amazement at the achievement of walking upright for the very first time.

'Aren't you wonderful?' Dropping down on her knees, Katie opened her arms wide and caught Connor to her in an exuberant hug. She saw the same glow of love and pride in Alexandros's lean dark face. A lump formed in her throat when she watched him comfort Toby, who had tried and failed to emulate his brother's feat and burst into floods of tears.

Pelias joined her later, when she was helping to put the children down for a much-needed nap. 'Calliope is so excited about having Toby and Connor to stay with us this week. Of course we'll have your nanny to help out, but we have so many treats planned. When they wake up, we'll take them.'

'I'm going to miss the little rascals,' Katie confided ruefully. 'But it *is* only for a week.'

The bridal couple were to spend their wedding night at Dove Hall and leave for their Greek honeymoon the following day.

'A week for the grown-ups to enjoy being newly married and alone.' Pelias Christakis studied her with warm approval. 'I had almost given up hope of seeing it happen, but you have transformed my grandson's life.'

'I've turned it upside down,' Katie slotted in ruefully.

'Alexandros deserves a normal marriage and family life. We are sincerely happy for you both,' Pelias told her gruffly.

As she went back downstairs, that phrase, *a normal marriage*, made her a frown. It seemed an odd thing for Pelias to have said. Had it been a veiled criticism of his grandson's first marriage? Doubtless it had been a reference to Ianthe's infertility. Children, after all, were highly prized in Greek culture. But she was still a little surprised,

for all things considered it had been a rather unkind comment—and Pelias Christakis was one of the kindest, most
tactful men she had ever met.

Cyrus approached her. 'Leanne Carson is taking photos
with her phone,' he informed her.

Katie blinked, and the pink bled out of her cheeks.
'Are you sure?'

The older man nodded confirmation.

'Does…my husband know?'

'Mr Christakis said that you would want to deal with it.'

Her tummy knotted at the prospect of that unpleasant
challenge, but accompanied by Cyrus, she went downstairs to confront her friend. Leanne just laughed when
reminded that there had been an embargo on photos printed
on her invitation. The phone was a very expensive high-
tech model. Katie suspected that the other woman had deliberately come armed with the means to invade their
privacy and that of their guests. Was some newspaper
already standing by, waiting to hear from her?

Leanne needed little encouragement to show off the
pictures she had taken, and Katie was horrified to see that
the twins featured—as well as certain celebrity guests
caught unawares. Leanne only lost her temper when Katie
passed the phone to Cyrus to delete the photos. A car was
already waiting to take the furious brunette to the train
station. Her vindictive final comments hurt Katie more
than anything else that had taken place, and she was seriously worried that another newspaper article might appear.
Had Leanne managed to send any of the photos before their
deletion? And would a tell-all scoop of a story appear in
print regardless? After all, Leanne would still be able to
describe their entire wedding day.

Alexandros said nothing. Unaware of what had taken

place, Pelias and Calliope took their leave with Toby, Connor and the nanny. Maura and Dermot left next, and Katie hugged her mother close. Her mother and stepfather were planning to spend a week visiting friends and relatives before flying back to New Zealand.

Soon the steady hum of cars and helicopters marked the departure of the guests, and the bride's tension began to climb like a pressure gauge. As the moment of revelation with regard to their wedding night came closer, Katie could feel her store of courage shrinking.

'Where are you going?' Alexandros asked when he saw her near the top of the staircase.

'Well…er…to get changed,' she mumbled through stiff lips, all composure threatening to desert her.

'But why?' Alexandros mounted the stairs to join her on the landing. He closed light hands to her shoulders and turned her away from the direction in which she had been about to head. 'Our bedroom is this way, *agape mou.*'

'It's been a really, really lovely day…'

As Leanne's shocking behaviour swam back into Katie's memory like a giant man-eating shark, she was silenced. She waited for Alexandros to make a sardonic comment on that same score but he did not.

'The very best…' Alexandros agreed, with remarkable restraint.

With careful hands he turned her back to face him and then bent down and swept her up into his arms.

'What on earth are you doing?' Katie gasped.

'I like the fact you're mine, lock, stock and barrel now,' Alexandros shared, striding down the corridor and shouldering his passage into a room bedecked with so many glorious flowers that her jaw dropped as he lowered her to the carpet. 'Calliope flew in Greek florists. She really goes for all the traditional stuff. This is a mark of her affection for you. But I told her not to bother rolling a baby on the bed…'

'I beg your pardon?' Katie echoed weakly.

'It's another tradition. But fertility is not one of our problems.' Laughing huskily, Alexandros drew her back into the shelter of his big, powerful body. 'I love our sons, but I would like to wait a little while before we extend the family. I want my precious wife all to myself,' he breathed thickly.

Within the strong circle of his arms, Katie felt as at risk as a bale of straw within reach of a match. She had still to drag her mesmerised attention from the bed, which had been transformed into a romantic floral bower. It was all so gorgeous—but now she had to say what she had to say, and he was going to hate her…

Easing free of his light hold, Katie spun round and backed off a couple of steps. 'I have something I have to say to you…'

His breathtaking smile lit his lean, strong features and made her heart hammer like a road drill. 'And I have something I have to say to you.'

'Me first,' Katie countered hurriedly, keen to get her little speech over with. 'I'm not going to sleep with you tonight. Now, please don't get mad about that.'

Alexandros had gone very still. Dense black lashes dipped almost to his stunning cheekbones, then slowly lifted again on glittering golden eyes filled with level enquiry. 'This is our wedding night. Why would you decide not to sleep with me?'

Katie closed her hands tightly in on themselves. 'Because you blackmailed me into marrying you, and that was wrong.'

'Blackmail is an evocative word. I wanted to marry you, and I cut through all the…nonsense.' Alexandros selected that final word with care, and squared his stubborn jawline. 'And here we are, married and with our whole lives before us. Please don't tell me that you're planning to destroy that.'

Katie made a tiny movement with a jerky hand, her normal relaxed motion restricted by the reality that the level of tension in the room was truly horrendous. 'I'm not planning to destroy anything—'

'Then why give me grounds for divorce on our wedding night?' Alexandros demanded wrathfully 'What *is* all this?'

CHAPTER TEN

ANGER burnishing his challenging gaze, Alexandros was unable to wait for her to answer that demand for clarity. 'This is some petty revenge because I saw what was right for us and I went for it on my own. You didn't like my methods?' he queried. 'Tough. My methods get results. If I'd left you in charge, we'd still be in limbo and nothing would be decided!'

'Well, it's good to know that your conscience won't be keeping you awake at night,' Katie responded, fighting the fact that her nerves had gone into panic mode at that reference to divorce. 'You need to accept that what you did was wrong, Alexandros—'

'How's it *wrong*? You're my wife now. My children will take on my name—'

'I want our relationship to be about *us*, not about the children—'

'Then stop behaving like a child!'

Katie breathed in deep, mentally buckled herself into defensive armour and held up a finger. '*One*…I married you because you threatened to contest my custody of the kids—'

'I wouldn't have done that to you!' Alexandros grated,

with a flash of his even white teeth. 'Don't you know *anything* about me yet?'

'Two—'

'*Siopi*…quiet!' Alexandros cut in. 'Holding up fingers and counting is bloody irritating.'

'*Two*…' Katie launched defiantly. 'I don't want to sleep with a guy who makes me feel that I'm only good enough for sex!'

'I don't want to sleep with a wife who thinks that she can use her body like a bargaining chip!'

'*Three,*' Katie continued doggedly. 'I—'

Alexandros threw up both hands in an explosive demonstration of rage. 'I'm out of here!'

'No…don't be like that!' Katie gasped, racing past him at breakneck speed to plant her back against the door and block his exit.

'Move.'

'But we need to talk—'

'I'm not in the mood. Move.'

'No…'

In response, Alexandros scooped her up off her feet, crossed the room in two strides and dumped her down on the bed. He came down over her and she lay there, looking up at him with huge green eyes full of surprise and uncertainty. 'Alexandros…'

'When you say my name it's an invitation.' Tawny eyes smouldering gold with aggression, he took her lips with a passionate urgency that melted her body into a honeyed compliancy that tore giant holes in her defences.

With a sob of regret in her throat, Katie pulled free.

Alexandros surveyed her with a savage condemnation that seemed to her to be all out of proportion to what she had done. His lean bronzed face might have been chipped out of granite, and he was pale below his dark skin.

'I swore I'd never marry again. I changed for you. I swore I'd never have children. I learned to accept and love our sons,' he breathed, with a bleakness of tone that made her break out in a sweat. 'And I thought you were different. Loving and giving and truthful. Well, where the hell has that all gone?'

His fierce bitterness cut through every layer of her skin. Suddenly she felt very much in the wrong, even if she did not quite comprehend exactly what that wrong was. What she did grasp was that in his eyes she had let him down, betrayed him, and that accusation hurt like hell. Who had he thought she was different *from*? She had never seen him reveal that much emotion before, and it shook her inside out.

The door closed. He was gone. She had done what she'd set out to do. She had stood firm, stuck like glue to her convictions. But she had not got to state the finer points of what she had intended to say. However, she had got across the basic message, she reminded herself, and, considering the hostility of her audience, that had been quite an achievement.

Her muscles were aching with the stiffness of extreme stress. Slowly, clumsily, she flopped back in her floral bower. She was still clad in her exquisite dress and tiara. *He* would have taken them off. Without any warning at all, she was racked by the most terrible doubts, and the tears started flowing.

The next day, Katie went down to breakfast at eight.

At one in the morning she had gone looking for Alexandros. Searching a house that contained two hundred and thirty two rooms had ultimately become too much of an embarrassing challenge as she'd run into or disturbed various members of the household staff. She'd rung his mobile, but it was switched off. Even if she had run him to earth, she had no idea what she would have said to him, and feared that, in the mood he had been in, she might actually have made things worse.

During the night, she had not slept a wink. She'd lain awake, hoping that Alexandros might come back to talk to her, and fretting herself to death when she had been left in splendid isolation. Suppose Alexandros demanded a divorce? Suppose he had left the country? Would he even go ahead with the honeymoon now?

She had got up at six to double-check her packing, then spent ages trying to hide the redness of her eyes with make-up. She'd put on a green skirt and top that she wasn't that fussed about but had bought purely because he liked her in short skirts.

The dining room was empty. She comfort-ate her way through a huge breakfast.

The wave of relief that assailed her when Alexandros strolled in, casually elegant in beige cargo pants and an Italian knit sweater, left her dizzy.

'Are you ready?' he asked.

A second wave of relief washed over her; the honeymoon was still on the travel schedule.

'Like the skirt,' he murmured, as she clambered with the greatest difficulty into the limo.

'Are you still talking to me?'

'Got any more skirts like that in your luggage?'

'Alexandros—'

He leant over and rested a silencing finger against her soft pink mouth. 'No—don't say it again, *agape mou*. "We need to talk" has to qualify as the phrase most likely to make the average guy run like hell.'

Green eyes huge, she nodded slowly. He lounged back into his corner, contriving to look absolutely gorgeous. She swallowed hard. They *did* need to talk, but now she was too scared to risk it. The night before he had told her that he had changed for her, and that declaration had shocked her, giving her another, not entirely welcome perspective of their relationship. Did he mean that marrying her and learning to be a father had been major sacrifices? She reckoned that he might well do, and she felt cut to the bone. There she was, always asking for more from him, and she knew that that was unfair and unreasonable.

A large contingent of the press awaited them at the airport. They were kept at a distance by Cyrus and his men. Alexandros closed a protective arm round Katie and ignored the questions flying their way. Someone said something about 'the latest story' and her blood went cold. *What story?* She cringed at the idea that Leanne's revelations might have made it into print again, and started praying feverishly. She could not work up the courage to ask Alexandros.

They boarded his private jet. She saw the neat rows of newspapers on the desk and riffled through them, to emerge with the trashiest—which bore a rather grainy depiction of them kissing on the dance floor.

Alexandros rested a lean brown hand over hers before she could lift the publication. 'Don't waste your time,' he advised.

But Katie was a glutton for punishment. She leafed through to find the centre spread. As far as embarrassing photos went, there was only one more, showing her in her bridal finery, but every detail of their special day was now public knowledge. Her eyes watered like mad and she stared into space, fighting for self-control. She felt so terribly to blame. She had been stupid and sentimental to trust Leanne again.

'I'm sorry about this,' she mumbled tightly.

'Forget it.'

But his forbearance was too much for her. Before the tears could overflow, she told him that she was going to lie down, and fled into the sleeping compartment. Sitting on the side of the bed, she struggled to hold the sobs back. The door opened thirty seconds later.

Alexandros sat down beside her and tugged her back against him. 'It's no big deal.'

'Everyone went to so much trouble and expense trying to keep our wedding private, and I blew it all sky-high!' Katie sobbed. 'I shouldn't have invited her—'

'You thought she was your friend.'

'That's what hurts…'

'Shush…' Alexandros sighed. 'I know.'

'Why aren't you furious with me?'

'I like the fact that you're like a chocolate with a soft centre,' he confided. 'If you were as tough as I am, you wouldn't be the same person, *agape mou.*'

She gulped in oxygen. 'Why are you being so nice?'

'I wasn't nice last night?'

A choked laugh was dredged from her, and she squirmed round to curl more intimately into the solid heat and strength of him. Love was running through her like a riot, and lust was following a close second. She was his, absolutely his, at that moment. She shifted closer, the tips of her breasts rubbing against the solid wall of his chest.

Alexandros reached down and straightened a pillow. He edged her away from him and slowly lowered her head down on to it. 'You're exhausted. You should get some sleep.'

'Where were you last night?' she whispered.

'Getting drunk.'

'Oh…' Katie just could not imagine that. And, knowing how much he liked to stay in control, could only feel that she had driven him into an act that was out of character.

'For what it's worth,' Alexandros announced from the doorway, lean, strong face grim, 'you were right about the blackmail. It was cruel. It was wrong. And I make no excuses. I knew what I was doing. I wasn't prepared to do the courtship thing…I wasn't even sure I *could* do it…I just wanted it—you and I—sorted.'

Katie wondered what 'the courtship thing' might have entailed. He had wanted it sorted? Yes, she understood that. He was very impatient, very stubborn, and very dominant—particularly in any field where he believed that he knew best.

'What do we do next?' she whispered.

'The honeymoon.'

Alexandros owned a private island. They flew in on a helicopter, which he piloted himself. From the air he showed her a sprawling white house, set in wooded ground above a white stretch of beach, and flew across the island to let her see the village. Down in the harbour, a ferry had docked. As they turned to head back inland a fisherman waved from a brightly coloured blue boat.

'We'll spend the rest of the week here, and then, if you feel like something more lively, we'll hit Ibiza at the weekend.'

At the house, cushioned wicker seating furnished the tiled terrace below stone arches that looked out to sea. The freshwater infinity pool shared the same incredible view. Decorated in Mediterranean blue and white shades that took on amazing clarity in the clear light, the interior of the house was pure enchantment. Rustic antiques were set off by natural cotton draperies and inviting sofas. And beyond the characterful charm and simplicity lay marble bathrooms to die for and a kitchen that a world-class chef would not have disdained.

'I love it…I really love it.'

Alexandros settled her luggage down in the fabulous master bedroom. 'As do I…it's always been a special place for me.'

Had he brought Ianthe to the island? Intelligence told her that he most probably had, and she scolded herself for being envious of a dead woman. But still she fell victim to mental images of the exquisite Ianthe posing out on the veranda, or draped elegantly across an opulent sofa, while Alexandros watched with helpless admiration.

They dined by candlelight on the terrace, and she sipped champagne. She wore the emerald and diamond ring and flaunted it as much as she dared. She had noticed that he was not touching her, and he hadn't put his luggage in the same room. Suddenly being apart from him felt really dangerous. If the distance between them got too great, maybe she would lose him altogether, she thought feverishly. All her insecurities were steadily mounting to the surface.

'Why won't you talk about Ianthe?' she asked him abruptly, and she really hadn't meant to say it. But there the controversial subject was, out on the table, like a giant rock suddenly surfacing from a clear sea.

Alexandros frowned in surprise and the silence stretched. He thrust back his chair and stood up. 'Why *would* I talk about her?'

Her nerves on edge, Katie forced a rueful smile. 'You were with her for the best part of a decade.'

Lean, darkly handsome face taut, Alexandros vented a sardonic laugh. 'And perhaps that's something I'd prefer to forget.'

That suggestion hung there while she gaped at him with steadily widening green eyes. 'Are you…? I mean, what you just said…er…I don't understand,' she fumbled shakily, unable to believe what he had just implied.

Alexandros shook his handsome dark head in apparent wonderment. 'Are honeymoons always this bad?'

Katie froze, and turned pale as milk.

Without another word, Alexandros strode off in the direction of the beach.

After a moment of paralysis, Katie scrambled up and chased after him, kicking off her high-heeled sandals to plunge into the soft sand in his wake. It was a clear night, and the full moon was shedding a lot of light. 'You can't blame me for being curious. You didn't tell me about her in Ireland, when we first met, and later, when I wanted to know more about her, you told me that I didn't have the right to know anything about your marriage!' she reminded him in a feverish rush.

'That was way back at the beginning. In Ireland I had no reason to talk about her. I knew you would be upset if you knew I'd been married and, like most men, I avoided the issue. I don't talk about her because I don't want to.'

'But I thought that if you'd really loved someone and lost them you'd want to talk about it…at least sometimes. Wouldn't that be healthier?'

'It wasn't like that between Ianthe Kalakos and I.' Alexandros stuck his hands deep in his pockets and stared out to sea, his bold, bronzed profile bleak.

'Then please tell me how it was,' Katie muttered. 'I really need to know.'

'I was twenty years old. She was twenty-four. My friends thought she was gorgeous, and they all said how lucky I was when she set her sights on me. She was up for anything, and at that age that was all I needed. I thought it was a casual thing. She said it was too. I was about to finish it when she told me she was pregnant.' Hearing Katie gasp, he turned his dark head and said grimly, 'Been there, done that, got the T-shirt…is that what you're thinking? It didn't turn out to be that simple, *thespinis mou*.'

But what he had already told her seemed to explain so much that Katie was knocked for six. He had been through the unplanned pregnancy scenario long before she came along with the twins. No wonder he had been so reluctant to credit that it could happen to him again. Lightning, it seemed, *could* strike twice in the same place. 'What happened?'

'I didn't even hesitate… I was a well-brought-up Greek boy. I married her, made two families very happy. A month after the wedding I accompanied Pelias to London for a business meeting, and when I got home Ianthe told me she had lost the baby.'

Katie winced. 'I'm so sorry.'

'Don't be. Ianthe was immediately determined to have a baby to replace the one she said she'd lost. I wasn't as keen. I was too young. But, had a child been born, I would have done my best. I did try to be as supportive of her needs as I could be. Five years after the marriage we were still childless, and I went with her to see her latest consultant because I was concerned by the weird treatment she was having. Quite accidentally I learned that she had never been pregnant in her life.'

Katie pressed a hand to her parted lips. 'Oh, my word… she lied to you about having conceived?'

'All that time we'd been living her lie. I couldn't believe that I'd been such an idiot. I was too naive to even *think* of asking her for proof before I agreed to marry her.' Alexandros sighed.

'You know…I imagined that you had had the perfect marriage with Ianthe,' Katie whispered apologetically.

'On the surface it did look perfect to a lot of people. Ianthe didn't have close friends, and our marriage *was* a perfect fantasy in her mind. But when I found out that she'd lied about the pregnancy, I told her I wanted a divorce…and she responded by trying to kill herself.'

'Oh, no…' Katie gasped in horror.

'That was when I realised that Ianthe wasn't really responsible for what she did. She was unstable—a fantasist who was obsessed with me,' he admitted, with a bleakness of tone that made her tummy clench. 'She couldn't bear to be on her own, and never stopped telling me how much she loved me.'

'And you felt trapped.' Katie was finally realising why such declarations weren't his style. Damon Bourikas had remarked that Alexandros had become a workaholic after his marriage. She imagined he had used work as an escape from the pressure of a relationship that must always have demanded more than he was able to give. For someone with his reserved nature, such emotional histrionics must have been an even greater challenge.

'I *was* trapped. She was my wife and my responsibility. Her parents were dead by then. I got her psychiatric treatment, but it didn't make much difference. She'd act a little more grounded for a while, and then slide back. She was taking heavy-duty medication when she crashed her car. She wasn't even supposed to be driving.'

The silence lay there until Katie finally picked up the courage to ask what she still longed to know. 'Did you ever love her?'

He released his breath on a stark hiss. 'No…not for a single moment.'

Katie blinked back hot stinging tears. 'I've been horribly

jealous of her, and yet she must've been so unhappy—and so must you have been.'

'When she died I felt incredibly guilty, because I knew I had my life back again and I'd wanted it back so badly I could taste it,' he grated in hoarse admission. 'I've never been able to forgive myself for that.'

'You did the best you could. You stuck by her,' Katie mumbled, half under her breath. 'Not every man would've done that in those circumstances. How much do your grandparents know about this?'

'Very little. But they must've had their suspicions that things weren't right. It was better that I didn't talk about it, though. It was easier to just do what I had to do and protect Ianthe by keeping up a front,' Alexandros told her flatly. 'Do you mind if I go for a walk?'

The abruptness of that request unbalanced her at a moment when all her concentration was focused on him. There was so much more she would have liked to have asked and said.

'No, of course not,' she lied, and headed straight back to the house. He wanted to be alone, and she was willing to bet that that had been a problem when Ianthe was around. Obsessive love was possessive, demanding and suffocating. His first marriage had been a nightmare that had to have poisoned his past with Katie and their present. How could it not have done? Of course he was wary of female love, expectations and commitment after such a ghastly experience. He had lost years of his life to a deeply troubled woman, and yet he had behaved with great honour. She realised in surprise that she loved him all the more for not having let Ianthe down. Yet in choosing not to confide even in Pelias and Calliope he had added to his burden of stress.

To have something to do she cleared up the dinner dishes, even though staff would come in the following day to take care of the housework. She went to bed but left her lamp lit, reckoning that it would show under the door. An hour later she heard him come back. She listened to the faint sound of the shower running next door and waited to see if he would come to her.

She lay in bed thinking about Alexandros and the state of their marriage. Not good, she concluded fearfully. He had admitted that he should not have used coercive tactics to get a wedding ring on her finger. How was withdrawing all intimacy likely to improve their relationship? Wouldn't it push them apart? He was so passionate. Why hadn't she thought of that? He had finally talked to her about Ianthe and she understood a lot of things much better now. In committing to marry a second time, he had made a much bigger leap in faith than she could ever have appreciated.

Confrontational demands did not seem much of a reward for that leap. She worried at her full lower lip and glanced at her watch. It was obvious that he was not about to join her— and why would he when she had said she would not sleep with him? Before she could lose her nerve, she got up again.

Alexandros was stretched out on the bed with his hands laced above his head, the sheet riding low on his hard flat stomach.

Moonlight revealed the wide-awake gleam of his gaze and Katie leant back against the door, her heart thumping like mad inside her. 'It's me…'

'What can I help you with?' he enquired lazily

Her face flamed, making her glad of the low level of the light. 'S-sex,' she stammered.

Alexandros resisted an unholy urge to grin and punch

the air in triumph. A suffering shared was a suffering halved. 'Come here…'

Anchoring a hand into her silky ringlets, he dragged her mouth hungrily down to his. She moaned under that urgent onslaught, heat pooling like liquid gold between her slender thighs.

He cupped her cheekbones between spread fingers. 'I can't think about anything or anyone but you, *thespinis mou*.' He dipped his tongue provocatively between her lips and eased her out of her nightdress.

'Neither can I…'

When she was all of a quiver with intense anticipation, he paused. 'Promise me you'll put on your wedding dress for me tomorrow, so that I can take it off…'

In a daze, she looked down at him, not quite sure she had heard him right. He ran a caressing hand over the swollen peaks of her breasts. Her stark indrawn breath was audible. 'I didn't bring it with me.'

'I'll organise a special delivery.' Binding her slender body to his hair-roughened muscular chest with a strong arm, Alexandros sat up and murmured in earthy challenge, 'So, wife of mine…will you dress up for me if I ask?'

'Yes…'

'You philistine,' he whispered huskily. 'How could you call anything this sublime just *sex*?'

So shamelessly excited she couldn't think straight, Katie closed her eyes beneath his demanding mouth and revelled in the tide of his hungry passion.

Four weeks later, Katie parked down at the harbour in her four-wheel-drive. She was early, so she lifted Toby and Connor out of their seats and buckled them into the light buggy she always carried in the boot. Her sons struggled against their harnesses and complained. Every since they had begun to learn to walk they had grown increasingly less tolerant of such restraint on their movements.

'Behave,' she told them sternly, copying the tone that Alexandros used when his sons played up.

'Mum-mum,' Toby murmured in a pathetic tone, all big brown eyes and charm.

Connor just stuck out his arms and gave her a big hopeful smile.

Helpless love surging through her, Katie crouched down and hugged each one in turn. A slim bright figure in a turquoise sundress, she walked up the village street. Several old people sat out on chairs at the front of their homes, and some children were playing with a ball. She smiled and responded to greetings, pausing now and then to allow the boys to be admired. She made liberal use of the Greek phrases Alexandros had taught her, and was delighted whenever she managed to add to her vocabulary.

She had a soft drink in the taverna, and sat out in the evening sunlight, enjoying the glorious view of the sea and the wonderful sense of relaxation she had. Alexandros did honeymoons really well. Just to think that she had another four weeks of the same bliss to look forward to made her feel positively giddy. He had already taken her shopping and clubbing and sailing and fishing.

The first week had been filled with lazy sun-drenched days when they had never been apart for more than a moment. Nothing had ever been so intense for her. She had never dreamt that she could feel as close to him as she now did, or that he could be so tender and affectionate. The barriers had come down after he'd told her the truth about Ianthe. The only time she had seen that cool reserve of his since was when some tourists had come ashore to stage a raucous party on their private beach.

Indeed, Katie had never been so happy in all her life. They had talked endlessly about so many things—even what it had been like for her when she was pregnant. That she had had to undergo that experience alone still bothered him. He was so good to her. She had bought designer clothes in Corfu town and modelled them for him. She was steadily acquiring a collection of contemporary jewellery. She fingered an earlobe, newly healed from being pierced to carry exquisite platinum and pearl earrings. She had been rather nervous, but he had held her hand through that experience. He spoiled her. He kept her awake at night in all sorts of infinitely fascinating and seductive ways. She was more madly in love with Alexandros Christakis than ever.

She watched his yacht skimming in and sailing into the harbour with sure skill. Alexandros appeared, and his crewman vaulted lithely on to the jetty to tie the craft up. Relief filled her. She wasn't into fishing, so that was the one thing he got to do alone. But, even though the sea had been smooth as glass all day, she could never quite relax until he came back again.

Evening sunlight providing pleasant warmth on her back, she walked down to the harbour to greet him. Clad in disreputable cargo shorts and a black T-shirt, Alexandros uncoiled his lithe, powerful frame from the yacht. He needed a shave, and it made him look like a very sexy pirate. She felt that little clenching sensation deep down inside her that only he could evoke, and stilled.

His beautiful eyes glittered, and he lowered his tousled dark head to kiss her with long, slow, intoxicating sweetness. He jerked back from her and looked down in surprise.

Toby was hauling on the hem of his shorts to demand his father's attention.

'I'm kissing your mother…have some pity,' Alexandros censured, reaching back for Katie.

Belatedly aware of the amused looks their amorous behaviour was attracting, Katie backed off and began to unclip her sons from the buggy. 'Let's go home.'

'It's such a long way…and I hate waiting, *agape mou*,' Alexandros growled, pressing his sensual mouth hotly to the nape of her neck as her ringlets cascaded over to one side.

Katie went breathless. Having watched him stow their sons in the four-wheel drive, she got in. 'What does it mean?' she asked across the bonnet.

'What does what mean?'

'*Agape mou…*'

Alexandros sprang into the driver's seat. In the silence, thinking that perhaps he hadn't heard her, she repeated the question and pointed out that he used the expression a lot.

He drove off. His handsome mouth compressed, he shrugged. 'It means…my love. That's all.'

Katie's eyes opened to their fullest extent. She dared not look at him. He'd sounded so dismissive of the endearment that it was clearly just an expression. Had her question made him uncomfortable? He said not a word all the way back along the twisting road that led to the house. Their smiling nanny emerged to take charge of Toby and Connor, and Alexandros gripped Katie's hand and dragged her into the house.

Giggling and blushing as he urged her into their bedroom and kicked shut the door behind him, she protested, 'Alexandros…'

'There's been something I've been meaning to say to

you...' Alexandros incised tautly. 'It's your own fault I didn't say it on our wedding day.'

Dismayed by his tone and tension, Katie whispered, 'Say what? *What* was my fault?'

His lean dark face clenched, lashes sweeping down as he studied the floor. 'I just feel so stupid saying it. I love you...okay? Right? I fell in love with you in Ireland, but I didn't recognise it for what it was. My emotions were so strong that I couldn't believe it was normal to feel that way.'

Katie blinked. 'Are you serious?' she mumbled dizzily.

'Yes. It was very destabilising stuff.'

Katie was honestly afraid she would faint with shock. 'Destabilising?'

'There I was, working at getting over a bad marriage, and then in you walked. I went straight off the rails into territory I didn't know even existed,' he admitted in a driven undertone. 'I'm the guy who plans everything, and nothing that happened with you was planned. I didn't realise it was love. I thought it was my unbalanced state of mind after Ianthe's death...that I was upset, out of control.'

'Our timing wasn't very lucky. So you loved me,' she conceded, striving to adjust to what he was telling her but very challenged to do so. 'No wonder I was so devastated when it all ended. I'd felt so sure of you up until that point...'

His dense lashes lifted on his brooding golden gaze and there was a definite appeal there for her understanding. 'When you told me you loved me, all I could think about was Ianthe. It was not that you reminded me of her in any way. But her confessions of love that I could never return still haunted me then.'

'Maybe you needed that time to get over what had happened with Ianthe. Were you really going to tell me you loved me on our wedding day?'

'You blew it,' he reminded her ruefully. 'You told me the wedding night was off.'

'It would have been full speed ahead if you'd mentioned love! When did you find out that you loved me?'

'I ignored my sneaking suspicions until the day I went into your apartment and thought for all of thirty seconds that it was you, rather than the nanny, who was shagging Damon Bourikas. Suddenly my mental fog cleared,' Alexandros confessed raggedly. 'The belief that you might have found consolation with another man almost killed me...almost killed *him* too.'

'My goodness, is that why you pulled the blackmail thing to get me to marry you?'

Alexandros nodded warily.

'Oh, that's so sweet.' Katie hugged him, thinking that fear of losing her was an award-winning excuse. 'And the picnic I rubbished. It was more real than I could've appreciated.' Her mind continued to rove over the blanks, and now she had him talking she had no intention of holding back any questions. 'But why did you keep on harping on about how it was just sex?'

'At first I thought it was, and then it seemed safer to keep it on that level—'

'You almost broke my heart!' Katie heard herself confess, and she was appalled, but a great surge of emotion had welled up inside her and a strangled sob emerged.

Alexandros grabbed her with a satisfying lack of his usual cool. Apologising in Greek and English, he covered her damp face with comforting kisses. '*Signomi*...I'm sorry. I can't be happy without you. Nobody else can make me feel the way you do, yet until it was almost too late I didn't understand why.'

'You must have been really stupid!' she hissed in tearful condemnation.

Alexandros wrapped both his arms tightly round her and rocked her against him until she had calmed down. 'I know I don't deserve you, but I really do love you, *agape mou.* You and the children have brought me back to life and I wake up every day feeling blessed,' he swore gruffly.

She subsided against him and held him close. 'I love you too,' she whispered happily. 'I can finally say it again.'

'I'll never stop saying it, *agape mou.*'

'What a little precious,' Calliope Christakis sighed, peeping into the cot at her newest great-grandchild, a little girl named Athena. 'She's dainty, just like her mother. And to think you and my grandson said there would be no more children for a few years!'

Katie blushed and grinned. Athena was now three months old. Not much planning had gone into her conception. Alexandros had merely murmured one night that he would love to see her body ripen with his child, and birth control had been abandoned there and then. Athena had been on the way within weeks.

Toby and Connor were now three years old. Energetic and talkative pre-schoolers, the twins were thick as thieves when plotting mischief, but each had a distinctive personality. Toby was a quick-tempered livewire, Connor the more thoughtful and calm leader of the pair.

They had flown out to the villa in Italy with his grandparents only two days before. Pelias and Calliope, however, weren't staying for long on this occasion. The older couple were about to leave on an escorted tour of their favourite Italian cities. Leaving the children in the tender care of the staff, Katie strolled downstairs with Calliope and kissed her goodbye. She waved at Pelias, who was already waiting in the car and tapping his watch, shaking his head in teasing rebuke of his wife's tardiness.

Sometimes Katie found it hard to credit that she had been married for two whole years. Her mother and her step-father had been over for a lengthy visit at the start of the summer. Alexandros made sure she saw her family as often as possible. He went out of his way to make her happy and she loved that in him. Their marriage had gone from strength to strength as their trust in each other blossomed and added a sense of warm mutual security. They both very much valued what they had together.

Alexandros had taken some drastic measures to cut down on his working hours. That had not been easy for him, and at first she and the twins had shared some of his trips abroad. But when she'd fallen pregnant with Athena, he had been afraid that she would overtire herself. He had made changes, and she saw a great deal more of her handsome husband now and loved the fact.

In actuality this very day was the day of their second wedding anniversary, but in answer to all enquiries she had told everyone that no, they weren't doing anything special. That was a complete lie. Some things, however, weren't for sharing. Some celebrations were of a more private nature. She adjusted the narrow pearl shoulder straps on her short swirling green organza dress and set off for the tower.

She walked down the woodland path and saw him through the trees. Her steps quickened without her even being aware of the fact. The romantic scene of luxurious quilts, cushions and a marble table overflowing with tasty food was every bit as beautiful as she recalled, and her sunny smile broke out. Alexandros, lounging back against the cushions with a glass of wine cradled in one lean brown hand, began to get up.

'Don't move,' Katie urged softly. 'You look like a Roman emperor.'

'Bring on my dancing girls.'

'There's just me…will I do?'

Alexandros ran smouldering golden eyes over her and extended his hand. 'I like the dress… I like you in it, but I'll like you even more out of it, *agape mou*,' he confided, with the earthy honesty that was so much a part of him

In response, Katie shimmied her slight shoulders and swung her hips. With one lingering glance he could make her feel like the most beautiful, sexy woman alive. 'You are so predictable, Mr Christakis.'

Laughing, his lean strong face alive with humour and a powerful look of tenderness, Alexandros tugged her down beside him with possessive hands. He settled her back against the cushions and extracted a lingering kiss. 'Isn't it great to know we've had less than three years together and there's hopefully another forty-seven at least ahead of us?'

Touched by that reference to his grandparents' lifelong happiness as a couple, Katie told him how much she loved him. He reciprocated with fervour, and the drowsy heat of the afternoon passed while they reaffirmed their joy in having found each other.

THE ITALIAN'S
BLACKMAILED
MISTRESS

JACQUELINE BAIRD

Jacqueline Baird began writing as a hobby, when her family objected to the smell of her oil painting, and immediately became hooked on the romantic genre. She loves travelling and worked her way around the world from Europe to the Americas and Australia, returning to marry her teenage sweetheart. She lives in Ponteland, Northumbria, the county of her birth, and has two sons.

Look for the most recent title by Jacqueline Baird, *Untamed Italian, Blackmailed Innocent*, available in March 2010 from Mills & Boon® Modern™ romance.

CHAPTER ONE

MAXIMILIAN ANDREA QUINTANO—Max to his friends—
walked out of the bathroom wearing only a pair of navy
silk boxer shorts. Just the effort of bending to pull them
on had made his head spin. He needed air and, walking out
onto the balcony that ran the length of the suite, he willed
the pain behind his eyes to vanish. It was his own fault. It
had been his thirty-first birthday two days ago, and
although Max owned a penthouse in Rome and a house in
Venice, he had done what was expected of him and spent
the day at the family estate in Tuscany with his father, stepmother, Lisa, and other family members.

But on his return to Rome yesterday, after he had taken
his yearly medical exam for insurance purposes, he'd met
up with his best friend Franco and a few others from his
university days for lunch. The party that had ensued had
ended up with Franco belatedly remembering his wife
was expecting him home in Sicily. Max, due to fly there
the next day anyway, had agreed to accompany Franco to
the island to carry on the party there.

Finally, at four-thirty in the morning and feeling much
the worse for wear, Max had got a taxi to the Quintano

Hotel, the hotel he was scheduled to arrive at that same afternoon in place of his father.

Ever since Max's grandfather had built his first hotel on the island, before relocating the family to Tuscany, it had become a tradition for the Quintano family to holiday at the Sicilian hotel during the month of August. For the last decade Max had rarely visited, leaving it to his brother Paulo and the rest of the family to carry on the tradition.

A deep frown suddenly creased Max's broad brow as he thought of his older brother's tragic death in a car accident just four months ago. When Paulo had enthusiastically entered the family business and become a top hotelier, Max had been given the freedom to pursue his own interests, and he knew he owed his brother a lot.

An adventurer at heart, Max had left university with a degree in geology, boundless energy and a rapier-sharp brain. He had headed to South America, where on his arrival, he'd acquired an emerald mine in a game of poker. Max had made the mine a success and started the MAQ Mining Corporation, which over the last nine years had expanded to include mines in Africa, Australia and Russia. The MAQ Corporation was now global, and Max was a multimillionaire in his own right. But, as he had been forcibly reminded a few months ago, all the money in the world could not solve every problem.

Deeply shocked and saddened by Paulo's death, Max had offered to help his father in any way he could with the hotel business. His father had asked him if he would check the running of the hotel in Sicily and stay a while to keep the tradition going. The loss of Paulo was too fresh for

Paulo's widow Anna and their young daughters to go, so of course Max had agreed.

Max rubbed his aching temples with his fingertips. The way he felt at the moment he was glad he had agreed to his father's request—he desperately needed the break. *Dios!* Never again, he vowed. By some miracle, when he'd arrived at the hotel just before dawn he had retained enough sense to instruct the night porter to keep his early arrival quiet. Nothing and no one was to disturb him....

Max stepped from the balcony into the sitting room. He needed coffee—black, strong and fast. He stopped dead.

For a moment he wondered if he was hallucinating.

A tall, feminine figure with a mass of flowers in her arms seemed to glide across the room towards him. Her hair was pale blond, and swept back into a long ponytail to reveal a face ethereal in its beauty. Her breasts he could only imagine, but her waist was emphasised by a black leather belt neatly holding a straight black skirt, which ended a few inches above her knees. The simple skirt revealed the seductive curve of her hips, and as for her legs... A sudden stirring in his groin said it all. She was gorgeous. *'Ciao, bella ragazza,'* he husked.

Sent up by the hotel manager to deposit the flowers and check the suite before the arrival of its illustrious owner, Sophie Rutherford was startled by the sound of the deep, masculine voice. She jerked her head towards the open French doors, the flowers falling from her hands at the sight of the huge man standing before her.

Frozen in shock, she swept her green gaze over him. Thick black hair fell over a broad brow, and dark, heavy-lidded eyes were set in a square-jawed, ruggedly handsome face. His bronzed muscular body was wide shouldered, with a broad chest lightly dusted with black hair that arrowed down over a flat stomach and disappeared beneath his dark shorts. His legs were long and splayed. He looked like some great colossus, she thought fancifully, and her green eyes widened in awe at so much masculine power.

Then he stepped towards her…. 'Oh, my God!' she cried, suddenly remembering where she was and belatedly realising he had no right to be there. 'Don't move! I'm calling Security.'

The scream echoed though Max's head like a razor on the bone. He closed his eyes for a second. The last thing he needed was someone calling the deity down on him. Then his less than sharp mind finally registered that her words had been spoken in English.

Max slowly opened his eyes, but before he could make a response she was disappearing out of the door. He heard the turn of the key in the lock behind her and could not believe it; the crazy girl had locked him in his own suite….

Shaking his head in amazement, he picked up the telephone and revealed his presence to Alex, the hotel manager. The he ordered some much needed coffee, and strode back into the bedroom to dress. Once he had shaved and dressed he returned to the sitting room, to find a maid cleaning away the flowers and Alex placing a coffee tray on the table. There was no mistaking the barely contained amusement in Alex's eyes as he greeted his old friend.

'Max, it's good to see you. I guessed you were the undesirable *giant* about to rob the place,' Alex said and he burst out laughing.

'Very funny, Alex. It's good to see you, too. Now, tell me, who the hell is the crazy girl?' Max asked, pouring himself a cup of coffee and downing it in one go, before collapsing onto one of the sofas.

'Sophie Rutherford,' Alex answered, joining Max on the sofa. 'Her father, Nigel Rutherford, is the owner of the Elite Agency in London. They handle the arrangements for a lot of our European clients, and Nigel asked me if his daughter could work here for a couple of months during her university vacation to improve her language skills. She is studying Russian and Chinese, but she also has a good grasp of Italian, French and Spanish. I thought, given the international clientele we attract, she could be very useful. She has certainly proved her worth already in the month she has been here. She is happy to work anywhere, and nothing is too much trouble for her.'

'If she is as good as you say, then I trust your judgement.' Max grinned at the older man. 'But my guess is the fact she is so beautiful might also have affected your decision,' he mocked.

'You would say that.' Alex grinned back. 'But, unlike you, it takes more than a pretty face to influence me—especially at my age.'

'Liar,' Max drawled, a knowing, sensual smile curving his hard mouth as the image of the young woman flashed up in his mind. 'Any man with breath in his body can see she is gorgeous, and I for one would like to get to know her a whole lot better.'

'Sophie is not for you, Max,' Alex said suddenly

serious. 'She is only nineteen, and in the absence of her father she is under my protection. Much as I like you, I do not think she is your kind of woman. She is serious about her studies and not the type of girl to have an affair—she is more the marrying kind.'

Max could have been insulted, but he wasn't. Alex was like an honorary uncle to him, and knew him well. As much as Max loved women, and they loved him, he had no intention of marrying for years—if ever. Since Paulo's death his father had begun to hint that it was time he married, constantly reminding Max that if he didn't there would be no male to carry on the great name of Quintano. But Max didn't want to settle down. He wanted to travel the world, doing what he loved. And with more money than he knew what to do with, Max was quite happy for Paulo's family to inherit their rightful share of his father's estate—as they naturally would have done if Paulo had lived. The last thing Max felt he needed was a wife.

'That's a shame.' His firm lips twisted wryly. 'She is delectable. But have no fear, old man, I promise not to seduce her. Now, shall we get down to business?'

Later that afternoon Max walked through the semicircle of trees that fringed the secure hotel beach and scrambled over the rocky headland to the small cove he had first discovered as a boy. He loved to dive from the rocks, and it was here that he had first become interested in geology. Today, however, the only rocks that concerned him were the ones in his skull, and he knew a swim would clear his head and cool him down.

Just then, a flash of pale gold against the backdrop of dark stone captured his attention. His dark eyes narrowed intently as he realised it was the girl from this morning. As he watched she flicked the shimmering mass of her hair over one shoulder and stretched herself out on a towel.

Silently Max moved towards her, his body reacting with instant masculine enthusiasm as his dark gaze swept over her. The pink bikini she was wearing was quite modest, compared to some he had seen, but the figure it graced was the ultimate in feminine allure. Her eyes were closed, and her glorious hair lay in a silken stream over one high firm breast. He had been right about her legs— they were long, slender and very sexy—and her skin was as smooth as silk, with just the shimmer of a tan. Max couldn't take his eyes off her, and he was instantly regretting his promise to Alex to leave her alone.

As he moved closer his shadow fell over her and she opened her eyes.

'Sophie Rutherford, I believe?' he drawled smoothly, and held out his hand. 'I am Max Quintano.' Max watched as she shot to her feet as though electrified. 'This morning did not seem to be quite the right time to introduce myself. Please forgive me for any embarrassment I may have caused you.' He smiled.

'Sophie, yes…' She blushed and took his hand. 'It is nice to meet you, Mr Quintano, but I think it is I who should apologise to you, for locking you in your room.'

Max felt the slight tremble in her hand and looked into her gorgeous green eyes. There he saw embarrassment, but also the feminine interest she could not hide—and miraculously his hangover vanished. 'Please, call me Max. There is no need to apologise—it was my fault—I must have startled you. Anyway, it is much too hot to argue, and as it happens you are occupying my favourite beach.' He smiled again. 'I wouldn't want to chase you away—I have already done that once today—please stay and allow me to show you that my apology is genuine and I am not some *giant* burglar.'

Sophie pulled her suddenly tingling hand from his and almost groaned. 'Did Alex tell you I said that? How embarrassing.'

Never before had she felt such instant and overwhelming attraction for a man. She had taken one look at him this morning and, shocked witless, had behaved like a terrified child.

Now, desperate to improve his impression of her, she added with a wry smile, 'But, in my defence, you really *are* very tall.'

'I'm six foot five—and there is no need for embarrassment, Sophie. I can assure you I am not in the least embarrassed by it. However, you do look rather red in the face—how about a swim to cool off?' Max suggested. Not giving her time to answer, he added, 'Race you to the water!'

Of course Sophie followed him. He hadn't doubted for a moment that she would; women had chased him all his adult life.

Wading into the water, Max turned and splashed her, and saw her smile broaden to light up her whole face. He also saw the gleam of mischief in her eyes just before she bent down and splashed him back.

The horseplay that followed did nothing to cool Max's suddenly rampant libido. Had she any idea that when she bent forward her lush breasts were bobbing up and down and almost out of her top? he wondered.

Eventually Max could stand it no longer, and he scooped her up into his arms. 'Trying to splash me, are you? You're going to pay for that, lady,' he declared, and waded farther out until the water lapped at his thighs.

'Don't you dare!' she cried, wrapping her arms firmly around Max's neck, her green eyes sparkling with laughter.

'There is nothing I wouldn't do to have you in my arms, Sophie,' Max teased, his dark gaze clashing with hers.

For a long moment their eyes locked, and the teasing stopped as desire, fierce and primitive, raced between them.

Sophie's green eyes darkened as for the first time in her life she felt the sudden rush of sexual desire for a man. She was intensely aware of Max's arm under her thighs, his other across her back and under her arm, the pressure of his long fingers splayed against the side of her breast. Her stomach churned and her pulse raced as the rest of the world seemed to stop. She simply stared into his eyes as though hypnotized, and the air between them grew heavy and shimmered with sexual tension.

Her gaze fell to his wide, firm mouth, and instinctively her lips parted as she imagined how his lips, his kiss, would feel.

The next second Sophie was under the water, swallowing what felt like half the ocean. Spluttering and gasping, she stood up and wiped the water from her eyes, to find Max watching her with a strange, almost regretful look on his face.

'I think we both need to cool off a little. I'm going to swim to the headland—see you later, Sophie.' And, like a sleek dolphin, Max dived out to sea, his strong brown arms cleaving the surface without so much as a ripple in the water.

Only later would she realise that a shark would have been a more appropriate metaphor….

Sophie watched him, helpless to do otherwise. Nothing in her nineteen years had prepared her for a man like Max Quintano.

After the death of her mother, when she was eleven, she had been sent to a girls' boarding school by her father. By the time she had reached the age of thirteen she had sprouted up like a beanpole to five feet nine and had become terribly self-conscious. She'd had few friends, and had spent the school holidays at home in Surrey, with Meg the housekeeper, while her father had worked.

A late developer, only in the past year at university had she felt her confidence grow in leaps and bounds. She'd been delighted to discover that being tall was no deterrent to making friends of both sexes, and she had even dated a few boys.

But never had she felt anything like the stomach-flipping, spine-tingling excitement Max Quintano's teasing smile and playful touch aroused in her.

A dreamy smile curved her wide mouth as she walked back up the beach and sat down on her towel, her besotted gaze focusing on his dark head, which was now a distant dot in the water. She could still feel the imprint of his arms as he had lifted her, the touch of his fingers against her breast on her heated skin…. Was this love or just fascination? she mused, unable to take her eyes off him.

Max turned in the water and struck back towards the shore, his tumescent flesh finally quietened by his strenuous swim. He had not had a woman since returning to Italy from Australia at the news of Paulo's death. He had endured four months of celibacy and was certain that this was the reason for his extreme reaction to the lovely Sophie.

Holding her in his arms, he had known she wanted him to kiss her—and he had certainly been aching to taste her lips and a lot more. But he had done the right thing and had left her alone, as Alex had requested. Alex was right. She was too young.

Feeling quite self-righteous, Max strode out of the water and flicked the hair from his eyes. He could see that she was still there on the beach, and as he approached she sat up and smiled. All his good intentions vanished. He was going to be in Sicily for a while, so what was wrong with a little flirtation with a beautiful girl?

'Come on, Sophie.' He reached a hand out to her. 'You have had too much sun. I'll walk you back to the hotel.' As she rose to her feet Max pressed a swift, soft kiss on the curve of her cheek. He heard the sharp intake of her breath, saw the sudden darkening of her incredible eyes his kiss had provoked, and before he made a complete fool of himself added, 'I'll show you the secret of the maze.'

As one week slipped into two Sophie didn't know if she was on her head or her heels. She was hopelessly in love for the first time in her life. Just the sight of Max Quintano set her heart aflutter, and when he spoke to her she was breathless. He treated her with a teasing friendliness, but his casual invitations to join him for a swim or a walk when she was off duty were enough to send her into seventh heaven. Of course she agreed like an eager puppy, and though they were not really dates they were both an agony and an ecstasy to her foolish heart. Max was the perfect gentleman at all times, and as much as Sophie wanted him to he never progressed past a kiss on her cheek.

Two weeks after first meeting Max, Sophie walked out of her bedroom and into the sitting room of the chalet she shared with her friend Marnie, the head receptionist of the hotel. Sophie was sure that tonight would be the night all her dreams would be fulfilled. Max had asked her out to dinner at a restaurant in Palermo—at last, a proper date!

'So what do you think, Marnie?' Sophie asked as she made a quick twirl. She had bought the sophisticated green silk designer gown from the hotel boutique that afternoon, hoping to impress Max.

'Let me guess—you are meeting Max Quintano?' Marnie quipped.

'Yes.' Sophie beamed. 'But do I look okay?'

'You look stunning! Max will be knocked for six. But are you sure you know what you are doing?' Marnie asked with a frown. 'I've warned you before about Max and his women. I even showed you a magazine article, remember? I can understand how you feel, but he is a lot older than you, and a sophisticated, experienced man. You're young, with your education to complete. Don't throw it all away on a brief affair—because that is all it can ever be.'

Sophie stiffened. 'I know, and I've heard all the rumours, but I'm sure those stories are vastly exaggerated.'

'Believe what you like—teenagers usually do,' Marnie said dryly. 'All I am saying is be careful. Max is a multimillionaire with a matching lifestyle. He rarely stays here for more than the odd weekend. The only reason he is here now is to fill in for his father and his family after the death of his brother. But that is about to change, because I heard today the rest of the family are coming soon—and when they do, Max will not hang around for long.'

'You don't know that for sure,' Sophie said, her heart plummeting in her breast at the thought of Max leaving.

'No, I don't. But Max and his father do not have the closest relationship in the world. I understand that although he gets on well with his extended family, the person he cares the most about is his stepsister, Gina. It's well known that they have had an on-off relationship for years. Some say she tolerates his other women because she is dedicated to her career as a doctor and not interested in marriage. But rumour has it that Old Man Quintano told Max ages ago he would not countenance such a relationship. As far as he is concerned they are brother and sister, and anything else between them is unthinkable. But circumstances change, and Max is very much his own master, and if and when he does decide to marry I wouldn't be surprised if Gina was his bride. So be warned, Sophie, and don't do anything foolish.'

Sophie was saved from responding by the ringing of the doorbell, but her happiness of five minutes ago had vanished. However, it returned the moment she opened the door and saw Max, starkly handsome and elegantly clad in an immaculately tailored suit. His tall figure oozed sex appeal, and Sophie's already pounding heart leapt in her breast.

Max turned a smiling face towards the open door and looked at Sophie. For a moment he was struck dumb. Her mass of blond hair was swept up in an intricate knot on top of her head. Her exquisite face was delicately made up to enhance her superb bone structure and fabulous green eyes. As for what she was wearing—the mid-thigh-length sheath of emerald-green silk outlined every feminine curve and lay straight across her high firm breasts. Damn it, he was getting aroused just looking at her.

'You look amazing—and remarkably you're ready,' he said, thinking that she wasn't the only one—he could have quite happily ravished her there and then.

'Yes.'

She smiled at him and the breath left his body. Max had to remind himself once again that he had promised Alex he wouldn't seduce her—but the trouble was, Sophie intrigued him on every level. She made him laugh, she was clever beyond her years and she was a great companion. As for her physical appearance—he only had to look at her to want her. He should never have asked her out tonight, he realised, because he did not trust himself to keep his hands off her.

Sophie sensed none of Max's doubts, either during the short car ride or as he took her arm and led her into the restaurant—she was simply too excited.

Max ordered champagne, and when their glasses were filled he raised his and said, 'To a beautiful girl and a beautiful night.'

Sophie's face heated at his mention of night. Did he mean what she hoped he meant? Was he at last going to move their relationship to the next level? Kiss her and then make love to her? Yes, she decided as his deep, dark eyes smiled into hers and they touched glasses. With that simple exchange, the mood had been set for the evening.

Sophie let Max order for her, and as course followed course and the champagne flowed freely she fell ever deeper under his spell. They talked about everything and nothing, and Max punctuated their conversation with a smile or the touch of his hand on hers. He fed her morsels of food she had never tried before, watching her every reaction with amusement and something more. By the end of the meal Sophie knew she was totally in love with Max.

'That was a perfect meal.' She sighed happily as Max paid the bill.

Perfect food, maybe, Max thought. But pure torture for him. He was white-knuckled with the strain of keeping his hands off her. He must have been mad to think he could have just a mild flirtation with Sophie, and when he slipped an arm around her waist and led her out of the crowded restaurant it was nearly his undoing. She was tall, and when she leant into his side they were a perfect fit, her hip moving sexily against his thigh.

'I am so glad you brought me here.' She turned her head to smile up into his face. Her teeth were even and brilliant white against the light golden tan of her skin and he felt his body tighten another notch.

He was no masochist. This had to stop or he was in real danger of losing control—not something he ever did. Dropping his arm from her waist, Max opened the car door for her—but it did not stop his heart hammering in his chest. She looked so utterly exquisite and so damn naïve she hadn't the sense to hide her feelings.

'My pleasure,' he said, and abruptly slammed the door.

By the time he slid behind the wheel and started the car he had his body under control. As he manoeuvred the vehicle along the winding road back to the hotel he glanced at Sophie and realised he had no right to be angry with her. It wasn't her fault she had the looks and the body of a temptress and stopped men in their tracks, he thought dryly as he brought the car to a halt outside her chalet.

After their laughter and intimacy over the dinner table Sophie sensed Max's mood had inexplicably changed, and when the engine stopped she glanced up at him and wondered what she had done wrong.

'Home again,' she said inanely, and blushed as she realised she was way out of his league in the sophistication stakes. But in the next moment he proved her wrong.

'Ah, Sophie,' he drawled huskily. 'What am I going to do with you?'

She saw the sensual smile that curved his firm lips as he reached to slide his arm around her waist and pull her close to the hard wall of his chest. He growled something softly, something she did not understand, and then his mouth covered hers and she didn't care.

It was as though a starburst exploded in her brain, sending shock waves to every nerve-ending in her body. He slid his tongue seductively between her softly parted lips, exploring the sweet, moist interior, and her hands involuntarily reached up to clasp around his neck. His kiss was more than she could ever have imagined, and Sophie closed her eyes and gave herself up to the wonder of his embrace. She felt his hand stroke up to cup her breast, and as his thumb grazed the silk-covered, suddenly taut peak, a fiery wave of desire scorched through her veins.

'*Dio!* How I want you,' Max groaned.

Sophie's fingers were tangled in the sleek dark hair of

his head, and her tongue—at first tentatively and then tenaciously—duelled with his as an ever-increasing hunger consumed her.

Max heard her moan when he finally lifted his head, and saw the passion in her dazzling green eyes. He knew she was his for the taking. He almost succumbed—after all, he was not made of stone, and denying his body was not something he was used to. But he had made a promise to Alex, so he had to rein in his carnal impulses.

Gently he pushed her back against the seat, and got out of the car, drawing in a few deep, steadying breaths as he walked around to open her door. 'Come on, *cara*.'

Hazy-eyed, Sophie glanced at the hand Max held out. It took an enormous effort on her part to still the shaking in her own hand and take the help he was offering, and step out of the car.

She looked at the staff chalet and back at Max, her body still strumming with excitement, not sure what to do, what to say.

Sensing her uncertainty, Max curved an arm around her waist and led her to the door. Once there, he turned her in his arms and narrowed his dark eyes on her bemused face—he would make it easy for her.

'Thank you for a lovely evening, Sophie. I won't come in. I have some international calls to make—different time zones, you understand.' He brushed his lips against her brow and said regretfully, 'I am leaving tomorrow, but maybe we will dine out again the next time I am here?'

Max wanted her, but he had a growing suspicion that once with Sophie would never be enough. He didn't believe in love, but he was astute enough to recognise that what he felt for Sophie and how he lost control around her could very easily become dangerous to his peace of mind.

'Thank you—I would like that,' she murmured.

Max saw the naked adoration and the hurt in her eyes, and much as he wanted Sophie he knew Alex was right—she wasn't for him. He had watched her with the guests, the staff and with the children she quite happily looked after whenever she was asked. She was so caring and everyone adored her. Sophie deserved the very best, and he was far too much of a cynic to believe in love and happy ever after—whilst she was too young and too much of a romantic for the kind of affair he enjoyed. The timing wasn't right. Maybe in a few years, when she had completed her studies, and if she was still single…who knew…?

'Good night, sweet Sophie.' Because he couldn't resist touching her one last time, he lifted a finger and traced the outline of her lips, saw her smile. 'That's better. A young girl like you should always be smiling,' he drawled softly, his dark eyes enigmatic on her beautiful face.

He opened the chalet door, and with a hand at her back urged her inside with a wry twist of his lips. She was temptation on legs, and far too responsive and eager for her own good—not every man had his self-control.

'And be careful,' Max warned her as frustration rose up in him. He spun on his heel and left. His decision was made. He would take a flying visit to Russia, to iron out a few problems with the manager of his Russian operation. As he recalled, the company's receptionist, Nikita, was a very inventive lover. With the arrogant confidence of a wealthy man in his prime, he told himself the world was full of beautiful women more than willing to share his bed. He didn't need Sophie, and he would dismiss her from his mind.

Sophie watched Max walk away, wishing he would at least look back and give her some sign that he cared. But it was in vain.

Later that night, when Marnie found her curled up on the sofa, red-eyed from weeping and looking miserable, she gave Sophie the benefit of her opinion.

'What did you expect after one dinner date? An avowal of love? Cheer up, girl. Max Quintano can have any woman he wants and he knows it. You were a pleasant diversion while he was here.' She shrugged. 'Who knows? If he returns he might take you out again, and if he does just remember what I told you before: a brief affair is the best any woman can hope for from him.'

Marnie's words didn't help, but at least they made Sophie face up to reality. Her first ever crush on a man and it had to be on Max Quintano—a much older, super-rich mining tycoon, and a womaniser by all accounts. Where had her brain been? He was as far out of her reach as the moon. Her mistake had been in mistaking a teenage crush for true love, she told herself flatly, and she had to get over it. At least she hadn't slept with him….

But somehow that thought gave her no comfort at all.

CHAPTER TWO

Seven years later

ON SATURDAY afternoon Sophie parked her ancient car on the drive and, taking her suitcase from the back she breathed a sigh of relief as she entered her old home. Timothy, her brother, ran down the hall to meet her and, dropping her suitcase, she swept him up in her arms and kissed him.

'Hello, darling,' she said as she carried him into the elegant living room to find his mother and their father.

Sophie looked at her stepmother, Margot, and then at her father. Immediately she sensed the tension in the atmosphere and wondered what was wrong.

'Oh, good you have arrived,' Margot said.

No, *Hello—how are you*? Sophie thought dryly, and sat down on the sofa, still holding Tim.

'I suppose we should be honoured you can spare the time to visit your brother with your jet-setting lifestyle. Where is it this time?'

'Venice, for a three-day international conference on global resources. But I don't have to leave until tomorrow night, so I have more than enough time to babysit this little man.' Sophie hugged Timothy closer on her knee and added, 'Why don't you and Dad make a night of it and stay at the hotel until tomorrow? I don't mind.' That should put a smile on Margot's face, she thought.

Two hours later Sophie was sitting in the stainless steel kitchen of the house she had been born in, feeding Tim his favourite tea of fish fingers and mulling over how her life had changed.

Five years ago, when she had graduated from university, Sophie had taken a year off to go backpacking around the world. On her return she had discovered that her father's new secretary was also his pregnant girlfriend. Marriage had followed, and Meg the housekeeper had departed at Margot's request—much to Sophie's disgust. And four months later her adorable young brother had arrived.

Sophie had been besotted with Tim ever since, and if she was honest he was the main reason she tended to go along with whatever Margot wanted. He was why she had agreed to Margot's last-minute request for a babysitter so they could attend a glamorous charity ball at a top London hotel.

Sophie glanced around the ultra-modern kitchen. The family home in Surrey had been totally renovated by Margot, and she barely recognised the interior any more. But at least, with the help of a small legacy from her mother, Sophie had her own apartment, overlooking the sea in Hove. The commute into London was not something she would like to do every day, but then she didn't have to. She was a brilliant linguist, and her work as a freelance translator took her all over the world. She had built up an impressive list of corporate and private clients.

She had spent the last eight weeks with a trade delegation, travelling around China, and before that six weeks working in South America. This weekend was the first time she had been home in months. It wasn't that she disliked Margot—after all, she was only two years older than Sophie—in fact they should have had a lot in common, but unfortunately they didn't. Margot was a social animal who loved the high life—the best restaurants and the right places to go and see and be seen. But to give her her due Margot, for all her love of society and designer clothes, was a good mother and would not leave Tim with anyone she didn't know.

Much as she loved her brother, it was with a sense of relief that Sophie left the next afternoon to catch her flight to Venice. She wasn't imagining it—the atmosphere between her dad and Margot really had been no better when they'd returned at lunchtime than it had when they'd left the evening before. Something was not right in their relationship. But as long as it didn't affect Tim, she wasn't going to worry.

She had enough to worry about going to Italy again for the first time in seven years. The very thought brought back a host of unwanted memories of her one and only love affair—and of what a complete and utter idiot she had been. She had fallen for Max Quintano like a ton of bricks, and when he had left the hotel in Sicily where she worked, she had been hurt. But when he had returned a week later she had fallen into his bed without a moment's hesitation. After he had taken her innocence she had leapt at his proposal of marriage, and had even agreed to keep it a secret until he could meet her father.

For all of two days she had been deliriously happy—
that was until she had discovered the kind of open
marriage he had in mind....

A cynical smile twisted her lush lips. Still, she had
learnt a valuable lesson from the experience—men were
not to be trusted. That lesson had been reinforced over the
years as she'd seen how a lot of them behaved as soon as
they arrived at a conference well away from wife and
family. Sophie had lost count of the number of times
married men had hit on her, and she had developed an icy
stare and a cool put-down to perfection.

The following Tuesday evening Sophie walked into the
ballroom of a top Venetian hotel on the arm of Abe
Asamov. Abe was a fifty-something, barrel-chested and
bald-headed Russian who barely reached her shoulder.
She had been delighted to see him arrive at the hotel this
morning, for the second day of the conference, because his
was a friendly face amongst a sea of strangers.

Abe was witty, and took great delight in fostering a
ruthless reputation. Only Sophie knew he was devoted to
his wife and family. In her last year at university she had
spent her summer vacation in Russia, teaching his four
grandchildren English.

When Abe had asked her to be his partner at this gala
dinner-dance, she had agreed. The company she was temporarily contracted to had been overjoyed, because Abe
Asamov was a billionaire oilman and owned a great deal
of Russia's resources. Sophie wasn't sure she believed
Abe's claim that he spoke only Russian, but she didn't care
because she was glad of his company.

'You realise, Sophie, that they will all think you are my lady-friend.' Abe said in his native Russian, grinning up at her as the waiter showed them to their table. 'No ordinary man could look at a beautiful blonde like you and imagine you have a brain.' He chuckled. 'I think I will enjoy fooling people tonight.'

'Watch it, Abe.' She grinned, knowing he was no threat to her. 'Remember you are a married man—and if that was meant to be a compliment it was a bit of a backhanded one.'

'You sound just like my wife.' Abe grinned back, and they both laughed as they took their seats.

Seated comfortably and with a glass of champagne in her hand, Sophie glanced around the room, taking in the other guests there that evening. Many she knew through her work. There was the ambassador, Peter, and his wife Helen, and next to them a couple who worked for the Italian government—Aldo and his wife Tina. There were also two Spanish men—Felipe and Cesare—whom Sophie was seated next to. Very pleasant company, she decided, and, taking a sip of her drink, she began to relax and look at her surroundings.

The dinner tables were set around a small dance floor, and at one end on a raised dais a jazz band played background music. The evening was a glittering showcase of the powerful elite of Europe. The men looked immaculate in dinner suits, and the women were dressed in designer gowns and jewels worth millions. But Sophie did not feel intimidated. Over the years she had worked and mingled with some of the richest people from all around the world—even crowned heads of countries. As a result, she had acquired the social skills and sophistication needed in such company.

At home, jeans and a sweater were her favoured form of dress, but she had amassed what she called her 'business wardrobe'. The black satin Dior gown she wore tonight was one of her favourites, as were the crystal necklace and earrings. She knew she looked good and could hold her own in any crowd.

Feeling relaxed, Sophie glanced across the dance floor as a group of late arrivals took their seats and her green eyes widened in appalled recognition…Max Quintano and his stepsister Gina. Her shocked gaze skimmed over his hard, handsome profile and moved swiftly away. She was almost sure he hadn't seen her.

With her heart pounding, Sophie manoeuvred her chair so she could turn her back slightly towards his table and hopefully remain unnoticed.

She turned to Cesare, seated on her left, and asked in Spanish, 'So, what do you do?' On hearing his response she focused all her attention on him. 'An earth scientist? How interesting.'

Fool that she was, Sophie could not believe she hadn't made the connection between global resources and Max Quintano before now.

Across the other side of the room Max Quintano smiled at something Gina said, not having registered a word. He had recognised Sophie Rutherford the minute he had entered the room. Her blond head was unmistakable, with the fabulous hair swept up in an elegant pleat, revealing her long neck and the perfect set of her bare shoulders. The cut of her gown displayed the silken smoothness of her back and the slight indentation of her spine. A spine he had once trailed kisses down. His body tightened at the memory.

He saw the exact moment when she recognised him, and watched as the cold-hearted bitch turned away in fright. He had despised her with a depth of passion he had not known he was capable off when they had parted, and the way he had dealt with it had been to ruthlessly blot her out of his mind for many years. Then, on the death of his father four months ago, due to a massive heart attack, the name of Rutherford had reared its ugly head again in the shape of Nigel Rutherford. Surprisingly, two months later on a brief trip to South America, Sophie Rutherford had been the object of much speculation. Twice in as many months he had been confronted with the very name he had tried to forget.

As executor of his father's estate, and with his stepmother distraught at her husband's death and in no fit state to concentrate on the running of Quintano Hotels, naturally Max had stepped in to help. An audit of the family's business had disclosed that it was running at a very healthy profit, but there were one or two bad debts outstanding. The largest one was the Elite Agency, London—Nigel Rutherford's firm. Max had soon discovered that they were not just slow at paying their clients' accommodation bills, they had not paid at all for almost a year.

How it had been overlooked Max could only surmise. Maybe his father had been in failing health for some time without believing it. He could relate to that feeling, because he had done the same thing seven years ago. When Max had been told he might have cancer he hadn't wanted to believe it, and a couple of nights in the lovely Sophie's bed had fed his illusion of invincibility. How wrong he had been…. So he could not blame his father for doing the same.

On further investigation into the bad debt he had discovered that Quintano Hotels was not the only firm owed massive amounts of money by Nigel Rutherford. Max had joined with the rest in calling for a creditors' meeting, which was to be held next Monday in London. However, Max had no intention of going—he was leaving it to the lawyers and accountants to take care of. He could not care less if the Elite Agency went under, along with its owner, as long as Quintano Hotels got paid.

But now, with the beautiful but shallow daughter only thirty feet away, sipping a glass of champagne and smiling as if she hadn't a care in the world, a different scenario sprang to mind. If *he* attended the meeting in London he knew he would have no trouble convincing the other creditors to bankrupt her father's firm; he was a very persuasive man.

Sophie was occupied at the moment, but next week he would make it plain to Nigel Rutherford that he wanted to meet his daughter *again*! He had already waited years, so a week or two longer wouldn't matter. With ruthless cynicism Max decided it would be interesting to watch Sophie squirm when she realised who was responsible for her father's downfall, and very satisfying to see how far she would go to save him.

Sophie Rutherford was the only woman who had ever walked out on him, and it had taken him a long time to get over the insult. Now fate had once again put her back in his life—and in his power, if he wanted to use it. With his body hardening at the mere sight of her he knew he did, and the iniquitous plan took root in his mind.

* * *

It had been an appalling trick of fate that had sent Max dashing back to Sicily and Sophie seven years ago. He had returned from five days in Russia to his apartment in Rome still celibate, and still resolved to stay away from Sophie. He had called an old girlfriend and arranged to have dinner that night, and also arranged to have lunch with Gina the following day—Friday.

His date had not been a success, and he had gone to his office early the next morning and finally caught up with the personal items of mail his PA had not opened. A casual glance at the report from the medical he had taken a couple of weeks earlier had told him there was a query about one of his results and that he would need to contact a Dr Foscari.

Two hours later Max had been sitting numb with shock as Dr Foscari informed him that his urine test had revealed irregularities in his testosterone levels—a sign of testicular cancer. The doctor had gone on to explain that it was the most prevalent form of cancer in males between the ages of twenty and forty-four, but was easily treated. He'd told Max not to worry, because the test wasn't certain, but as a precaution he had made an appointment with a top consultant at the best hospital in Rome for the following week.

Max had walked out of the clinic with fear clawing at his gut. But he had been furious at the mere suggestion he could be ill, and had determined to seek a second opinion. Gina was an oncologist; she would know the leading specialist in the field. He would talk to her over lunch, tell her his fears, knowing she would keep his confidence.

By the time lunch had been over Max had known more

than he'd ever wanted to know about his suspected illness. Gina, in her forthright manner, had immediately called Dr Foscari, and after speaking to him had told Max not to panic. She had explained that there might be other causes for the irregular testosterone levels, and that anyway there was now a ninety-five per cent success rate in the treatment of testicular cancer. At Max's insistence she had gone on to outline the worst-case scenario if it *was* cancer. She had asked him if he had noticed any little lumps, if he was feeling unusually tired or suffering any loss of libido—all of which he had vehemently denied.

When she had then begun to explain in detail the treatment and the side effects—the possible loss of virility, the freezing of sperm as a precaution against infertility—Max had actually felt sick. To reassure him, Gina had offered to contact a colleague at a clinic in America who was a renowned specialist in the field, in case a second opinion was needed.

He had suggested flying straight to America, but she had told him not to be so impulsive and added that as nothing was going to happen in the next few days he should try to have a relaxing weekend.

Max hadn't been able to ignore Gina's opinion because he trusted her completely. He had done since their parents had married, when he was four and she was five, and they had instantly become as close as biological siblings, with a genuine liking for each other that had lasted into adulthood. She had supported him in his ambition to be a geologist, and he had done the same for her in her medical ambition and in her personal life.

'Max? Max!'

The sound of his name intruded on unpleasant memories of the past. He looked across the table at Gina, and the other two people in their party—Rosa and her husband Ted.

Gina and Rosa were lovers, and had been for years. Ted had his own reasons for keeping the secret—Rosa was the mother of his two children, and Max knew he had a long-term mistress. As for Max, he kept the secret because Gina wanted him to. She was convinced that their parents would be horrified if they knew the truth, and that the potential scandal of the relationship might harm her career prospects.

'Sorry, Gina.' He smiled. Personally, he thought Gina was wrong, and believed that not many people were bothered about a person's sexual preference in the twenty-first century, but it wasn't his secret to reveal.

'You have seen her? Sophie Rutherford?' Gina prompted. 'Are you okay?'

'Yes, fine.' He saw the concern in her eyes and added, 'I can't say I am impressed by her choice of partner.' He cast a glance at the blond-headed Venus in question, his mouth curling in a cynical smile. 'But I'm not surprised.'

Always a man of action, Max was not given to moods of reflection. But now, as he ate the food put before him, he found it hard to concentrate on the present when the woman responsible for so many painful memories of his past was seated just a few yards away. Seeing Sophie again had brought to mind in every vivid detail perhaps the worst episode in his life all those years ago....

Max had left Gina outside the restaurant, his mind in flux, and slowly walked back in the direction of his office.

For a self-confident man who prided himself on always being in control, a man who made business decisions involving millions on a daily basis and never doubted his course of action, it had been sobering to realise he was just as susceptible as the next man to the unfamiliar emotions of doubt and fear. He enjoyed his work, was very successful and very wealthy, and he had gone his own way for years with very little thought to the future. But now he'd been forced to face the fact he might not have one, and suddenly everything he had achieved didn't amount to much.

If he dropped dead tomorrow his family and a couple of friends might grieve for a while, but eventually it would be as though he'd never existed.

A few days before Max had thought he had all the time in the world, that marriage and children were something he wouldn't have to consider for years. He had thought in his arrogance that the *timing* had not been right for an *affair* with Sophie—that he didn't need her. But with the threat of serious illness hanging over him *time* had suddenly become vitally important.

Impulsively he had called his pilot, and an hour later had been flying back to Sicily—and Sophie. Alex be damned! He needed Sophie's uncomplicated company, her open adoration, her stunning body, and he wasn't going to wait. He was going to have her—and she might just be the last woman he had in this life.

Max had glanced around the familiar view of the hotel gardens. His dark eyes had narrowed on a group of three young boys in the swimming pool, playing water polo with a girl. The girl had been Sophie, and as he'd watched she had hauled herself out of the water and flopped down on a sunbed, the young boys sprawling on the ground around her.

The mere sight of her in the familiar pink bikini had knocked any lingering doubt from his brain and he'd felt his body stir and strode towards her.

'Hello, Sophie. Still playing around, I see,' he drawled mockingly, and tugged lightly on the long wet braid of her hair falling down her back.

Her head turned and her green eyes widened to their fullest extent. 'Max—you're back! I didn't know.' And the rush of colour and the welcoming smile on her face were all Max could have hoped for and more.

'Dare I ask if you are free for the evening?' Of course her answer would be yes. He never doubted it for a moment. And the events of the morning in Rome were pushed to the back of his mind as his dark gaze lingered over her scantily clad form. 'I thought a drive along the coast, and a picnic, perhaps?' He wondered why he had denied his own desire the day he met her, three weeks ago.

'I'd love it,' she said, a smile curving her luscious mouth, and he couldn't resist pulling her into his arms and kissing her.

Lifting his head, his brown eyes dark with need, he searched her lovely face. *Dio!* How he wanted this woman. There was certainly nothing wrong with his testosterone levels. In fact, if he didn't get away fast the rest of the guests around the pool would be well aware of that, too.

He sucked in a deep, steadying breath and gently pulled her away from him. 'I'll pick you up at eight.' And he turned and walked away.

Sophie watched Max's departure, her eyes drifting

lovingly over him, the misery and doubt of the last week forgotten in her euphoria at seeing Max again.

Later that evening Max helped her out of the car and, lifting a hamper from the back, he took her hand firmly in his.

'Where are we?' Sophie asked. He had stopped the car at the harbour of a small town, and she glanced around her with pleasure. Coloured lights danced in the darkness, following the curve of the harbour that had a dozen yachts bobbing in gently lapping water.

'La Porto Piccolo,' he said, looking down at her with a reminiscent smile on his starkly handsome face. 'It was a favourite haunt of my friend Franco and I when we were younger. We bought our first yacht together when we were nineteen and hoping to impress the girls. We have always kept it here, away from our families' prying eyes. It is small, but we had some great times.' Taking her hand, he helped her on board.

Sophie wasn't sure she liked the implication in his words. Was this some kind of love boat? And just how many girls had Max entertained on board? But then she spotted a table and two chairs set out on the polished wood deck. 'We are eating here?' she asked.

'Yes.' He placed the hamper on the table and drew her gently into his arms. 'It is a beautiful night, and I thought you would appreciate dining on the deck.' He brushed his lips against her hair. 'You have no idea how much I want to please you, in every way.' His lips lowered to brush gently against her mouth and she was stunned by the gentleness in his gaze.

Max cared, he really cared for her, and involuntarily

Sophie raised her hand to rest on his broad chest. 'You already do,' she said with blunt honesty. 'I missed you so much when you were away. I missed your unruly black hair, your teasing smile…' She flicked a silken lock from his brow. 'I'm glad you are back.'

'You can show me how much later.' Max covered her hand on his chest with his own and bent his dark head so that his mouth lightly nuzzled her neck. Sophie shuddered when she felt the flick of his tongue against her sensitive skin. 'But first a tour of the yacht, and then food,' he prompted.

With his arm around her waist, his fingers splayed across the soft skin of her midriff, Sophie was too aware of the magic of his touch to notice the boat. She had a fleeting view of one small cabin, and heard Max's comment about 'two berths', and then he was opening a door into the only other cabin.

'Duck your head,' he instructed, ushering her inside and closing the door behind them. The cabin was tiny, and lit only by the lights of the harbour, which were casting flickering shadows on the double bunk that almost filled the space. 'It is only for sleeping,' he murmured, his breath warm against her brow.

Sophie had never felt less like sleeping. And when Max's hand tightened on her waist and turned her to face him all she felt was breathless. She looked up, every nerve-ending tingling at the close proximity of his great body, and stared as if mesmerised by his glittering dark eyes, any thought of caution vanished.

Then his mouth found hers, his tongue moving within it with a deeply erotic passion, and Sophie was lost to everything but the incredible sensations shooting through her body.

He lifted his head and looked searchingly down at her.

'You want this?' he prompted huskily, his voice barely audible as he gently brushed a strand of silken hair from her cheek.

'Yes,' she gasped, and in moments they were naked on the bed.

A long time later Sophie lay collapsed on top of him, breathless and shaking—she had never known such pleasure existed. Max gently lifted her chin with his index finger. 'You should have told me I was your first.'

'And my only,' she sighed. 'I love you so much.'

'Oh, Sophie, I adore you. You are truly priceless— don't ever change,' he drawled softly.

'I am changed now, thanks to you,' she whispered.

'I know.' Max kissed her swollen lips again—he couldn't help himself. 'But it is I who should be thanking you. You have given me something precious and worth much more than you can ever imagine.'

Never before had he made love to a virgin, and never before had he met with such a wild reciprocal passion. He had lost touch with everything but the incredible agonising pleasure he had felt as he came inside her.

But that was the problem. He had done just that— forgotten protection. He looked into her happy love-lit eyes, about to tell her, but couldn't bring himself to spoil the moment. Instead he heard himself say, 'Marry me.' And realised he meant it…. Whatever the future held, Sophie was to be his and his alone….

With anger simmering just below the surface, Max cast a hard, cold glance at the catalyst of his trip down memory lane. With the benefit of hindsight he realised his proposal had probably been a simple gut reaction to the massive blow his male ego had suffered at the thought of testicular cancer. But at the time, after having sex with her, he had deluded himself into believing it was something more and asked her to marry him.

Max glanced across at Sophie again, and this time his gaze lingered, his dark eyes narrowing as he saw her smiling and charming the men either side of her. He saw Abe Asamov stroke her cheek with one finger, and his mouth curled in a bitter, cynical smile—a smile that was strained to the limit as she got up to dance with the man. The easy familiarity between Sophie and Abe was unmistakable.

Dio! Sophie was certainly sleeping with him, and it could only be for one reason—money. Disgust churned his gut. When he saw them leave the dance floor, and watched her kiss the fat Russian on the cheek, he dismissed any notion of waiting a week or two to speak to her. In fact another minute was too long, and he changed his plan accordingly.

It was said that revenge was best taken cold, and Max told himself he felt nothing but ice-cold anger for the beautiful Sophie and what she had become. He rose to his feet and excused himself. He had once thought the timing wasn't right for an affair with Sophie, and then changed his mind. Two days later he had been dumped unceremoniously by the heartless witch. Now he had changed it back again, and this time he would be the one to walk away. But not until he had sated himself in her gorgeous body....

CHAPTER THREE

EVERY SELF-PROTECTIVE instinct Sophie possessed was telling her to turn and run. She'd known coming back to Italy was not a good idea, and seeing Max confirmed it. But she knew she had to get through this dinner—if only to prove that she was a true professional and Max Quintano meant nothing, in fact less than nothing, to her.

Luckily for Sophie, Abe had asked her to interpret Cesare's conversation and she readily agreed; if she kept her eyes on Cesare and Abe she could almost pretend that Max and Gina didn't exist.

Back at university, after her brief affair with Max, it had been hard—but with the help of her friends and by throwing herself into work she had finally got over him and convinced herself she didn't care. Now it was galling to have to admit that it still hurt to see Max with Gina.

For the next hour Sophie ate, drank and smiled in all the right places, but she was intensely conscious of Max Quintano's powerful presence. She felt as though his eyes were on her, and that made the hair on the back of her neck stand on end. It took every bit of will-power she had to chat normally and avoid glancing back at the hateful man. The realisation that just the sight of him could upset her so much after all this time gnawed away at her. To compensate she sparkled all the brighter with the clearly admiring Cesare, so much so that Abe picked up on her distress.

He raised a finger to her cheek and stroked her jawline. 'Sophie?' She looked into his shrewd blue eyes. 'You are trying too hard—whoever it is you are trying to avoid, my dear,' he murmured, 'use me, not young Cesare. You could hurt him. But I have broad shoulders, and I don't mind playing the game.'

'You see too much,' Sophie sighed, and when Abe asked her to dance she managed an almost natural smile and rose to her feet, going gracefully into his arms.

Surprisingly, for all his bulk, Abe was a good dancer, and Sophie relaxed into the music, her tall, graceful body drawing the eye of many appreciative males—and one in particular.

'You're a very beautiful woman, as I've told you before,' Abe said as the music ended and with a guiding hand around her waist he led her back towards the table. 'Whoever he was, he was a fool, and he didn't deserve you in the first place. You are worth the best, and don't you forget it.'

She looked at Abe's hard face and realised that not only was he an extremely nice man, but also extremely astute—no wonder he was a billionaire oil mogul.

'You're right.' She smiled and kissed his cheek. 'Thank you.' Why was she wasting her time getting upset all because she had had one disastrous love affair with a womanising bastard? It was time she moved on with her life, she thought determinedly.

'Excuse me,' a deep, dark voice drawled mockingly,

and Max Quintano appeared in front of them. 'May I claim your partner for the next dance?'

Abe looked up at Max, not in the least intimidated by his great height, and slowly let his eyes inspect the man, before quirking an enquiring brow at Sophie and demanding in his own language to know what had been said. She was too shocked by Max's sudden interruption and request to think of lying, and she told Abe.

'Ah.' He looked back at Max. 'You want my woman?' he managed in English, and his blue eyes danced with a wicked light.

Sophie knew Abe was enjoying himself, and she glanced up at Max through the thick veil of her lashes. The look of cynical contempt on his harshly handsome face infuriated her. Abe had implied that she was his lover, and it was obvious Max believed him. He had a nerve to sneer at her, when *he* was the one with a legion of lovers and his long-term lover sitting at the other side of the dance floor. So why was he insisting on dancing with her given his obvious distain?

'I hope you will allow me the pleasure of dancing with your charming companion. Sophie and I are old friends.' His dark eyes narrowed challengingly on Abe.

Abe let go of her waist and threw up his hands in a theatrical gesture. 'I am not her keeper—ask her.' Abe suddenly seemed to know a lot more English than anyone had given him credit for—Sophie included.

Max's dark head turned and his gaze captured hers. 'May I have this dance, Sophie? Your partner does not seem to mind,' he opined, with a sardonic curl of his firm lips.

'Max—what a surprise,' she said coldly. Words couldn't begin to describe the anger that had swelled up inside her as the two men talked over her as if she wasn't there. 'I didn't know you could dance. Did Gina teach you?' she asked pointedly. The two-timing toad had the nerve to take a dig at her in front of everyone, and still demand that she dance with him.

'As a matter of fact she did. Amongst other things,' he said, grinning.

Shock kept her silent for a moment, his brazen reply adding insult to injury. Then, realising that standing in silence, sandwiched between two men on the edge of the dance floor, was arousing the antennae of the company around them, she said sweetly 'I'm sure she did. And, given she is your companion for the evening, shouldn't you be dancing with her?'

'No, Gina has other things on her mind,' he replied with an amused glance across at his table.

His callous indifference amazed her, and she allowed her gaze to rake angrily over him. He hadn't changed much. His black hair was cut shorter, and liberally sprinkled with grey, and the lines bracketing his mouth were slightly more pronounced. There was a hard edge about him, which was in direct contrast to the laughing, teasing man she had known, but he was still strikingly attractive.

'I'm surprised you want to dance with me,' she finally said bluntly.

Max moved closer and held out his hand. 'You shouldn't be, Sophie. After all, we were once *extremely* close friends.' His glittering eyes mocked her, and for a moment she hesitated. But she didn't trust him not to blurt out something even more compromising if she refused, and the gossip it would cause was not something she wanted.

'I'd be delighted to dance with you, Mr Quintano,' she said with a coldly polite social smile, and put her hand in his.

Max sensed she hated the idea but was too polite to say so, and he deliberately linked his fingers through hers and felt the slight tremble in her hand. 'Now, that wasn't so hard,' he said, dipping his dark head to murmur in her ear as he led her onto the dance floor. He had won the first battle without her putting up much of a fight

As he stopped, he caught her other hand and deliberately held her at arm's length. 'You are looking well.' He allowed his dark gaze to sweep insolently over her. She was. Sophie Rutherford had turned into an exquisitely elegant lady—even if she did have the morals of an alley cat. 'More beautiful than ever, in fact. But I've been watching you, and some things never change. You are still as eager as ever where men are concerned—and Abe Asamov is quite some catch! You do realise he is a married man?' Max prompted cynically, and did what he had been aching to do since he'd first set eyes on her tonight. He pulled her close against his hard body and guided her expertly around the floor to the slow music.

The brush of his long legs against hers, the familiar warmth and scent of him, sent a tremor of what Sophie hoped was revulsion down her spine. His callous reference to her pathetic eagerness with him so long ago was making her squirm inside at how naïve she had been. A lamb led to the slaughter sprang to mind... But she didn't let it show. That girl was long gone. She was now a confident, sophisticated woman who could hold her own in any situation.

'So?' she said, with a casual shrug of one shoulder, even whilst tensing against the inevitable close body contact. 'I'm not looking for a husband.'

'No,' Max drawled, glancing down at her with hooded eyes. 'I more than most should know that you want wealth and pleasure. But the stress and strain of marriage, of caring for a husband—' he gave a wry grimace '—is certainly not for you.'

'You know me so well,' she said sweetly, and felt his strong hand stroke up her naked back and press her closer, until she was in contact with his broad chest. Much to her dismay, she was helpless to control the sudden tightening of her nipples, or the leap in her pulse-rate.

'You've got that right.' He slanted a glance down at the soft curve of her breasts revealed by the low-cut neckline and a sardonic smile twisted his firm lips. 'And I wouldn't mind getting to know you all over again. What do you say, Sophie?' he queried arrogantly. 'Me instead of the ape Abe? You know we were good together, and they do say a woman never forgets her first lover.'

With a supreme effort she hid her shock at his statement. Max was certainly direct, if not downright crude, and it seemed impossible to her now that she had ever thought she loved this man.

'You're disgusting,' she finally said bluntly, attempting to lean back from him. Being so close to him was playing havoc with her nervous system. Age hadn't dimmed his powerful animal magnetism, and even though she despised him she was drawn to him like a moth to a flame. She felt exactly the same as the first time she had set eyes on him, and she hated the powerless feeling he ignited in her.

'Maybe.' She felt his lips brush against the top of her head. 'But you haven't answered my question.'

'It isn't deserving of an answer.' She looked up into his hard face, her green eyes turbulent with the mixed emotions of fear and anger—at her own weakness almost as much as with him. 'I don't know why you even asked me to dance, given when we parted you never wanted to set eyes on me again. Or why I allowed good manners to influence me to agree, because *you* certainly have none.'

That Max thought she was capable of having an affair with Abe was bad enough, but that he actually had the nerve to suggest she swap lovers! 'I have not seen you in seven years, and if I don't see you again in seven times seven years it would still be too soon.'

'My, Sophie, what a shrew you have turned into—and here I was, trying to be kind,' he said silkily. 'I may not be quite as wealthy as Abe, but I can certainly keep you in the manner to which you have become accustomed. The gown is Dior, but your lover has short-changed you. As my mistress you would be wearing diamonds, not crystal, I promise you,' he ended mockingly.

'Why, you…' Words failed her. She didn't have to put up with this, she wasn't a star-struck nineteen-year-old any more, even if her traitorous body was still excited by the man. That he should endow her with his own despicable morality was the last straw, and she attempted to wriggle out of his grasp.

'Stop it,' Max warned, and his hand moved up her back

to hold her firmly against him, his long fingers splayed just below her shoulder blades. 'For your sake more than mine, I would prefer us to reach a mutual beneficial agreement without the avid interest of this crowd.'

'Agreement! What the hell are you talking about?' she demanded, beginning to feel like Alice in Wonderland when she fell down the rabbit hole…. No, more like the Mad Hatter, she amended.

When the music thankfully stopped, Sophie placed her hands on his chest to push him away, but his other arm tightened about her and she was unable to move.

She looked bitterly up at him, saw the flare of raw anger that hardened his eyes and watched his dark head lower. He wouldn't dare kiss her in public, she thought— just before his mouth brushed over hers in a brief, hard kiss. She was too surprised to resist, and her hard-won icy control shattered into a million pieces as the awareness she had been trying to deny from the moment she saw him again heated her blood and coloured her face.

When he lifted his head her hands were resting on his chest. She didn't know how they had got there, but she was humiliatingly aware that to anyone watching it must look as if she had consented to his kiss. 'God! You have no scruples at all, you bastard.'

'Where you are concerned, no. And now maybe Abe will have got the message. You were mine before you were his, and you will be mine again.'

'Have you lost your mind?' Sophie asked, but with her head spinning from the dizzying effect of his kiss it was her own mind she was worried about. 'I wouldn't have you gift-wrapped with bells on.'

'Yes, you will.' He disentangled his arms and laid a hand on her waist. 'Your reaction told me all I needed to know,' he said as he led her back to her table, his head bent solicitously towards her as he continued talking. 'I have heard glowing reports about you from a friend of mine in South America. Apparently, your career has really taken off. It seems you are in great demand—and not just for your language skills,' he drawled sardonically.

'You've heard?' She was horrified to think Max Quintano might know some of the people she worked for, but suddenly she realised how blind she had been. Of course he moved in the same sphere as a lot of her clients—why wouldn't he?

'The Chilean ambassador's son—a fantastic polo player—was quite besotted with you. Apparently when you arrived at his last cup match he couldn't take his eyes off you, and as a result he fell off his horse and broke a leg. But needless to say you didn't rush to his side.'

Sophie remembered the incident, and the gossip it had caused—which had shocked her because she barely knew the man in question. But she shrugged off his comment with a terse, 'So what?'

'I also heard your father is married again and you have a little brother.'

'Yes,' she answered mechanically. It was taking all of her will-power simply to walk beside him, when all she really wanted to do was run and hide. Away from him— and the curious eyes that were watching them.

'If you value their security, you will meet me tomorrow for lunch to discuss it. I will call at your hotel at noon,' he commanded, as they reached the table.

'We have nothing to discuss,' she muttered, as he pulled out a chair for her to sit down. She looked up into his taut, cynical face and wondered why on earth he wanted to see her again when he had the doting Gina—and what it had to do with her family.

'Be there,' he said with a silky smile. 'And thank you for the dance. It was very illuminating.' But the smile never reached his eyes and she watched numbly as he turned and said, 'Thank you, Abe,' his narrowed eyes glittering with triumph as they met the older man's.

Abe took a long time to answer, his cool blue gaze holding Max's, and then he shook his bald head. 'I do not need the thanks,' he said dryly. 'You have my…' He turned to Sophie and asked for the word for sympathy. She told him and he repeated it. 'My sympathy.'

'What do you mean by offering Quintano your sympathy?' Sophie asked Abe as soon as Max had walked away. 'I thought you were my friend. I can't stand the man, and I'm certainly not having lunch with the arrogant devil.'

'The Ice Queen cracks.' Abe grinned. 'And if you don't know why I offered the man sympathy, then maybe I am wrong and all is not lost,' he answered cryptically. 'In which case Quintano does not need my sympathy and we shall continue the game.' He called the waiter and ordered more champagne, toasting Sophie and teasing her with, 'My wife will be delighted when I tell her the story. We have been waiting for this for a long time—you are far too lovely to be alone.'

Sophie denied she had *any* interest in Max Quintano, and tried her best to appear unaffected by her encounter with him, but it was an uphill struggle. She sipped the champagne and joined in the conversation, but her emotions were all over the place.

She felt angry with Max for intruding into her life again and deliberately humiliating her by kissing her in front of a crowd of people—but also angry at herself for letting him. He was still with Gina, and if he had been serious about propositioning her then he was also still a womaniser and beneath contempt. But then she already knew that, and the only thing to do was to dismiss him from her mind. As for his demand that she should have lunch with him—in his dreams!

She drained her champagne, and when Abe suggested coffee she agreed. They left shortly after.

Max watched them leave, his dark eyes burning with an unholy light. Abe Asamov would never get another chance with Sophie, he decided with ruthless implacability. He had the power to make sure she was his again for as long as he wanted her delectable body, and he was going to use it.

CHAPTER FOUR

BACK AT THE HOTEL Sophie stripped off her clothes and headed for the bathroom. She washed, then removed her make-up, and after brushing and braiding her hair pulled on a cotton nightshirt and slipped into bed. She was weary beyond belief and, sighing, she closed her eyes and snuggled under the covers.

But sleep was elusive. She moved restlessly, turning onto her stomach and burying her face in the pillow, trying to block out the image of Max from her brain—but it was no good. Meeting him tonight had stirred up a host of memories that she had tried her damnedest to forget.

From the first day she had met Max she had been totally besotted with him, and when he'd left the hotel two weeks later, after their one and only dinner date, she had been devastated. But with Marnie's help she had almost convinced herself it was for the best. Max Quintano was streets ahead of her in every way. As a mega-rich mining tycoon he was too old, too worldly and too wealthy to be tempted by an innocent young student, and she had begun to recognise that she had been extremely foolish to imagine otherwise.

That was until he had returned unexpectedly a week later. All her doubts and reservations had vanished like smoke in the wind when he'd asked her out again.

Much later, when trying to account for what had happened next, Sophie would realise she had been set up and seduced by an expert. But when he'd taken her to his yacht—a boat he'd actually told her had been more or less bought for the purpose—she had made no complaint. When he'd led her to the cabin, stripped her naked and laid her on the bed she had made no protest. Naked before a man for the first time in her life, she should have been nervous—but with Max she hadn't been. And when he'd joined her and begun to kiss her face, her eyelids, the soft curve of her cheek, she had reached for him.

Sophie could see his smile in her mind's eye even now, all these years later. His heavy-lidded eyes molten with desire as he took her mouth in a deeply passionate, hungry kiss—then her breasts, her stomach, everything else, until she was moaning and writhing, her whole body shaking. She had never felt such pleasure, and he'd taken her into realms of sensuality she had never known existed.

When he had discovered she was a virgin he had stilled for a moment, then moved again slowly. With erotic caresses from his hands and mouth he had driven her ever wilder, and thrust even deeper, until they'd moved together in perfect rhythm. Finally, with more powerful strokes, he had filled her to the hilt and driven her over the edge into a delirious climax, and, crying out, had joined her.

Stifling a moan, Sophie squirmed in the bed. Whatever else Max was, there was no denying he was a magnificent, considerate lover. She doubted that any woman had ever had a more incredibly satisfying initiation into sex—one that had been topped off with a proposal of marriage. Delirious with happiness, she had accepted immediately, and agreed that their engagement would remain secret until he had spoken to their respective fathers.

Wryly, she conceded that at the time she would have accepted black was white if Max had said so. But her state of euphoria had lasted just one more night, and their final day was etched into her brain for all time....

Eyes closed, she could picture Max perfectly as he had walked out of the hotel dining room after lunch on the Sunday afternoon.

Casually elegant in pale chinos and a loose cotton shirt, Max had moved with a lazy grace to lean against the reception desk, where Sophie had been helping out for a few hours, his gleaming dark eyes holding hers and a sensual smile playing around his lips.

'I was hoping we could enjoy a siesta,' he said, his long, tanned fingers closing over hers on the desktop Even after two nights of Max's incredible lovemaking and their secret engagement she still reddened. 'No need to blush, Sophie.' He chuckled. 'It is what all engaged couples do—in fact it is a tradition here in Sicily. And you would not want to upset the locals,' he teased, tongue in cheek.

'You are insatiable, sir,' she teased back. 'And I am not off duty until four.'

He glanced at his wristwatch, and then his knowledgeable eyes met hers again, a wealth of tenderness in their depths. 'Two hours—I suppose I can wait that long, but it will be hard,' he said, with a tilt of one ebony brow and a wicked grin, and Sophie burst out laughing.

But Sophie's laughter faded as someone distracted him by calling his name. He spun around, and she watched in surprise as Max dashed to the small, gamine-looking woman with close-cropped black hair approaching the desk, swept her up in his arms and kissed her on both cheeks. A tirade of Italian followed for the next five minutes, interspersed with much hand waving, before Max turned to walk back to the desk with his arm firmly around the other woman.

'Sophie, I want you to meet my sister Gina,' he declared. 'She decided to make a surprise visit.' And, smiling down at the other woman, he said, 'This is my friend Sophie.'

Sophie smiled shyly at Gina and held out her hand to the woman who would be her future sister-in-law. 'Pleased to meet you.'

Gina acknowledged her with a bright smile. 'The pleasure is all mine. You're very lovely.' She shook her hand, then immediately turned back to Max. 'Staying true to form, I see. It would take a bulldozer to flatten you!' She laughed, and although Sophie didn't get the joke, she thought to herself that Gina seemed friendly enough.

'Sophie, be a dear and order a light lunch and coffee to be sent up to my suite. Gina hasn't eaten yet, and we have a lot to discuss. I'll catch you later.'

Sophie watched Max walk away and enter the elevator with his arm still around Gina—and without a second glance for her. Slightly disturbed by his offhand manner, she felt her happy mood sink a little as she rang through to inform the kitchen of Max's requirements. Only after she had replaced the receiver did Marnie's warning come back to haunt her.

Gina wasn't his sister but his *step*sister—and the woman it was rumoured that Max had been having an affair with for years. Suddenly Sophie's shining confidence in her lover, her *fiancé*, took a nasty knock.

It didn't help when Marnie came in at four to take over from her. When she told her that Gina had arrived unexpectedly, the sudden pity in her friend's dark eyes simply increased Sophie's doubts. Feeling dejected and suspicious, she returned to the staff chalet and stripped off her uniform and took a shower. Grasping a big fluffy towel, she dried her body—and grimaced at the telltale stain.

Maybe it was the time of the month that was making her feel jealous and moody, she thought as she walked back into the bedroom and dressed casually in Capri pants and tee shirt. It also meant no lovemaking for a few days, which lowered her mood still further.

Too restless to settle, she prowled around the chalet, her eyes constantly drawn back to the telephone. Surely Max would ring soon, stepsister or no stepsister. He knew she was off duty at four.

When it got to five she could not stand to be cooped up inside any longer, so she decided to go for a walk around the gardens to the maze where Max had taken her the first day they met.

Sophie rolled over onto her back and squeezed her eyes tight to hold back the tears that threatened, even now, after all these years. She could hear their voices as clear as if it had been yesterday.

'Max, you have to tell the girl, if you really do intend

to marry her. Young women are much worldlier nowadays; she might handle the situation without so much as batting an eyelid.' Sophie recognised Gina's voice, and the urgency in it, and slowed her pace a little.

'Do you think so? I'm not so sure. She is very young, and not very worldly at all—unlike most women I know.'

What situation? Sophie wondered, all her earlier feelings of jealousy and doubt flooding back as she walked slowly towards the end of the hedge—and, if she had but known, towards the end of her dreams...

'In that case, why are you even contemplating marrying her?'

'Because, among other things, I was careless and didn't use any protection. She could be pregnant.'

Sophie heard his response and froze in her tracks. So bewitched had she been by the wonder of his lovemaking, his proposal, it had never crossed her mind she might get pregnant. How could she have been so dumb and blind? It was obvious Max had realised the implication of unprotected sex straight away. Was that why he'd asked her to marry him? Was that the real reason for their secret engagement, which obviously wasn't secret where Gina was concerned? He had told Gina he had asked Sophie to marry him, and mentioned the words *careless* and *pregnant*, but the word *love*, the most important reason for marriage, had never passed his lips.

Sophie's heart squeezed in her chest and she had trouble breathing as pain sharp as a knife sliced through her. Max had told her he *adored* her, he had said she was *priceless*—but, sickeningly, she realised he had never once mentioned *love*.

Was the secrecy he had insisted upon less to do with informing her father and more to do with Max keeping her sweet until he discovered if she was pregnant?

'I might have guessed.' Gina's scornful voice cut through her tormented thoughts. 'I warned you not to do anything impulsive, but no. You reacted like most men do at the sight of a willing woman. Well, whatever happens, you can't marry her without telling her. She hardly knows you, and in my opinion she is far too young to marry anyway. She hasn't even finished her education. And she has the right to choose whether she wants to be involved in this situation. So if you don't tell her, I will.'

To Sophie, it was another nail in the coffin of all of her hopes, and that Max should submit to such a scolding from a woman without any comment stunned her. He thought very highly of Gina, that much was obvious, and she had to be very sure of her standing in his life to lecture him in such a way.

'Sophie might be dumb enough to fall into bed with you—what girl wouldn't? Even I can't keep count of the number. I've given up trying,' Gina drawled angrily. 'But from what you have told me about her academic achievements she cannot be that stupid. She would soon guess something was wrong if her new husband kept disappearing from the marital home on a regular basis, probably overnight, and then when he did return did not have the energy to make love—which we both know is almost inevitable.'

'I will tell her—I will,' Max declared. 'But not yet. It has only been a couple of days.'

'Ah, Max, I do love you. But you are a typical man—impossible!' Gina replied.

'I know,' he chuckled, 'and I love you. I don't know what I would do without you. But look on the bright side—with any luck I may not need to tell Sophie anything at all.'

Suddenly, with blinding clarity, Sophie saw it all.

Marnie had been right. Max and Gina were lovers, and the only reason Max had proposed marriage to Sophie was because he might have made her pregnant. He had never even mentioned the possibility to *her*, his so-called fiancée, and tellingly she realised he had been careful to use protection every other time. What did he intend to do? She answered her own question—wait and see. And if she wasn't pregnant he would use her, then drop her like he did all the other women in his life.

If she *was* pregnant the pair of them were discussing how Sophie might handle their ongoing love affair as the pregnant wife left at home. She couldn't even blame Gina. She was all for telling the truth; it was Max who was the devious, lying one of the pair.

Pain and anger such as she had never felt in her life before consumed her. Tears pressed against the backs of her eyes, but she refused to let them fall. She wanted to rage and scream at the man who had seduced her so completely, stolen her heart and her innocence. How could she have thought he loved her? She was as dumb as Gina had said she was for falling for Max's charm, and the knowledge was soul destroying.

It took every bit of will-power she possessed to carry on walking to the entrance of the clearing. Maybe, just maybe, she was mistaken and there was some other explanation, her foolish heart cried. But the sight that met her eyes was the death of any hope that she might be wrong.

They were sitting on the bench, their arms around each other, their whole body language screaming long-term intimacy, and her heart turned to stone in her chest.

From somewhere she got the strength to move forward, and it was pride and pride alone that allowed her to declare, 'You are right, Max—you don't need to say a word. I heard everything, and—' *You don't need to marry me.* But she never got the chance to say it as Max cut her off.

'You heard everything?' He jumped to his feet. 'I'm sorry. I should have told you the truth. I didn't mean you to find out this way.' He walked towards her, a regretful, almost shameful smile on his handsome face. But she held up a hand to ward him off.

'No need to be sorry…. Gina's right. I am far too young to marry, and your situation does not appeal to me at all. I am leaving at the end of the week anyway, as my two months are up, so I'll say goodbye now. And wish you luck.'

'No, Sophie, you can't mean that!' he said, reaching for her. She took a step back; she couldn't bear for him to touch her. 'It is not as bad as it seems. Come and sit down, and we can talk it over with Gina. '

Not as bad! Disgust curled her mouth. It probably *wasn't* that bad in their sophisticated, decadent world, and that realisation was enough to numb all feeling in Sophie. 'No.' She shook her head, her green eyes glistening with anger, sliding contemptuously over him from head to toe. Her hero…her lover… The conniving, lying rat actually had the gall to suggest she sit down with him and his lover and discuss—what? A three-way relationship? Career woman or not, parental disapproval…whatever! Why Gina put up with him she had no idea.

'I have heard it all and there is nothing more to say. It was an interesting experience, but under the circumstances not one I wish to continue. I am not in the least interested in the kind of future you have mapped out, and luckily for me I discovered today there is no chance I am pregnant, so you have nothing to worry about except yourself.' She almost added *as usual.*

Max had never really cared about her. Even his love for Gina was not something Sophie recognised as true love. And she finally realised Max was the most arrogant, manipulative, selfish man she had ever had the misfortune to meet.

Sophie saw him straighten his massive shoulders and tense. For a second she imagined she saw a flash of raw pain in his dark eyes, but she must have been mistaken because when he looked at her his handsome face was a taut, expressionless mask.

'You are not the girl I thought you were. And you're right, there is nothing more to say—except there is no need for you to stay until the end of the week. Please oblige me by packing as soon as possible. I will square it with Alex and have your flight tickets waiting at the desk. I never want to set eyes on you again.'

Thinking about their parting now, Sophie saw again the hostility in Gina's eyes, and the hard, cold anger in Max's, and wondered why she had let the memory bother her for so long. They deserved each other, and she was well out of it. As for meeting Max for lunch—not likely... And on that defiant thought she finally fell asleep.

But the next day, at the end of the morning conference, as she was deep in conversation with the organiser, Tony

Slater, her defiance dipped when Max Quintano suddenly appeared in the foyer.

'Sophie.' He nodded his head in her direction and held out his hand to Tony Slater. 'Good to see you again, Tony. Sorry I could only make the dinner and not the meeting, but I hear the conference has been a great success. I believe that some very positive ideas have been formulated, which may be put into practice in the future. Maybe we can get together and discuss it further?'

Sophie's mouth fell open in shock. She could not believe the nerve of the man, interrupting their conversation, but if the expression on Tony's face was anything to go by *he* could not believe his luck—the great Max Quintano, suggesting a one-to-one, with *him!*

'Yes, that would be great.' Tony beamed, much to Sophie's disgust.

Max's dark triumphant eyes flicked mockingly over her and he chuckled softly as he addressed Tony again. 'Sophie and I are old friends and I am taking her out for lunch. I believe there are only closing speeches this afternoon, so please do me a favour and make Sophie's apologies to any interested parties for her early exit from the conference. I would like to show her something of Venice before she leaves tomorrow.' Withdrawing a card from his pocket, Max added, 'This is my number. Give me a call in the morning and we can arrange a meeting.'

Sophie tried to object; she had to fulfil her contract, and that meant staying until the end. But with the organiser of the conference declaring it was not necessary, that he would square it with her clients, before Sophie knew what had happened Max's hand was at her elbow and he was leading her out of the hotel. A male conspiracy if ever there was one, Sophie thought bitterly, with the sound of Tony's eager suggestion to enjoy her lunch ringing in her ears.

She shrugged off Max's hand as soon as they made the pavement and spun around to face him. 'I suppose you think you're clever, manipulating Tony Slater into excusing my absence? Where do you get off, interfering in my work?' she snarled, so angry she wanted to hit him.

He was staring down at her from his great height, all arrogance and powerfully male. The autumn sun was gleaming on his black hair and highlighting his chiselled features. Clad all in black—black jeans and a black cashmere sweater—he looked like the devil himself, she thought. But she was too mad to be frightened of him.

'Well, I have news for you, Quintano: I am *not* having lunch with you. Not today, not ever.' And, pulling her shoulder bag a little tighter over her shoulder, she added facetiously, 'But, hey, thanks for the day off.' And, swinging on her heel, she walked away.

Max let her go, because she was moving in the right direction. His motor launch was tied up fifty yards along the canal, and, although he was quite prepared to drag her kicking and screaming onto the launch, watching Sophie stride along was a lot more interesting. Her hair was loosely pinned with a mother-of-pearl clip at the nape of her neck and flowed like a curtain of pale silk down her back. Her pert bottom in a slim-fitting, short navy wool skirt was a pleasure to watch, and her legs—covered, he guessed, in silk stockings—were a pure joy.

Sophie didn't look back—she didn't dare! She was marching along the side of the canal, congratulating herself on her easy escape, when suddenly an arm snaked round her waist and she was lifted bodily into the air. She let out a surprised yell and began to struggle—only to be dumped unceremoniously onto a leather seat in the back of a boat. Before she could rise fully to her feet Max started the engine and cast off, which sent her crashing into the bottom of the vessel.

'You're crazy,' she yelled at Max's broad back. 'Stop this boat this minute, or I will have you arrested for kidnapping!' And to her utter astonishment, he did. She heard the engine die and, lifting her head, saw that Max had turned around and was leaning against the wheel, gazing down at her, his handsome face hard.

'If anyone is to be arrested it will be your father, Nigel Rutherford, for fraud.'

What the hell was he talking about now? Sophie thought furiously, tilting back her head to face him. A frisson of fear slid down her spine at the implacable intent in the cold black depths of the eyes that clashed with hers as he added, 'Unless you do exactly as I say.'

'You're mad! You can't threaten me or my father,' she blustered. Suddenly she recalled Max's comment last night about her family. She had thought nothing of it at the time, but now she wasn't so sure. Unease stirred inside her—how did he know her father was married again and had a son?

'I don't have to,' he responded calmly.

'Then why?' she asked, and stopped. She could read nothing in his austere features, but she knew for a fact that her father did not know Max. When she'd returned from Italy seven years ago her father had asked her if she'd enjoyed the break. In the conversation that followed he had revealed he had only met the owner, Andrea Quintano once, but he knew Alex. She supposed Alex might have mentioned her father's marital state. She had to wonder what else Alex might have mentioned.

Did Max know something about her dad's business? Was there something wrong? The tension between Margot and her father had been glaringly obvious at the weekend. Worriedly, she gnawed at her bottom lip—maybe they had money problems she knew nothing about. Dear heaven, the way Margot spent money it was certainly possible.

She was beautiful, Max acknowledged. With her skirt riding up around her thighs, her long legs splayed out in front of her, he saw he'd been right about the stockings— he could see the ribbons of her garter belt. The jacket of her suit was open, and the white silk blouse she wore underneath fitted over the high, firm curve of her breasts, revealing an enticing glimpse of cleavage that encouraged the eye to linger.

Reluctantly he raised his eyes to her face and saw the exact moment when she realised he was not joking. The angry glitter faded from her incredible eyes and her small white teeth nibbled at her full bottom lip. His body tightened—very soon *he* was going to nibble on her lush lips, and a lot more, and he did not intend to wait much longer.

'Because the law will, when his creditors get together next week,' he drawled sardonically. 'Unless I help you, of course—and that comes at a cost.'

'His creditors? And what do you mean—help *me*?' Suddenly realising she was at a distinct disadvantage sprawled at his feet, she struggled to sit up on the leather seat.

'I think you know. If you don't, have a guess,' he said with mocking cynicism, 'while I take us to lunch.' And with that he turned his back on her and started the engine.

For a moment Sophie stared at his back and wished she could stick a dagger in it, but it wasn't an option. Instead she ran their conversation over and over again in her head, and the more she thought the more worried and angry she became. But she did not dare argue with Max—not yet—not until she knew exactly what was going on.

Sitting on the edge of her seat, incapable of relaxing, she tried to focus on the beauty of her surroundings rather than the oppressive presence of Max at the wheel.

Venice in mid-October, cooler and with the worst crush of summer tourists gone, was a magical place. The sun-washed buildings edging the canals, the various crafts skimming through the water, the intricate bridges arching over the smaller canals—she should have been fascinated. And in any other circumstances she would have been. But she was too tense and too aware of Max to concentrate on anything.

CHAPTER FIVE

SOPHIE heard the tone of the engine change and, lifting her head, realised they were approaching a landing stage. She glanced up and saw a large, elegant pale-pink-washed house with a massive stone stairway leading up to it from two sides. She saw the huge double doors open and a man run down one side of the steps to catch the rope Max threw to him. Within seconds the launch was tied up.

She began to rise to her feet, and Max took her hand to help. She tried to pull free, but his fingers tightened. For a moment his eyes flared with anger, and when he spoke his voice was dangerously soft. 'Sophie, behave. I will not have you embarrassing me in front of my staff—understand?'

Glittering green eyes lifted to his. 'I don't want to be here. So we can solve both our problems if you just let me go,' she drawled facetiously. He had the nerve to laugh.

'Nice try, but no.' A moment later, with Max's arm firmly around her shoulders, she'd been introduced to Diego, his factotum, the man who had tied up the launch, and was walking up the steps to the impressive entrance doors, Diego leading the way.

The house was incredible; Sophie stood in the great entrance hall and simply stared.

The floor was a magnificent marble mosaic in cream and earthy tones, the walls magnolia, with elegant gold mouldings and works of art tastefully displayed all around. Marble columns formed a framework for the huge reception hall, an open door between two of them revealing a long dining table laid for lunch. She tilted her head back to look up at the ceiling and gasped at the centre dome, painted to rival the Sistine Chapel, and the huge chandelier that had to be Murano crystal. It took her breath away. The impressive steps outside were mirrored, and outclassed only by the fabulous marble staircase inside, which swept up to a central landing and divided again to a vast gallery that she presumed led to the bedrooms.

'Welcome to my home, Sophie.'

Awestruck, she glanced at Max. 'It's amazing!' she exclaimed. 'But I never knew you lived in Venice.' The Quintano family had been a constant source of gossip in the hotel when she'd worked there. She knew Max had an apartment in Rome, but no one had ever mentioned Venice. If she had known she would never have set foot in the city.

'When we first met I had just bought this place. It was a rundown *palazzo,* and I had it faithfully restored to its original style. Do you like it?'

'Like it? You are joking—it's fabulous.' She smiled, forgetting her animosity towards him for the moment, but she was brutally reminded of it two seconds later.

'Good. Then you will have no problem with living here for a while,' he said smoothly.

'Wait just a damn minute. I—' She never got the chance

to reiterate that she didn't even want to stay for lunch, because he pulled her possessively into his arms.

His dark eyes glittered golden with some fierce emotion, and his mouth settled on hers with a passionate intensity that caught her completely off guard. She flattened her hands against his chest, trying to push him away, but he simply pulled her tighter against him so she could not move. It was a kiss like nothing she had experienced before—a ravaging, possessive exploration that horrified her even as she shuddered at the fierce sensations he awakened.

Sophie closed her eyes and tried to will her body not to respond. As the kiss went on and on and he plundered her mouth, one hand swept feverishly up and down her spine, urging her into ever closer contact with his hard thighs. His other hand dipped below the neckline of her blouse to cup her breast, long fingers slipping beneath the lace of her bra to stroke a burgeoning nipple. An ache started low in her stomach and snaked down to her loins as a long-forgotten passion ran like wildfire through her veins.

When he finally allowed her to breathe, she was gasping for air, shaking all over with the shock of her arousal. He didn't give her time to recover but began to trail kisses down her throat, sucking on the vulnerable hollow where her pulse beat madly.

She never heard the discreet cough, only felt Max's head lifting and glanced up to see anger and desire mingling beneath his heavy-lidded eyes as he told Diego they'd be there in a few minutes.

'What do you think you are playing at?' she demanded, fighting for breath and trying to move out of his arms without much success.

'Tasting the merchandise,' Max said with brutal honesty. 'If I am going to bail your father out of debt, then I need to know it will be worth my while.'

Finally the penny dropped, and she realised his *living here* comment made horrible sense. Sophie looked at him with wide, appalled eyes. 'You actually imagine I will stay with you to get my father out of a fix?' she murmured. 'That is what all this is about?' She shook her head as if to clear it, fury rising inside her to give her eyes a wild glitter. 'Sorry to disappoint you, but my father is a grown man. If he is in any trouble—which I very much doubt—he is old enough to get out of it on his own,' she said with bitter sarcasm, hating Max with a depth of feeling that was almost frightening.

'He is your father. You should know.' He set her free and she took an unsteady step back, relieved he had given up on his demeaning proposition. But her relief was short lived. 'Maybe being bankrupted will do him good—though how it will affect your young brother remains to be seen.' He shrugged. 'But you probably know that better than I.'

'You bastard.' Sophie was goaded to retaliate at the mention of Timothy. 'You make me sick. If my father needs money I will willingly give him all I have, even borrow for him—there are plenty of ways of doing it. But take money from you? Never.'

His dark eyes narrowed cynically on her flushed furious face. 'Never is a long time, and your father only has a few days until the creditors' meeting. You should also know I got a call a couple of hours ago from your friend Abe. He knew I was having lunch with you and he asked me to say goodbye for him and told me to look after you. Of course

I said I would. Apparently he's flying to the Caribbean to join his wife and family on his yacht. So if you're counting on running to him for money, forget it.'

She swallowed the sudden lump that rose in her throat. How like Abe to put his mischievous oar in. She wouldn't mind betting he was laughing all the way across the Atlantic. But *she* wasn't laughing. Anger raged inside her that Max had had the arrogance to tell Abe he would look after her—as though she was a parcel to be passed around. But with the fury came an underlying sadness that Max, whom she had once thought she loved, could happily live in such a moral vacuum.

'Nothing to say?' he asked smugly.

She shook her head in disgust. 'I take it you're not married yet?' He couldn't be. Surely not even Max would have the gall to bring her here if he was? 'But, just out of curiosity, what would Gina say if I did agree to your disgraceful proposition?'

'There is nothing she can say—though obviously she won't be very happy, after last time. But as my mistress you won't need to meet her.'

She almost pitied Gina. Max's callousness appalled her. For one wild moment she considered walking out of his house, taking a water taxi to her hotel and then the next flight back to England, back to sanity. But the thought of Timothy held her back.

Max Quintano was not the sort of man to make mistakes—at least not in business. Much as she would like to, it would be foolhardy to just assume he was wrong about her father and dismiss the man. She needed to know the facts.

Max saw the indecision on her beautiful face and knew what she was thinking. 'If you don't believe me, call your father and ask him.' He indicated the telephone on a console table. 'Be my guest.'

He wanted Sophie more than any other woman he had ever known, and he had finally faced that fact when fate had put her in his path again last night. It had made his blood boil to see her with Abe Asamov, to see what she had become. The idea of the fat Russian enjoying her body—a body that *he* had initiated into sex—had sent a totally alien streak of possessively charged sexual desire raging through him.

Sophie was the only woman he had ever asked to marry him, but luckily he had discovered in time that she was the type to be economical with her wedding vows. As he recalled, the old English vow was *With all my worldly goods I thee endow.* She was obviously all for that but when it came to *in sickness and in health* she didn't want to know. She had dropped him like a shot when she'd heard he might have cancer.

It had taken him a while to recover from the cancer, and it had taught him to be a lot more circumspect in his sex life. But it hadn't stopped him wanting Sophie in the most basic way the minute he had set eyes on her again. Sexual desire took no account of the character, or lack of it, in the object of desire. It was simply there, twisting his gut.

He had denied it for seven years, because seven years ago he'd had more to worry about than her betrayal, but now he was damned if he was going to let her get away with deserting him unscathed. Now he was going to indulge his passion until the desire faded and he could look at her with nothing but the contempt she deserved.

Sophie looked at him standing before her, overpowering and arrogantly male, with an aura of silent, deadly strength that was decidedly threatening. 'I'll use my cellphone,' she said, determined to exert what little bit of control she had left over the situation. 'And I would like some privacy.'

'I will wait for you in the dining room,' Max drawled, and she watched him turn before she retrieved her cellphone from her bag.

Sophie switched off her phone and switched off her life, as she knew it, for the foreseeable future.

Surprisingly, she had contacted her father easily at home. When she'd told him she had bumped into Max Quintano at dinner last night, and he had told her there were rumours in the hotel trade that his company was in trouble, her dad had been amazingly frank. A group of creditors *were* due to meet next Monday, varying from airlines to hoteliers. Apparently he had delayed payment of clients' money and spent it.

He'd been sure he could put it right if he sold the house and rented something small until he had a chance to straighten out his business, but Margot hadn't accepted the fact so he had been trying to raise money from the banks. Last week Margot had finally accepted the house had to be sold, but she wasn't happy about it. The reason he was at home in the middle of the day was because he was expecting the estate agent.

Hence the atmosphere last weekend, Sophie thought bitterly, moving reluctantly towards the dining room. Her father's last comment was ringing in her head: 'I'm sure

I can convince the creditors to hold off until I sell up, but whatever you do, don't upset Max Quintano. His father died a few months ago, and it was only when he looked into the family business that the discrepancies in payment came to light. If he had left his mother, who ran it with her husband for the last few years, in sole charge then this would not have happened so fast.'

Her father had never had a high opinion of women in the business world. Being such a chauvinist, it was surprising he allowed Margot to push him around.

She entered the dining room. Max was sitting at the top of a long table, with the light from the window catching the silver streaks in the gleaming blackness of his neatly styled hair. No sign of the errant locks that used to fall over his brow, or the teasing brilliant smile that had haunted her dreams long after she'd left him.

He had changed; he was leaner, harder, more aloof. But he could still make her pulse race just by looking at her. Sophie's stomach muscles clenched into a tight knot of tension as she stared down the length of the table at him.

'Did you speak to your father?' he asked.

'Yes.' She made herself walk forward until she reached the place-setting Diego had laid on Max's right. 'And you are correct.' She watched as he rose and pulled out the chair for her, ever the gentleman. She almost laughed at the hypocrisy of the man; why treat her like a lady when he was intent on turning her into little better than a prostitute? But she said nothing and sat down.

'I usually am,' he drawled, arrogantly resuming his seat, and at that moment Diego entered with a champagne bucket and placed it beside Max. 'Thank you, Diego. I will do the honours.' Taking the bottle, he uncorked it expertly and filled the two fluted glasses on the table. He held one out to Sophie.

'Take it, Sophie. A toast to old friends and renewed lovers,' he said sardonically.

'I haven't agreed to anything,' Sophie protested, but it was a weak protest and he knew it.

'Your very presence at this table tells me you have agreed,' he declared, his eyes lit with mocking amusement 'Otherwise you would have been out of this house in a heartbeat.'

He was right, damn him! Hot, angry bitterness swept through her, but she was not prepared to give up without a fight. 'My father is putting the family home on the market as we speak. Given time, he can clear his debts,' she said defiantly. But deep down she knew she wasn't going to see her little brother homeless and her father ruined.

'He does not have time,' Max asserted softly, his firm mouth twisting with cynical derision. 'I made sure of that this morning.'

'You... But how?' Sophie demanded tensely, green eyes flaring across the table at him.

'I had a very productive morning and bought out your father's creditors. I am now his sole creditor, and as such his fate is in my hands.' An ebony brow arched sardonically. 'Or yours...'

'You swine!' she exclaimed. 'You really expect me to sleep with you to pay my father's debt?'

'Sleep is not what I have in mind,' he said with silken emphasis. 'And outraged virtue ill becomes you when I know Abe Asamov was the most recent in no doubt a long line of lovers.' Dark, insolent eyes mocked her fierce tension, and he lifted the glass again. 'Take this. You look like you need it.'

Sophie could feel angry colour rising in her cheeks at his casual destruction of her character. But with her father's warning ringing in her head she fought back the fury that threatened to engulf her and took the glass he offered from his outstretched hand. The slight graze of his fingers on hers made her flinch, and her skin tingled with a multitude of sensual yearnings that shamed and inflamed her. She raised the glass to her lips and took a large swallow of the sparkling liquid—she *did* need it!

Max was so damn arrogant, so confident in his ability to get what he wanted in business and in his private life. Look at the way Gina still clung to him. Yet he must have hurt her a thousand times with his decadent lifestyle—a lifestyle he was intent on dragging Sophie into.

'No argument, Sophie?' he queried, leaning back in his chair, the trace of a satisfied smile quirking his wide mouth.

She affected a casual shrug, but inside she was seething with a mixture of emotions—the uppermost a burning desire to knock the smug look off his face. 'I don't believe in fighting. A reasoned debate is more my style,' she said coolly.

'So sensible, Sophie,' Max opined mockingly. 'But are you able to pay your father's debt by next Monday?' he demanded, his challenging gaze capturing hers.

Tension crackled in the air, and suddenly Sophie felt seriously threatened. He quoted a figure slightly over a million, and she stared at him in mute horror. The amount was nothing to a man of his wealth, but a fortune to most people—herself included. The house in Surrey had been the family home for thirty years and, given the astronomical rise in property prices in London and the home counties recently, the sale might fetch that much, but her father would be left with next to nothing.

Minutes earlier she had been determined to play it cool, but now every vestige of colour drained from her beautiful face.

'I take your silence as a no. And, that being the case, you will agree to be my lover until such time as I tire of you or your father repays me.'

'Not if…*when,*' Sophie asserted vehemently, but a chill was invading her body, and with it the growing certainty that she had no escape. How long would it take to sell the house in Surrey? she wondered. Set in an acre of garden, it was a highly desirable residence, with five bedrooms and five bathrooms, thanks to Margot's expensive modernization. The irony of the situation didn't escape her. It was an easy commute to London, and it should sell quickly.

How hard could it be to have Max as a lover for a month or two, maybe three? Millions of women would leap at the chance…. If she could get over the fact she despised the man it might even cure her of her helpless physical reaction to him. Then afterwards she could move on with her life and maybe meet and marry a decent man, have a family….

'Then we are agreed?'

Reluctantly she nodded her head, just as Diego arrived with a silver platter and proceeded to serve the meal.

She picked at the mushroom risotto, her stomach churning in sickening protest at the bits she tried to swallow. The veal cutlet that followed she ignored, while Max tucked in to everything with obvious enjoyment. The only words spoken were a few conventional comments on the food. On the inside Sophie was almost overwhelmed with a sense of frustrated anger at her situation, and her hatred of Max was building with every passing minute.

'More wine? Or would you prefer coffee?' Max asked. 'Then we can get down to business.'

She glanced at her half-empty glass, realising she had drunk too much already on a near empty stomach, and clipped back, 'Nothing, thank you.'

'I must say, Sophie, you have surprised me,' he said, subjecting her to a long, lingering scrutiny that roamed over her face and then down, to pause over the proud thrust of her breasts. 'I didn't think you would accept my proposition quite so quickly.'

The arrogant devil knew damn well that she'd had to. With her nipples hardening simply at his glance, she was shamed and furious at the same time.

She had dated and kissed a few other men over the years, but none had aroused her enough to want to do anything more. Yet with just a look this man could make her body react like the dumb teenager she had once been. It wasn't fair.... But then life wasn't fair, she thought bitterly, or she wouldn't be here now. She glanced at him, big, dark and dangerous. A couple of hours in close proximity to Max had strained her nerves to the limit, but he was so arrogantly sure of himself that she decided to strike back.

'Well, as you said, Abe has left for the Caribbean, and my father tells me time is of the essence.' She smiled slightly and deliberately let her eyes roam slowly over him before adding, 'You're not a bad alternative, I suppose.' She drained her glass. 'Now, as you said, we should get down to the nitty-gritty.' Filled with Dutch courage, she continued, 'As well as settling my father's money problems, I would like to know how much you are going to pay *me*. I have a well-paid job, and I stand to lose a lot if I have to hang around with you. I'm not sure of the going rate for a mistress, so I will have to trust your wealth of knowledge on the subject.' She saw his thunderous frown and warmed to her theme. 'Do I have to stay here, or do I get my own apartment? I need to know all these things, and obviously I need it in writing.'

CHAPTER SIX

BAITING a man like Max Quintano was a stupid idea, Sophie realised almost immediately. To say her response had infuriated him was an understatement. He leapt to his feet, grabbed her wrist and hauled her to hers, then spun her around to face him in one fluid movement.

'*Dio*! You would tempt the devil himself with that smart mouth,' he grated, his dark eyes glittering with inimitable anger. 'You obviously need some training in how to be a mistress. For a start it is bad form to mention past lovers. My study—now.'

Sophie took a deep, steadying breath as he almost dragged her from the room and into another that was obviously his domain. Books lined one wall, and a state-of-the-art computer set-up stretched along another. There were armchairs either side of a large fireplace, and in front of the window there was a massive desk with a winged-back chair behind it.

His hand tightened briefly on her wrist, and then with a muffled oath he thrust her into an armchair. 'Stay there and don't move.' She cringed at the force of his barely leashed fury as he strode over to the desk and flung himself down in the hide chair. 'You want it all legal? Then that is what you shall have,' he declared, and picked up the telephone.

An hour later he dropped a document on her lap, but Sophie was past caring. She was thoroughly disgusted with the whole affair. She had always known Max was a ruthless man, but she had never realised quite how brutally blunt he could be.

He had called his lawyer and the man had appeared within fifteen minutes. The following conversation had been the most shaming in her life. Max, as her father's only creditor, had agreed not to demand payment of the debt and bankrupt the company if in return Sophie would live with him until he decided to end the arrangement. At that point the debt would be wiped out. In other words, Sophie was the collateral for her father's debt. At her insistence, a clause had been added to say that she was free to go immediately if her father repaid the debt. This clause was unnecessary, according to the lawyer, but she didn't trust Max an inch.

She had tried to brazen it out, and had suggested again that men usually provided a mistress with an apartment, and did not have her living in their own home. Only to have Max respond that with her track record he didn't trust her out of his sight. She had shut up after that.

The lawyer had presented the finished document and signed it, and witnessed her total humiliation along with Max. But she had signed it, so what did that make her?

'Satisfied?' a laconic voice drawled, and she looked up to see Max towering over her like some great avenging angel.

Getting to her feet, she picked up her shoulder bag. 'Yes, you have made my position perfectly clear. Now, if you don't mind, I need to go back to the hotel and consult my diary, make some calls and rearrange my schedule for a week or two. I'll get back to you tomorrow,' she informed him coldly.

'No. You can do that from here. Now it is time for *my* satisfaction.' Without another word he swung her into his arms and carried her up the stairs, oblivious to the blows she landed on his broad chest.

'Put me down,' she snapped. 'I am quite capable of walking.'

'You're not getting the chance,' he asserted as he shouldered open a door and lowered her slowly down the long length of his body until her feet touched the floor. 'Because your first lesson as my live-in lover starts here,' he declared, his dark gaze hard and chilling in its intent as he closed the door behind him. 'A mistress is always ready and willing for her man.' He reached for her, his hands catching her shoulders. 'And she never strikes him.' He paused. 'Unless asked to in the pursuit of pleasure of course,' he mocked.

In that moment the enormity of what she had agreed to finally hit her. She glanced wildly around the luxuriously appointed room, her eyes widening in fear at the enormous bed. 'Oh, my God. What have I done?' she groaned, her gaze lifting to the man holding her.

'Nothing, so far.' His sensuous lips curved in a sardonic smile. 'But that is about to change.' He pushed her further into the room and stopped by the bed. 'Take off your jacket,' he demanded, his hands sliding down her shoulders to the curve of her hips. 'And the rest—except for the garter belt. I rather like the idea of removing that myself.'

'How do you know—?' But he cut her off with a finger to her lips.

'Sprawled in the boat. But no more questions now.' He moved back and sat down on the edge of the bed. 'I want to inspect the goods and see if you are worth what I am paying.'

He wanted to humiliate her—as if he hadn't done that enough already. But for the first time in hours Sophie began to think clearly and wonder why. She let her gaze roam over him. He was aggressively male, with a fantastic physique and rugged good looks; he could have any woman he wanted. So why blackmail her into his bed? Because basically that was what he had done, by using her love for her family against her. Why was he so mad about it?

They had parted years ago. She supposed technically she had jilted him, but under the circumstances he had nothing to complain about. Yet she could sense the latent anger lying beneath his apparent casual control and she could see no reason for it—unless it was some dubious desire for revenge. Maybe she had bruised his ego by walking out on him—not many women would, if any— but why bother after seven years?

'Did you plan this? Did you know I was going to be in Venice?' She asked the questions she should have done at the beginning, her gaze lifting to his, searching for the truth.

'No,' he said smoothly, and the expression in the eyes that held hers was contemplative. 'The first time we met, my brother had died four months earlier. This time my father died four months ago. The Japanese consider the number four unlucky—the devil's number. I am not superstitious, but you seem to have a knack of appearing in my life after a tragedy.' He shrugged his broad shoulders. 'Fate or sheer chance—take your pick. I saw you with Asamov, looking more beautiful than ever and obviously more experienced, and—knowing the state of Nigel Rutherford's finances—I decided to have you.'

'And that is why you are doing this?' She drew a deep, unsteady breath, a snippet of conversation from years ago coming back to her.

Gina had told him she'd warned him not to do anything impulsive when he had revealed he might have got Sophie pregnant. Max obviously hadn't changed that much—he still took what he wanted on a whim. Suddenly she felt heart sick, because the really sad thing was that deep down, in the sensual part of her being, a part she had denied for years, was a secret longing to be back in his arms…and even now she didn't want to believe he was as cruelly amoral as he appeared.

Max saw the puzzlement in her eyes, noted the pallor of her face and grimaced. She looked like some virgin being led to the sacrificial altar. Hell! She was doing it to him again—tricking him with her aura of innocence when underneath she had the heart of a bitch.

A cynical smile twisted his lips. 'I'm not doing anything. I am waiting for you to perform.'

Who was she trying to kid? Max had no finer feelings. Well, if he wanted a whore he could have one.

Fuelled by anger, she shrugged off her jacket and slipped the blouse from her shoulders. She unzipped her skirt and shimmied out of it, and stood hands on hips brazenly before him. 'Do you like what you see?' she prompted scathingly. He could look, but she was damned if she was going to lie down and surrender without a fight.

Max more than liked it... Her lush breasts were cradled in gossamer white lace, high-cut white lace shorts—so much more sexy than a common thong—enhanced her incredibly long legs, and the matching garter belt was all he had imagined and more.

He lifted his gaze to her face. 'So far, I do.' She looked sinfully sexy, her green eyes glittering with defiance, and slowly he rose to his feet. 'Except the picture is not quite right. The rest has to go—but first...' he reached for her shoulders and curved one hand around her neck '...*this* has to go.' Deftly he unfastened the clip that held her hair and ran his fingers through the pale silken mass. 'I prefer your hair loose.' He pulled the soft strands down over one shoulder and traced the length over her breast. 'Try to remember that.'

A shiver snaked down Sophie's spine and she tensed, her moment of bravado over, suddenly fiercely aware of his hand on her bare shoulder, the knuckles of his long fingers grazing her breast. 'Yes,' she murmured, lowering her eyes from his intense gaze, appalled at the ease with which her body responded to his slightest touch.

'*Yes* is good.' He drew her closer. 'You're learning fast,' and Max was fast losing what little control he had left.

She felt his fingers gripping her shoulders and glanced up through the shield of her lashes to his mobile mouth. She knew he was going to kiss her.

She wouldn't respond. She would *not,* Sophie silently vowed, her hands curling into fists at her sides. But when his lips found hers her resolve was strained to the limit. His kiss was hungry, punishing, and passionate. She didn't struggle, but neither did she respond. He lifted his head, his hands dispensing with her bra, and she stifled a groan as he palmed her breast.

'There is no escape now, Sophie. You will only delay the inevitable and hurt yourself in the process if you try to deny me.'

His voice was implacable, and a shiver ran through her. Max saw this and snaked an arm around her waist. He drew her against him, his mouth finding hers again, and he kissed her with such power that it made her senses swirl. Together, the caress of his hand against her bare breast and the demanding power of his mouth conspired to defeat her resistance, and helplessly her traitorous body surrendered to the heat of arousal surging through her.

A whimpering cry escaped as his mouth left hers to bite the curve of her neck, his hand stroking over her full breast, cupping the firm flesh with his fingers, teasing the sensitive peaks into aching buds of need. He lifted his head, his dark eyes burning down at her, and she grabbed his shoulders, afraid she would fall as her bones turned to water. But the arm around her waist held her firm, his fingers edging beneath her lace briefs.

'I swore I would make you strip, make you squirm,' he rasped. 'But somehow it does not seem important any more.'

She saw the savagery in his glittering gaze and for a second she was afraid. But with a low groan Max captured a rigid rosy nipple in his mouth and she was past all conscious thought. He licked and suckled with tormenting tender bites that sent quivering arrows of need cascading through her body.

'Yes, tremble for me,' Max grated and, lifting her off her feet, he swung her onto the bed and wrenched her briefs down her long legs. 'This is how I pictured you,' he growled, his eyes devouring her. The white lace garter belt and silk stockings were her only covering, and her glorious hair tumbled around her shoulders. Desire raged through him, and swiftly he dragged off his clothes, all the time feasting his eyes on the sensual splendour of her spread out before him.

Breathless and lying on her back, Sophie widened her eyes in helpless fascination on his tall tanned body. He was totally aroused—all hard, urgent male, and she wanted him with the same passion, the same eagerness, as the first time they'd made love. She knew later she would hate him again, but now she was not even embarrassed by their nudity.

'Look all you like,' Max said, with a low, husky laugh of masculine pleasure as he knelt on the bed beside her. He reached to brush her hair from her shoulders, and somehow his words hit a nerve—was she still so obvious to him?

'I will—and don't forget protection,' she said, in an attempt to reassert some control, remembering the first time she'd been with him and the awful aftermath. 'I want no repercussions from this sordid affair.'

'I'm not that careless. I don't know where you have been,' he lashed back. For a second his hands tightened on her shoulders, his dark eyes blazing down at her with a contempt he did not try to hide. He felt a primitive determination to drain every ounce of satisfaction from her exquisite body, to imprint his mastery over her so all her past lovers faded into oblivion. But first he reached for the bedside table and protection.

'Be my guest,' he drawled, sinking back on his knees and holding it out to her.

'I…' She stretched out her hand and then dropped it. 'No…you.' And the heat that coloured her skin was not so much sexual as a total body blush.

He offered her a mocking smile and leant over her to brush the hair away from her brow. He saw the tumult in her green eyes. 'Not so forward now.' Actually, Max was amazed she could still blush—but it didn't make any difference to the need pounding away in his blood, the need to dominate and captivate this sexy siren who had haunted his dreams for far too long. With that in mind, he dipped his head to claim her mouth, all of her…

At the touch of his lips on hers Sophie was once again swept away on a wave of sensuality. His tongue tasted her mouth, and when the need to breathe moved him his lips brushed down her throat and bit gently on the madly beating pulse he found there, then moved lower to her taut breasts.

She touched him then, letting her hands slide over his shoulders to feel the tension in his mighty body. She stroked her fingers down his back, lost in the wonder of him, of his satin-smooth skin beneath the pads of her fingers. His tongue licked her breast and she groaned, her fingers digging into his skin as he took the aching bud into his mouth and suckled with fierce pleasure, first one and then the other. The feel of his tongue, hot and wet, sent a renewed explosion of passion though every part of her.

Max lifted his head and knelt back, so her hands fell

from his body. He stared down at her, his heavy-lidded eyes glinting with fiercely leashed desire.

'Patience, *bella mia.*' His hands stroked tantalisingly slowly up from her ankles over her silk-clad legs to settle on her thighs. He parted them and moved between her legs, bending his dark head to kiss the band of naked skin above her stockings, and she groaned out loud, her thighs quivering at the subtle caress. She needed to touch him and tried to rise, but Max placed a hand on her stomach and pushed her back down. 'Not yet.'

Helplessly Sophie watched him gaze down at her naked thighs, at the golden curls guarding her femininity, with dark, intense eyes. His fingers slipped beneath the two white suspenders, flicking them open with hands that were not quite steady, then very slowly he peeled the stockings down her legs. And then just as slowly, with hands and mouth, he stroked and kissed his way back up, until she was a trembling mass of mindless sensation.

She gasped as his fingers reached the short golden curls to part the soft velvet folds beneath. His head dipped again, and she cried out as his teeth grazed the nub of her sex, then lost all control and gave herself up to the wondrous torment of his lips and tongue.

Her hands stretched out to clutch at his shoulders, her fingers feverishly stroking up into his thick black hair. She felt him tense and pull back.

'*Dio!* The taste of you is so sweet,' Max groaned, and slipped his hands beneath her thighs, kissing his way up her quivering flesh to her stomach, her breasts and finally her lips.

As his tongue plunged deep into her mouth he parted

her thighs wider and in one smooth thrust entered the hot, pulsing centre of her. Sophie winced at the slight pain—he was hard and thick, and it had been so long—but her legs and arms instinctively locked around him. And when he moved inside her time stopped. There was only the rapture, the ecstasy, of his awesome body possessing her.

She cried out as he moved in her with ever deeper powerful strokes, until she was sobbing his name over and over again. Her inner muscles clenched around his throbbing length as she was swept into a violent climax, and before her orgasm had time to subside he joined her, his great body shuddering uncontrollably with the powerful force of his release.

Max lay over her, his head on the pillow beside her, and Sophie held him, her slender hands stroking down his broad back, glorying in the weight, the scent of him, the heavy thud of his heart against her breast. For a while the real reason for her presence in his bed was completely forgotten. But she got a rude awakening when Max rolled over and slid off the bed.

Unashamedly naked, he stared down at her, his black eyes glinting with pure male satisfaction. 'The chemistry is still there—you still want me. That wasn't bad to begin with,' he drawled, in a deep, dark voice, and a chill invaded Sophie's bones at the mocking tone. 'But I never did get to take off your garter belt. Stay where you are until I get rid of this, and then we can continue.'

She watched him walk across to a door on the far side of the room—the bathroom, she guessed. The afternoon sun shone through the windows, gleaming on his big bronzed body, and stupid tears burnt the back of her eyes.

What had she expected? Tenderness? Caring...?

Blinking hard, she slid her legs off the bed and stood up. No way was she going to wait for him like some besotted fool. Been there, done that....

CHAPTER SEVEN

THE NEXT MORNING Sophie opened her eyes and yawned, and for a moment she was blissfully unaware of her surroundings and her situation. She stretched languorously and flinched, as muscles she hadn't known she had ached, reminding her of the humiliating truth. She had given herself to Max as she had done when she was nineteen—but it had been very different.

Because after seven years of celibacy, and with Max presuming she was vastly more experienced than she really was, he had subjected her to a lesson in eroticism and introduced things she had never imagined were possible. Worse still was the knowledge that she had responded with an eager mindless sexuality that she had no control over. She glanced across the huge bed. The only sign that Max had been there was an indentation in the pillow, and the lingering scent of him on the bedlinen and her body.

She drew in a deep, steadying breath and sat up, pulling the sheet around her neck. The clock on the bedside table said eight. She glanced warily around, as if she expected him to leap out at her at any moment.

She couldn't face him...not yet. Slowly she swung her legs off the bed and stumbled to the bathroom. She stepped into the huge circular shower stall and turned on the water, flinching as a dozen powerful jets pounded her body. She let her head fall back and closed her eyes—and a kaleidoscopic picture of the last twenty-four hours whirled in her head....

Max returning from the bathroom, his tautly muscled body still totally naked... The ease with which he had changed her mind and removed the garter belt... Her breasts swelled at the memory.

The tender lovemaking of her youth hadn't prepared her for the full force of Max's sexual expertise—or the wild woman she had become in his arms. She didn't know herself any more.... Turning off the shower, she stepped out and wrapped a bathsheet sarong-style around herself, and a smaller towel around her hair, then padded back into the bedroom.

She didn't want to think—to remember the humiliation when later Max had accompanied her back to the hotel to collect her belongings, or his brooding silence over dinner. When she had tried to speak, tried to assert some independence and insist she had to return to England to make arrangements for her apartment to be taken care of, he had coldly dismissed her suggestion and taken her back to the bed that was the scene of her earlier downfall.

At one point, buried deep inside her, driving her mad with a torturous pleasure, he had stopped. Sophie had begged him to continue, arching up, her nails digging desperately into his firm flesh, but he had resisted her every effort. And she had opened her eyes and registered the triumph in his molten black gaze, his taut features, as he'd grated, 'Did Abe make you feel like this?'

She'd given him the 'no' he wanted, and seen the glitter of masculine supremacy in his eyes as he took her over the edge.

Glancing at the rumpled bed now, she twisted her lips wryly as she recalled Max pointing out, as he'd left, that this was *her* bedroom. Where his was she had no idea. At least she didn't have to actually *sleep* with him, she thought, determined to try and be positive about their arrangement. But oddly the thought was not as much comfort as it should be.

Bending her head, she began to ferociously towel-dry her hair, in the hope of knocking every image of her shameful capitulation of him out of her mind.

'Here—let me do that.'

She jerked upright in surprise at the sound of his voice. 'Where did you come from?' she demanded. Six feet plus of arrogant male was standing in front of her, dressed casually in navy pants, a navy shirt and leather jacket. But to her shame the instant picture in her mind's eye was of the same body naked. His dark gaze met hers, and the gleam of sensual knowledge in his send a red tide of embarrassment over her pale face.

'I'm sure you would like to think I had sprung up from hell,' he drawled sardonically. 'But nothing so dramatic. This is the master suite. We share the bathroom and dressing room. I'm surprised you did not notice the connecting doors.'

Of course she had—the same way she'd seen the up-to-the-minute bathroom, all white and steel, with two vanity basins and a massive circular pedestal bath. But it had not registered. In fact, nothing much had registered in her head since yesterday afternoon, except the dynamic, powerful presence of the man standing before her, and it had to stop.

But, before she could formulate a cutting response, Max took her unresisting hands from her head to slide them gently down her sides. Catching her shoulders, he pulled her close, and to her amazement began drying her hair.

For an instant she was tempted to rest her head on his broad chest and let him continue. But what little pride and self-respect she had left after her helpless surrender to him in the physical sense would not let her. Planting her hands on his chest, she pushed him away and he was left holding the towel.

'There is no need for that. I can use a hairdryer.'

His hooded eyes ran slowly over her wild tumbling hair, and lower, to the towel that slanted across her breasts. 'Need—maybe not. But want—well, *want* is a very compelling emotion.' To her surprise he chuckled, making a deep, sexy sound. 'And with that towel threatening to fall at any second, it is one emotion I am becoming very aware of.'

'What?' She glanced down and saw the towel sliding, and grabbed it up around her breasts as his arms captured her. His mouth came down to cover her own. She couldn't struggle, not without losing her only covering, and as his tongue stroked over hers she didn't want to. Her body melted against him as though tuned to his touch, and the familiar heat flared up inside her.

'Much as I would like to continue,' Max murmured, taking his mouth from hers, 'we have a flight to catch at ten.'

'A flight?' she exclaimed in confusion.

'Yes.' His hands fell from her. 'We have an appointment with your father for lunch. I arranged it last night, before dinner.' He looked at her stunned face with a gleam of mockery visible in his dark eyes. 'You have kept your part of the bargain more than adequately so far. Now I have to keep mine. But I want to meet the family who drove you to be so—obliging,' he said in a deep, cynical voice. Stepping back, he turned and walked over to the door, opened it, then stopped to fling over his shoulder, 'I'll see you downstairs in forty-five minutes. Don't keep me waiting,' and then left.

Sophie found the dressing room, and her few clothes neatly hanging in a wardrobe. It took her less than thirty minutes to get ready, she was so angry. After refusing her request yesterday, to return home to sort out her apartment, he had some nerve arranging to meet her family. But why was he doing it? To humiliate her further?

She gave a quick glance at her reflection in the mirror. Her hair was tied back with a red scarf, she'd applied minimum make-up and was wearing the same navy suit as yesterday. Someone had obviously pressed it, and, teamed with a red cotton top and flat red loafers, it gave a more casual effect. Her choice reflected her new status as a scarlet woman, she thought wryly—but she hadn't much choice. She had packed sparingly for her trip: a business suit, an evening dress and a selection of tops. The only casual item she had with her was a tracksuit she wore to run, or to lounge around in. Somehow she couldn't see the sophisticated Max appreciating his mistress in a track-suit. She tensed at the thought. When had her mind accepted she *was* his mistress?

She remembered reading the definition of the word in her mother's dictionary years ago, when Meg had mentioned her father's latest mistress. By definition a female *paramour*—a woman *courted* and beloved. If only, she grimaced. It certainly wasn't the connotation most people put on the word today—*kept and paid for* was the common assumption, and unfortunately in her case it was the truth.

Telling herself she didn't care, she straightened her shoulders and, with a defiant tilt to her chin, walked downstairs.

Max was waiting for her, and though she had told herself she would be perfectly composed, her stomach somersaulted as he let his gaze rake blatantly over her.

'A punctual woman.' His sensual mouth twisted with amusement. 'Or were you just keen to see me?' he mocked.

'No,' she said grimly. 'But I *am* keen to know why on earth you would want to meet my father with me in tow. Surely it's enough you will see him at the meeting next week? Even *you* can't be such a bastard as to tell him the truth about our arrangement.'

He shot out a powerful arm and yanked her against him. 'I've warned you before about your smart mouth.'

Sophie was trapped by the savage brilliance in his dark eyes. Her heart raced as his head dipped, taking her mouth in a deep, powerful kiss that was meant as a punishment.

She wanted to pull away, but the familiar musky scent of him teased her nostrils. Her toes curled with pleasure and with a will of their own her hands lifted to curl around his neck. She kissed him back, hungry for the taste of him. Then, without warning, he pushed her away.

'Call me all the names you want, but you *do* want me,' Max drawled, his dark eyes scanning her flushed face with cruel amusement. 'You worry too much.' He didn't bother to hide the derision in his tone as he added, 'Given the circumstances, your father will be delighted to see you, I have no doubt.'

'But what—?'

'What am I going to tell your father?' he said, reading her mind. 'The truth, of course.'

'Are you crazy?' she declared, eyeing him in horror. 'You can't possibly do that! He may not be the greatest dad in the world, but I *am* his daughter. He'd probably kill you!'

To her amazement, he laughed in her face. 'Ah, Sophie.' He shook his dark head. 'When I said the truth, I meant *my* version of it.' He reached an arm around her waist, and once again his dark head bent to take her mouth with his.

She shuddered beneath the brief, forceful passion of his kiss, and it took her a while to register what he was saying after he took his mouth from hers.

'We met and became *friends* years ago, in Sicily, and again in South America, and then again in Venice. For want of a better word—you are now my girlfriend, and as such I can't see you upset over your father when I can help…'

'You're definitely crazy. My father is not likely to believe that.' But bitterly she realised that Max was smart; there was just enough truth in his words to make them plausible.

'Yes, he is—because he will want to. I understand that as a widower he was quite a ladies' man, and spent generously on his woman. According to my information, his present wife costs him a fortune. I think we can safely say he will swallow the story whole, as long as you give me your full co-operation.'

Max was right about her father. In the years after her mother's death she would have had to be blind not to notice his penchant for the ladies. She had tried not to let it bother her, and mostly she had succeeded. How Max knew, she had no idea—and she wasn't sure she wanted to find out. In a way, they were two of a kind, she thought bitterly.

Letting none of her feelings show, she glanced coldly up at him and asked, 'What exactly do you mean by that?'

He grasped her chin between his fingers and looked deep into her eyes. 'You shall play the part of the eager and besotted lover—you did it once before to great effect, so you shouldn't find it too difficult. Especially after last night.' He pressed one last brief, punishing kiss on her mouth before, with her firmly held to his side, they walked out to where Diego waited with the launch.

An hour later Sophie, tense and trying to marshal her turbulent thoughts, sat in his private Citation X jet. According to Max, his enthusiasm evident, it was the world's fastest business jet, and could fly close to the speed of sound. It allowed up to eight people to travel the world and hammer out business deals at the same time. Talk about toys for the boys—multimillion pound toys, in this case, she thought dryly as the jet winged its way to London.

She glanced at Max in the seat next to her. He was wearing glasses and all his attention was on the papers he had withdrawn from a large briefcase—and had been since they took off, over an hour ago. Nervously she chewed on her bottom lip; they would be landing in another hour, and she still wasn't convinced the story Max had outlined to tell her father would work.

'Max,' she said beginning to panic, 'my father is not a fool—though he behaves like one at times,' she amended with feeling, still not able to fully grasp the ramifications of her dire situation. 'Are you sure…?'

His dark head turned towards her, and he slipped the glasses from his nose and rubbed his eyes.

'I never knew you wore glasses,' she said, diverted by his action.

'There is a lot you don't know about me, Sophie.' His mouth twisted cynically. 'But you have plenty of time to learn. As for your father, he will believe what we have already discussed. He is an experienced man with eyes in his head.' Curving a hand around her nape, he captured her mouth with his in a deep kiss. 'And you, Sophie, have the glow of a *satisfied* woman,' he drawled with silken satisfaction.

Did it show? Sophie wondered, flushing as she remembered last night. His last sentence effectively silenced her—as did the habit he seemed to have developed of kissing her without a second thought.

Seated to the left of her father, with Timothy beside her, Sophie tried her best to appear happy. But with Max and Margot opposite she was fast losing the will to live….

From the moment they had arrived from the airport by chauffeured limousine, and seen the 'For Sale' sign at the entrance to the drive, Sophie had been walking on eggshells. She'd had a brief respite when Timothy had demanded a ride in the limousine, and Sophie had gone with him while Max spoke privately with her father. She had shown the chauffeur the way to the village pub and back again, but when they had returned so had her tension.

Apparently Max had boldly announced to her father that he wanted to help him out of his present difficulties because he could not bear to see Sophie worried about her family, and a deal had been made.

Everyone was happy—especially Margot, who had taken one look at Max and started to flirt shamelessly. Max had cleverly fielded her innuendos and played the ardent suitor to perfection, keeping Sophie pinned to his side, and only letting her go when Margot had told them where to sit at the table.

Before the main course was finished, and after far too many personal questions from Margot, Max smoothly explained that he had had a soft spot for Sophie ever since he had first met her, when she was nineteen. He went to explain that they had met up again, purely by chance, in South America a few months ago—which wasn't strictly true. They *had* both been there; they'd just never met up.

Sophie could almost marvel at the way he avoided telling a direct lie, and when he said that their relationship had become serious in Venice, he turned his shining brown eyes to hers to add, 'Isn't that right, *cara*?'

'Yes.' What else could she say? She blushed scarlet at the gleam of mockery only she could see in Max's gaze, and that blush confirmed the story for her father.

It got worse when Margot asked her to help with coffee and cornered her in the kitchen.

'My goodness, you *are* a dark horse. I can't believe you've pulled a man like Max Quintano—but thank heaven you have. Play your cards right and he might even marry you. You want children, so get pregnant. That way even if he won't tie the knot you will be made for life.'

Sophie had often wondered if Margot had got pregnant deliberately, and now she knew—but she couldn't be angry because she loved Timothy so very much.

Sophie began to say, *I am quite happy with my life as it is*, but stopped, realising it would be a lie. She had only been happy until she had met Max again.

Margot shook her head and loaded the coffee tray. 'At least we get to keep the house. Whatever you do, don't upset the man until your father's debts are settled.'

'No, Margot, you don't understand. The house still has to be sold.'

'Don't be ridiculous. You're as bad as your father. Even if the house *is* sold, after the mortgage is paid off it won't make a fraction of what is owed. But for some reason Max fancies you—maybe you are good in bed.' She cast Sophie a brief doubting glance. 'I have heard he is a great lover. Maybe the attraction is in teaching you... But, whatever it is, one word from you and he will not see your family home sold to strangers. So start talking, quit worrying and pass me the cream and sugar.'

Trailing behind Margot back into the dining room, Sophie barely glanced at the others as she resumed her seat. She drank the coffee Margot poured without lifting her head. From the couple of months she had envisaged as being Max's mistress, her sentence seemed to have become open-ended. She knew that on the death of her mother the mortgage on the house had automatically been paid off by joint insurance—her father had told her so. It had never entered her head that he would remortgage it. How stupid was that? But with a young and expensive wife like Margot it was inevitable, and she supposed she should have guessed.

Barely two minutes after serving the coffee, Margot was leaning towards Max. 'More coffee, Max?' Her avid eyes were almost eating him alive. 'Let me fill you up—or perhaps you would prefer something else?' she prompted with an arch look, before adding, 'A cognac, or champagne to celebrate?'

Sophie could stand it no longer; she pushed back her chair and dragged Timothy out of his. 'Come on, Tim, you have sat still long enough. We will leave the adults to their drinks and go for a walk.' And she was out of the dining room and into the kitchen like a shot.

Opening the back door with Tim's hand in hers, she walked out into the crisp autumnal air. She took a few deep breaths, trying to cleanse her mind and her body from the shame she felt about what she had done and what was happening inside.

Tim tugged at her hand. 'Can we climb to the tree house?' he asked eagerly.

Looking down into his happy, innocent face, her heart swelled with love and she knew she had made the right decision. She would do anything to keep her brother in a happy home, with both parents, and if that meant saving her dad from bankruptcy, so be it....

Margot was young, attractive. Sophie didn't see her as the type to stay with a much older husband who was broke. Cynical, she knew, but realistic.

She smiled at Tim. 'Yes, of course, darling.' They set off down the path that wound round sculptured flowerbeds and manicured lawns to where a box hedge half hid the lower garden of fruit trees and pasture. A well-used child's swing and a slide stood in a clearing among the apple trees, and at the bottom was a hawthorn hedge with a large beech tree at the end. It had been Sophie's favourite place as a child. She had an abiding memory of her mother, pushing her high in the air on the swing, and sweeping her up in her arms as she careened to the foot of the slide.

Moisture hazed her eyes as they approached the beech tree and the rickety platform built across a fork in the trunk that Tim euphemistically called the tree house. Sophie had built it with her mother's help when she was eight. She had reinforced it last year. Now, giving Timothy a hand up, she climbed up behind him. Memories, she thought wistfully, looking at Tim's happy and excited face. They had no price. She knew she had done the right thing in accepting Max's dishonourable proposition.

'Really, Sophie, what must poor Max think? Climbing trees at your age.' Margot's tinkling laughter brought Sophie's attention down to the ground where Margot, clinging to Max's arm, was leading him down the path and smiling up into his face. 'I swear sometimes Sophie is more a child than Timothy, and I've told her over and over again not to let him climb.' She shrugged her elegant shoulders as they stopped beneath the tree. 'But she takes no notice of me.' She flicked a glance up at Sophie. 'Come down this minute.'

Seeing Sophie, her hair spiked with a few autumn leaves, tumbling free from the scarf that fought to contain the silken mass, her skirt around her thighs, didn't make Max think of her as a child—quite the opposite. She had the little boy firmly in her hold, and the two of them looked very similar, he realised. Sophie also looked childishly guilty.

'You heard what your mother said, Sophie,' Max prompted, tongue in cheek, his dark eyes glinting with amusement.

'I'm not her mother,' Margot said indignantly, and Sophie had to stifle a laugh.

Max ignored Margot and tipped his head back, his eyes taking in Sophie's lovely face and the humour twitching her lips. 'Come down this minute,' he commanded sternly, his gaze flickering over her slender body on the precarious perch, before lingering on her thighs, straddling the planks. 'Better still—hand me Timothy.' He held out his hands and glanced up, a brilliant smile slashing across his face. 'Then I will come and get you.'

His smile was so natural and so unexpected that Sophie laughed and handed Timothy into his arms. Before Tim was on his feet Sophie had swung out of the tree and was standing firmly on the ground.

Sliding a casual arm around her waist, Max pulled her into his side. 'You are a strange mixture, Sophia.' He drawled the Italian version of her name as he scanned her exquisite features. 'A beautiful, elegant woman—and yet you can act like a child.' His dark gaze held hers with compelling intensity. 'I have settled with your father—you have nothing to worry about. After seeing you with Timothy, I understand you a little better.'

Sophie very much doubted that—he thought she'd had

a host of lovers, for a start—but with his arm around her waist she felt oddly protected, and she wasn't about to argue with him.

But she *did* argue with him when her stepmother suggested they stay for dinner and the night and Max accepted.

'No—we can't possibly.' She shot Max a vitriolic look. He was seated on the sofa next to Margot in the drawing room, his long legs stretched out casually before him, looking perfectly at home, with a glass of brandy in his hand. 'I have to check on my apartment and make sure everything is okay with my neighbour.' Stiffly she rose from the armchair, and crossed the room to stare down at Max. 'If that is okay with you, Max?' she said, with a brief attempt at a smile.

It was a novel experience for Max to be looking up at Sophie. A Sophie who was actually asking his opinion instead of spitting defiance at him. For a moment he was tempted to deny her request just for devilment. But as his gaze slid appreciatively over her, and his body responded predictably, something stopped him. His tall, beautiful lover looked positively fragile. He saw the tension in her slender shoulders, the strain on her lovely face, and realised she was near breaking point.

'Yes. Of course.' He rose to his feet and read the flicker of relief in her guarded green eyes as she stepped back a little. He moved to slip a protective arm around her waist and took his cellphone from his pocket. 'I'll call the driver.' She glanced up at him and he felt her relax slightly. 'Ten minutes and we'll leave…okay?'

'Thank you,' she said softly. 'I'll just go and freshen up.'

She slipped from his hold. He watched her walk to the door, saw the effort she made to straighten her shoulders and hold her head high as Margot objected.

'Really, Sophie, we hardly ever see you. And that little apartment of yours can look after itself, for heaven's sake. You and Max *must* stay.'

He saw her head turn. 'No, I'm sorry, Margot. We must go.' She carried on out of the door, and for the first time since he had set eyes on Sophie again Max questioned what he was doing.

He looked at her so-called parents, and realised that two more self-centred people would be hard to find. He recalled Sophie telling him that her mother had died when she was eleven and she had gone to boarding school. Her father cared for her, but not enough to disrupt his lifestyle, and he was quite happy to take Max's offer to save his skin without so much as a private word with his daughter to ascertain how she really felt.

Max flicked open his cellphone and made the call, the realisation that he had behaved in just as cavalier a fashion—if not worse—making him feel as guilty as hell. Not an emotion he appreciated.

Sophie didn't go back downstairs until she saw the car arrive, and their goodbyes were mercifully brief. Her father kissed her cheek and Margot kissed air. Only Timothy was really sorry to see her go. She lifted her brother up and hugged him, smothering his little face in kisses and promising him he could come and stay with her again by the sea next summer, as he had before. She then slid into the back seat of the car.

'Are you okay?' Max asked, noting the moisture in her

eyes as he slid in beside her, after telling the driver to make for Hove.

She brushed a stray tear from her cheek, before looking bleakly at him. 'Of course. You have solved my father's problem in a day—I couldn't be happier. What do you expect me to say?' she prompted, with a negative shake of her head. And, not expecting an answer, she looked away.

Max had never seen her look more disgusted or more defeated, and unexpectedly his conscience bothered him. He had bulldozed his way into her life and into her bed without a second thought. He had taken one look at her with Abe Asamov and a red-hot tide of primitive posses-siveness had blinded him to everything except a burning desire for revenge on the only woman who had ever walked out on him. But now he wasn't so sure...

'*Thank you* would be good, but not necessary.' Max caught her chin and made her face him. 'But I consider it not beyond the bounds of possibility that you might be happy with our arrangement.' He watched her green eyes widen in disbelief. 'Our sexual chemistry is great—' the slight colour rising beneath her skin encouraged him to continue '—and, contrary to the impression I might have given in the last day or two, I'm not an ogre. And with a bit of goodwill on both sides we could rub along very nicely.' Bending his dark head, he took her mouth in a quick, hard kiss. 'Think about it during the journey, while I get on with some work.' Parting his legs slightly, he lifted his briefcase to his lap, extracted the latest mining report on a new excavation in Ecuador and began to read.

Rub along very nicely—was he for real? she asked herself, her lips still tingling from his kiss. The only thing rubbing around here was his thigh against hers, with the motion of the car, and *nicely* was not an adjective she would use—*naughty*, more like. She cast a sidelong glance at his granite profile; he was so cool, so calm, so in control. How did he do that? she wondered. He was far too ruthless, too lethally male to ever be associated with the word *nice*, and she was surprised it was even in his vocabulary.

As for goodwill on both sides! She edged along the seat to put some space between them. She could just imagine how *that* would play out. An all-powerful, arrogant male like Max would consider his will good for both of them.... He certainly had so far.

Yawning, she closed her eyes. She had barely slept for two nights, and she was bone-weary and tired of thinking.

CHAPTER EIGHT

'SOPHIE...SOPHIE, wake up.' She heard the deep voice from a distance and slowly opened her eyes—to find herself with her head on Max's chest. Her arm was burrowed under his jacket and her fingers grasped the back of his shirt, while his arm was looped across her shoulders and under her other arm.

She jerked her head up. 'I fell asleep,' she murmured, stating the obvious and blushing scarlet.

'With you plastered to my chest, I did notice,' he quipped, his eyes smiling down into hers. 'But we have arrived.'

Pushing on his chest, she scrambled back to a sitting position and ran her fingers through her hair, straightening her skirt over her legs. 'I am sorry. I must have stopped you working,' she said, too embarrassed to look at him.

'Don't be. It was my pleasure,' he chuckled, and stepped out of the car.

Her apartment was on the first floor of a double-fronted detached Victorian house on a main road overlooking the beach and the sea.

'Great view,' Max remarked, glancing around as he took her hand and helped her from the car.

Standing on the pavement, it suddenly struck Sophie that she didn't want Max in her apartment. It was her private sanctuary, and when this affair was over she wanted no spectre of Max hanging around her home.

'There is no need for you to come in.' She slanted a smile at him that faded slightly as she met with intense dark eyes, studying her curiously from beneath lush black lashes. He really was incredibly attractive, and for a moment her intention wavered as she enjoyed looking at him.

She blinked rapidly and continued fighting back the blush that threatened. 'Why don't you have the driver show you around the area? He can't park here anyway, and Brighton is just along the road and very interesting,' she pointed out, with admirable cool. 'It won't take me long to pack a few things, and I have to visit my neighbour. You would be bored.' She tried to casually free her hand from his.

An ebony brow arched sardonically. 'You cannot be serious, Sophie.' In an aside he quietly dismissed the driver for the night and tightened his grip on her hand. 'I have had enough of driving around for one day.'

Sophie fitted her key into her front door lock and walked into the elegant wood-panelled foyer.

'I live on the first floor,' she murmured, and was very aware of Max's eyes on her as she walked in front of him up the enclosed staircase, and unlocked the door at the top that led into her hallway.

'Not quite up to your standards,' she said bluntly, as she led him into the sitting room. Without thought, she heeled off her shoes, dropped her bag on the usual sofa table and turned to face him. 'But I like it.'

Max gaze skimmed over her. She was bristling with defiance, and he knew she did not want him here. 'I'm sure you do,' he said smoothly, glancing around the room. 'It is charming.'

It had a sophisticated elegance, with its high ceiling and light oak floor. A grey marble fireplace housed an open fire, and a deep wide bay window that overlooked the sea was fitted with a comfortable window seat. The décor was mostly neutral, with a touch of colour in the rug and the sofas, and on one wall a waist-high long mahogany bookcase was filled with books. Above it a group of paintings were displayed.

'Would you like coffee, or a glass of wine?' Sophie asked, uncomfortable with the growing silence.

'Wine, please. Your English coffee is terrible.' Max strolled across the room and, shrugging off his jacket, draped it on the arm of the sofa and sat down.

'I left a bottle of South African chardonnay in the fridge, but I can't guarantee it will be better than the coffee,' she responded dryly.

The sight of him sprawled at ease in her home, looking as if he belonged there, confirmed Sophie's worst fears. She'd never get the image of him out of her head, she just knew it, and she was glad to escape to the kitchen-diner off the main hall.

She took off her jacket and hung it over the back of a pine chair. Taking the bottle from the fridge, she opened it and filled two large crystal glasses. She took her time, sipping a little of the wine, feeling reluctant to face him, and then realised her mistake—the quicker she got him out of here the better. She drained her glass and replaced the bottle in the fridge.

Moments later she walked back into the sitting room and placed the crystal glass on the table. 'Enjoy—the bottle is in the fridge if you want a refill. I'll just go and pack—it won't take me long. A quick call to my neighbour and we can be gone.' She knew she was babbling, but he made her nervous.

A strong hand wrapped around her wrist, and with a jerk he pulled her down beside him.

'What did you do that for?' she demanded, struggling to sit up. Another tug pulled her back, a strong arm clamping around her shoulders.

His dark eyes made a sweeping survey of her mutinous face, and he just grinned. 'Relax, Sophie; you have a lovely home—unwind and enjoy it. We are not going anywhere tonight. When you decided after lunch that you had to come here, I gave my pilot the rest of the day off—he started at ten, and he is only allowed to work twelve hours.'

His hand was warm through the fabric of her top, his thumb and fingers idly kneading her collarbone, making her achingly aware of the dangerous sensuality of his touch. Her breath caught and she had difficulty speaking for a moment. She swallowed hard, determined not to give in to his overpowering sexual attraction. She glanced at the clock on the mantelpiece. They'd left Italy at ten, and they could be back by ten if they hurried.

'It…it's just six.' She couldn't help the stammer, but carried on urgently. 'I can pack, and we can be at the airport by seven if we hurry. It is only a two and a half hour flight—we can be there by nine-thirty.'

'I'm flattered you are eager to return to my home, and your mathematical attempt on my behalf is quite impressive. Unfortunately, *cara*, you haven't allowed for continental time being an hour ahead.' Max looked at her mockingly. 'So it is not possible.'

'You can't sleep here.' Her eyes widened on his in appalled comprehension—it was her own stupid fault he was here at all. It was bad enough having him in her sitting room, but it would be a hundred times worse having him in her bedroom.

'Would you mind telling me why not?' Max enquired smoothly, his hand stroking up the side of her neck and his long fingers wrapping around her loosely tied hair.

His wide shoulders were angled towards her, and she was strikingly aware of the virile male body, the glimpse of golden skin beneath the open-necked blue shirt. She blurted out the first thing that came into her head. 'You have no clothes.'

'You are wrong. Surely you know that I am always prepared? Not that it matters—remaining naked with you will do just fine.' He grinned. 'Come on, Sophie, we both know the game is over and I won.' He tugged on her hair and tilted her head back, his glinting dark eyes capturing hers. 'Cut out the pretence. You're mine for as long as I want you—here or anywhere.'

'Only until the house is—' She tried rather futilely to deny his assumption, and was silenced by his abrupt bark of laughter.

'After meeting Nigel and Margot, I know that is never going to happen unless I make them. And I won't.'

That he had seen so easily through Margot didn't surprise her, but, forcing herself to hold his gaze, she said, 'You're probably right. But it does not alter the fact I'd rather we didn't stay here. A hotel…'

'A hotel?' His brow pleated in a frown. 'Afraid I will discover signs of your last lover in your bedroom?' His amusement vanished.

'No, of course not,' she shot back, incensed, and then wished she hadn't as his expression became strangely contemplative.

'So something else is bothering you?' His piercing black eyes narrowed shrewdly on her face and suddenly she was afraid.

'I've been away since Saturday—there is no food in the house,' she said, swiftly tearing her gaze from his, frightened he would see more in her expression than she wanted him to know.

'Is that all?' She sensed rather than saw the smile an instant before his lips brushed hers. 'I am a big man, and I need my food, but there must be a restaurant around here. We won't starve.'

Her green eyes focused on his starkly handsome face, saw his mouth curved in a sexy smile, and for a moment she was transported back in time, to the laughing, teasing Max of her youth. She felt again the heavy beat of her heart, as though it would burst from her chest, the incredible lurch in her stomach that accompanied her every sight of him, and it terrified her.

'You're right.' She forced a smile to her lips. 'Drink your wine. I need to shower and change,' she managed to say steadily. 'Climbing trees is a messy exercise.' She indicated the TV remote control on the table. 'Watch the television, if you like. I might be a while.'

Intense dark eyes skimmed over her face and lingered for a moment, then he calmly lounged back on the sofa as she rose unhindered to her feet. 'I'd rather share your shower,' he prompted softly.

'It isn't big enough,' she said without turning around and she walked slowly out of the room, closing the door behind her.

She leant against the wall, physically and emotionally drained. It had hit her like a thunderbolt when she had mentioned Saturday and made the excuse about food. Five days—it had only been five days, and her life had changed for ever. His easy dismissal of her excuse about food and her reaction had shocked her to her soul. Suddenly she realised the futility of trying to keep him out of her bedroom. It wouldn't matter where or whom she was with; the image of Max would always be in her mind.

Making herself move, she walked down the hall and into the bathroom. She stripped off her clothes and felt a chill down her spine as she realised with a sense of inevitability that she was in very real danger of becoming addicted to Max's undoubted sexual charisma all over again. She refused to call it love....

Turning on the shower, she pulled on a shower cap and stepped under the spray, her thoughts in turmoil. She had tried to dismiss her feelings for Max as a teenage crush the first time they'd been together, and had convinced herself—until last night. Now her mind was at war with her body, and the internal battle was tearing her apart. That she was Max's mistress was a huge blow to her pride, her self-respect, but the pleasure she had felt at the touch of his lips, his hands on her body, the wonder of his possession she could not deny. She could not fool herself anymore—she wanted him with a ferocity that frightened her, and he must never find out. Because if he did that would surely destroy what little self-respect she had left.

Stepping out of the shower, she dried and dressed, wondering all the time how was it possible to lust after someone when she hated the kind of man he was—and certainly didn't trust him.

Dressed in jeans and a sweater, Sophie was still asking herself the same question when, forty minutes later, she walked back into the sitting room. Max was still seated on the sofa, his briefcase open beside him and some papers in his hands. He looked up as she entered.

'Quite a transformation.'

'Not really. I always dress like this when I am at home.' She flicked a cold green glance his way. 'If there is a dress code for a mistress you should have told me.'

Max knew she was angry with him for forcing her into this situation, and in a way he didn't blame her, but on another more cynical level he didn't see what she had to complain about. She was no longer a starry-eyed virgin, not by a long way.

'Not that I am aware of. An *un*dress code, yes. Any time I say so,' he stated bluntly, his dark gaze skimming over her. She looked stunning—her long shapely legs were covered in close-fitting blue denim, and a deeper blue sweater clung to the firm thrust of her breasts. The pale blond hair was swept back into one long braid and reminded him forcibly of the teenager he had first known—and of the reason they'd parted.

He reached for her, his hands palming each side of her head, and looked deep into her angry, resentful eyes. Infuriated, he took the lush mouth with his own in a bitter, possessive kiss. If anyone had a right to be angry it was he; she had walked out on him without a second thought, at the lowest point in his life.

He felt her fingers link around his neck, the softening of her gorgeous body against his, the response she could not deny. And, disgusted with himself as much as her, he lifted his head and pushed her away. 'Where is the bathroom? I need a wash.'

As rejections went, it was a bad one, and Sophie learnt a valuable lesson. Sucking in a deep breath of air, she forced her chin up, her face expressionless. If she was to get through the next weeks or months she had to be as cool and emotionless as Max. 'First door on the right along the hall,' she replied.

Max heard the laughter as he approached the sitting room door minutes later. Light and sexy, it ripped open a Pandora's box of memories he could do without. For a moment he stood in the open door, watching her. She was sitting in the window seat, her lovely face wreathed in smiles.

'Oh, Sam, you are impossible.'

At the name Sam, Max stiffened and stepped into the room. He must have made a sound, because she turned her head towards him and the smile vanished from her face.

'Look, I can't talk now, but I promise I will try my best to get back in time. Okay?' She put the telephone down and rose to her feet.

'Sam is a friend of yours, I take it?' he prompted, and sat down on the sofa, swallowing the bitter taste that rose in his throat. How many men had sampled Sophie's luscious charms? he wondered. It was not something that had ever bothered him with his other women, and the anger surging through him felt suspiciously like jealousy.

'Yes. We spent a year backpacking together when we finished university.'

'How nice.'

Sophie glanced at him. So the word *nice* was in his vocabulary—but by the tone of his voice and the way he used it it was anything but. 'Yes, it was brilliant,' she said defiantly. Letting him know she hadn't pined for him was a good idea. 'Now, if you're ready, it is quite a pleasant night. I thought we could walk along the seafront to my favourite Italian restaurant. It is probably not in your class, but the food is great.'

'I'm relieved to hear you appreciate something about Italy,' Max grated, rising to his feet.

With him looming over her, big and threatening, she bit back the comment that sprang to mind. *It was only Max she didn't like*. Instead she said, 'If you don't mind, I'll call on my neighbour on the way out to tell her my change of plan. It won't take a moment.'

He raised an ebony brow mockingly. 'Lead on. I am in your hands.'

It was after eleven when they left the restaurant, and Sophie was feeling quite relaxed for the first time in days—though it might have had something to do with the three glasses of wine she had consumed with the meal.

Max took her hand and tucked it under his arm. 'Are you okay to walk, or shall I get a cab?'

'You should be so lucky.' She grinned up at him. 'The

pubs close at eleven—this is the rush hour for cabs. If you haven't booked one you have no chance.'

Of course he proved her wrong, by flagging one down two seconds later.

'You were right about the food—it was good. And I have never had such fast and efficient service in my life. Though I think that had more to do with your presence than mine,' Max said dryly, looping an arm around her shoulder in the back seat of the cab. 'You seem to know the family very well; you must go there a lot.'

'Oh, I do—two or three times a week when I'm at home.'

'The owner's two sons, Benito and Rocco, seem to be very friendly with you.' *Friendly* wasn't the word he really wanted to use. Fixated would be more appropriate. The two young men were clearly completely besotted with her, and, as he glanced down at her now, it wasn't hard to see why. It had been an eye-opening experience for Max.

Ironically, Max had been cross-examined by the owner as if he was Sophie's father—something Nigel Rutherford should have done earlier, but hadn't. As for the two sons, they had virtually ignored him except to shoot dagger glances at him when Sophie wasn't looking. They were much the same age as Sophie, and entirely too familiar with her for Max's liking.

'Yes, we are great pals. Sam and I met them when we were in Australia on our world travels, and they linked up with us for the last six months of our tour. We all came back to England together, and we have stayed in touch ever since.'

Dio! She had a trail of men lusting after her; they might have already had her for all he knew. 'That does not surprise me,' he snarled, his hand tightening on her shoulder at the unpalatable thought. He saw the surprise in her eyes, and with a terrific effort of will he reined in his temper. But he couldn't resist touching her, and he tilted her chin, slid a hand around the nape of her neck to hold her head.

She was a beautiful, vibrant young woman, and he had introduced her to sex—unlocked her passionate nature in what had turned out to be the most sensually exciting experience of his life, he had to admit. It was only natural she had taken other lovers after they'd parted; she wasn't cut out to be celibate.

The Abe Asamovs of this world he could deal with, but seeing her tonight, with two young men of her own peer group, so obviously relaxed and at ease with them, he'd been forcibly reminded of how much older he was than Sophie. He realised he should be thanking his lucky stars he had got her at all—she truly was priceless.

He caught her lips beneath his and explored her mouth with long, leisurely passion, before trailing a teasing path down to the beating pulse in her throat.

The cab stopping halted any further exploration, but Max kept an arm around her waist as they walked up the stairs and into her apartment. As soon as the door closed behind them he turned her in his arms.

'Your bedroom, Sophie,' he demanded, and saw the hectic flush of arousal in her face. He nipped playfully on her lower lip. 'Quickly would be good, *cara*.'

He stared down at her and, held against his big, taut body, Sophie realised that what was to follow was as inevitable as night following day. With every cell in her body crying out for what he was offering—why fight it? And, easing out of his arms, she reached for his hand and linked her fingers with his, leading him along the hall to the door opposite the sitting room and opening it.

Max laughed out loud, a rich, dark sound in the stillness of the utterly feminine room. The carpet was a soft ivory, and along the wall furthest from the door was a four-poster bed, draped in yards and yards of white muslin tied with pink satin bows. A delicate dresser and matching wardrobes in antique white, delicately painted with roses, plus a matching chaise longue were arranged around the other walls. But it was the big bay window that amused him.

'How on earth do you sleep with all those eyes watching you?' The window seat was lined with a startling array of dolls in every form of dress, and on the floor in the bay was a Georgian-style dolls' house.

'Very well, as it happens,' Sophie declared, abruptly recovering from the sensual daze he had evoked in her. Pulling her hand from his, she said, 'And what has it got to do with you, anyway?' He was never going to come here again, if she could help it.

Dark eyes glinting with amusement sought hers, and a predatory smile revealed brilliant white teeth. 'I'm intrigued as to why a woman of your intelligence and sophistication would have a bedroom like this.'

'The dolls' house was my mother's, and as for the dolls—some I have had for years, and I've got into the habit of collecting others from every country I visit,' she said defensively. 'I do have another bedroom you can use. I'll show you.' She grasped the chance and turned to leave.

But he stopped her, his arm snaking around her waist to keep her clamped against him.

'No, Sophie, this will do just fine,' he informed her softly, and he bent his head just enough to brush his lips against her own.

She jerked her head back in rejection. 'In Venice you have your own bedroom. At least let me keep the same distinction in *my* home,' she demanded.

'Remember our deal—sex anywhere, any time, my choice,' he drawled, and he caught her mouth again and this time didn't stop.

Helplessly her eyelids fluttered down, and she raised her slender arms to wrap them around his shoulders, her body arching into his. Her tongue traced the roof of his mouth and curled with his, her blood flowing like liquid heat in her veins. His hands were all over her; his long fingers finding the snap of her jeans and sweeping up her spine under her sweater to open her bra, then sweeping around to find the thrusting swell of her breasts.

Her hand darted down to tear at his shirt, and she whimpered when his mouth left hers. Her eyes still closed, her slender body shaking with need, he lifted her onto the frilly white coverlet and with a deftness that underlined his experience she was soon naked.

At the touch of cool air on her skin her eyes opened, and her gaze fixed on the masculine perfection of Max standing by the bed. Big and formidable, his muscular, hair-roughened chest was rising not quite steadily, and his lean hips and hard thighs framed the great dynamic power of his sex.

How often had she lain in this bed with the image of a

naked Max haunting her dreams? The erotic fantasies she had built in her mind of him appearing and declaring his undying love while she drove him mad with desire had left her sleepless and frustrated.

'Max,' she murmured throatily, her fantasy now a reality, and her green eyes darkened as with a slow, seductive smile she lifted her arms to him.

He chuckled a deep, sexy sound that vibrated across her nerve-endings and, leaning over her, curved his hand around her throat. He looked deep into her eyes. 'Yes, Sophie—say my name.'

His hand slid down over her breast and her stomach to settle between her legs. He held her gaze as a finger slipped between the soft folds and stroked once, twice, and she shuddered, groaned out her frustration when he stopped. Then he was beside her on the bed, his dark head dropping, his mouth taking the groan from her throat as his tongue stroked hers in a wicked dance of desire.

Lost between fantasy and reality, Sophie reached for him, her slender hand curving eagerly around his neck and raking into the silken hair of his head. Her other hand stroked down over his broad chest, her subtle fingers grazing a pebble-like nipple on their descent down his sleek, muscled body to his flat belly. She touched him where she had never touched him before, her hand closing around the long, hard length of his erection, a finger stroking the velvet tip. She felt his great body jerk in response, heard his groan and gloried in it as her hand moved inquisitively down to the root of his male essence. Then abruptly he caught her straying hands and, rearing back, placed them on either side of her body.

'Now you want to play?' he growled, his dark gaze sweeping over her body, lingering on the perfect rose-tipped breasts, and lower, to the soft blond curls at the apex of her thighs, then dropping to her spectacular long legs and moving back to her face. '*Dio*, you are exquisite.'

His compliment fed her fantasy as his avid glance seared her flesh. Sophie was on fire for him, liquid heat pooling between her thighs. She reached for him again, her hands stroking over his wide shoulders.

He looked down at her, his sultry smile a sensual promise, and parted her thighs to move between them. He took her mouth once more in a fiercely passionate kiss, his hand cupping her where she wanted him, his long fingers easing again between the sensitive folds.

She clung to him, the tantalising movement of his clever fingers driving her wild with want, and when his mouth dipped lower, to draw on her straining nipples, she cried out. 'Please, Max, please,' her whole body quivering with need.

At her cry, Max groaned hoarsely and lifted his head. Her green eyes glazed with passion, she was *so* wet and *so* ready. Lifting her hips, his great body taut with strain, his breathing harsh, he plunged into her. She was tight and hot, and, using all his skill and self-control, he moved— sometimes with shallow strokes, and then more intensely, with long, full strokes ever deeper. He wanted to make this last. He wanted to blot out every other lover from her mind.

Sophie had never known such almost painful pleasure existed as he swept her along in an ever-increasing ferocious tidal wave of tense, torturous desire.

Max rolled onto his back and lifted her above him, his

strong hands firm on her waist, crazy with need as she hovered on the brink and stared down into his dark face. He was watching her with a feral light in his night-black eyes, and he stilled for a second whilst she rushed head-long towards her climax. She cried out at the tug of his mouth on her rigid nipples, and at the same time the power of him filling her to the hilt with ever more powerful strokes sent her over the edge into a delirious climax. She was wanton in her ecstasy, pushing down hard on him with every increasing spasm. She felt his great body buck and shudder, and he called her name once in a voice that was close to pain as he joined her in a cosmic explosion of raw, passionate release that was completely beyond their control.

Sophie collapsed on top of him, breathless and shaking, burying her head in the soft curls of his broad chest. She had never known such intense sensations were possible. For a few blissful moments while she lay in the circle of her arms she could almost believe it was love: the familiar scent of him, the weight of him, the pounding of their hearts almost in unison. Then he moved her over onto her back and flopped down beside her, and the fantasy vanished as the silence lengthened.

Suddenly she felt cold; there was no love, only a prim-itive lust. Of course it was great…Max was an expert at sex, and so he should be…he'd had plenty of practice, by all accounts, she reminded herself. She clenched her fists at her sides, to prevent her weaker self reaching for him again.

The movement of the mattress told her he had stood up, but she didn't look; she couldn't, in case he saw the hurt in her eyes. She heard the door open, and moved to slip beneath the covers, a shiver of revulsion assailing her at what he had made her. A willing slave to her sexuality, nothing more....

She pulled the lace-covered duvet up around her chin and buried her head in the pillow. She heard the door close, and then nothing.... He had probably found the spare bedroom. It was no more than she expected, and she had to learn to live with it....

'Sophie.' He drawled her name softly and she turned, her eyes widening in surprise. He was standing by the bed stark naked, with two wine glasses in one hand and the half-full bottle of wine in the other.

'A nightcap? Or perhaps a drink before the second round?' he prompted with a wicked grin. And she couldn't help it—she grinned back.

Sophie yawned and opened her eyes. She blinked at the sunlight streaming through the window, and then blinked again as a dark head blotted out the sun.

'Max,' she murmured, and she was intensely aware of his long body against her own. 'You stayed all night.'

'I had nowhere else to go.' He dropped a swift kiss on her softly parted lips. 'Unfortunately I do now.' His hand curved around to cup her breast and she sighed. 'I know,' he said, and his thumb grazed her rosy nipple. 'Unfortunately we haven't any time. My pilot has a take-off slot in eighty minutes.' Withdrawing his hand, he rolled off the bed. 'Come on—the car will be here any moment now.'

Twenty minutes later, washed and dressed in a short red and black kilt-style skirt, with a soft black mohair sweater pulled hastily over her head and her feet pushed into red pumps, Sophie slid into the limousine.

She was still trying to make sense of this new, relaxed Max when they boarded his jet and a steward served breakfast.

CHAPTER NINE

DIEGO WAS WAITING with the launch as they exited the airport at noon, and their return to the *palazzo* was swift. Entering the elegant hall, Sophie was shocked to see a group of six smiling adults lined up to meet them. She was surprised to discover as Max made the introductions that Diego did not run the house on his own. Maria, his wife, was the cook, Tessa, their married daughter, was the maid and her husband Luke was the gardener…quite the family affair.

'I didn't know you had a garden,' Sophie said as the staff dispersed.

'Obviously you need a tour. Diego will take your luggage upstairs while I show you around.' Max waved around the ground floor. 'Dining room, study and morning room and grand salon. Beneath is the kitchen, utility room and Diego's apartment, and beneath that the cellars.'

Of course—the massive steps to the entrance concealed the fact this was actually the first floor, and not the ground, she realised as he led her around the back of the staircase and opened a large double door. To her surprise inside there was a fully equipped games room and gym, with a swimming pool half in and half out of the house. The exterior part had glass walls and a roof that opened to the sky. Steps led down into a walled garden.

'Feel free to use this whenever you like.' Striding back to the reception hall, he added, 'I have some work to catch up on, so I will leave you to your own devices—but remember lunch is at one-thirty.'

She saluted. 'Yes, oh master.' But he was not amused. The Max of last night, who'd drunk wine in her bed, was gone, and the autocratic tyrant was back.

'That is exactly what I am, and don't you forget,' he replied stiffly, and without another word disappeared into his study.

Sophie made her way upstairs to her bedroom just as the young maid Tessa was disappearing through the open door of the dressing room with the smallest case in her hand. 'No—please, I can unpack myself,' Sophie said with a smile. From what she had seen so far there was precious little else for her to do around here—except await her master's bidding.

But she was too late. After Tessa had left she occupied her time by placing a few personal items—her make-up, jewellery box and perfume—on the small, ornate antique dressing table. It was just for show, however, because she had no intention of using the dressing room for anything other than storing clothes now that she knew she shared it with Max. And at that moment he appeared.

'I forgot to give you these,' he said as he walked towards her. Stopping at her side, he dropped something on the dressing table. 'I have opened an Italian bank account for you, as agreed, and that is your credit card.' He glanced at her. 'After lunch we are going out, and much as I like that short, flirty skirt I don't want you wearing it in public. Get changed.' And, swinging on his heel, he left as abruptly as he had arrived.

What did he *want* her to wear? Sackcloth and ashes? Sophie fumed as she stripped off and headed for the shower. She had lived on her own and been her own boss for years. Kowtowing to a man was not in her nature— especially not to an arrogant, ruthless man like Max.

She frowned as she stood under the soothing spray. Sophie knew herself well. She was not cut out to be a mistress; she was far too independent. But the trouble was, until her father's business was secure she had no choice.

Deep in thought, she walked back out of the bathroom and into the dressing room. What she needed was a strategy for living with Max that would not leave her an emotional wreck when they parted. Inexperienced as she was, she knew Max was right: they *were* sexually compatible, dangerously so, and it would be very easy for her to become addicted to the man. She had to guard against that at all costs.

Slipping into white briefs and a matching bra, she opened the wardrobe door, her hand reaching for a pair of denim jeans, and stopped. She wasn't at home; this *palazzo* would never be her home. Max had told her that a mistress agreed with her man at all times, and an inkling of an idea occurred to her.

She entered the dining room half an hour later, dressed in a sage-green double-breasted jacket with only a bra beneath, and a matching slim-fitting skirt that ended just above her knees. She had scraped two swathes of hair back and fastened them in a loop at the back of her head. The rest she had left loose, to fall down her back. Her make-up was perfect, but a lot more than she would usually use, and on her feet she was wearing three-inch-heeled stilettos.

Max was standing by the drinks trolley, a glass in his hand, and turned as she walked in. His hard, dark eyes swept slowly over her from head to toe, lingering on the plunging V of her jacket and even longer on her legs. He was examining her like some a master in a slave market. She could feel angry colour rising in her cheeks, but she fought it down.

'You have taken my advice, I see. Would you like a drink?'

'Yes, please.' Her temper rising at his arrogant certainty that she would do as she was told, she had almost said no. But, mindful of the part she had decided to play as she had dressed, she agreed. Hadn't Max told her a mistress always said yes? The beginnings of a smile twitched her lips. This might even be fun.

'Do you always eat in here?' she asked, and smiled up at him as she took the glass of wine he offered her. It was a large, elegant room, but her preference would be to eat somewhere less formal.

'Yes, when I am here. Which is not that often.'

'Well, if you don't mind, when I am on my own would it be all right for me to eat somewhere smaller—the kitchen, perhaps?' she asked.

'If you like.' Max pulled out her chair for her as Diego entered with the first course, then took his own seat.

As the meal progressed Max grew puzzled. Sophie had changed from the tiny skirt into an elegant suit, as he had suggested, but it did not help him much. Because although

her legs were halfway covered, he could see her cleavage—and he was pretty sure she wore nothing under the
jacket. She had left her gorgeous hair loose, and she was
smiling and talking perfectly politely, agreeing to everything he said. So why did he get the feeling something was
wrong?

'So, where are you taking me this afternoon?' Sophie
asked as she took a sip of coffee, the meal over.

Max knew where he wanted to take her—straight to
bed. But he reined in his baser impulse; there was something different about her and it infuriated him because he
could not pinpoint the change. 'I am taking you to the jewellers to fulfil my side of the bargain,' he said, shoving
back his chair and standing up. 'I promised you diamonds
instead of crystal.'

'Oh, yes. I forgot.' Sophie stood up as well. She didn't
want his damn diamonds, but in her new role she had to
agree. 'But there is no hurry,' she couldn't help adding.

'I'm a busy man, and I am never usually here on a
Friday. As I am here, I want to get the matter settled now.'

Sophie bit down hard on her bottom lip. 'Yes, of
course,' she replied and headed for the door before she lost
her cool and landed him a slap in the face. He was talking
to her as if she was some blond bimbo. But then that was
what he *thought* she was....

'Sophie?' Her skin prickled at the way he drawled her
name, and a long arm slipped around her waist, halting her
progress. 'We don't *have* to go out....'

She glanced up at him, saw the intention in his dark
eyes. The warmth of his arm around her waist was making
her temperature rise—and with it her temper.

'Yes, we do,' she said sweetly, and her plan to say *yes* to everything suddenly seemed very easy.

Half an hour later, when they walked into the jewellers, it was not quite so easy. The jeweller saw them seated and then presented a staggering array of diamond necklaces, earrings and bracelets for their perusal.

'Do you like this set?' Max indicated a stunning waterfall of diamonds.

'Yes,' she said, and continued to say yes to everything he suggested.

'Oh, for heaven's sake, chose one,' Max snarled, finally losing his patience, and he saw her luscious lips curve in a secretive smile.

She turned wide, innocent green eyes up to him. 'You choose, Max. After all, you are paying for it so it has to please you.'

Then it hit him. The little witch had been saying yes to everything, agreeing with everything he said, since the moment she'd come down to lunch. It was every man's fantasy to have a lover who said yes to everything, so why did it feel so damn irritating?

Indicating the waterfall set, he bought and paid for it, ignoring Sophie, and then, taking her arm, he pulled her to her feet and they left the shop.

'I am on to you, lady,' he drawled, turning her into his arms, his dark eyes gleaming down into hers. 'Will you jump into the canal for me, Sophie?' He felt her stiffen in his arms. 'Or kiss me, here and now?' And he saw the guilt in her green eyes. She knew she had been found out. God, she was a stubborn creature—but beautiful with it. He made it easy for her. 'Say yes to the latter. You know you have to,' he chuckled.

The broad grin and the laughter in his eyes were Sophie's undoing. 'Yes,' she laughed, and he bent his head, taking advantage of her open mouth to slip his tongue between her parted lips. Her hands slipped up around his neck—and that was how Gina found them.

'Max? Max—what on earth are you doing?'

Max lifted his head but kept an arm around Sophie's waist. 'Gina.' He grinned. 'You're a doctor—and you don't know?' He felt the sudden tension in Sophie and tightened his grip. She had to face his sister some time—the one witness to her brutal dismissal of him years ago. 'I didn't know you had stayed in Venice.'

'Even doctors are entitled to a holiday. But I am surprised *you* are still here. Though I can see why,' she said drolly, with the lift of a delicate brow in Sophie's direction.

Sophie looked at the small dark woman and her companion, another slightly older woman, and wished the ground would open up and swallow her whole. To be caught kissing in broad daylight was bad enough, but to be caught by Gina, his ex-lover—or maybe not ex—was doubly embarrassing.

'You know Sophie, of course,' Max said suavely, and glanced down at her. 'And you remember Gina, *cara*?'

As if she could forget. 'Yes,' she said slowly, and gave Gina a polite smile. 'Nice to see you again.' Why on earth had she said that? She couldn't give a damn if she never saw either her or Max ever again.

'Nice to see you, too,' Gina agreed. 'This is my friend Rosa.' She made the introduction. 'We thought we would do some shopping, then stop for a coffee at Florian. What are you and Max up to?'

'The same.' Max answered for her. 'Except we have finished our shopping.'

'My God, Sophie, I don't believe it—you actually got the world's worst chauvinist to take you shopping!' Gina laughed. 'If you hang around longer this time he might even become halfway human.'

Confused by Gina's obviously genuine laughter, and the lack of malice in her tone, Sophie gave a wry smile. 'I doubt it.'

A husky chuckle greeted her words and Max glanced at his stepsister. 'Watch it, Gina. I don't want you frightening Sophie off with your biased view of me.' He drew Sophie closer to his side.

'So it would seem,' Gina said, slanting an amused look at the pair of them. 'It is to be hoped—'

'Are we going for coffee or what?' Rosa intervened. 'I need my caffeine fix.'

'Yes—sure. Why don't you and Sophie join us, Max?' Gina asked.

An hour later, when they left the coffee shop, Sophie was none the wiser about Max and Gina's real relationship. On the launch going back to the house she replayed the meeting in her mind. Surprisingly, the conversation had been easy. Rosa, she had discovered, was married with two boys—who sounded like holy terrors from the anecdotes she had shared with them. It was obvious Max and Gina were close, and totally at ease with each other, but whether it was sexual Sophie didn't know. She had sensed under their apparently friendly conversation and laughter a kind of tension—and it wasn't just the tension *she* always felt around Max. It was something more, but she couldn't put her finger on it.

'Rosa was funny—and Gina was quite pleasant,' she said slowly as they entered the house.

'Were you surprised?' Max asked with a sardonic lift of an ebony brow. 'You shouldn't be—she almost always is.'

'Yes, if you say so,' she murmured.

With his finger and thumb he tilted her chin. 'Have I missed something?' he demanded. His dark eyes narrowed intently on her upturned face. 'Or are we back to the yes game again, I wonder?' His astute gazed dropped to the lush curve of her mouth and his hand tightened slightly.

She knew his intention, felt it in the sudden tension between them.

'No to both,' she said hurriedly, and lowered her lashes to mask her own reaction.

'You look tired. Have a rest before dinner.'

'I know your kind of rest,' she said with biting sarcasm, and, shrugging off his hand, she headed for the stairs.

But she didn't escape completely.

She was standing in front of the dressing table, having kicked off her shoes and shrugged off her jacket, and was about to remove her make-up when Max walked in.

'You forgot this.' He strolled over and dropped the jewellers box on the table, his cold dark eyes meeting hers in the mirror. 'The deal is finalised. I always keep my word— just make sure you keep yours.'

Over breakfast the next morning Sophie could barely look at him. He had come to her bed last night and made her wear the diamonds while he made love to her—no, *had sex* with her. And she had never felt so demeaned in her life.

'I am going to the family estate this morning,' he informed her coldly, rising from the table. 'Since the death of my father I need to help out with the running of the Quintano hotels. I'll be back Sunday night. In the meantime, if you want to go out you are not to go alone. Diego will accompany you at all times—understood?'

It was a very different Sophie who, six weeks later, looked in the same dressing table mirror and slipped a diamond drop earring into her earlobe. They were going to a charity dinner, and she could hear Max moving around in the dressing room. He had returned an hour earlier, from a week-long trip to Ecuador, and they were in danger of being late because he had joined her in the shower....

Max was an incredible and determined lover, and she had long since given up on trying to resist him. He was also very generous—her lips twisted at her reflection in the glass. The Versace emerald-green evening gown revealed more than it concealed, a pair of designer green satin shoes were on her feet, and the large diamond Van Cleef earrings with matching necklace completed the look. Yes—she looked what she was: a rich man's mistress.

In bed, she had no defence, and only a strong sense of self-protection stopped her revealing her ever-deepening feelings for Max. But paradoxically her image in the mirror satisfied her, because it made it easier to play the part of a cool sophisticate around him.

Surprisingly, it seemed to work, and they did—to use

Max's words—*rub along* quite well. Every night he was in Venice he came to her bed and aroused her with a slow, deliberate eroticism, aware of every nuance of her response until she cried out for release and he tipped her over the edge into ecstasy. Sometimes he came with her, and sometimes he followed her. Either way, they ended up breathless and spent—but also silent. Sophie didn't dare speak, and she guessed Max had no reason to; he had got what he wanted. As often as not he stayed till the morning and they made love again. And sometimes when she was locked in his embrace she almost believed it was love instead of lust....

Over the weeks she had developed her own routine to make life bearable, and the kitchen had become her favourite room in the house. She got along well with Maria, Tessa and her three children, and she took great pleasure in teaching the young ones English—the adults benefited as well.

She had quickly realised Max worked incredibly long hours. Sometimes he was here, in his study, but he was just as likely to fly halfway around the world for a couple of days. When he was at home he spent at least two or three days a week—always including Friday—at his head office in Rome.

Sophie had travelled to Rome with him only once, about a month ago. He had worked all day, taken her shopping in the evening, then to dinner in an intimate little restaurant, and finally to bed in his penthouse apartment. She had thoroughly enjoyed the experience; somehow in Rome she had not felt like a mistress.

But the following morning, after Max had left for the office she had again. She'd taken a shower and, looking in the bathroom cabinet, hoping to find a toothbrush, had discovered a bottle of perfume and various other female toiletries—plus a large black hairslide and a bottle of prescription medicine in Gina's name. The slide she knew could *not* be Gina's—the woman had close-cut hair.

The next time Max asked her to accompany him to Rome she refused, with the excuse that it was the wrong time of the month.

Sophie frowned now, as she clipped on the other earring. He had dismissed her excuse as irrelevant— saying there were many routes to sexual pleasure—and it had only been when she'd insisted she felt ill that he had given in. She had seen in his sardonic smile as he'd said, 'Have it your way,' that he didn't believe her.

Sophie knew from Maria that she was the only woman Max had brought to live in the *palazzo*. To the romantic but conservative Maria that meant they would marry, and Sophie didn't like to disillusion her. Sophie now accepted that Max shared her bed—honesty forced her to admit she couldn't resist him—but she couldn't accept sharing his bed in Rome. Not when he had all his other lovers.

Sophie spent quite a lot of time on her own. Max, she presumed, continued to go and visit the family estate— though he had never told her so since that first time—or perhaps he stayed in Rome. The fact that he never asked her to accompany him again didn't bother her. At least that was what she told herself. And when he telephoned her occasionally she never asked him where he was; she was afraid to show too much interest.

She enjoyed the freedom to explore Venice—not that she was entirely free; Diego had strict instructions to accompany her when she went out. But, on the upside, Diego was a fount of information. She had visited St Mark's and sat outside the Café Florian, sipping coffee and watching the world go by. They had visited the Guggenheim and the Accademia, and many more smaller art galleries, which she would never have known existed without Diego, plus countless churches filled with stunning masterpieces that one would not normally expect to see outside a museum.

The city itself was probably the most beautiful and romantic in the world—but how much better it would have been to explore the tiny alleys and hidden *piazzas,* to linger in the small cafés with someone she loved, she thought sadly. Someone like Max....

If she was honest she missed him when he was away— she kept telling herself she hated him and it was just sex, but it was becoming harder and harder to do. He occupied her thoughts all the time. Like now, she realised, her forehead pleating in a frown.

'Why the frown?' a deep, dark voice drawled.

Sophie turned her head to see that Max had emerged from the dressing room and was watching her with a look of genuine concern in his eyes. Her heart squeezed in her chest. He had his dinner jacket in one hand and was wearing black trousers and a white evening shirt that con- trasted brilliantly with his tanned complexion. He looked staggeringly attractive. But then he always did to her. And it was in that moment she knew she loved him. She could fool herself no longer. She loved him, probably always had and always would, and the knowledge terrified her.

Sophie looked back at her reflection in the mirror, to give herself time to get over the shock of realising how she truly felt about Max and to try and compose herself. 'I was wondering if these earrings were too much,' she finally answered, turning back to him with her face a sophisticated calm mask—she hoped.

'Not a bit—you look exquisite,' he declared, dropping his jacket on the bed, His gaze swept appreciatively over her. A slight smile quirked the corners of his sensual mouth and she saw the gleam of gold in his dark eyes and recognised that look. Given it was no more than half an hour since they had indulged, and given the scary knowledge that she loved him, she resented the ease with which he aroused an answering response in her own body.

She lifted her chin—an angry sparkle in her green eyes. 'You paid for it,' she snapped, and his eyes narrowed fractionally at her sudden outburst.

'True,' Max said, and stepped towards her. 'I also pay for your services.' He stretched out his arm.

'We haven't time,' she gasped, taking a step back.

'Oh, Sophie, you really do have a one-track mind—not that I am complaining,' he mocked. And, grasping her hand, he dropped a platinum cufflink in her palm. 'Fasten this for me.' He shook his outstretched arm, amusement dancing in his dark eyes. 'I can never manage the right as easily as the left.'

Her lips twitched. 'You, Max Quintano, can and do manage *everything*,' she said, but fixed the cufflink, admiring the fine dark hair on his wrist as she did so.

'And that is what irks you, my beauty.' Slipping an arm around her bare shoulders, he brought her into close contact with her hard body. His mouth closed over hers in a long deep kiss. 'How about we skip this party and stay here? I have been away too long, and I have not had nearly enough of you yet.'

'You're actually asking my opinion?' she prompted, with the delicate arch of a fine brow. 'Now, that *is* a first. You usually do as you like.'

'True,' he said, all arrogant virile male, his hand sliding down over her bottom. 'But you also like.' He smiled as he felt her shiver.

'Maybe.' She recognised the sensual amusement in his dark gaze. 'But you're crazy if you think I got all dressed up like this just for you to undress me.'

'Crazy about you—yes,' he said, with a wry smile that completely stunned her. It was the closest he had ever got to hinting that he cared, and a tiny seed of hope lodged in her heart. He moved his hand to curve it around her waist and added, 'But I promised to attend this charity dinner, so the undressing will have to wait until we return.' He ushered her towards the door. 'Though maybe we can fool around in the launch on the way. What do you think?' he asked, with roguish lift of his black eyebrows.

He looked like a swashbuckling pirate, Sophie thought, and, shaking her head, she laughed. She couldn't help it. At moments like this she could almost believe they were a happy normal couple.

The dinner-dance was a select affair held at Hotel Cypriani, and with Max's hand linked in hers she walked into the elegant room. The first person she saw was Gina, in a group of half a dozen distinguished-looking people. She turned her head and laughed at something that had been said, then caught sight of Max and came rushing over.

'Max, *caro*.' She grabbed his arm and stood on tiptoe,

her body pressed against his side, to give him a kiss full on his lips. Still clinging to his arm, she turned to Sophie.

'Sophie, I'm surprised to see *you* here. I didn't think this was your thing. But we do need all the support we can get,' she said with a smile, and turned back to Max. 'It's weeks since I've seen you. I am so glad you could make it.'

Gina could not have made it plainer that it was Max who interested her and she only tolerated Sophie's presence at his side, Sophie thought, her new-found love making her hypersensitive as jealousy, swift and painful, sliced through her. When had the conventional public kiss on both cheeks developed to a full-blown kiss on the mouth?

Then, out of the blue, a distant memory hit her like a punch in the stomach. Old Man Quintano had strongly disapproved of Max and Gina's relationship, but now he was dead there was no one to object to them marrying.

Suddenly Max's desire to have her as his mistress made more sense, and the blood turned to ice in her veins as the reality of the situation sank in. Max was a highly sexed man—as Sophie knew all too well. One woman would probably never be enough for him. As a teenager *she* had been the prospective bride, because she might be pregnant, and Gina the lover; now the situation was reversed, and *she* was cast in that role.

'You're right—this isn't my thing.' And Sophie didn't mean the dinner. She meant Max and Gina's relationship. 'In fact, I will quite happily leave.' Sophie saw no reason to pretend any more. A ménage à trois had never been and never would be for her, and she tried to pull her hand from Max's.

Max's jaw tightened in anger. Enjoying Sophie's exquisite body, he had almost dismissed the reason she had left him, excusing her behaviour by telling himself that she had been young and naturally frightened of the prospect of tying herself to a sick man. Now he knew better—she didn't give a damn about anything but her own pleasure. What kind of man did that make him? Lusting after a heartless woman who had quite happily been Abe Asamov's mistress and heaven knew how many more?

He gave her a hard look, saw the beautiful, expression-less face and the cold green eyes, and said with chilling emphasis, 'This is Gina's night—her cancer charity.' He smiled coldly and twisted Sophie's hand around her back to pull her against him in what looked like a loving gesture. 'You will stay and be civil to everyone,' he murmured against her ear. 'You will act the part of my loving con-sort—something I know you are good at. After all, that *is* what I pay you for,' he reminded her with sibilant softness. He felt her tense, and simply tightened his grip.

Then he turned his attention to Gina. 'I am sure your night is going to be a great success. Don't mind Sophie. She did not mean to offend you. Did you, *cara*?' His hard black eyes turned on her.

'No, it was a joke,' Sophie said feebly. But the joke was on her. She had finally recognised in her heart and mind that she loved Max, only to find out half an hour later nothing had changed.

Sophie sank into the seat Max held out for her, glad to be finally free of his restraining hold. But it was only in memory of her mother that she sat down at all. She was sick to her stomach and simmering with anger. From the teasing lover of an hour ago, he was once more the ruthless, autocratic swine who had forced her to be his mistress. She hadn't missed the threat in his words, and he couldn't have spelt out more clearly exactly where his loyalty lay. And with that knowledge the faint seed of hope she had nurtured earlier of something more than sex between them died a bitter death.

She straightened the slim-fitting skirt of her gown over her thighs, fighting to retain her composure, and when she did lift her head her lips twisted cynically as she noted the seating arrangement. Gina was seated on Max's left and she was seated on his right—now, why didn't that surprise her?

She forced a smile to her lips as introductions were made all round, and realised they were mostly medical professionals. She accepted the wine offered and did her best to ignore Max. It wasn't hard, as Gina engaged him in conversation—for which Sophie was truly grateful.

As course followed course and the wine flowed, the conversation became more animated. But Sophie took very little part. These people were probably all very good and clever, but she was in no mood for talking.

Beside her, Max wore the mantle of dominant and so-phisticated male with ease, his input into the conversation witty and astute. His occasional comments to Sophie were smoothly made with a smile, and to any onlooker he appeared a caring partner, with a touch on her arm, an offer to fill her glass. Only she could see the restrained anger in his gaze, and it took all her will-power simply to respond to him civilly. The way she felt right now, she couldn't care less if she never spoke to him again.

She'd got over him once and she would again, Sophie

vowed. But although she tried to ignore it, the pain in her heart refused to go away.

For the rest of the meal she avoided his glance, with her head bent down, concentrating on her food, although she had never felt less like eating in her life.

It was when coffee was served that the conversation really became boisterous. Sophie gathered the discussion was about ways of raising money for cancer research and involving patients at the same time. But she wasn't paying much attention; it was taking every atom of self-control she possessed simply to stay seated at the table with Gina and Max. Her mind was reeling at the thought of them together—and heaven knew how many other women had shared the pleasure of his sexual expertise.

'Why not have an auction, with the beautiful Sophie selling kisses?' a voice declared loudly, and at the sound of her name Sophie raised her head. A man sitting opposite her, whom she had noticed earlier staring at her cleavage and ignored, was ogling her again. 'The patients could buy them as well. I know if I was seriously ill a kiss from a gorgeous woman would do me good.' Everyone laughed, and all eyes were on her.

'That would never work.' Gina chuckled. 'Sophie is a beautiful, decorative woman, but not cut out to visit the sick. She'd probably give them a heart attack. Isn't that right, Sophie?' Gina quipped, and everyone laughed.

It was a hurtful thing to say, and for a moment Sophie was struck dumb. Gina knew nothing at all about her—and yet she felt able to pass comment on her. She glanced around the table; nobody here really knew her, she thought, so why bother to argue?

'If you say so,' she murmured.

'I wouldn't allow her to anyway,' Max drawled, and reached for her hand.

But she avoided his hand *and* his glittering gaze by picking up her glass and draining it before she put it back down. She wished she was anywhere in the world but here.

A veined hand patted hers on the table. 'It was just a joke. We medical people *en masse* tend to lose our sensitivity a little—don't take it to heart.' It was the professor seated next to her who spoke, quietly seeing what no one else had noticed.

Sophie was touched and grateful for his intervention, as it allowed her to turn her back on Max and look up with moisture-filled eyes into the old man's face.

'Thank you,' she said, trying to smile. 'But it is an emotive subject for me,' she explained quietly. 'My mother died of breast cancer when I was eleven. For two years before that I did my best to nurse her, but I was still a child and obviously not up to these people's standards.' She attempted to joke.

'Forget it, and do me the honour of this dance.' The professor stood up. 'If you do not mind, Signor Quintano?' he asked Max over the top of Sophie's head.

Max glanced at him, and sharply at Sophie. Her body was angled towards the professor, all her attention on the older man. The witch had the nerve to ignore him and then captivate the eminent Professor Manta, right before his eyes. The old fool was grinning all over his face as if he had discovered the cure for cancer. How the hell did she do it?

'Be my guest.' He couldn't do much else with Gina tugging on his arm again. Since when had his sister become such a chatty type? he wondered in exasperation as he watched Sophie and the professor take to the dance floor.

'Feel better now?' the professor asked Sophie, his brown eyes twinkling into hers.

'Yes—yes, I do.' She relaxed in his formal hold. 'I am not usually so emotional, but the comment about me not being cut out to visit the sick caught me on the raw and I didn't see the joke. You see, the anniversary of my mother's death was the twenty-fifth of November—three days ago.' And also she had realised she loved a man who didn't deserve to be loved.

'You are a lovely, emotional little woman—and that is nothing to be ashamed of,' he reassured her gently.

Sophie did smile at that. 'Hardly little.'

'Maybe not, but you are extremely feminine. Something, I am afraid, that in my experience can sometimes get knocked out of female doctors over the years.'

'Feminine I like,' she chuckled, appreciating the distinguished-looking man more by the minute—even if he was a bit of a chauvinist.

'Good. Now, a change of subject is called for, so tell me about you. Are you on holiday here? And what do you normally do when not visiting our fair city?'

Whether he knew of her connection with Max or not she didn't care. Because she instinctively knew the professor was a gentleman.

'I am visiting a friend for a while, but I'm a linguist and I work as a translator. Sometimes I teach, but at the minute all I do is teach English to the cook's grandchildren.'

With his next words, much to Sophie's surprise, Professor Manta was offering her a job. Apparently he was on the board of governors at the private school that his grandchildren attended, and they were looking for a language teacher—someone to fill in for the rest of the term, as the present teacher was on extended sick leave.

'I'm flattered, though I'm not sure it will be possible,' she said, but she took the card the professor offered and promised to ring him tomorrow, to let him know one way or the other.

Max couldn't believe it. He saw her take the card from the old goat as they approached the table and he had had enough. He rose to his feet and, with a stiff smile for the grinning professor, wrapped his arm tightly around Sophie's waist.

'It is time we left now.'

Sophie felt his proprietorial arm around her and tensed, but refused to look at him. Instead she said good night to the professor, and a general good night to the rest of the company. Gina she ignored. But Max's prolonged goodbye to his stepsister more than made up for Sophie's lapse in manners.

CHAPTER TEN

'YOU are very quiet, *cara*.' He dipped his head towards her as they exited the room. 'Upset that I took you away from your latest conquest?'

His words were soft, but she heard the angry edge in his tone, and when she tilted her head back she saw his eyes glittering hard as jet.

'The professor is not a conquest but a gentleman,' she snapped. 'Something you would know nothing about.'

'Maybe not,' he said, his smile cruel. 'But I *do* know you're no lady. The fact is you are available to the highest bidder, and at the moment it happens to be me. So hand over the card he gave you—he is not for you.'

'God! Your mind never lifts above the gutter!'

She stared at him. His face was a mask of barely contained anger, and for a fleeting moment she wondered if he was jealous. No…for that he would have to care, and all he cared about was getting his money's worth. He had just said so.

'It just so happens that Professor Manta offered me a job. Not everyone sees me as just a body. That distinction appears to be a peculiar trait of you and Gina.'

'A job?' he sneered. 'We both know as what. But I hate to tell you, *cara*, distinguished as he is, he cannot afford you.'

She was about to snap back with the truth, but they had reached the foyer and a member of staff arrived with their coats.

What the hell? Why bother to explain? It wouldn't make a blind bit of difference to the way Max felt about her. He saw her as an experienced woman with dozens of lovers, thanks to Abe, and tonight there was no longer any point in telling him the truth. Because she no longer cared.

She looked at him, tall, dark and stony-faced, as he held out the rich sable coat—another one of his presents she really didn't appreciate. He had dismissed her arguments on wearing real fur in his usual autocratic manner. Venetian women in winter *all* wore fur. Maybe he was right, and she had actually seen children in fur coats, but it didn't make her like it—or him, she thought as he helped her to slip it on, keeping his arm around her shoulders.

It was a miserable night—a thick fog had descended, along with drizzling rain. Luckily the launch was waiting, and she stepped on board, shrugging off Max's restraining arm, and walked down into the small cabin and sat down.

She heard Max talking to Diego and hoped he would stay on deck. Sophie let her head fall back and closed her eyes; she could feel the beginnings of a tension headache—hardly surprising, under the circumstances. It was impossible to believe she had left the house with a smile on her face a few short hours ago, confident she could handle her relationship with Max, fooling herself that they got along well and he was genuinely beginning to care for her. Only for the evening to turn out an unmitigated disaster. It had opened her eyes to a reality she didn't want, couldn't accept, and made her realise she had been in danger of succumbing to living in a fool's paradise. Well, no more....

Rising from the seat, she exited the cabin. Max was leaning against the roof, with Diego at the wheel. Diego's head turned. 'Well timed, Signorina Sophie.' He grinned at her as he swung the boat in to the landing stage.

She smiled back, ignoring the looming figure of Max. It was Diego's hand she took as she stepped off the boat, and she didn't wait but ran up the steps and into the house. She slipped the sable from her shoulders, not caring where it fell, and she didn't stop until she reached her bedroom and closed the door behind her. She kicked off the killer heels and, withdrawing her earrings, walked to the dressing table and dropped them in a box. The necklace quickly followed. She stepped out of her dress and slipped on a towelling robe. With the outward signs of Max's ownership gone, she heaved a deep sigh of relief.

She picked up a sliver of lace that in Max's opinion passed for a nightgown and, walking into the bathroom, locked both doors. Now all she had to worry about were the inward signs of his ownership, and she had a nasty suspicion they would be a lot more difficult to deal with. She pulled on a shower cap, had a quick shower, twisted her hair into one long braid over her shoulder and slipped on her nightgown and robe again. Unlocking both doors, she walked back into her bedroom—only to find Max standing there, a glass of whisky in his hand.

'Running scared, Sophie?' Max fixed her with an unwavering glare. 'Or an act of defiance?'

'Neither,' she said flatly, ignoring the angry tensing of his jaw as she met his gaze. 'Just an overwhelming desire to be clean after an evening spent with you and Gina.'

'What the hell do you mean by that?' he demanded, and she shivered, her stomach muscles knotting at the anger evident in his dark eyes.

Max saw her tremble, and for a moment the fury inside him subsided, his eyes narrowing astutely on her flushed but stern face. Thinking back, he recalled other times when Sophie had made remarks about Gina. Given that Sophie had only met her a couple of times, it made no sense. He drained the glass of whisky and crossed to put it on the bedside table before walking back to stare down at her.

'Tonight you made your distaste plain the moment we arrived. I can understand that the thought of cancer scares you—I know it does a lot of people,' he prompted. 'But what have you got against Gina?'

Sophie paled. Good, Max thought savagely, he was on the right track. 'I want the truth, and I am in no mood for any more of your sly innuendos.'

Pale with fury at his sanctimonious comment about understanding her fear of illness, Sophie threw him a venomous glance—the only sly person around here was Max, and she had had enough.

'Oh, please,' she drawled, her eyes spitting fury. 'What do you take me for? An idiot? You and your sainted stepsister Gina have been having an affair on and off for years and everyone knows it.' A short laugh of derision left her lips. 'My God, she flung herself into your arms tonight and the pair of you kissed like long-lost lovers. It was disgusting.'

'*Basta*,' he roared, and she took an involuntary step backward. But it was futile. In one lithe stride Max had narrowed the space between them. Steely hands caught hold of her arms and hauled her hard against him, his dark gaze sweeping over her swift and savage.

'Oh, no, you don't,' he grated, and his eyes narrowed as she began to struggle. 'Stop!' he commanded furiously, and his fingers bit into her soft flesh.

'You're hurting me.'

'Right at this moment I don't damn well care,' he swore. 'I would flatten *any* other person without the slightest hesitation for even *implying* what you have just said,' he revealed harshly.

Sophie stared at him defiantly. 'You can't face the truth, that's your trouble.'

Max saw the determination and conviction in her eyes and realised she actually believed what she was saying. For once he was speechless. He heaved in a strangled breath. 'You actually believe I...' He couldn't say it, and with a shake of his head he shoved her away. 'That is some sick opinion you have of me.'

'Not an opinion. Fact.'

'Fact—Gina is my stepsister, period. She kissed me because she was pleased to see me—a quite common occurrence in my culture. As for anything more, that is only in your head.' He looked at her lovely face, saw the childish braid over her breast rise and fall as she took a deep breath and wondered how anyone so beautiful could harbour such evil thoughts. Maybe it was jealousy. For some reason that did not seem so bad, if a bit extreme. 'If you're jealous—'

'Jealous?' Sophie cut him off. 'Don't flatter yourself—

and don't bother lying.' She swallowed nervously. 'I was there, remember? Seven years ago. The stupid teenager with the enormous crush on you. Marnie warned me about you. She told me about your legion of women and I refused to listen. She even showed me a magazine article about you, with photographs of some of them. Finally she told me about your affair with Gina, *and* the fact that your father didn't approve of the relationship. But I still refused to believe what kind of man you were. I was the dumb kid you seduced and asked to marry because you thought I might be pregnant.'

Her eyes filled with anger. 'The idiot who believed you—until I walked through the maze and heard you and Gina talking about me. To give Gina her due, at least *she* said you had to tell me about her if you really intended marrying me. I heard you both discussing whether I was worldly enough to accept the situation—and you call *me* sick?'

Sophie didn't see the colour drain from his face; she was swamped by memories she had tried to suppress. But no longer. 'What a joke!' She laughed—a raw sound. 'And when Gina asked why you were marrying me your response was a real eye-opener—*because you were careless and I might be pregnant*. Then came her descriptive account of how life would be for the pregnant bride, with a husband who took off at regular intervals to stay overnight with his lover and then came back too tired to make love to his dumb wife.

'My God, it was a revelation,' she spat at him. 'And how could I ever forget your comment that it had only been a couple of days, and with luck you wouldn't have to tell me

anything at all. Well, you got lucky,' she mocked bitterly.
'I wasn't pregnant. And I had no intention of joining a
three-way relationship then and I haven't now. So don't
try and fob me off with Italian culture or any other excuse.

'As I walked round into the centre of the maze I heard
you say you loved each other, and I found you in each
other's arms. Last month in Rome I found her medicine
in the en suite bathroom cabinet, along with signs of your
other women.' She paused, then added with a shake of her
head, 'The only thing that amazes me is why Gina puts up
with you. I have no choice—as you so often remind me.
You are a despicable excuse—' She raised her eyes, and
for a heart-stopping moment she thought he was about to
strike her. His face was contorted with rage, and she
shivered at the cold black fury in his piercing gaze.

'Shut up—just shut up.'

Max had listened with a mounting horror that had quickly
turned to red-hot rage. He wanted to grab hold of her and
shake her. He couldn't believe that Sophie, the woman he
had made love to for weeks, had all the time been harbour-
ing these cancerous thoughts about him. No pun intended,
he thought blackly. And that stopped him. His brain rerun-
ning what she had just said, recalling the conversation, the
circumstances at the time, he could begin to see why, fed
by gossip, she had jumped to the wrong conclusion.

'*Dio mio!*' Max curved a hand around her neck. He
could feel the rapid beating of her pulse against his fingertips, and he looped an arm around her waist and hauled
her hard against him. 'You actually believed that rubbish?'
he snarled, his dark eyes sparking with outrage. 'You crazy
fool! You listened to gossip and believed the worst of me.'

'The magazines didn't lie.'

'I was over thirty—of course I had slept with a few women.' His hand tightened on her throat. 'But as for the rest—you got it all wrong in your stupid juvenile mind.'

'I heard you, remember?' Sophie shot back, refusing to be intimidated by the towering proximity of his great body bristling with outraged fury.

'You said you heard everything, but you didn't.'

'I'm—'

'Shut up and listen,' he roared, his hand moving higher to grasp her chin, turning her face to his, forcing her to meet his eyes. 'The day you overheard me talking to Gina we were *not* talking about a three-way relationship. I have never had one in my life. Nor have I ever had anything other than a brother and sister relationship with Gina. Her preference is for her own sex, as it happens—Rosa is her partner. You should have had more sense than to listen to the idle gossip of a middle-aged woman like Marnie.'

'She said it was common knowledge,' Sophie defended, but the revelation that Gina was gay and Rosa her partner...well, it made sense of the odd tension she had felt when they'd all had coffee together. Her voice lacked a little of her earlier conviction as she added, 'She had no reason to lie.'

'In her dreams,' he grated. 'What you *actually* overheard was Gina comforting me as a sister should—because two days earlier I had been told I probably had testicular cancer. At the same time she was advising me, as a doctor, that I couldn't marry you without telling you the truth, because you would be bound to find out when I went for treatment. Is that plain enough for you?'

He studied her face closely and then smiled mirthlessly. 'The reason she is a little restrained around you is because, as a caring professional, she believed from what you said that you wanted no part of me as a sick man or—in your words—the future I had mapped out. She is a serious woman, and she thinks you are beautiful but too superficial. You can't blame her. Her joke tonight at dinner was perhaps a little crass, but from her past experience perfectly valid.'

At the word *cancer* her stomach had plunged, and shock held her rigid. His dark eyes were cold and hard on hers, but she couldn't look away as a dozen conflicting thoughts whirled in her brain. The overriding one being that surely no man, and certainly not such an arrogantly masculine man as Max, would lie about testicular cancer.

But then again it was still hard to believe, given he'd had no problem making love to her years ago. And his sexual prowess in the bedroom certainly had not diminished over the years—quite the reverse.

'Are you sure you were ill?' She stared at him. 'You seemed remarkably fit to me.'

'Yes, I was.' He met her gaze with sardonic challenge and continued. 'But don't worry—I got over it, and I'm fine now.'

She eyed him uncertainly, remembering that conversation on the fatal day *verbatim*. Dear heaven, she had run it through her head over and over again after they'd parted, to remind herself what a bastard he was in the hope it would cure the hopeless love she felt for him. Could she have been mistaken? Max's explanation made a horrible kind of sense. And if Gina was gay, as he said... She saw again Max reaching his hand to her at the end, when she'd told him she was leaving.

'When you asked me to talk with you and Gina, you meant about your illness?'

'Correct. It was that one-track mind of yours that thought otherwise.'

Appalled, she looked at the face only inches from her own. 'You really *did* have testicular cancer?' she murmured.

'Yes,' he said, a curious blankness in his dark eyes, as though he looked through and beyond her to some bad memory.

'Oh, my God!' All the blood drained from her face. 'I'm sorry—so sorry. What must you both have thought of me?' No wonder Gina was offhand with her. And as for Max, the anger she had sensed in him since they'd met again was now easily explained. He wanted her body, but he thought she was heartless. 'If only I had realised…' Green eyes full of compassion fixed on his. She wanted, needed to tell him—what? That she would never have left him? That she loved him? No, she didn't dare. 'If I'd known you were ill I would—' But he cut her off.

'It would have made no difference,' he said flatly. 'It was caught very early, quickly treated, and I've been clear for years. I don't need your pity.' Drawing her closer to him, he slowly ran his hand down from her throat to lightly cup her breast. 'Only your body. That hasn't changed.' For interminable seconds he stared down at her in total silence, then gave a mocking laugh. 'And before you go beating yourself up over it—you were right. I *did* set out to seduce you. I heard the bad news in the morning and took you to bed in the evening to reaffirm my manhood. Apparently it's a common impulsive reaction with most men, according to Gina.'

'Thanks for that,' she snapped. 'Glad to be of service.' From feeling heartsick and sorry, she was suddenly angry—and yet aroused as his hand slipped inside her robe.

'My pleasure,' Max said sardonically. 'So we both made a mistake years ago? It doesn't matter—I much prefer what we have now.'

She stared at him with huge pained eyes. She knew exactly what he meant; he had never wanted a teenage wife—or any other kind—he much preferred a mistress. Nothing had changed...including her devastating physical awareness of him. But it wasn't enough, would never be enough for her....

As if he knew what she was thinking, he gave her a slight arrogant smile, his head lowering.

'No...' she murmured. 'No,' she said more forcibly, and, shoving hard at his chest, she twisted. But he quieted her by capturing her hands in his and folding his arms around her.

'Yes,' he mocked.

She flung her head from side to side, but he backed her to the bed, and then she was falling.

His impressive body came over her and his mouth covered hers. She tried to keep her lips sealed, but he circled them with his tongue and bit gently, until with a helpless sigh she opened for him. He clasped her head in his hands and kissed her with a deep, possessive passion that stole the breath from her body.

'Forget the past,' he murmured, and stripped off her robe, his dark gaze skimming over her thinly covered slender body. 'The present is all I am concerned about.'

'But—' she started, but he bent his head and kissed her again and again, until she groaned with pleasure. And when he left her for a moment, to strip off his clothes, she simply watched with dazed, hungry eyes. He came back to her and divested her body of the scrap of lace to cover it with his own.

Much later, lying in his arms as the aftermath of passion subsided, Sophie hugged him close and stroked her hands up his chest, her earlier burst of defiance forgotten as she thought of what he must have gone through. Her heart filled with love and compassion for what he must have suffered.

She murmured, 'I am truly sorry you were ill, Max.'

A barely stifled oath left his lips, and abruptly he rolled off her and the bed. 'I told you—I don't need your mawkish sympathy,' he said coldly. 'I never did.' And he left.

CHAPTER ELEVEN

SOPHIE GOT OUT OF BED late the next morning after a restless night, and felt sick. Hardly surprising: the enormity of her mistake about Max and Gina haunted her. Dear heaven, what a fool she had been at nineteen—and she wasn't much better now. Because, being brutally honest, last night, with the original cause of mistrust between them resolved, she had nursed a secret hope that he might grow to love her as she loved him. Well, he had certainly disabused her of that notion. When was she going to learn?

He was a giant of a man in every way—enormously rich, successful and supremely confident in his abilities to defeat anything or anyone who stood in the way of what he wanted. A silent laugh escaped her. Given his stamina in the bedroom, not even cancer had dared dent his virile power. But he had not stayed in her bedroom last night, and that said it all....

It was Friday; he had probably left for Rome. It crossed her mind to wonder whether he would tell Gina the truth, and realised bitterly it didn't really matter. She was still the mistress and would never be anything more.

She dressed and went down to the kitchen, and poured

herself a cup of coffee from the pot on the stove. She took a sip as Maria came bustling in through the back door.

'That is my job. You should have rung,' Maria scolded her. 'Now, what would you like for breakfast?' And she told her to sit down.

Sophie pulled out a chair and sat down, a bitter smile curving her lips. Everyone had a job but her, and being a lady of leisure was really not her scene. Even the coffee tasted bitter, she thought, but drained it down to the dregs. Unless she did something about the sybaritic lifestyle Max had ordained for her, she was in danger of becoming bitter through and through.

She picked up a banana from the fruit bowl in the centre of the table and rose to her feet. 'Don't bother, Maria, this will do,' she said, and left the kitchen to run back up to her bedroom.

She found the card Professor Manta had given her....

The revelations of last night had changed nothing— except now she knew what Max had really thought of her when they had met up again. Not only had he seen her as a promiscuous woman with a string of lovers, but also as the kind of heartless girl who would walk away from sickness. Her heart ached to think of him suffering, but he had told her quite bluntly he didn't want her sympathy. More chilling, he had also told her what deep down inside she had always known: he had deliberately seduced her years ago, simply to confirm his masculinity when it was threatened.

He didn't want her caring or her compassion. There was nothing more to do except play out the charade of being his mistress until he tired of the sex. And, going on his past record, that shouldn't be long.

But in the meantime she had had enough of bowing to his every order. She sat on the end of the bed and took out her cellphone to dial Professor Manta's number. When she rang off, she had made an appointment to meet him outside the school.

Much to Diego's annoyance, she flatly refused to use the launch, insisting she was going out on her own and wanted to try the *vaporetto,* the public transport. Before he could stop her she left.

The sense of freedom was exhilarating. She met Professor Manta, and after a short interview with the principal of the school accepted the job of teaching two mornings a week until Christmas.

Professor Manta insisted on buying her a coffee at Florian before he had to leave for his hospital clinic, and that was where Max found her....

Last night Max had been furious when he'd discovered the depths of depravity Sophie thought him capable of. But, rather than discuss the rage and resentment burning inside him, he had swept her into bed and made passionate love to her—the only sure way he knew they could communicate.

Even in his wildest days he had never kept two women at the same time. He had demanded fidelity in his relationships for however long they lasted. His affair with Berenice at university had taught him that, after he'd discovered she had slept with half of his friends as well as him.

But this morning, in the early light of dawn, his anger fading, he had finally begun to think straight. He had walked back into Sophie's bedroom, determined to talk to her, but she'd been sound asleep. He'd clasped the sheet and pulled it down, intending to wake her, but had stopped. She'd looked so precious, with her knees tucked up like a baby to her stomach, the childish braid falling over her shoulder and across her breast, and he hadn't had the heart to waken her.

He'd watched her for a long time and realised he had no right to be angry with her. She had been young and innocent. Because of his wealth and lifestyle he'd always been the subject of gossip. It had never bothered him, but to an impressionable young girl it must have been a cause for insecurity. A half-heard conversation and she had leapt to a conclusion based on that gossip. But he was older and wiser, and should have known better. He should have insisted on telling her the truth, made her listen, but instead, because of his own problem, uppermost in his mind, he had told her he never wanted to set eyes on her again.

His perception of her as heartless had coloured the way he had treated her over the last few weeks, and he wasn't proud of his behaviour. He had left her sleeping this morning with one thought in his head—to try and make it up to her.

With that in mind he had given Maria strict instructions that she wasn't to be disturbed, and had spent two hours in his study, clearing up some work. He'd called Rome, and the hospice he helped out at every Friday, and told them he couldn't make it. Then he'd made an appointment with his lawyer for lunch, intent on having the humiliating agreement Sophie had signed destroyed. That done, he hoped maybe they could start again. Finally he had hot-footed it to the jewellers. He wanted to buy her a present; he wanted to surprise her....

But it was he who was surprised. Max stood in the shadow of the buildings for a while and simply watched. She was sitting outside the coffee house sipping coffee and smiling at Professor Manta. Elegant in a mulberry-coloured trouser suit, her silken hair loosely tied back with a velvet ribbon, her face delicately made-up, she looked relaxed and happy.

His hand turned over the small velvet box in his pocket. He was going to surprise her all right. Not with a gift, but with his presence. He had been an idiot to think differently of her, but that did not mean he was going to give up what he had got. She was *his* very sexy mistress, and at the minute a disobedient one. He was damn sure he wasn't going to lose her to some old professor. Straightening up, a look of grim determination on his face, he walked across the square.

'Sophie. I didn't expect to see you here this morning.' He saw her head lift and a guarded look come into her eyes.

'Max what a surprise. I thought you had gone to Rome. You always do on a Friday.'

He barely had his temper under control after the shock of seeing her with the professor. But he saw she was nervous, her hands clenched and twisted in her lap, and he thought, *You have a damn good right to be.*

'Obviously not,' he drawled. 'I have a luncheon appointment with my lawyer.' He turned to Professor Manta. '*Buongiorno, Professore,*' he said, and, indicating a chair, '*Permesso?*'

'*Prego,*' the professor said, and stood up. 'How is the hospice going these days? Still expanding?' he asked Max.

'Yes,' Max said shortly.

'Good work.' Patting Max on the back, he added, 'I have to leave now. I'll give you the pleasure of escorting Sophie home. You're a very lucky man. I can't tell you how grateful San Bartolomeo is to have secured her services. *Arrivederci.*'

Max looked at Sophie for a long, silent moment. 'Explain.'

Sophie drew in a shaky breath. Dressed in a charcoal-grey business suit, and a paler grey shirt and tie, he looked tall, dark and austere—and decidedly dangerous. He was staring at her with cold dark eyes, but she refused to be intimidated.

'I told you. Professor Manta asked me if I was interested in a job.' She gave him a sweetly cynical smile. 'Teaching languages at his grandsons' school—San Bartolomeo. They need someone to fill in for a language teacher who is on extended sick leave until Christmas.' She picked up her coffee and drained the cup. 'I called him this morning and said I was interested. We have just been to see the principal. I start work next week, Tuesdays and Thursdays. Is that okay with you, oh lord and master?' she mocked.

He was taken aback by her vehemence, but he couldn't really blame her after what he had implied last night about the professor. The man actually had offered her a job. He wondered what else he had got wrong about her. But he wasn't about to let her get away with openly defying him. 'Where was Diego while all this was going on? I told you not to leave the house without him. You deliberately disobeyed my orders.'

She pushed back her chair and stood up. 'He is probably at your house, where I left him. As for your orders—I forgot,' she said lightly. 'Now, I am going to catch the *vaporetto* and return—if *that* is okay with you?'

His face grim, he got to his feet and grasped her arm. 'Such meekness. But I will escort you back, and we will discuss your idea of working later.'

'There is nothing to discuss. I have accepted the job at San Bartolomeo.'

'You already have a job. Me,' he reminded her succinctly. 'You also have credit cards and a generous allowance.'

'A salary, don't you mean?' Sophie heard herself snipe, very conscious of Max's steely grip on her arm as they walked to the landing stage.

'Call it what you like, but spend the damn money. Shop, lunch, do what other women do. You don't have to teach a bunch of kids.'

'But I love children—and I hate shopping.'

Max hand tightened on her arm. 'In my experience *every* woman likes shopping with unlimited money. Try it and see,' he drawled cynically.

'Your kind of woman, yes, but not me.' Her head lifted fractionally, and her voice was remarkably calm as she met his dark gaze. 'You really don't know me at all, Max.' The *vaporetto* had arrived and people were disembarking. 'Contrary to what you and Gina think for whatever mistaken reason, I *do* care about people. The only reason I stayed at that dinner last night after being the butt of Gina's so-called joke was not because you threatened me but for my mother. She died of breast cancer, and for two years Meg and I nursed her. The only reason I am here now is because I care for my brother Timothy. If you had the least interest in me in any way other than sexual you might have realised that.'

His hand fell from her arm and she saw a muscle jerk in his cheek. He didn't like that, but she was sick of pandering to what Max liked.

'I finally realised last night exactly how you see me. In your mind I am an experienced woman of the world, out for what I can get from any man and without a caring bone in my body. And do you know what really sickens me? Even believing that, you still had no scruples about enjoying my body. So what does that make you?'

Not waiting for a response, she walked on board the *vaporetto*, went inside the cabin and sat down.

A few moments later a stony-faced Max sat down beside her, the warmth of his hard thigh seeping into hers.

'I thought you had a lunch appointment,' she gibed, trying to move along the seat, but she was pressed up against the window already.

'*Non importante*,' he said, with a wave of his hand. 'You and I need to talk.'

'I know your idea of talking. A few brief commands that usually involve me being horizontal,' she said bluntly. 'But you're wasting your time today. Every Friday afternoon Tessa brings her children over. I give them an English lesson and we all have dinner together. My life does not stop when you're not around.'

She looked at him. His starkly handsome face was dark and taut, and she could feel the tension in the long muscular body so close to hers. 'And if you are going to tell me I can't accept the job at San Bartolomeo, forget it. The way I feel at the minute, the thought of working is the only thing keeping me sane. For two pins I would say to hell with you *and* my father and get back to my own life. So don't push it.'

'No, I don't mind you working at San Bartolomeo at all,' Max said swiftly. The very idea of her leaving him was not something he could bear to contemplate.

'Just as well,' she muttered, the wind taken out of her sails. Maybe Max was getting tired of her. That was her next thought. She turned her head and looked out of the window, for some inexplicable reason moisture glazing her eyes.

'This is our stop.' He took her arm and led her off the boat.

'Are you sure?' she glanced around. 'This is not where I caught the *vaporetto*.'

His hand tightened momentarily. 'This is quicker.' And, holding her arm like a vice, he strode forward. She stumbled to keep up with him. He never once slackened his pace, and he almost pulled her up the steps to the house.

'Where is the fire? she asked breathlessly, trying to shake off his hand as they entered the hall.

He stood looking down at her for a moment, towering over her, his eyes glittering with some fierce emotion. 'In me,' she thought she heard him say. But at that moment Diego came dashing from the kitchen.

'*Signor*, you are back.'

'Yes, and I want a word with you.'

With Max's attention diverted, Sophie slipped upstairs to her room. She kicked off her shoes as usual, took off her suit and replaced it with the pink tracksuit she favoured for visiting the gym and hanging around the kitchen with Tessa and the children.

Her stomach rumbled and she realised she was starving;

she had eaten only a banana at breakfast. She had her hand
on the door to go back downstairs when suddenly it was
flung open. Instinctively she put her other hand to her face
and went staggering back against the wall.

'Sophie!' She watched with eyes that were watering as
Max dashed into the room.

'You could have broken my nose, you great oaf.'
Blinking, she shoved the door back. 'As it is, my knuckles
will be black and blue for weeks. Are you raving mad?
Have you never heard of knocking?' she yelled, straightening up and rubbing her bruised hand with the other.

She was not aware of the fierce tension affecting Max's
tall frame. She was too busy checking out her own; her back
wasn't feeling too great after its sudden contact with the
wall.

'Yes, I *am* mad—about you,' Max said fiercely, and
suddenly he was in front of her, his hands reaching for her,
roaming gently over her head and her shoulders, down her
arms. '*Dio!* If I've hurt you I will never forgive myself.'

Wide-eyed, Sophie stared up at him and saw such pain,
such passion in his dark eyes, her breath caught in her
throat. She couldn't believe what she was hearing—what
she was seeing.

'I'll call the doctor,' he declared, his hands moving feverishly over her. 'My love, I couldn't bear it if I lost you.'

'What did you say?' she asked, stunned.

The austere, sophisticated mask Max usually presented
to the world had cracked wide open, and he looked absolutely frantic.

'The doctor. I'll call the doctor.'

'No—after that,' she prompted, a tiny ray of hope

lighting her heart as she saw his slight confusion. 'Tell me again.' She needed to hear him say *my love* so she could start believing it might be possible.

His hands stopped their urgent search and settled on her waist, his dark eyes holding hers. 'I couldn't bear it if I lost you,' he said, in a voice husky with emotion.

Sophie saw the vulnerability in his eyes and was amazed that Max, her handsome, arrogant lover, could be so unsure of himself.

'I did once, and I never want to make the same mistake again.'

'And why is that?' she asked, hardly daring to breathe, the ray of hope growing bigger and brighter by the second.

Max tensed, his hands tightening on her waist, a flush of colour burning under his skin as he looked at her. 'Oh, I think you know, Sophie.' Even now he had difficulty saying the words. Even when he knew his happiness, his life, depended on convincing the woman in his arms to stay with him. 'My love.'

He had said *my love* again; she had not imagined it. Sophie was suddenly conscious of the erratic pounding of her heart, and it took every shred of courage she possessed to ask the next question. 'Am I really your love, Max?

'Yes.' Max gulped, his eyes burning into hers. 'I love you, Sophie. I know I have given you no cause to believe me, but it is the truth. I love you.' From not being able to say the words, Max suddenly had no trouble repeating them. In fact he would tell her a million times over if he thought it would convince her to stay with him.

It was the answer she had prayed for, and Sophie drew a shaky breath. Only then did she raise her hands to touch him. She ran her fingers through his hair and cradled his head in her palms. 'You love me?' She paused, saw the answer he made no attempt to hide in his dark luminous gaze, and added, 'As I love *you*, Max.'

She finally told him the truth she had held in her heart for years. Because the impossible had happened; Max loved her. Tears of emotion misted her vision, a smile of pure joy that reflected her inner radiance lighting her beautiful face.

'You love me? You really mean that, after all I have done?' he asked roughly, and his doubt squeezed her heart.

'I fell in love with you the first moment I saw you. I still love you and always will.'

Max saw the truth in the glittering green eyes that met his intense gaze.

'Ah, Sophie. I don't deserve you,' he groaned, and kissed her with a deep tender passion. She clung to him and returned the kiss with all the love in her heart. His arms tightened around her and he lifted her off her feet to lay her gently in the middle of the bed. Quickly he shed his clothes, but Sophie was almost as quick pulling off her tracksuit and panties.

Max groaned, falling down beside her and scooping her into his arms. Their limbs entwined, she glimpsed the deep, throbbing desire in the depths of his smouldering eyes as his mouth met hers. She gloried in the hungry passion of his kiss and reciprocated with a wondrous abandon. He loved her, and she cried out his name as his mouth found her breasts, his caressing hands arousing and exploring until her every nerve was taut with quivering, aching desire—and more. Love had freed the hungry yearning inside her. Urgently her hands roamed over his hard muscled body, from his wide shoulders down to lean hips.

'Sophie,' he groaned, and he slid his hands under her back. Frantically she locked her legs around him as he surged into her with a primitive and powerful force that reached to her very core. In a wild wonderful ride, their mingled cries echoed a mutual pleasure of cosmic intensity as they reached nirvana, that joining of the souls with creation as one.

They lay, a tangle of welded bodies, breathless, shuddering and speechless, until Max raised his head to say, 'Sophie, my love,' and kissed her with a tenderness so profound her eyes filled with tears of happiness.

Eventually, as their breathing grew steadier, he withdrew from her, then wrapped her in his arms to cuddle her into his side.

'I thought the first time I made love to you was the most intense sexual experience of my life,' Max said thickly, staring down into her flushed face. 'But now…' He was lost for words. '*Dio*, how I love you.' He gave up and kissed her love-swollen lips, slowly, gently and with aching tenderness. He swept a damp tendril of hair from her brow. 'I know I have treated you abominably in the past, and I also know that if I apologise to my dying day it will not be enough.'

'Shh…it doesn't matter,' Sophie murmured, placing a finger on his lips. 'As long as I know you love me now, that is all that matters.'

'No.' Max took her hand and saw the red knuckles, gently brushed them with his lips. 'You're hurt, and I know

I have hurt you in other ways. I need to talk—to explain.' He dropped her hand and she stroked it teasingly up his chest.

'You're sure about that?'

'I need to talk. And I am not going to give in to temptation again until I have,' he said with a wry smile, and recaptured her hand.

'Spoilsport,' Sophie teased

'Maybe.' He grinned and lay back, his deep, husky voice serious. 'But for too long I have used sex as the only way to communicate with you. Now I am determined to tell you the truth.'

'That sounds ominous.' Sophie pushed up on her elbow to stare down at him and threw her other arm over his broad chest, her fingers stroking through his curling chest hair. 'Are you sure you wouldn't rather do something else?'

'Witch.' He grinned again. 'I know what you're trying to do, but I refuse to be sidetracked.'

'Pity!'

He clasped her hand on his chest. 'I am serious, Sophie.' The determination and the intensity of his dark gaze kept her silent. 'From the minute I first set eyes on you in Sicily I wanted you. But Alex warned me off you; you were too young and under his protection. I accepted that, as up until then I'd preferred mature women who knew the score, not dewy-eyed romantic teenagers.' Sophie stiffened. 'Please don't be offended—I am trying to tell you the truth as I saw it at the time.'

'Okay,' she murmured. She was not pleased to think that

Alex had warned Max off, but it *did* explain Max refusing to touch her at first, and she had to admire his restraint.

'I very quickly realised I couldn't keep away from you. I told myself there was no harm in having a light flirtation with a beautiful girl, and I had no intention of taking it any further. I liked my freewheeling lifestyle. But that night when I took you out to dinner, in the car after, I very nearly… Well, suffice it to say it took every bit of will-power I possessed and then some not to follow you into the chalet and make love to you. I left the next day, determined not to see you again.

'In my conceit, I thought there were plenty of willing ladies around without getting embroiled with a teenager. I even convinced myself that the time wasn't right, but if I bumped into you a few years later it would be okay.'

'That was some conceit,' Sophie could not help saying.

'Yes, I know. But a few days later I was already weakening,' he said with a wry smile. 'I went to Russia intending to get rid of my sexual frustration with a lady there. But I didn't. I returned to Rome and made a date with an old flame for that night. I left her at her door, still frustrated.'

'I'm not sure I like such determination,' Sophie murmured.

'Nothing happened, I swear,' Max said quickly. 'On the Friday morning I went though my personal mail in the office and there was a letter informing me to get in touch with the clinic I had attended earlier for a medical. There was some doubt about a sample I had given. I made the appointment the same morning, and it was then I discovered I might have cancer. I'd already arranged to meet Gina for lunch, and she filled me in on the facts. It was easily treatable, with a very high success rate, and did not necessarily affect a man's virility. But as a precaution I should freeze some sperm just in case I couldn't father a child naturally.'

'Oh, my God! You must have felt terrible!' Sophie said, blinking back the tears pricking at her eyes and squeezing his hand. But he let her hand go. He still wasn't prepared to accept her sympathy, she realised sadly.

'No, what I felt was furious—and scared. I couldn't believe it was happening. From thinking I had all the time in the world, I was wondering if I had any. It seems selfish now, but the one thought in my head was that if I was going to die I was going to make damn sure I had you first. And I ordered the plane to take me to Sicily.'

How like her impulsive, arrogant, but adorable Max, Sophie thought, a husky chuckle escaping her.

'It wasn't funny,' Max chided her. 'When I saw you by the pool all I could think of was making love to you. I suppose I did deliberately seduce you. But when we made love it was the most wonderful experience in my life. Until now.'

Max reached up and tenderly outlined her lips with one long finger, his dark eyes burning into hers. 'I would like to say I knew I loved you then, but I have to admit that afterwards I did wonder if it was a subconscious reaction at the thought of having cancer—a need to prove there was nothing wrong with me as a man. All I do know is that when you lay asleep in my arms I thought I wouldn't mind if you were pregnant. And when I asked you to marry me I did mean it. Later, of course, when Gina arrived, it all fell apart. And now we know why.'

Sophie could understand his uncertainty, but she chose

to believe he had loved her from the start. Raising her hand, she gently stroked his cheek, her green eyes gleaming with love. 'That was my fault. I should have listened to you.'

'No. No, it was mine. I was older and should have explained. Instead I dismissed you as a heartless young girl. I was determined to put you out of my mind and concentrate on getting better. The latter I succeeded in doing quite easily. But forgetting you was not so easy.'

'Good, I'm glad.' She let her hand stroke over his shoulder and moved closer, to stretch one long leg over his thighs.

'Yes, well… I am trying to confess here, Sophie, and you are trying to do something else.' His mobile mouth quirked at the corners. 'And it is not going to work. At least not yet.'

She responded by slumping on top of him, her breasts against his chest. 'Okay, go on.' She wriggled, and he laughed.

'When I saw you again at that dinner, looking so beautiful with Abe Asamov, I saw red.'

'I was never *with* Abe, the way you mean. I spent a summer vacation from university in Russia with his wife and children, teaching them English. He is just a friend,' she explained quickly. 'I hadn't seen him for ages, and he just acted like that for fun.'

'Yes, well, it doesn't matter now.' Max believed her— he had to, for his own peace of mind. 'But at the time I think I went a little crazy. I had been helping out with the hotel business, and your father's name had come up—as you know.' He grimaced. 'I decided it was fate. I should never have forced you into being my mistress, but once I had, and you were so responsive in my arms, I told myself that was all I wanted. Until last night. I stormed from this bed because I didn't want your sympathy. But I came back and watched you sleeping, and knew then that I loved you quite desperately. Because I wanted so much more. I wanted back the love you once said you felt for me.'

'You should have wakened me, then,' Sophie said softly

He smoothed a hand over her cheek and swept back the long swathe of her hair, his dark eyes holding hers. 'No. I was determined not to make mistakes this time. I arranged to meet my lawyer for lunch, to cancel that demeaning contract I made you sign, and then I went out to buy you a present—to surprise you, to ask if we could start again. But you surprised me. I saw you with Professor Manta and I was mad with jealousy.' His lips curved in a self-deprecatory smile.

'But it got worse. I discovered he really had offered you a job teaching, and then came your revelation about your mother, your flat refusal to spend your time and my money shopping, like all the other women I have known.'

She didn't like *all the other women*, but she let it pass. He was hers now.

'I had misjudged you over and over again. You were right when you said I didn't know you at all. I stood for a moment, paralysed with fear, and watched you board the *vaporetto*, certain I was going to lose you. I followed you on board determined to make it my life's work to remedy that and keep you at any cost.'

'You've succeeded,' Sophie said, her voice husky with emotion. That Max, her arrogant, magnificent lover, should bare his heart to her had convinced her beyond a shred of doubt that he really did love her. She looped an arm around his neck. 'If you've finished talking...' she smiled, a slow, sensuous curve of her lips '...can I do what I want now?' And she pressed her lips against his throat, then to the hollow of his shoulder blade, whilst her slender fingers traced his silky chest hair and she teased a hard male nipple.

'It depends what you want,' Max said, on a strangled groan.

Pushing on his chest, Sophie sat up, straddling him. Tossing her head back, her green eyes gleaming, she said, 'I want to make love to you. I always want to; it is just what you do to me.'

Max had never heard, felt or seen anything more seductive in his life. Her beautiful face was flushed pink, her glorious hair falling in a tumbling mass around her shoulders, playing peek-a-boo with her lush breasts, and as for her thighs gripping him...

'Feel free,' he murmured.

In the silence of the afternoon, with the sun pouring through the window, Sophie did just that. She was like a child in a candy shop as she kissed and licked her way down his great torso, tracing his belly button and lower, stroking his thighs, and by the time she was kneeling between them he was painfully aroused. Fascinated, she stroked her hands up his inner thighs.

'I never knew a man could be so...beautiful,' she said, glancing up at his taut, dark face. She grinned a broad, beautiful smile. 'You are perfect.'

For a long moment Max stared at her with the strangest look in his eyes, and then said, 'What about Sam?'

Sophie frowned in confusion. 'What about Sam? I'm going to be her bridesmaid in February,' she murmured.

'*Her* bridesmaid—Sam is a *woman*?' he choked. 'Tell me, Sophie, how many lovers have you had?'

'Well…' She pretended to think as it dawned on her that Max was very definitely jealous, and had been from the minute they'd met again. First Abe, and now Sam. 'Let me see, including you—one.'

He pulled her down to take her lips with his in a fierce, possessive kiss, and then, grasping her thighs, he thrust up into her sleek wet heat in a paroxysm of passion.

Sophie collapsed on top of him, her heart pounding fit to burst as she felt the lingering spasms of their mutual climax in every nerve-ending of her body. With his arm wrapped securely around her, his hand gently stroking her hair, calming her down, she closed her eyes.

'Are you all right?' Max asked.

She heard his huskily voiced question and opened her eyes, looking up at him, a languorous smile curving her full lips. 'Surprised, but never better,' she sighed.

'Surprised… *Surprise*!' he exclaimed, and pushed her away. He leapt off the bed and picked up his trousers.

It *was* time they surfaced, she supposed. Heaven knew what the staff must think. And she swung her legs off the bed—only to see him drop his trousers again.

'Max?' she queried, and to her amazement he fell to his knees and grasped her left hand.

'I almost forgot your surprise.' He opened a velvet box and held up a magnificent emerald and diamond ring.

'Will you marry me? I swear I will love and cherish you to my dying day.'

His starkly handsome face, taut with strain, filled her vision, and tears of emotion flooded her eyes. 'This was my surprise?'

She swallowed the sob in her throat. He wanted to marry her—he had already bought the ring.

'Yes,' he said, and, taking her hand, slipped the ring on her finger. He stood up, pulling her with him. 'Now, all you have to do is say yes.'

'Yes,' she cried, and their lips and hearts met in a kiss like no other—a kiss that was an avowal of love and a promise for the future.

'Are you sure about this?'

Sophie fingered the pearls at her throat, her wedding gift from Max, and glanced up at him with a wealth of love and laughter in her sparkling green eyes. Today was her wedding day, and with her family and friends from England, and Max's family and friends in attendance, they had married, in a moving church service in Venice.

Sam and Gina had been her bridesmaids, and Timothy a pageboy. Gina, on learning of the gossip and the trouble caused by her hiding her sexuality, had come out, and her mother had accepted the fact.

The wedding breakfast had been held in an elegant restaurant near the church, and now they were going home by gondola, to change and adopt a more modern form of transport to fly to Paris for a short honeymoon.

'Trust me,' Max said huskily. He had never seen Sophie look more exquisite, in a long white velvet gown, her magnificent hair loose, entwined with a crown of rosebuds, and a velvet muff decorated with the same flowers on one wrist. She looked like some fey medieval princess and she took his breath away. She already had his heart.

He caught her hand and helped her into the gondola. Sitting down, he drew her to his side. 'It is a tradition that Venetians travel in a gondola on their wedding day.'

'You're not Venetian,' she pointed out teasingly, and a great cry went up from the crowd gathered at the landing stage as the vessel, covered in garlands of flowers, began to move.

'True—but we would never hear the end of it from Diego and Maria if we didn't,' Max offered, looking down at his beautiful blushing bride.

'You're such a pussycat, really, Max Quintano.' Sophie laughed.

'And you, Sophie, are my wife—Signora Quintano,' he said, with pride and heartfelt satisfaction. And he couldn't resist; the kiss in church had not been nearly enough. Closing his arms around her, he kissed her again.

The gondola rocked and the crowd cheered again, but the two locked together heard nothing but the pounding of their two hearts as one.

Much later that evening, after they had consummated their marriage, they lay with their limbs entwined in the huge bed of the bridal suite in a luxurious Parisian hotel, and Sophie gave Max her wedding gift.

'You know you told me Gina insisted you freeze your sperm just in case you couldn't father a child?' She felt him tense and kissed his jaw. 'Well, there was no need. I'm pregnant.'

He grasped her hand and their eyes met, and she was sure she saw moisture in the luminous depths of Max's. 'That's incredible—a miracle. But are you sure? How? When?'

'Well…' She linked her fingers through his and cuddled up to him, secure in his love for her. 'A certain guy walked into my bedroom and laughed at my dolls, and then he made love to me and left for a while. Then later he returned, with a bottle of wine and two glasses and nothing else, and he made love to me again.' She knew the exact moment, and as he remembered his mouth curled in a broad smile.

Max chuckled, and the grip on her hand tightened. 'It must have been all those eyes watching me that made me forget protection.' He drew her to him, the look in his eyes one she knew very well.

'Or maybe I should have mentioned that a couple of the dolls I collected on my travels are fertility symbols.'

He threw back his dark head and laughed out loud. 'Ah, Sophie, *amore mia*, you are truly priceless and all mine—now and for ever.' And he proceeded to show her what he meant, with her enthusiastic co-operation.

THE SPANIARD'S
BLACKMAILED BRIDE

Trish Morey

Trish Morey is an Australian who's also spent time living and working in New Zealand and England. Now she's settled with her husband and four young daughters in a special part of South Australia, surrounded by orchards and bushland, and visited by the occasional koala and kangaroo. With a life-long love of reading, she penned her first book at age eleven, after which life, career and a growing family kept her busy, until once again she could indulge her desire to create characters and stories – this time in romance. Having her work published is a dream come true. Visit Trish at her website, www.trishmorey.com

Look for Trish Morey's latest exciting novel, *Forbidden: The Sheikh's Virgin*, **available in May 2010 from Mills & Boon®** **Modern™ romance.**

For Anne Gracie, who introduced me to Diablo.
One fantastic author.
An even better friend.
Thanks, Anne, this one's for you!
☺

CHAPTER ONE

IT WAS much too late for a social call.

Briar Davenport crossed the entrance hall uneasily, the click of her heels on the dusty terrazzo tiles echoing in the lofty space while a premonition that all was not right in the world played havoc with her nerves.

Late-night visitors rarely meant good news.

The chimes rang out yet again and she reined in an unfamiliar urge to yell for whoever it was to hang on. But Davenports never yelled through doors—even when their senses were strained tight from trying to work out which family heirloom to send next to auction—it was bad enough that these days they were reduced to opening them.

Her hand hovered over the door handle for a moment while she took a deep breath, trying to calm her frayed nerves and think logically. It didn't *have* to be bad news. Sooner or later their run of bad luck had to change. Why not tonight?

Then she pulled open the door and bad luck just got worse.

'You!'

Diablo Barrentes leant into the open doorway, one arm propped high above her head, his black-clad torso arching over hers, and it was all she could do not to reel back from the sheer force of his hard-wired body. In the spill of the entry lighting he looked more like an extension of the night sky than a man—dark and filled with untold dangers. Tonight his shoulder-length black hair was pulled back into a short ponytail that did nothing to detract from his masculinity and everything to emphasize his dramatic buccaneer looks, but it was the flash of triumph in those black-lit eyes, the slight upturn at the corners of his full lips, that turned her thoughts to sudden panic and had her fingers itching to jam that piece of timber right back where it had come from.

Instead she forced herself to stand her ground, jagging her chin higher as if it might increase her already not insubstantial height. In heels her eyes fell but an inch short of his.

'What do you want?'

'I'm surprised,' he said, one side of his mouth rising higher as if amused by her efforts to match his height. 'I half expected you to slam the door in my face.'

Oh, Lord, the last thing she needed was to be reminded of how much her fingers itched to do just that. Already her grip on the door had turned her knuckles white as she schooled her voice to clipped civility. 'Then I don't need to tell you you're not welcome here.'

'Still, I am here.'

Four words, four simple words, and yet spoken in the remnants of that rich Castilian accent like a threat. Fear tracked a spidery path through her veins.

'Why?'

'And how delightful to see you too, *Briar*,' he said, ignoring her question while emphasizing her incivility. But being polite was hardly a concern to her right now. Not when his accent curled around her name as if he were devouring it.

As if he were devouring her.

She shivered. If he thought that, then he was definitely reading the wrong menu.

'Believe me,' she squeezed out, battling to keep her voice even, 'the pleasure is all yours.'

He laughed, barely more than a chuckle, a low sound that rumbled, somehow insinuating itself into her flesh and right through to her bones.

'*Sí*,' he agreed, his eyes making no apology as they traversed her length, all the way from her eyes, searing a trail over her curves and down her designer denim-clad legs to her pink leather boots, and then all the way up again.

The slow way.

The hot way.

His eyes, heavy with raw heat and firm possession, finally returned to hers and it was all she could do to remember to breathe.

'It's been my pleasure, indeed,' he murmured.

Anger bubbled to the surface with her very next intake of air, overtaking the slow sizzle his hooded gaze had left in its wake. How dared he look at her that way—as if he owned her? He had no right! Diablo Barrentes was kidding himself if he ever thought he would possess her. He'd never even come close.

Even so, she couldn't stop herself crossing her arms over her chest. If her nipples looked anywhere near as rock-hard as they felt, he would be in no doubt as to how that seemingly lazy once-over had affected her, and she didn't want him to know about it. She would rather not have to acknowledge that fact herself.

'You still haven't told me why you're here.'

'I've come to see your father.'

'I doubt it. I seriously doubt my father would ever want to see you again—not after everything you've done to undermine his business and ruin our lives in the process.'

He shrugged, lifting his thick dark eyebrows in a way that told her he didn't care what she thought, infuriating her even more.

'Your doubts are not my concern. My business, however, is, and right now you are preventing me from conducting that business. So, if you'll just move aside?'

She straightened, not budging an inch. 'It's late. And, even if it weren't, you're wasting your time. You're the last person my father would want to do business with.'

His jaw shifted sideways as he leaned forward, his black eyes coming closer.

'Then obviously you have no idea *what* your father is capable of.'

His warm breath brushed her face, testosterone laced with coffee overlaid with something far more potent—

Was it ruthlessness?

Or cruelty? And for the first time her fear became tangible. Now it wasn't only the sight of him or the sound of his hard words in a smooth accent that she had to deal with; now she had the very essence of him assailing her lungs, assaulting her senses, testing her sanity.

And it was too much.

In spite of the balmy autumn night she could feel the heated moisture break out on her forehead; she could feel every muscle tightening in preparation for fight or flight.

What had brought this man here tonight? Why would he possibly think he would be offered entrée into their house— after doing his utmost to bring her family and two hundred years of history crumbling down with them?

Right now, it didn't matter. Because there was one thing she registered instinctively—that, whatever this man was doing here, no good could come of it. And he'd made her family suffer enough as it was.

The answer was as patently simple as it was critical. Diablo Barrentes wouldn't cross this threshold, not while she rode shotgun.

'Briar? Who is it, dear?'

Surprised her mother was still awake, she still only let her head tilt slightly in the direction of her voice. There was no way she was taking her eyes off the dark nemesis before her. 'It's no one important. I've taken care of it.' And with a rush of satisfaction she reached for the handle and attempted to ram the door home.

She didn't even come close. Like a lightning bolt, his hand shot out, palm flat and long fingers outstretched, arresting the path of the heavy door dead. Then, with just one cast-iron shove, he pushed it right back and clean out of her grasp.

'What do you think you're doing?' she cried out in both fury and shock as the door swung wildly past her, leaving him standing exposed in the open doorway like some angry black spider determined that its meal was not going to escape.

'Briar!' her mother cried, her voice tense and sharp as a rapier. 'Let Mr Barrentes in.'

She turned to face her mother fully this time. 'You can't be serious. Not after—'

'I *am* serious,' the older woman said in barely more than a whisper, one arm held tight around her chest, the fingers of her other hand nervously clutching at her throat. 'Your father's been expecting him. Come in, Mr Barrentes. Cameron's waiting for you in the library. I apologise for my daughter's lack of decorum.'

Briar reeled as if she'd been slapped in the face. But her mother had a point. So much for her Davenport breeding; it had gone out the door the moment she'd opened it, no match at all for dealing with a man like Diablo.

'It's quite all right,' he said, striding past Briar's stunned form with barely an acknowledgement. 'I find there's nothing I enjoy more these days than a woman with spirit.'

Her mother closed her eyes and seemed to sway on her feet for a moment. 'Quite,' she said, after recovering her composure, not quite able or willing to meet her daughter's concerned gaze. 'Well, if you come this way, Mr Barrentes…'

'What's going on?'

Carolyn Davenport turned to her daughter, or rather *almost* to her, focusing on a point somewhere over her shoulder.

'Perhaps you could close the door, dear; there's a real chill in the air tonight. Then maybe you could get the men some coffee and brandy? I'm sure they have plenty to discuss.'

Her mother had to be kidding. If there was a chill in the air it had more to do with the black cloud she'd just admitted into the house rather than the ambient temperature. And be damned if she'd serve what little was left of the good brandy to the likes of Diablo Barrentes, the man who'd almost single-handedly cost one of the oldest and most respected Sydney families its fortune.

'I'll get my father anything he needs,' she conceded, swinging the door closed, realising she was abandoning any hint of good breeding and yet unable to stop herself. 'But I'm sorry, Mother, Diablo can fend for himself.'

Half an hour later she was still simmering over the presence of their unwanted guest when her mother found her sitting alone in the kitchen.

'Has he gone?' she asked.

Her mother shook her head and Briar felt her blood pressure spike before forcing her attention back to the screen. Not that she could concentrate when her head was full of one take-no-prisoners Spaniard. Damn the man! What could he possibly want of her father now? There was nothing left for him to take. Even the family home—the last remaining asset—was now mortgaged to the hilt.

'What are you doing, sweetheart?' her mother asked as she came around behind her, placing a hand on her shoulder and stroking with gentle pressure. Briar smiled as she leaned her head into the caress, feeling some of her tension dissipate under her mother's touch.

'It's that schedule I've been working on, listing the furniture and artworks you and Dad decided you could bear to part with. I've spoken to the auctioneer and, rather than sending everything off in one big lot, it looks like if we send the right pieces to auction every two or three months, we'll still have enough to meet our commitments.'

'Oh? Is that right?' Her mother's hand stopped moving and she shifted to the stool alongside, the tight frown that marred her brow as she contemplated the detail of the spreadsheet's contents adding at least ten years to her age.

And suddenly Briar regretted her earlier behaviour at the front door. Carolyn Davenport had been barely more than a shell of her former self lately, her skin pale and drawn, her emotions brittle. The stress of their money troubles was taking its toll on all of them, but on none more so than on her mother, who was still feeling the loss of her eldest child two years before. Almost too reluctant to venture downtown any more, she'd been constantly humiliated by the newspaper articles documenting the family's downfall and the endless pitying looks from one-time society friends. And, despite the provocation of the most arrogant male in the world, Briar hadn't helped the situation by behaving more like a teenager in a snit than the twenty-four-year-old woman she was.

With a few quick clicks of her finger, she saved the spreadsheet and closed down the computer. Being reminded of the family heirlooms that would soon no longer be theirs was no doubt the last thing her mother needed right now. 'Don't worry; I'm sure it's not as bad as it looks. We'll work our way through this, I know we will. And if that job I was promised at the gallery comes through, things will be even better.'

Her mother placed her hand over hers and patted it lightly. 'You're so good to do all of this. And with any luck we might not have to sell everything after all. Your father's hoping there might just be another way out of this mess.'

Briar swivelled around to face her mother, her hands held palms up. 'But what else is there? We've done the rounds of the banks and the financiers; we've tried everything going. I thought we'd run out of options.'

'All except one,' she said, her eyes taking on a sudden spark. 'Just today it seems we've been offered something of a lifeline. The loans paid off and a settlement—a large one, enough for us to get the staff back and live like we used to, without having to sell everything and scrimp and save. It'll be just like before— like nothing ever happened. Except…' Her mother's fast and furious speech ran down as she turned her head in the direction of the library, a look of bleakness extinguishing the spark, turning her eyes grey and cold, frosty needles ascended Briar's spine.

'Oh, no! You can't mean Diablo? Please tell me this has nothing to do with why *that* man is here tonight.'

Her mother didn't answer and despair pumped unchallenged through her system. She launched herself off her stool and put her hands up in protest. 'But this is all his fault! He's almost single-handedly brought about the downfall of the Davenport family. Why should he then turn around and offer help? It makes no sense. There's nothing left for him to take.'

Her mother stood and came closer, tucking one renegade tendril of hair behind her daughter's ear before running her hands down her arms, squeezing them at her elbows. 'Right now we're hardly in a position to be choosy.'

'But he's so awful! The way he swaggers around Sydney like he owns the place.'

Her mother raised her eyebrows on a breath. 'Well, these days that's probably somewhere close to the truth.' She smiled weakly. 'But just think, he can't be all bad. He must have some redeeming features, don't you think?'

Briar snorted. 'They're well and truly hidden if he has.'

'And he is a very good-looking man.'

'I guess, if you go for the bandit look.' She frowned, the direction her mother's arguments were taking suddenly niggling at her. 'Anyway, we're talking about Diablo Barrentes. The same Diablo Barrentes who has set out to bring down the Sydney establishment, and the Davenport family first and foremost. What's it matter what he loo—'

'Briar—' her father's gruff tones interrupted them from behind '—I'm glad you're still up. Can you spare me a minute or two?'

She breathed a sigh of relief. Her father's appearance meant Diablo must have gone at last, and good riddance to him. She was sick of feeling on tenterhooks in her own home. And at least now she might find out what was going on. If her father was planning on accepting help from Diablo, she'd have a few things to say about it first.

'You go with your father,' her mother urged, her smile too thin, too unconvincing, as she gestured towards the door. 'We've finished anyway.'

She caught the loaded look that passed between her parents. Something was going on. Why didn't her parents look happier if there was a lifeline in the offing?

Or were Barrentes's terms too costly?

A sick feeling snaked in her gut. Nothing would surprise her. Diablo would be sure to want to stick the boot in now that he had her father down.

Damn the man. She'd do everything possible to ensure they could avoid his greedy clutches.

'Actually,' her mother piped up, catching her daughter's hand in a sudden change of heart, 'maybe I should come along with you.'

'No!' insisted Cameron, insinuating himself between the two women and breaking their grasp. 'You stay here,' he directed at his wife. 'This won't take long. And then I could probably use another coffee.'

'So are you ever going to tell me what's going on?' Briar asked her father a few moments later, wishing he would say something—*anything*—as he led her through the house. His silence was unsettling. 'What did Diablo want?'

Just outside the library he paused and turned to her, taking both her hands in his, the look on his face almost one of defeat, and this close up she was shocked to see how dark and heavy those circles under his eyes really were. It might be late but it was clear the stress of their circumstances was eating away at him, too. From inside the library the old grandfather clock ticked away the seconds ominously.

'Briar,' he said on a sigh, 'before we go any further, I want you to know that I didn't want this to happen, you have to believe that.' He peered at her so intently she could feel his utter desperation, his bony hands cold and unsettlingly clammy around her own.

She swallowed. 'You didn't mean what to happen?'

'I need you help,' he continued, evading her question, 'even though I know that what I am asking of you may be too much.'

'It's okay,' she replied with a confidence she didn't feel, squeezing his hands back. She tried desperately to raise a smile but a racing heart and a mind filled with shadows and creeping foreboding wouldn't let her. 'So what is it you want me to do?'

A dark flicker of movement wrenched her attention away from her father as a prickle of awareness skittered along her skin.

Diablo! So he hadn't left after all! And now he stood leaning casually against the doorway. Although the look on his face was anything but.

Victory, his features proclaimed.

It was there in the dangerous glint in his eyes. It was there in the voracious tilt of his smile. And it was there in the menacing darkness of his attitude.

'It's really quite simple,' Diablo announced, answering for her father, his teeth flashing dangerously as he levered himself away from the door and closer to her.

'Your father merely expects you to marry me.'

CHAPTER TWO

'IF THAT'S your idea of a joke, Mr Barrentes...' Briar's voice sounded strangely calm in spite of the explosions going off behind her eyes '...I'd say you were seriously overdue for a sense of humour transplant.'

He laughed. Or rather he rumbled, that low rolling sound that vibrated uncomfortably through her.

She bristled, trying to dispel the rush of heat that came with his proximity. 'I'm afraid I don't see the joke.'

His mouth quietened, his eyes stilled. *On hers.* 'That's because it is no joke. Your father has agreed that you will marry me.'

For a moment she was speechless. But only for a moment. Then it was her turn to laugh, wiping away his wild assertions with a sweep of one hand. 'You're crazy! Dad, tell him how ludicrous he sounds. There's no way you'd ever expect me to do something so absurd as to marry someone like *him*.' She looked at her father, inviting him to agree—*imploring him to agree*—but her father said nothing, his eyes more desolate than she'd ever seen them, and the laughter died on her lips just as hope died in her heart.

'Briar,' he said in the bare bones of a whisper, reaching for her shoulder, 'you have to understand—'

A hitched moment of realisation passed and then, *'No!'* She recoiled from both his touch and from what his eyes told her. 'There's nothing to understand.'

'Please,' her father pleaded, 'before you mother hears us.' He motioned them both into the room before closing the door behind them. 'You must listen to me.'

Her mind a blur, she let herself be bustled inside the room before she turned on her father, blurting out just how she felt. 'How can I listen when what you say makes no sense?'

'And how can you say it makes no sense,' Diablo argued from the sidelines, one arrogant eyebrow cocked, 'if you don't listen?'

She snapped her head around in his direction. 'If I'd wanted your opinion, I would have asked for it.'

He didn't look nonplussed. Far from it. In fact he looked altogether too pleased with himself as he leant back against her father's desk, his hands planted wide either side of him, pulling his shirt taut across a muscled chest that looked far better than any man's had a right to. The open V of his shirt revealed olive skin that was impossibly smooth, almost glossy, and a hint of dark chest hair. She forced her eyes higher, aware that she'd been staring. Her mother was right. Diablo Barrentes was one good-looking man. Why did someone so detestable have to be blessed with such good looks and such a killer body? There was clearly no justice in this world.

He smiled then, as if amused by what her face betrayed of her thoughts. 'You are as prickly as your name suggests, my wild rose.'

'I am *not* your wild rose! Don't you understand? I don't want to marry you. And there's no way on earth you can make me.'

She turned her attention back to her father as another cog suddenly slipped into place. Suddenly her mother's 'he must have some redeeming features' discussion made sense, though not the sudden secrecy. 'What's this really about? Why did you make us come into the library? Mother knows about this arrangement, doesn't she?'

Her father looked grey. 'She knows something of the proposal, it's true.'

Briar's gut churned. '*Something of the proposal*'? What more could there possibly be? What she was hearing already set her stomach roiling. And the very concept that her future had been mapped out by her own parents—the two people she'd always assumed loved her and wanted the best for her—was too much.

'So you've discussed this then, between yourselves like some kind of domestic transaction. I can just imagine how the conversation went: *"Shall we renovate the beach house? Maybe trade up to the new Mercedes? Oh, and while we're at it, maybe we can marry Briar off to Diablo Barrentes."'*

She swivelled her head and firmly fixed Diablo in her sights. 'You've worked out between yourselves that you're going to marry me off to the person this family detests more than anyone in the world. How could you do that?'

Diablo didn't flinch at her words, his eyes merely glinting menacingly. Her father, however, was getting more agitated.

'Briar, calm down, we have no choice!'

'There's always a choice! Like I have a choice. Because there's no way I'm marrying Diablo Barrentes. I wouldn't marry him if he was the last man on earth.' She swung around in Diablo's direction and looked square into his dark fathomless eyes. 'I'd rather die!'

This time the merest tic in his cheek was the only indication that her words had met their mark. 'It's drama you studied at university, then,' he delivered in a tone that told her how unimpressed he was with the proceedings. 'I was obviously under a misapprehension.'

'I studied fine arts,' she hissed. 'Not that it's any business of yours.'

He raised his eyebrows. 'You surprise me, given you have such a flair for the dramatic.'

'And you have such a flair for the insane! How could you possibly imagine I would marry you? What were you thinking? That you could marry your way into Sydney society? It won't work. People aren't going to forget how you rode roughshod over everyone in your path to get to where you are today.'

He surveyed her through half-hooded eyes that failed to hide those dark simmering depths. 'You resent me for building my own fortune, instead of having it bestowed on me through some accident of birth like you and your kind?'

'I resent you because you've built your fortune by pulling others down, my father included.'

'Is that so? And yet now I'm offering your father a chance to get re-established. He can see the sense in the offer. And yet still you resent me.'

'I will *always* resent you.'

She turned in frustration to her father. 'Please, tell me this is all a joke. You can't really expect me to marry this arrogant Spanish import. This is twenty-first century Sydney, after all. We don't do arranged marriages!'

Her father shook his head sadly. 'Briar…' His voice choked off as he sank down into an armchair, dropping his head into his hands. 'Oh God, I've been such a fool.'

She rushed to him and knelt at his side, latching both hands on to his forearm, willing him some of her strength and hope. 'Dad, listen to me. We don't need Diablo's money. I've got it all worked out. We can survive just like we planned—with my job and by auctioning the good furniture periodically. We don't need to go crawling to people like him. We don't need his money.'

'It's not that easy,' her father murmured, shaking his head from side to side.

'It *is* that easy,' she assured him. 'We don't have to make this deal. I haven't had a chance to tell you yet—because we can survive without it. So what that we won't have servants?—We can cope. We've been coping. And I'll have a job soon.'

'We're not coping! Look at the state of the house—it's killing your mother that she can't keep up with everything.'

'Who cares if the floors don't get cleaned every day? Things will get better, you'll see.'

Her father grabbed her by the shoulders, his desperate fingers clawing into her flesh so hard it hurt. With his hurt, she knew. 'No, it's not that easy,' he reiterated. 'You have to listen. We have no money left. No credit. Nothing.'

'We do,' she argued, wanting to stop his pain. 'Or we will, and enough to keep us going and to get us through these times. We don't need anyone else's money, let alone his. Let me go and get the schedule I've been working on. I'll prove it to you. I've worked it all out.'

'Briar,' was all he said as he dropped his grip to her hands, holding on to them for all he was worth, not letting her rise. 'Thank you. You're such a good child. I'm so proud of you.'

She looked into her father's eyes and saw his approval beaming out at her. She relished the moment as he pulled her close, wrapping her securely in his arms, and for a moment they were the only two people in the room. Nobody else counted. Nobody else mattered. Her father thought he had been carrying the entire burden of their debt on his shoulders. Now he knew that Briar had also been searching for solutions. And everything would look different when he'd seen her calculations. She'd soon show him they didn't need to resort to people like Diablo for the funds to ensure their future.

'So when are you going to tell her?' jarred a voice from outside her perfect understanding. And she stilled within the circle of her father's arms as dread turned her blood to ice.

'Tell me what?' she asked huskily, drawing back to search her father's face. What the hell else could there be?

He looked down at her with his empty eyes and it was impossible not to feel his despair drape around her, damp and pungent. 'There's nothing left.'

'What do you mean?' she asked, willing life into his eyes, searching for the merest flicker of hope. *"Nothing left"?'*

'It's all gone. All of it.'

'But we've still got the house and the furniture! I told you…'

But, even as she was speaking, his head was shaking from side to side.

'Gone,' her father said. 'All that was left is gone. It's Diablo's now. Everything. The house, the furniture. Everything.'

Fury took charge of her senses. She rose up and wheeled around. 'You bastard!' She moved closer. Never before had she had an urge to tear someone limb from limb but tonight was becoming a night for firsts. Her first arranged marriage. Her first fiancé. Why not her first homicide? She lifted one hand, resisting the desire to lash out at his smug face, instead curling it into a fist between them.

'You scheming bastard. Not content to obliterate four generations of work, you couldn't let up until you had taken every last thing, even our family home, and consigned us to the gutter. What a hero. Do you feel proud of yourself now?'

In the space of a blink he'd ensnared her wrist, the heat from his grip like a brand on her arm.

'I'm offering a way to keep you all out of that gutter. I've told your father—he can keep the house and everything in it along with a sizeable lump of cash every year. All you have to do is be that good daughter your father seems to think you are. All you have to do is marry me and all your family's unfortunate financial problems will be a thing of the past.'

The grip around her wrist tightened, forcing her towards him, closer to his dark eyes and his tight body and his masculine heat. If his gaze at the door had been sizzling hot, his hold and his closeness was like an incendiary device set to slow burn. Already her skin sizzled into life; how long would it take to get to flash-point?

'Put like that, it seems you leave me no choice,' she said through gritted teeth, watching his eyes flare with an anticipated victory.

'I'm glad you're willing to see reason at last,' he said, loosening his grip.

'Oh, yes, I see reason. I'll take the gutter over you any day!'

She took advantage of his shock by wrenching her arm free, massaging the burning skin as she wheeled away.

'You don't know what you're letting yourself in for!' Diablo countered. 'You have no idea what it's like to live in poverty, always desperate to find your next meal, never able to make ends meet, and with your pampered upbringing you won't survive ten minutes out in the real world.'

She spun on her heel, lifted her chin determinedly. 'Oh, we'll survive.'

He scoffed. 'What—you see yourself as the noble poor? Allow me to let you in on a secret—there are no noble poor. There are only the poor, the hungry and the desperate. There's no place for nobility in that line-up. The gutter is no fairy tale romantic notion.'

She regarded him levelly. 'What a coincidence,' she mustered. 'Neither, it seems, is marrying you.' She turned to where her father still sat, looking like an empty shell of a man, a fallen ruler, vanquished and heartsick for what he'd lost, and pain for what he was feeling now encompassed her like a tide rolling in.

'I'm sorry, Dad. I can't do it. I just can't marry him.'

Her father nodded his head and she knew that it was not in agreement but in resignation. He seemed to shrink before her eyes. 'I understand,' he croaked. 'I should never have had to ask you. It's all my fault—my fault. Now I just have to find a way of telling your mother that we no longer have a home.'

Briar's heart plummeted.

'Oh, God, you mean she doesn't know? I thought she must have been in on this crazy idea.'

'She doesn't know we've lost Blaxlea. I didn't want to worry her unnecessarily. But now…'

'Oh, Dad, no…'

The grandfather clock clicked loudly in the ensuing silence as the mechanism for the chimes kicked in, the prelude for ringing out the midnight hour.

Diablo strode between them. 'Can you do that to your mother, then? Deny her the chance to see out her days in this house rather than some doss-house? What kind of a daughter are you really?'

She said nothing, just let her eyes tell him how much she hated him while inside her heart ached for her mother. Because Diablo was right—how could she do that to her mother after what she'd been through? After losing Nat, then the business and along with it their fortune, to lose the family home would kill her.

'I can see you need more time to think about it,' Diablo decided. 'So I'm prepared to give you one more chance. You have until the clock strikes twelve to decide once and for all. Marry me and your family live in comfort for the rest of their days. Turn me down and you'll be out of this house by the end of the week.'

'You can't do that!'

'Watch me,' he said. 'It's not as if you have anything left to pack.'

'Even you couldn't be so cold-hearted!'

'It's not up to me any more,' he said as the clock finished its chimes and made the first of twelve strikes. 'It's up to you what happens next. Luxury or poverty, it's your call. Will you abandon your parents in their hour of need or will you restore your parents to the life they desire?'

The clock struck again. 'That's two,' he said. 'I hope you're thinking.'

Oh, she was thinking all right. Panicked thoughts with no beginning and no end and no hope. And, between them all, the clock struck again.

Would it kill her to marry him? Maybe not, but there was no doubt it would definitely kill her mother to leave Blaxlea, her childhood home and the seat of her mother's family for generations.

And would she ever forgive Briar for rejecting the financial lifeline that Diablo was now offering?

The clock struck again and she looked up in panic. Had she missed one? How much time was left? There was too much to consider.

Why, oh, why, did it all have to come down to her? *Oh Nat*, she pleaded, *what should I do?* But she knew without question that if her big brother had survived the crash that had cut short his life, he wouldn't hesitate to help. He'd do whatever it took to help his parents out, even if it meant sacrificing his own career and his own future into the deal. So why did the thought of sacrificing her own chances seem so abhorrent? After all, all she had to do was to marry Diablo.

Marriage…

The clock sounded again, straining her nerves to breaking-point. It was almost time.

Marriage sounded so final. But then hadn't she always planned on getting married one day? Indeed, she'd been groomed from the day she was born for being a society wife with a rich husband… Would it really matter if it was to Diablo? And it didn't have to be for ever. He'd get sick of her before too long—she'd make sure of it—and then he'd have to agree to divorce her. How long would it take—one year? Two? She'd make sure there were no children to suffer in the fallout. And then she'd have her life back. It wouldn't kill her. Marrying Diablo didn't have to be a life sentence.

All too soon it was just an echo that rolled around the room. The clock had rung out for the last time. The witching hour was here—the time when bad things crawled out of the night and ruled supreme. Diablo, the Spanish devil, was nothing if not faithful to the old legends.

She looked across at her father, who sat there looking like the beaten man he was. He looked up at her as if he'd realised too that this was it, his eyes bearing a rare spark of defiance. 'Don't do it,' he urged in a gruff entreaty as he rose to his feet, some measure of his fighting spirit renewed. 'This is my fault—all of it. You shouldn't have to pay for my mistakes. We'll make it through somehow.'

She smiled and mouthed a silent thank you.

'Well?' demanded the Spanish devil, drawing closer, obviously impatient to seal the deal. 'What have you decided?'

'That I hate you,' she snapped. 'With all my heart and soul.'

He lifted a hand to her face quickly and she recoiled, but his touch, when it came, was surprisingly gentle as he ran the backs of his fingers along the line of her jaw. She shuddered at the sizzle of flesh against flesh as his eyes bored into hers, rendering her breathless, unable to move. 'Hate is such a useless waste of passion.' He sighed and turned away and she dragged in air hungrily.

'But so be it. Under the circumstances,' he stated coldly, 'I want you all packed and out of here by the end of the week.'

'No!'

He spun around. 'What do you mean, "no"? My terms were clear.'

'It means we won't be leaving.'

'Briar,' her father implored, 'don't do it. You can't—'

Diablo held up one hand that silenced her father in a heartbeat as he scrutinised her face, the barest hint of a smile returning as the dark vacuum of his bottomless eyes sucked in hers. 'Tell me,' he insisted.

She took a deep breath and prayed for strength. Because she needed strength if she was going to do this. And she had no choice *but* to do this.

For my mother, she told herself, *for my family*.

'I'll do it,' she whispered, feeling like a swimmer out of her depth, going down for the third and final time.

'I'll marry you.'

CHAPTER THREE

'WHAT'S taking you so long?' asked Carolyn Davenport, bustling with excitement as she swept into Briar's room, holding her turquoise gown's ample skirts up high and trailing a silky layered train in her wake. 'It's just fabulous downstairs,' she announced. 'Everyone's here. Even with the short notice, I think the whole of Sydney society has turned out.'

Only out of morbid curiosity, thought Briar cynically as she applied the finishing touches to her make-up. No matter what story Diablo's spin doctors had concocted to release to the press, there wasn't a chance anyone believed theirs was a love match.

Anyone, that was, apart from her mother.

Carolyn Davenport had taken the news of the impending nuptials like the true society doyenne she was, swinging into mother-of-the-bride mode as if she was born to it. Any hint that she'd known about a link between her daughter's rushed marriage and the fact that now suddenly they had servants again, with the funds to pay for them and much more besides, like her brand new Lisa Ho gown, for example, seemed to have been conveniently deleted from her memory. Her mother seemed all too ready to believe in the whole sorry fairy tale.

'Fairy tale romance', my eye, Briar thought, reflecting on the latest headline as she snapped the blusher compact closed. But

even the business pages hadn't been immune to the press bombardment.

'*Marriage Merger*' had been their angle—'*a blending of new money with old, the brash success of the young entrepreneur merged with the proven track record of the establishment*'.

How the papers would lap it up if she came clean with her own version of the headline—'*Blackmail Bride—sold to save her family from financial ruin*'. But that story would never come out, no matter how true.

'You could do with more colour than that,' her mother protested, as Briar dropped the blusher back into a drawer. 'You look so pale tonight—I knew we should have got your make-up done professionally. Are you feeling nervous?'

'Not really.' *Feeling sick, more like it.* Briar looked briefly back in the mirror to check—even against the white silk of her simple toga-inspired gown she looked pale—but then, what make-up was going to be a match for her mood? There was only so much you could do with powder and paint.

'Never mind,' her mother said, when it was clear her daughter was going to make no attempt to redress the issue. 'I'm sure a glass of champagne will soon put some colour in your cheeks.'

Briar's stomach clamped down in rebellion. Champagne was the last thing she needed. After all, tonight was hardly a celebration.

'Come on, then,' her mother urged. 'Diablo's waiting for you downstairs. Just wait till you see him; he looks so dashing tonight.'

'That's nice,' she responded absently, slipping her feet into heels. Who cared what he looked like? He could be the most handsome man in the world, but it would still be the devil in disguise waiting for her. And frankly, he could just keep on waiting. Just because she'd agreed to marry him didn't mean that she'd be dancing to his tune any time soon.

She'd done a lot of thinking over the last two weeks and she'd worked out her own musical score for this marriage. Diablo craved respectability and an entrée to Sydney society. He didn't care about her and he almost certainly didn't even like her. Given that the feeling was mutual, it shouldn't take much to convince him that the best way to make this marriage work was for them both to lead separate lives. At least until he tired of her and agreed to a divorce. That way life might be bearable. She could put up with a year or two of inconvenience if she knew that at the other side of it she'd be free.

'Oh, hasn't Carlos done such a wonderful job with your hair?' her mother exclaimed with delight. 'It suits that gown perfectly. Although I still don't understand why you wanted to wear that old thing. It is a special occasion, after all.'

Not *that* special. And this 'old thing' was barely twelve months old and only worn once as it was. But still, she turned and smiled at her mother's never-ending enthusiasm. Someone had to be enthusiastic about this wedding and who better than her mother? Already she looked so much better than she had just two short weeks ago when this crazy marriage plan had been unleashed, her features less drawn, her frown vanquished. It wasn't just that their financial situation had taken a turn for the better, she knew, but because her mother genuinely seemed to want this marriage to work out.

'I'm just saving my splurge for the big event,' she told her, with a passion she didn't feel, taking her mother's arm and pulling her in close. 'Come on, let's go meet these guests.'

The champagne flowed so freely it seemed the huge ballroom was awash with it. Champagne, old money and the celebrity A-List blended together in the Blaxlea ballroom, which fairly gleamed since the team of cleaners Diablo had organised to go over the place had done their bit. Huge arrangements of flowers were doubled in the enormous mirrors, their colours reflected in the crystal chandeliers, while a full wall of feature windows welcomed in the diamond lights of Sydney Harbour at night.

It was some place all right and it could have been his outright—indeed it had been, for just one night. But he was happy with his deal—they could keep the title to the house. Tonight he would gain himself something much more important than just bricks and mortar and a few hundred feet of prime Sydney Harbour frontage. Tonight he'd cement his place and his future with the society that had resisted him for so long.

Already he could sense the change in the way he was perceived, by the constant string of congratulations he'd received from people who would have crossed the street to avoid him in the past, as he stood alongside Cameron Davenport waiting for the ladies to appear. In marrying Briar there was no way they could ignore his hold on the Sydney property industry any more. Now he had the Davenport seal of approval. Now there would be no stopping him.

How fortunate that a man so unskilled in the ways of his business should have had such a suitable daughter. For there was no one he'd rather cement his future with than Briar Davenport. She would make the perfect wife. The bonus was she would also make a pleasant bed-warmer. Siring children with her would be no hardship.

There was a stir amongst the crowd before everyone hushed and his eyes drifted upwards to where the two women stood at the top of the stairs, the older woman in plumage peacock-bold, the daughter so deathly pale as to render any other mere mortal invisible.

But not Briar. Her skin might be pale but her eyes shone like dream stones, amber and intense. And the dress might be colourless but it could not disguise the exquisitely feminine form beneath. A tiny waist that only accentuated the lushness of her breasts and hips, and legs that went forever and then some.

Briar. Like the rose that grew wild, spreading branches rambling, *soon she would be clambering all over him*. Already he could feel those long limbs wrapped around him, clinging to him, supported by him. Already he could hear her crying out, begging him for release. His body stirred in anticipation as the women slowly descended the wide staircase.

Oh, no, siring children with her would be no hardship at all.

The women reached the foot of the stairs. Carolyn took her husband's arm. Diablo held out his hand for Briar and for the first time she looked at him.

Something jolted through her as their eyes connected, a prelude for the bolt of electricity that was unleashed when their hands touched. His dark eyes narrowed and regarded her strangely.

'You look beautiful,' he said. 'Like a virgin sacrifice about to be tossed to the lions.'

How appropriate, she thought, though hardly willing to buy into that particular discussion. 'And you,' she replied, 'look like the proverbial cat that got the cream.'

He drew her hand closer, pressing his mouth, warm and moist, to her skin while his eyes held hers. 'Not yet; so far I only have the unopened package. But, I must confess, I'm looking forward to opening it up and then—' his eyes narrowed and focused like dark torchlight '—and then sampling the treasure within.'

She dragged in air and turned her head away, suddenly too uncomfortable, too giddy, too *hot*. She didn't need a mirror to tell her that there was plenty of colour in her cheeks now. Diablo's words had achieved in an instant what the finest cosmetics in the world had failed to do.

Yet it wasn't just his words heating her body. Her mother hadn't been exaggerating. Tonight he looked magnificent in clothes that would have made a lesser man look ridiculous and yet on Diablo merely accentuated his masculine power. A snow-white shirt contrasted with his smooth olive skin and black fitted trousers that finished above hand-stitched leather boots. Over it all he wore a long black jacket with a Nehru collar that emphasized his long, lean length. With his hair tied back, all he needed was a gold hoop in his earlobe and he could have been a pirate out on the town celebrating his latest conquest.

And, if that wasn't enough, just breathing the same air, laced with the heady tang of his aftershave, was like getting a shot of testosterone.

And damn him but somehow that scent was like a lure, snagging on her defences, tangling with her resistance. Purposefully she stiffened her spine. She would not be attracted to such a man. It couldn't happen.

Someone—her father—made a toast and the room erupted into applause and congratulations. Briar made out not a word of it as she scanned the crowded ballroom without taking in a thing. She was too busy working out what to do next. They would have to talk—privately—and soon. Diablo had to be made to see under what terms she was prepared to marry him and that those terms in no way included him sampling *anything*!

'Darling? Briar?'

It was hearing her name that brought her back and she turned to him, ready to protest that she was hardly his darling, but something in his eyes stopped her in her tracks.

'Didn't you hear the guests? They're waiting for us to seal our betrothal with a kiss.'

And, before she could protest this latest indignity, that there was no way she would kiss him, least of all in front of two hundred people, his mouth was on hers and any protest was muffled, *melted*, by the sheer impact of his lips.

They were soft, she realised with surprise—soft but sure. He looked so powerful dressed as he was all in black, hard and unyielding, and yet his lips moved over hers with an elegance of movement and a grace that was as surprising as it was intoxicating.

Heat rolled through her in waves, a surging tide of warmth that crashed and foamed into her extremities and set her flesh to tingling and her protests all but forgotten. The room shrank around them until there was just this kiss, these sensations, this mouth, weaving magic on hers.

And then he lifted his mouth from hers and sounds and colour and people invaded her numbed senses once more. She blinked as the crowd cheered; she blinked as her state of daze sloughed away; she blinked as Diablo smiled back at her, success lining that passionate slash of mouth, as she realised what she'd done.

Dear God! She'd let Diablo Barrentes kiss her, in public. And his expression told her he was gloating about it. She lifted one hand, touched the back of it to lips that still hummed from his touch, but he stilled the movement, pulling her hand down within his.

'You don't wipe me away that easily.'

She didn't doubt it, her mouth still full of the taste of him.

'We have to talk,' she croaked as her parents were absorbed into a circle of guests and a buzz of conversation went up all around them. 'Tonight. In private.'

The spark in his eyes flared, one dark eyebrow lifted in surprise. 'I did not expect you to be so accommodating quite so readily.'

Already rattled by his kiss, she was in no mood for his easy confidence.

'We have to *talk*! We need to set down some ground rules for this arrangement.'

He took two glasses of champagne from a passing waiter's tray, handing her one. 'Oh? That sounds very important.' He took a bored sip of his wine that told her he thought it sounded anything but. 'In that case we will talk. But later.' He took her free hand, surrounding it in his warmth, and headed into the ballroom. 'First the happy couple must mingle with our guests seeing they've come especially to wish us well.'

'You mean they've come to knit at my execution. They're

nothing but ghouls, wanting to witness the ultimate degradation of one of their own.'

He stopped dead and lowered his head to hers, his body close, his voice a clipped whisper in her ear. 'You had a choice. You did not have to agree to this.'

'I had *no* choice, and you know it. You left me without any choice at all.'

'Wrong,' he hit back. 'You could have walked away from me and—' he swept his champagne-bearing hand around the room '—and all of this.'

'I couldn't—'

'No! You could have, but you *didn't*—for whatever reasons you had, you chose not to! And, having made your decision, I expect you to live with it. Now, I suggest we meet some of our guests.'

It was many hours and many more cases of champagne later that the party wound down, leaving only a few of Cameron's colleagues, who seemed all too content to settle in for brandy and cigars in the library. Carolyn had excused herself an hour ago, pleading too much excitement, and Briar sympathised.

It had seemed an endless night, moving on from one group of people to the next, filling the time with the same small talk, trying to instil the right measure of excitement into her voice. She could see the doubts, she could see the cynical way half the attendees accepted the marriage, the questions they asked, aimed to find any chink in the story, seeking out the truth they knew was there if they just dug in the right place.

She could even see the looks of envy that were fired her way from women who obviously thought Diablo was some kind of catch. Just because he hadn't been embraced by Sydney society didn't mean there wasn't a queue of women lining up to be photographed on his arm.

Diablo had carried himself through the night like a consummate professional, letting his answers trip from his tongue—*their attraction had surprised them both but now they couldn't wait to be married, and the icing on the cake was his father-in-law-to-be's sudden change in fortunes.*

And all the while he'd bluffed his way through the potential minefield of the evening, he'd never let her stray more than inches away, his arm proprietorialy looped over her shoulders or around her waist, or just reaching out to stroke her arm, or tuck a strand of hair away from her face. Briar, on the other hand, had smiled through gritted teeth at the pointed questions and gentle caresses and wished the whole evening over. After what felt like an eternity, thankfully, it nearly was.

'Now, you wanted to talk.'

They had just bid farewell to the last of the departing guests at the front door. She shook her head, revelling in being able to put some distance between them at last. At last the pretence was over. But the strain of deflecting their barbed queries coupled with Diablo's constant presence at her side had left her with such a thundering tension headache that all she wanted to do now was to go to bed. The last thing she wanted to face was an all too revealing statement of how she saw their marriage working.

'It can wait,' she conceded, rubbing her temples. 'I'm just glad this farce of an evening is over.'

But Diablo was talking to a passing waiter and she didn't think he'd heard her.

'Why do you call it that?' he said, turning back to her a moment later and proving her assumption wrong. 'Our engagement is no farce, nor will our marriage be.'

'You know it's a farce! And having to pretend that this relationship is anything other than the business transaction it is, it's just impossible.'

His eyes narrowed. 'You think this marriage is merely a business transaction?'

'Isn't it? It's hardly a love match.'

He ushered her into a small sitting room opposite the ballroom just as the waiter returned, bearing a tray with two glasses, one a tumbler of what looked like Scotch, the other a tall frosty glass, its contents sparkling. He lifted them both from the tray and held out the tall glass as the waiter exited, closing the door behind them.

'What is it?' she said, not taking it.

'Drink it. It's an old Spanish headache remedy. It will make you feel better.'

Briar eyed the glass suspiciously. There was no telling what ingredients might go into making an 'old Spanish headache remedy'. 'And you care how I feel? I don't think so.'

He shrugged, still holding the glass even as he took a sip from his own. 'You would rather keep your headache?'

She murmured her thanks as she took the glass, aware she was being churlish, wondering at his ability to rub her up the wrong way. She sniffed tentatively at the glass, took a sip and, with surprise, instantly recognised the slightly bitter taste of paraceta-mol. 'Old Spanish headache remedy' indeed. She lifted her eyes to meet his and found them creased at the edges, a smirk tugging at his mouth.

He was laughing at her.

'Now,' he continued, 'let's stop wasting time. Tell me about these "ground rules" you're so keen on implementing.'

'Do we have to do this now?' she protested, after finishing the contents of her glass. She wasn't up to going ten rounds with anyone right now—let alone with Diablo. 'It's late. Can't it wait?'

'No. We will be married in two weeks and for much of that time I have business overseas. If you want anything incorporated into our pre-nuptial agreement, then you best tell me now.'

His cold words broke over her like a rogue wave, catching her unawares, tumbling her into the sandy depths. 'What pre-nuptial agreement?'

'Oh, come, come.' He swept away her protest with one potent hand. 'Surely you didn't expect we would be married without one? As you say, ours is hardly a love match.'

For a moment she bristled at his ready agreement with her summation. Only then common sense prevailed. If his terms for this marriage could be in writing, so too could hers. Two could play at that game.

'Of course, you're right,' she conceded, feeling a surge of confidence. 'A pre-nuptial agreement would be for the best. Then we both know where we stand.'

He downed the rest of his drink in one mouthful and she watched as he swirled the smooth liquor around his mouth and kick back his jaw as he sent it southwards. And through it all his eyes smouldered, never shifting from her, as if weighing her up, evaluating her.

'Sí, exactly. So tell me, Briar, where do you stand? What terms would you like included in the arrangement that outlines our future life together?'

'You mean our marriage together,' she corrected.

He smiled in a way that made her shiver. 'I said what I meant. Now it's your turn.'

She swung around and laced her fingers together, taking a couple of breaths before she was ready to face that bottomless dark gaze once more. She could feel her colour rising again and gave thanks for the low lighting. What she had to say was difficult enough without one hundred watts to illuminate it. 'It's really quite simple,' she began, turning. 'As you agreed, this marriage is hardly a love match. And, in that case, I think it's sensible that we understand what we bring to the marriage—in your case, it's money. In mine, it's my family connections.'

She hesitated. Diablo's body language as he sprawled into one of the wing-chairs and looked up at her was not giving anything away.

'You think all you have to offer is your family connections?'

'Isn't that the reason you came up with this plan?'

He said nothing. Just surveyed her some more. In apparently excruciating detail. Her skin bristled with irritation under his deep-seated gaze, her senses fusing.

'Go on,' he urged at last, without bothering to answer her question.

'So I've come up with a plan as to how we're going to work this out. Clearly, we have no choice now but to go ahead with this marriage but, equally clearly, it's obvious that neither of us is completely happy about the arrangement.'

'Says who?'

'Says both of us! We're both doing this out of necessity, nothing more. And, like the performance I put on tonight, I want you to know that I'm prepared to put on a public face after we're married that says we're man and wife.'

'How accommodating of you.'

'Well, I understand how important this is to you—and to me and my family. I'll do my best to make it work, to give a convincing performance as your wife.'

'And in private?'

'I beg your pardon?'

'You talked about how things would be in public. I'm wondering what you have in mind for our private life, when nobody else is watching.'

The heat continued to build under her skin. Of course, he wasn't about to make this easy for her. She stiffened her back, kicking up her chin resolutely. 'Then we live our lives separately, just as we have until entering this sham of a marriage. In public I agree to play your wife, even your adoring wife on the occasions that demand it. Out of the public eye we will lead separate lives. If you want this marriage of convenience to satisfy your need for connections, then so you shall have it, but you can't expect anything more.'

His only response was a blink of his eyes, slow and loaded. Then he leaned forward.

'And just how separate a life do you expect to lead while you occupy my bed?'

She snorted, outraged at the idea. 'That's just it. I won't be. Given your track record, I'm sure you'll have no trouble finding yourself someone who is more willing in that department. All that I ask is that you be discreet about it.'

He brushed aside her slur with a shake of his head. 'You haven't thought this through.'

'Of course I have…'

'No. Clearly you have missed something. For how are you to bear my children if you won't at least share my bed? Or are you merely suggesting a much *kinkier* way of getting pregnant?'

The heat under her skin flared into a sizzle, spreading its warming tentacles out to her furthest regions. He wanted her pregnant? He wanted her to *bear his children*? *But that would mean making love with him!*

Making love with Diablo. What would that be like? All olive skin and lean muscled limbs, control and power and heat. She shivered.

'In your dreams!'

Because there must be no children to complicate this marriage, no fallout for when they divorced, as she'd already decided they would.

His smile started and ended at his lips, his eyes refusing to get involved. 'So you know about my dreams? How convenient. Because soon I won't just have you in my dreams. Soon I will have you underneath me, in my bed—or out of it, as you clearly seem to be advocating.'

She battled with shredded senses to regain some kind of foothold in this argument. But she was slipping, losing grip. She was supposed to be stating her terms. When had this become a discussion about where the act of sex itself would take place?

'Why do you try to twist everything I say? I'm trying to be reasonable here.'

'And you think it's not reasonable for a wife to bear her husband his child?'

'In normal circumstances, certainly. But this marriage is in no way normal. You know as well as I do that this arrangement is no more than a contrivance, to pay off my father's debts and to make you look better in the world.'

He paused, his eyes narrowing. 'If you say so. But think how much better I will look with a wife *and* a clutch of children. They will be half Davenports after all, socially acceptable, born into the same society that tried to keep me out for so long. Because I'm not operating under any misapprehensions—tonight I was accepted because you were on my arm. But people don't change their colours so quickly. If anything were to happen between you and me, if our marriage was to end acrimoniously without children, I have no doubt the door to Sydney high society would soon be slammed in my face once again. And I have no intention of that happening. Children are what I want and children are what you will give me.'

'So that's why you want me—as some kind of brood mare, to bear your *devil's spawn*.'

The corners of his mouth curved up. 'Are you so disappointed it's not for your sweet nature?'

She fumed with irritation. 'You can't make me sleep with you.'

He was out of his chair and before her in an instant, his stance dangerous, confronting. He reached out to her and his attitude suddenly softened. He touched fingertips to her cheek, trailing down below her chin and raising it closer. His other hand slipped around her neck.

'No,' he whispered, so close to her face she was sure he must hear the slam of her blood in her veins. 'But maybe I can convince you.'

She could hardly breathe, let alone respond, as his fingers stirred into a slow caress at her neck that left her dizzy and swaying on her heels, her headache all but forgotten under his searing touch on her bare skin. She gasped in air, his face so close that the taste of him filled her senses, and memories of those lips and a stolen kiss resurfaced into a solid, shocking need for a replay.

'You're trembling,' he said.

'I... I'm cold,' she lied.

He drew her closer, pressing his lips first to one cheek and then the other before drawing back.

'I think,' he whispered, 'it could be fun warming you up, convincing you that making love would not be such a bad thing between us.'

She pressed her eyes shut, but behind closed lids she could still see him, larger than life, supremely confident, could still feel the sensual dance of his fingers against the bare flesh of her back.

'And if you're not enough for me?' she gasped breathlessly, looking up in challenge, desperate for any kind of defence against this slow, sensual onslaught. He answered by gathering her full length against him and shock rendered her speechless. Through their clothes, she could feel his power pulsing, straining, waiting to be unleashed.

Unleashed inside her!

It wasn't just shock that kept her from protesting. It was fascination she felt, a desire to explore more of these new sensations, a yearning for something forbidden, something carnal that this man promised, that held her mute.

'Oh,' he murmured, tugging on one diamond stud in her ear with his teeth, 'I will be *more* than enough.'

And then he let her go so swiftly she almost collapsed to the ground. She spun away, panting and dizzy, not doubting him, the throb of her pulse echoing in newly awakened flesh, already aching and ready and lush.

'So,' he said so calmly that it was as if the last few minutes had never happened. 'Now that we've settled that, if you have no further suggestions for inclusions into our pre-nuptial agreement...?' He hesitated a moment or two. 'No? Then I'll see you at the wedding.'

She was still catching her breath, her heart still thudding, as he turned and swept from the room, his long coat swinging in his wake like a cape. Her skin still tingled from his touch, her senses still humming.

So much for her resolve to keep separate lives. How long would it take him to 'convince' her that her place was in his bed? She clutched her arms about her as she remembered the feel of his lean body pressed against hers and the way her own body had responded. Probably no more than five minutes based on what had just transpired.

Damn the man! But it didn't have to be the end. So it wasn't going to be as easy as she'd hoped—she'd just have to change her plans accordingly.

He might think he'd won that round, but there was still one hell of a battle to come.

It wasn't over yet!

CHAPTER FOUR

'I'M SO sorry, Briar, this is all my fault.'

Briar squeezed her father's hand as they waited for the organ music to come to an end. How strange it was that she should be the one calming him down right now.

'Don't worry, Dad,' she assured him with a confidence dredged up from somewhere. 'You had no choice.'

'But Briar—' he began.

'*None* of us had any choice,' she insisted. 'He never gave us a chance. But at least now we've managed to save Blaxlea from his clutches.'

Her father squirmed in his dark suit. 'Briar—'

But her father's words were cut off with the strains of the wedding march ringing out, signalling that it was time to walk down that aisle and meet her fate, signalling that it was time to meet her soon-to-be husband. A quiver of sensation zipped through her, leaving her blissfully numb in its wake, so that when her father tugged her forward into the church she went without resistance.

'I now pronounce you man and wife.'

It had to be a dream—a bad dream. Any second now she'd wake up in her own bed with the morning sun streaming through the curtains and this nightmare would fade with the darkness and she'd laugh at how ridiculous it had all been...

'You may kiss the bride.'

Oh, God. A brain spinning with the effects of weeks of barely sleeping suddenly clicked into gear and registered the truth.

There would be no waking up to the light. There would be no laughter. Instead her nightmare stared down at her, his dark eyes chasing away the morning, chasing away all hope. They regarded her now, the heated possession contained within terrifying as he drew closer, collecting her into his arms.

Her eyes looked too big for her face, her skin so pale and her limbs so fragile it was a wonder she didn't snap. Instead she came softly into his arms in a rustle of creamy silk, unprotesting rather than willing, and he swallowed back a sudden and totally unfamiliar urge to comfort her. But he didn't have to comfort her. She was his now. She would accept her fate eventually.

And then his mouth slanted over her cool lips and heat arced between them in a rush.

He felt the jolt that moved through her; angling her mouth into a better fit, he felt the heat suffuse her flesh, melting her to him, and suddenly his kiss took on a life of its own and anticipation of contact more carnal hummed through his senses. If she responded this readily to just a kiss, then how much more might he heat up her temperature tonight, when they were alone?

He drew back, watched the tawny colours in her eyes eddy and swirl before coolness once again iced their depths and turned them defiant and glinting like topaz. She couldn't disguise her cheeks so readily, though, the bright slashes of colour evidence that even if her spirit wanted to fight, her flesh was more than willing. It would be a pleasure seeing her skin flush all over. And then it would be more than a pleasure bringing her spirit into line.

Organ music soared through the lofty chapel as he laced her hand through his arm as they prepared to walk back down the aisle together as man and wife, the battery of bridesmaids and groomsmen her mother had organised from the ranks of cousins hanging behind. With Briar's two best friends now living overseas and unable to make the wedding, Carolyn had only been too pleased to take matters into her own hands and organise everything.

Her mother stopped them before they'd gone two paces, hugging her daughter tightly and greeting her new son with a kiss as tears of joy streamed down her face.

'If only Nat were here to see you now,' her mother cried, and Briar bit down on her bottom lip. At least he'd been saved from witnessing this humiliation. Her father added his quiet congratulations as slowly they continued down the length of the aisle, having their progress constantly interrupted by the babble of family members, friends and colleagues, all of them from the bride's side of the church.

The press had occupied Diablo's side; only now they'd vacated their seats to form a camera-wielding posse in front of them, leaving a sprinkling of actual guests on the groom's side of the church. Did this scattering of individuals constitute all of Diablo's family and friends? She'd heard that he'd lost both his parents, but what kind of man operated so alone in the world that he had so few other contacts? And while he was frequently featured in the social pages, he'd never been seen with the same woman twice. What kind of lone-wolf had she married?

She slid a glance up at him and his eyes and jaw gave her the answer in an instant. Hard. Uncompromising. *Difficult.*

No wonder he had no friends.

Then they were outside in the bright sunny afternoon and enduring what felt like a never-ending round of poses and photographs.

'Smile,' the photographers called, reminding her once more

to paste one on. Because it was expected of her. Because it was supposed to be the happiest day of her life.

But how did you smile when you'd just been bound legally to a man you hated, when you'd been forced into a marriage because you had no other choice, for without it your family would be reduced to nothing?

How did you smile when it was the last thing in the world you felt like doing?

The official photographer requested one more pose before they headed for the reception. He arranged them in yet another clinch, this time with Diablo behind, his arms circling her waist, and she stood stock-still, trying to ignore his warm breath in her hair and the tingling of her scalp. He nuzzled his face against her hair and breathed deeply.

'Mmm,' he whispered, the sound vibrating right down to her toes, 'you look and smell delicious enough to eat.'

Breath snagged in her throat as a wave of heat roiled through her. Those lips had taken her unaware during the wedding—it wasn't hard to imagine them pushing a trail southwards, kissing, suckling, devouring. She shivered. She didn't care what he thought and she most certainly didn't want to hear it or anything that reminded her of what lay ahead. She swivelled her head away from the photographers and hissed, 'Rest assured, it's not for your benefit.'

'And does that matter?' he asked, lifting one of her hands in his own and pressing his mouth to the back of it as camera flashes went off wildly all around them, desperate to catch the apparently gallant gesture. 'When it is indeed me who will benefit. Do you realise how much I am looking forward to this night, to peeling this garment away and seeing how beautiful you are underneath, how beautiful you are everywhere?'

Remnant heat from his last assault sparked inside her, flames licking sensitive flesh to life. She squeezed down on her muscles, hoping to clamp down on the effect of his words. 'How unfortunate,' she bit back unsteadily, 'that the feeling isn't mutual.'

'When the time is right,' he growled, with just a hint of aggravation, 'all of what we feel will be mutual. I am a generous lover, my wife; you will not be disappointed.'

She gasped and tried to push herself away but suddenly the air lacked oxygen, burnt up in the blast furnace atmosphere his words generated and in the stirring press of solid flesh behind her. Instead of letting her go, his grip around her waist tightened, keeping her impossibly close to him and his burgeoning hardness. Right now there was fabric between those places they touched, fabric that still seemed tissue thin, but later—later there would be nothing between their skin but air—and, later still, not even that.

The photographer signalled an end to the formal shots. 'You can let me go now,' she protested. 'We're all done.'

'No,' he disagreed, while still easing his grip around her waist enough so she could spin away in a flurry of silk and exasperation. 'We're not done—not by a long shot.'

'We're leaving in ten minutes. I want you to be ready.'

Briar jumped. If the low voice whispering in her left ear hadn't been enough reason to scatter her thoughts and send her pulse jumping, her new husband's seemingly casual gesture of running his fingers up her right arm certainly had been. She excused herself from the group of guests she was talking with and followed the path Diablo had taken from the enormous marquee that had been set up in the grounds.

'Diablo,' she said, hitching up her skirts and skipping after him as he entered the house, 'where are we going? There's a suite been prepared here. I assumed…'

He spun around and smiled suddenly, disarming her as he stopped in front of the majestic staircase. 'Is it not traditional in this country for a groom to take his new bride away for a honeymoon?'

'You know it is. But ours is hardly a traditional marriage. Our honeymoon is likely to be over before it's begun. Frankly I can't see the point.'

His smile widened. 'Oh, you will. This night is too special not to make the most of it, don't you agree?'

She didn't, as it happened. '"*Special*" isn't exactly the word I'd use.'

'Oh, and how would you describe it, then?'

A wedding night with Diablo? She shivered as a frosty wave of trepidation washed through her. How would anyone sane not feel fear at the thought of that lean, powerful body being unleashed on her own? Ruthless in the boardroom, ruthless in his dealings with her, why would he be anything but in the bedroom? But there was no way she'd admit she was afraid. She stiffened her spine and looked him squarely in the eye. 'As a night to be endured.'

The movement in his jaw betrayed the grinding teeth below. 'You do not enjoy the sexual act? I'm surprised…' he raked his eyes over her length '…when you look purpose-built for it.'

Camera finish make-up would help to disguise her flaming cheeks, but she knew, there was nothing to disguise her thundering heartbeat. He had to be able to hear it. Just as he must have noticed the swelling of her bustline, the peaking of her nipples.

Would he feel cheated when he discovered just how inexperienced she was? Would he find it amusing and use it as yet another tool in his arsenal of humiliation?

She turned her eyes away, gathering up her skirts. 'If you've made up your mind then, I might as well go and get changed.' She'd only reached the second step when he placed a hand to her forearm, tugging her gently back.

'You don't need to change,' he said. 'I've had a bag packed for you. I want you to accompany me just the way you are.'

'But why?' she asked, shrugging her gown's skirts in her hands for emphasis. 'Why would you want me to wear my wedding gown? I'll feel ridiculous travelling in this.' She ascended another couple of steps. 'I'm getting changed.'

'No!' He leapt up behind her and this time there was nothing gentle in his hold as he halted her progress, turning her to face him. 'I want everyone to know you are my bride and that this is our wedding night.' His eyes lingered on hers, their dark secret depths rich and thick. 'And I want everyone to know exactly what we will be doing later.'

She looked down at his hand on her arm, his golden olive skin almost glowing against her own flesh in this lighting, before lifting her gaze to his eyes. 'That's some kind of sick.'

'No. That's some kind of pride. Every man will envy me. And I want them all to know you're mine. And that tonight I will have you.'

She swallowed. 'You're kidding yourself if you think that. You don't *have* anyone merely because of one simple act.' But, even as she spoke the words, she knew that sex with Diablo would never be simple. It would be as intense as his eyes—highly charged, like that kiss at the wedding that had been no mere meeting of lips but more a bolt of electricity.

'Come now, Briar,' he soothed, urging her down the stairs. 'Nobody said anything about having you only once. I do hope you enjoyed your meal. You're going to need the stamina.'

'Whatever for?' she questioned, feeling amazed they could be so openly bantering such a topic. 'I assumed you were man enough to take care of everything.'

He drew her closer to him, a smile tugging at his lips. 'I can see I'm going to enjoy tonight immensely.'

'At least that makes one of us.'

His eyes swirled with something that looked like challenge and for a moment she half expected him to argue the point. Instead he repeated just one word.

'Immensely.'

If she'd expected to be paraded through airports in her

wedding dress she was wrong. Shortly after they'd said their goodbyes and left the reception in Diablo's red TVR Tuscan sports car, it was clear that they were heading in the wrong direction for the airport. But it didn't matter where they were going really; she knew all too well what was waiting for her when they got there—Diablo had made that more than crystal clear.

For now she was content to settle back into the prestige convertible's black leather seats, enjoying the throaty purr of the engine as it ate up the miles. Heads turned around them as the car snarled its way north up the motorway, powering through the curves with fail-safe security.

It made sense that Diablo would possess a car like this—all lean lines and rumbling power, making toast of everything else on the road. The devil's car—red and racing, its curved bonnet suggestive of the three prongs of a pitchfork, with the devil himself behind the wheel.

'You're very quiet,' he said when they'd been travelling for half an hour, the lights of the city now way behind.

'I was thinking about your car,' she said.

'Oh?' Clearly, she'd surprised him. 'Tell me.'

'I was thinking how very like you it is.'

'You don't like my car?'

She resisted the urge to laugh. He almost sounded wounded. But of course he'd make that connection.

'I mean it's very stylish and powerful and…'

He looked at her. 'And?'

She'd been going to say *wicked*, but somehow that sounded too playful and there was nothing playful about Diablo. And she dared not say *dangerous*. That would be admitting way too much.

'And powerful.'

He surveyed her for a second or two till he returned his eyes to the road. 'You already said that.'

'Did I?' she asked ingenuously, closing down the conversation by pretending interest in the dark shrouded view outside her window and trying to forget the heated prickle his eyes had burned into her skin.

Some time later she must have dozed. She came to as he pulled off the main road, making his way coastward. The lights of a small seaside town beckoned but he turned off before then to a large property on a headland overlooking the ocean.

Electronic gates opened slowly in response to Diablo hitting a button on a remote and low lighting welcomed their approach up a long driveway.

'We're here?' she asked as they pulled up outside the imposing front doors of a house that seemed to go forever, its style reminiscent of a rambling hacienda.

He turned off the engine. 'We're here.'

'Where are we exactly?'

'A place called El Paradiso, about four hours north of Sydney.'

That far? She'd more than dozed; she'd slept most of the trip away.

'Come inside,' he said. 'I'll give you the tour.'

She lifted her long skirts and let him lead her up the steps to the entrance. She'd do the tour; she'd welcome it. Anything to delay the inevitable. The inevitable that stared her in the face when they concluded the tour more than a score of spacious rooms later in the biggest bedroom she'd ever seen.

A wall of windows spanned one side, the view over the dark sea even now breathtaking, the line of surf as waves crashed into the shore turned electric-blue under the full moon's power.

But it was hardly the view that snagged her attention and turned her mouth ashen dry. It was the bed. *Their bed.* An ocean wide itself, it held pride of place opposite the wall of glass, mocking her, reminding her of exactly why she was here.

Diablo crossed the room, slid a bolt and opened a door to a

deck that stretched out seawards. Avoiding the bed, she followed, breathing in the fresh air like a salve.

'Make yourself comfortable,' he said. 'I'll get the bags and something to drink.'

'I'm surprised you don't have a cast of thousands to run and fetch for you in a place this size.'

His eyelids slid half closed. 'I think I'm capable of moving a couple of bags. But as to staff, there's Joe and Luisa, a husband and wife team who maintain the house and gardens, who have their own detached accommodation close by. Luisa acts as housekeeper and cook when I'm here. I'll introduce you tomorrow.'

It was cool on the balcony, probably too cool, but tonight she didn't care, the air from the sea refreshing against her face, blowing away the last of her travel weariness. It might have been relaxing too, in other circumstances. But not tonight, not with what she knew was going to happen next. Despite the chill in the night air, she wasn't ready to go inside and face that bed.

And yet, even now her body seemed to be preparing itself, her skin tingling, her senses humming, on alert. Soon he would be back and then he would expect her to climb into that enormous expanse of bed and he would make love to her.

No!

He would have sex with her. Making love didn't come into it. He wanted children and she was no more than his brood mare. He'd no better than bought her and now he planned to drive her as ruthlessly as he drove his car. He would make her perform. He would use her like another of his possessions.

Or so he thought. She was here now and legally she was his wife. But be damned if she'd play incubator for his spawn, regardless of the terms of the contract they'd signed. She didn't even feel guilty about the arrangements she'd made to ensure that could never happen. A judge would never find her guilty for not wanting to bring a child into existence under these circumstances.

He studied her as she stood out there on the balcony looking out to sea, her long gown rippling in the soft breeze and glowing like shifting pearls under the moonlight, tendrils of her hair tumbling loose from the sleek coil at her head, their ends kissing that long sweep of neck. She looked like an ancient goddess, borne of the moon and made for loving. And soon he would be kissing that long sweep of neck, and places far beyond.

It was time.

He adjusted the interior lamps down to low before he joined her on the balcony, holding two flutes of champagne. She started at his approach, a tightening between her brows giving way to a tell-tale flutter at her throat and a panicked flaring of her eyes, betraying her otherwise cool façade.

'Champagne?' he offered. 'To calm your nerves.'

'Who said I'm nervous?' she asked as she took the glass.

'These,' he said, touching a hand alongside her eyes, 'and—' he moved to touch the pads of his fingers to that place on her throat where her pulse was still throwing out a frantic beat '—here.'

She stiffened and pulled away from his touch, retreating to the balustrade. He let her go, watching her as she took a sip from her glass.

She hugged her arms around herself, her shoulders tight. 'Are you cold out here?' he asked. 'Do you want to go inside?'

'No!' She blurted the word out before he'd hardly finished the question. 'I mean, it's not too cold. Just refreshing.' She took another sip of her champagne, as if to prove how relaxed she was, instead of the obvious bundle of nerves she was trying to contain.

'It's so beautiful here,' she said, looking over the lights of the town below, hugging the shoreline.

'You are,' he agreed. 'You look like a goddess in that gown.'

She raised her chin defiantly. 'You told me you wanted other men to see me, to know I was yours. But we saw no one.'

'And if I'd told you I wanted you to wear that gown because you look like a fairy tale princess, would you have believed me?'

She turned back to face the sea.

'I don't believe in fairy tales.'

'Who does?' he replied, joining her at the balustrade. 'But there are certain elements that appeal.'

'What, like happily ever after?' She gave a low laugh. *Not in this case.* 'I don't think so.'

'No,' he said emphatically. 'That concept belongs exclusively in fairy tales.'

She turned to look at him, her surprise giving way to cynicism. So he was bitter and jaded? So much the better. If he felt that way, it suited her purposes perfectly. Given his cynicism, he could hardly be surprised when she walked out of this marriage at the first chance she had.

She took another sip of her champagne, already thinking ahead to when she would be free again. 'At least we have that much in common,' she mused.

He looked at her and her half drained glass, his fathomless eyes suddenly speaking volumes. 'Maybe it's time to find out what else we have in common.'

Anticipation flowed through her in a rush. But she wasn't ready. 'A generous lover', he'd described himself as. Would she find that to be true? She didn't want to. She wanted reasons to hate him instead. So, instead of answering, she turned back against the balustrade, looking out to the sea.

'What is this place?' she asked as if he'd never spoken. 'Did you build it? It looks like something straight from a Spanish movie set.'

He recognised the change of topic for the avoidance technique it was, but he'd play along for a minute if it relaxed her. No longer than that, though. Already his body was tightening, its expectations for the night to come too acute to ignore. 'I built it for my mother.'

She turned her head. 'What happened to her? I know next to nothing of your family. You've never mentioned a thing about any of them.'

He shrugged. 'It's not important.'

'Of course it's important. You expect me to sleep with you, but I don't know the first thing about who you really are. You might as well be a stranger.'

'Strangers sleep together all the time.'

Briar stiffened. 'Not this little black duck.'

'So my new wife didn't spend her university days sleeping around? So much the better.' He had no doubt he'd soon obliterate her memories of each and every one of her former lovers but the last thing he wanted was her former boyfriends crawling out of the woodwork.

Her head spun around, her amber eyes sparking like shooting stars in the moonlight. 'If you say so,' she bit back, 'but surely it must have occurred to you that I might just have spent my university days sleeping around with all the people I *did* know.'

He downed the balance of champagne in his flute in an instant, flinging it sideways to shatter into a thousand crystal shards on the far side of the balcony. 'Then what is to come will hardly be a surprise to you. I can't see the point of delaying any longer.'

She crossed her arms defiantly. 'If that's your idea of foreplay, I'd suggest you borrow a couple of books from your local library.'

In a sudden and unexpected movement he'd trapped her against the railing, imprisoning her with his arms, his body so hard against the balusters she had to unlock her arms and throw them back to steady herself.

'Something you're about to find out, my lovely wife,' he crooned as he dipped his lips to the place where her pulse jumped erratically in her throat. 'I wrote those books.'

Talk about bloody-minded arrogance! She was just about to tell him how egotistical he sounded when his tongue touched the flesh of her throat, searing her skin and damn near cauterising her words dead. Flames radiated outwards from the path his tongue was taking like a rolling tide of desire. Her breasts firmed, her nipples aching and heat pooled low down inside her. And suddenly, the way his tongue had been unleashed on her throat, she didn't doubt his claims. If he could wreak such havoc by merely touching his mouth to her neck...

Just then he lifted his head, found her mouth and transferred his magic there, his lips insistent but gentle, coaxing, encouraging. And behind it all she could taste his hunger—hunger for *her*—and resolve took a back seat and she found herself kissing him back, joining in the sensual dance of lips and mouth and tongue.

It should have been easy to resist him, to push him away, but the feelings he was unleashing inside her and the warm tingling rush of preparedness stripped down her defences. She didn't want to feel this way about Diablo! She didn't want her body to respond to someone who was so self-serving, who wasn't interested in her but for her name and her baby-bearing capabilities.

And yet her knees threatened to buckle, her spine weakening under the onslaught of his mouth and the press of his body against hers.

He lifted his head away from hers and she had to blink to clear her vision to focus on those dark eyes, almost black in this light, fully intent upon hers. But his brief absence gave her breathing space—vital breathing space—and she wasn't about to miss the opportunity to regain some kind of coolness between them. He might have the piece of paper that bound them legally together, but he had no rights over her heart and soul.

'I see,' she managed, pretending to be unmoved in a voice that sounded more like heavy breathing, while at the same time pushing against the barrier of his arms. 'In that case, I might as well go and get undressed in preparation for the main event.'

She attempted to edge out between him and the balustrade but he stopped her, one hand at her throat, his thumb gently stroking as he moved even closer. 'Oh, no, you don't,' he murmured, swinging her into his arms as easily as if she weighed nothing at all.

'Undressing you is *my* job.'

CHAPTER FIVE

DIABLO'S mouth arrested her gasp, cutting off any protest more effectively than if he'd argued the point, only this time the gentleness and sensuality of his kiss was gone, replaced by a ferocious sexuality so raw she could feel the impact to her core. He swung her into his arms as if she were weightless, moulding her to him, cradling her like a prize as he carried her inside, his mouth moving over hers with a fierceness that left her senses reeling and any protest abandoned.

She didn't have to hold him—there was no way he was about to drop her—but somehow it felt necessary to wind her arms around his neck and splay her fingers through his hair, and to graze her peaking breasts against his broad chest as she pulled herself closer to his mouth.

Diablo growled, deep in his throat, and the sound reverberated through her, sweeping to and fro like a hot tide that concentrated down to one pulsing point between her thighs.

Once inside he released her legs, letting her feet slowly slide down to the ground while his hands moulded her against him, length against length. He cupped her behind, forcing her to embrace with her body the solid column of his erection.

He was so big, so alive, the sheer force of his hardness a fascinating thing—*a terrifying thing*. To imagine that somehow she

might take that length inside her… Fear jagged through her—
and if she couldn't?

Wouldn't that be too funny? What a way that would be for
Diablo to realise he'd chosen the wrong woman for his needs.
And then he slid her shoestring straps over her shoulders and
peeled her bodice away, releasing her swollen breasts into his
hands, and a feeling akin to insanity told her it would be *she* who
would be the loser.

How could she ever have imagined she could resist him? As
soon as he touched her, she was on fire for him.

He leaned down and took one pebbled peak between his lips,
flicking the tip of it with his tongue, and need crashed through her.
Her back arched involuntarily, pushing her breasts towards him like
an invitation. He accepted, filling his mouth with her aching flesh,
circling her nipple with his tongue, scraping his teeth evocatively
over her skin while he rolled her other nipple between his fingers.

She held on to him, clutching his head and shoulders, knowing
that if she didn't she would collapse, right here and now, on the
floor. Her fingers tracked through his hair, his ponytail tie pulled
out by her fingers, his thick collar-length black hair a silken
curtain on her hands.

He lifted his head from her breast and she twisted her hands
in his hair in desperation but he only turned to her other breast,
lavishing on that nipple the same devout attention, worshipping
her flesh with his mouth.

There was slight pressure behind her and then the long sensual
glide of her zip. His hands slid under the fabric, sweeping away
the sides, turning her spine molten as finally he lifted his head
and let her gown glide, a silken waterfall, to the floor.

Eyes, at once wild and desperate, regarded her in a hot display
of need, taking in her peaked breasts, her tiny scrap of underwear
and the lace-topped stockings. He dragged in a breath so hard
she felt the rush of air.

'*Dios*,' he rasped, 'but you are beautiful.'

Her own breathing was just as out of control. Fast and shallow, she felt light-headed and faint and never more in need all at the same time. He seemed to sense her condition and in an instant he'd swept her out of the circle of her gown and laid her reverently on the bed.

'So beautiful,' he growled as he wrenched off his jacket and shirt and threw them into the corner. Her eyes widened at the satin perfection of his olive skin, the play of light and shadow over the muscled walls of his chest. She ached to touch him there and to run her hands over that perfect surface, to where his tight waist disappeared into the waistband of his trousers—the waistband he was now unbuttoning.

His shoes and socks had gone while her eyes were elsewhere and now his trousers joined them. Her mouth went dry as his silken briefs outlined the burgeoning force beneath, bucking with its own life force. Oh, what was she doing? She was such a fraud. She couldn't do this!

And then he eased his underwear over and down and her mind went blank. He joined her on the bed, collecting her into his arms, and with trepidation tempered with relief she joined willingly in his kiss as his hands swept her curves, tracking over her super-charged flesh in an erotic dance.

Every part of her seemed on fire. Every part of her came alive as he followed the trail of his touch with his mouth. Once again he suckled her breasts and this time she was grateful she was lying down. She was past standing, past holding herself together. His fingers traced down her legs and up again, driving her crazy with both their proximity and their distance to that aching core, but when his hand lingered over her mound she tensed.

'*Diablo*,' she pleaded.

'I know,' he murmured as his tongue lazily snaked around her nipple.

But he didn't know. He couldn't. And when his hands had worked away her damp underwear and his fingers dipped lower, separating her and exploring her innermost flesh, circling one tight bud, she was too far gone to explain.

'So ready,' he murmured, 'so slick.'

And, as if to prove a point, he slid one finger deep inside. She gasped at the intimate intrusion at the same time that he groaned, a desperate kind of sound that he followed with a rush of words and action.

'And so tight!'

He lunged up the bed, positioning himself between her legs, nudging himself against her slick core.

'Diablo!' she cried as the pressure mounted below—unfamiliar pressure, pushing against flesh untested, unproven.

'So tight,' he repeated as he pushed through her final barrier in one long fluid lunge.

She tensed, expecting pain, but there was none. Only pressure, a feeling of fullness that stretched and filled her inside in a way she'd never dreamed possible.

His eyes sought hers, as if he sensed something wrong, even as he pulled slowly out of her. *Could he tell?* She felt her muscles contract around him, not wanting to let him go, but then he lunged into her again, and then again.

She followed his lead, the rhythm beating furiously between them, the tide rising, carrying her higher and higher up the shore, while his dark eyes continued to stare down at her, the beads of sweat on his forehead proclaiming both his effort and his control.

She held his eyes while she matched his movements, tilting her hips towards him, letting the tide sweep her up with his next deep thrust, until she couldn't hold his gaze any longer. Her head thrashed from side to side as he slammed into her, the tide lifting her one last time before it smashed her against the cliff face in an explosion of starlit sea foam.

He crashed right behind her, his body tensing before his final shuddering release, collapsing alongside her, bringing her still joined with him.

They lay together, their breathing slowly easing, their bodies spent. So that was sex, she mused, knowing it was better than she'd ever imagined possible. And if that was sex with someone you detested, what must it feel like to actually make love with someone you cared about?

She turned her head sideways, watched his face, his eyes closed, his breathing now slow and even as if he was sleeping. Now would be a good time to get out from under his arm and find something to cover her up.

She made a move to ease herself away but his arm tightened over her, preventing her escape. 'No,' he said, his eyes opening to reveal dark thunder as he raised himself up on one elbow over her.

'Why didn't you tell me you were a virgin?'

Silence stretched out between them, strained within a millimetre of breaking-point. So he had realised. But what did it matter? Was he now going to pretend contrition? He'd wanted her in his bed and he'd got what he'd wanted.

She swallowed, still feeling suddenly shy and nervous and exposed. 'How did you know?'

'Did you think you could hide the truth from me?'

She shrugged and turned her head away. 'I should have realised such a hot-shot lover would recognise a total novice in an instant.'

'Did I hurt you?'

'What do you care?'

'You should have told me.'

'Why? What the hell difference would it have made? Am I to suddenly believe you care how I feel? Not likely.'

His eyes hardened, their surface reflecting a play of light and dark like some shiny glinting stone.

'What does it matter? It matters because it means your father is a worse businessman than even I gave him credit for.'

'What are you talking about?'

'I would have settled upon him twice the amount if I'd known you were a virgin.'

'You bastard!' She pushed at his shoulders and attempted to wrench her leg out from under him at the same time. 'You can't buy and sell people like just one more of your precious properties. It doesn't work that way.'

'No?' he questioned, making a mockery of her attempts to escape. 'Well, it sure got me you, and...' He pressed himself to her side and, with a small cry of shock, she felt him hardening against her. 'It got me you, right where I want you to be.'

'You disgust me!' she said, trying desperately to edge away even as the knowledge he was hard again and wanting her caused her flesh to tingle once more in preparation.

'Do I?' he challenged, jamming her free arm back against the pillows, covering her mouth with a crushing kiss that took her breath away with its ruthless ferocity, so punishing was its intensity.

'Do I really disgust you?' he demanded, when finally he withdrew from the kiss, his lips hovering bare millimetres above hers. 'That's not the impression you gave me earlier.'

'So I was keen to be rid of my virginity at last. Don't fancy yourself—I had to throw it away on someone! You just happened to be the only one around.'

With a twist of his body he'd insinuated one knee between her legs, his body now hovering over her like a thundercloud.

'And I could have sworn you enjoyed every minute of it.' The words were squeezed out of a grimace chiselled from a granite-lined face.

'Sorry to disappoint you.'

'Really? So I didn't just make you come?'

She glared up at him. 'I was faking it.'

His eyes turned suddenly feral, glistening, and instantly she could see he'd taken her blatant lie for a challenge.

'Then how about I give you a chance to "fake it" again?'

'Diablo!' she cried, but he'd already positioned himself, his intentions clear. Immediately she regretted her foolish words, afraid of being swept away by the maelstrom this man conjured up in, but already he was nudging against that sensitive flesh, testing her newfound muscles as he pressed himself home, and her protest turned into a gasp as she received him, her back arching as he drew one peaked nipple into his hot wet mouth.

He drove into her, almost to the hilt, before withdrawing in a rush that had her gasping all over again with the sudden loss.

'You don't enjoy this?' he growled roughly against the flesh of her breast, his voice thick before his tongue curled once more around her nipple.

Then he drove into her again, this time deeper, withdrawing again only to power himself home once more.

'Or this?'

Spears of current coursed through her, forming an inner circuitry from her breasts to the muscles framing him, stretched and tight. It was impossible not to like it. It was just as impossible to utter more than a breath of appreciation every time he filled her.

His eyes glittered above her as slowly he built up the speed, burying himself ever deeper, ramping up the power, crashing and thundering into her like a storm front. And obviously satisfied she was faking nothing, he returned his attention to her breasts, tugging at her nipples with his teeth, filling his mouth with her aching flesh, every flick of his tongue lashing at her defences, every nip of his teeth drawing her further into the turbulence.

So she clung to him, going with him, fearful that if she let go she'd be spun and tossed away. She anchored herself against him, caught up in the raw energy he was unleashing in them both, reducing her entire world to this one intense whirlpool.

And when she came it was at the height of the storm, with a thunderclap like a roar from the gods splitting the heavens asunder, and she was thrown into the darkness, fractured and broken and spent, while the waves of shuddering slowly abated, rolling through her like thunder disappearing rumbling away into the distance.

Precipitation coated her cheeks in the storm's wake as she realised what she'd done. Once again she'd let her body betray her. Once again she'd let herself be carried away in passion by Diablo. She rolled herself away, taking advantage of his momentary inertia, swiping at his too-late grabbing attempt to stop her.

'Let me go,' she insisted on a sob, turning her head away so he wouldn't see the tracks of her tears as she bolted from the bed.

'Still faking it?' he called out behind her, his words a steely accusation.

'I'd say you made your point perfectly, wouldn't you?'

She snatched up her handbag on the way to the *en suite* bathroom, locking the door behind her before dragging on a robe hanging at the back of the door. It was way too big but right now she just needed something gentle against her skin, something warm and comforting after the cold fire that was Diablo. Then she dived into her bag, desperately burrowing through the contents until she found what she was looking for. She popped the bubble and pushed out the tiny pill into the palm of her hand.

The door handle rattled behind her. 'Briar!' he called. 'Are you all right?'

'You expect me to believe you care?'

'Let me in.'

'Go to hell!' she yelled. *Back where you belong.* The door rattled one more time before she heard a muttered curse and the sound of his irate footsteps receding across the jarrah floorboards. She took a deep breath as she turned back, shocking herself when she caught sight of her reflection in the mirror. Some time during the action her hair had fallen free of restraint to float wildly around her shoulders, her lips looked pink and tender, their edges smudged and ill-defined, and her eyes stared back at her, wide and lost. Some time tonight, maybe the moment he'd swept her up in his arms, she'd lost herself. She'd lost her way. She'd clung to him, wanting him to take her higher, wanting him to love her, even when she knew she shouldn't.

Tears slid silently down her cheeks. So much for her resistance. It had crumbled with one touch of his mouth. And the shame of it was that he could do it all again just as easily. Now she had but one defence.

She threw her hand to her mouth and swallowed the pill down, chasing it with a scoop of water from the tap, before stashing the pills back in her bag and zipping them down tight.

Because, damn him to hell and back, she might have to endure his passion and his bed, but she would *never* bear his child!

Diablo paced the room like a caged lion, eating up the metres of polished floorboards between each wall as if it was a shoebox rather than the massive suite that it was.

Why the hell hadn't she told him? He'd never suspected she was a virgin—she'd never so much as hinted—but then, when he'd driven into her, experiencing her impossibly sweet tightness, he'd wondered. She hadn't cried out but she'd tensed suddenly around him like a vice, her eyes wide open and startled like a doe's, and the half formed question in his mind had turned to suspicion.

But he still hadn't been sure, not totally, until she'd confirmed it with her quiet affirmation.

'How did you know?'

She'd admitted everything with those four simple words. He

paused before the sliding doors, looking out at the dark sea as it shifted, its surface glistening in the moonlight.

Dios! Why hadn't she alerted him? And then, damn her, why had she acted as if it hadn't mattered? As if it was nothing special?

He was pleased there had been no other lovers. Relieved. And yet he had rewarded her virtue by taking her roughly, *cruelly*, not once, but twice, the second time even *after* he knew how inexperienced she was.

This was no way to introduce a woman into the ways of the bedroom. She could be a willing pupil too, if he took his time, if he showed her what was possible, instead of acting like a monster in her bed. And he wanted her to learn. For her first time she'd been amazingly responsive—*no wonder he'd been uncertain*—her body melding with his, moving with his rhythm, matching it and meeting his rise and fall as if she was born to it. And when she'd come apart in his arms it had been real, for them both. No wonder he'd been so keen to take her again so quickly.

His body stirred, his blood quickening and collecting as he recalled her sweet curves, her deliciously smooth skin that felt like silk and tasted like honey. Oh, yes, he'd make amends by showing her how it could be between a man and a woman.

But not tonight. He looked down at himself and cursed. After what had happened before, the last thing she needed was to see him like this. And he didn't want her on guard, he didn't need her any more scared. He wanted her receptive and warm and eager. But if he saw her emerge from the bathroom now, all fresh-skinned and gleaming and dressed in little more than a towel, then he wouldn't be going soft any time soon.

Damn! What he needed right now was a different kind of exercise. He needed laps. Mind-numbing, body-punishing, repetitive laps.

He turned his back on both the view of the shimmering sea

and the promise of the glittering jewel that lay behind the door to the *en suite* bathroom and headed for the indoor pool.

He was gone. The dimly lit room wore his absence like a vacuum, expanding to twice the size without his aura to eat up the space. Briar let go a breath she'd been holding and pushed herself away from the door frame. She'd been braced for...what? Another confrontation? Another battle leading to sex? Whatever it was, she was relieved he had taken himself away some time while she'd stood under the shower and tried to scour all trace of his touch from her skin.

Not that it had worked. Her skin might be relieved of a layer or two of cells but what chance did mere soap have in eradicating the memories of the fires he'd lit under the surface? Even now her skin prickled with newly discovered sensations at the memories.

I hate him, she told herself, while she hated herself even more for the strange sexual fascination he'd awakened within her. Never before had she experienced such earth-shattering sensations. She'd be lying if she pretended she hadn't liked it...if she pretended she didn't want more...

With a shiver she pushed herself away from the door and darted across the room to where he'd left her bag. A quick run through the contents turned to two and still no nightgown. But why was that not a surprise? She could just imagine him giving the command for someone to pack her bag *sans* night attire. Well blow him, she thought, diving under the rumpled covers without removing the robe. As defences went, it wasn't much, but she felt safer just hugging it around herself.

Where was Diablo, anyway? Already sick of her? Or still seething after her stinging insult to his manhood? He needn't be; he'd more than proved she wasn't immune to his charms.

For a long time she lay there, her eyes flying awake at the slightest noise, her ears straining for the sound of an approaching footfall, but all she heard was the rhythmic whoosh of the ocean as it slid endlessly up and down the shore below, gradually quietening as sleep came up to claim her.

He watched her while she slept, her eyes closed, her lashes meshed together, her lips slightly parted, while burnished copper laced hair spilled loose beneath her on the pillow. A picture of innocence. But then, not quite so innocent any more.

A swell of masculine pride overcame him. She was his now and his alone. Nobody had had her before him. Nobody would again. Nobody but him.

It was enough to make him hard again, despite still feeling the effects of his ten kilometre swim. He shook his head as he eased himself into bed alongside her. He had chosen well indeed when he had decided on Briar Davenport for the mother of his children.

CHAPTER SIX

WARMTH enveloped Briar like a drug, holding her hostage to sleep, even as the lightening sky told her it must be morning. But it wasn't the sunlight infiltrating the curtains at the window that made her snap her eyes open, but the sudden understanding of the source of her comfort.

Diablo's body curved around hers, one arm thrown casually over her hip, a hip that nestled in dangerous proximity to another more carnal source of heat. She tensed and immediately regretted it. For even the tiniest movement meant friction between his naked body and the robe she still had tightly wound around her.

He shifted in his sleep, his hard length grazing her while his hand drifted north to come to rest at the under-swell of her breast. Oh, Lord, if even his unintentional touch through a layer of towelling sent sparks shimmying through her, then how much more so would it be when he woke and expected to make love to her? Already her breasts felt tight and full, her nipples at attention, longing for his hand to slip further around and tighten over them. Already flesh so tender it should ache for days seemed to tingle back into life.

How could it be so?

After last night she should hate him more than ever, but what her mind told her and what her body craved seemed to be two different things. Diablo had thrown a switch inside her that had her body wilfully ignoring her head.

Behind her Diablo stirred again and she held her breath. His arm dropped to her hip again and tightened, pulling her hard against his erection as he raised himself on one elbow and dropped his lips to her cheek.

'Good morning, Mrs Barrentes,' he growled in that way that rumbled right through to her core.

'Morning,' she replied thinly, on tenterhooks, waiting for him—*expecting him*—to push her robe away and take her right then and there.

Already her blood had thickened to a crawl, her breathing similarly hindered as she anticipated what was to follow.

Then his hand disappeared with a lurch of the bed and he launched himself from the other side. Anticipation turned to an unexpectedly bitter stab of disappointment.

'What would you like to do today?' he asked, padding across the floor to slide the door to the balcony open, seemingly unconcerned by his nakedness and his lingering erection as he breathed in the new day. She studied him, standing there. If she hadn't realised it last night, the cold light of morning told her just how perfect a male specimen her new husband was. His body was sculpted perfection, from his broad shoulders down to the muscled wall of his chest and tapering to those lean and powerful hips. The view from the back lacked nothing either—the dimples either side of his spine where his waist was most narrow and, further down, the tight symmetry of his behind. She forced her eyes away. She shouldn't stare.

Because she didn't care what he looked like, not really. It was just that she'd never had the opportunity to study the male animal in such detail before.

'Would you like to visit some local galleries?' he asked over his shoulder, not waiting for an answer. 'Or take a walk along the beach to the town?'

Confusion muddied her thoughts. For a man who last night had been as hungry as a wolf, and who looked ready to go another three rounds right now, the noticeable absence of a continuing-where-he-left-off-last-night option on that list of suggestions was damning. And no, not even the renowned Diablo Barrentes could believe himself so virile that his work was done and that she was pregnant already.

She pushed herself up in the bed. Was he already tired of her? She'd been sampled and found wanting, too inexperienced, too argumentative. He was no doubt more conversant with a more amenable lover. *All of which helped her case*, she realised with a jolt. If she didn't breed, which she most certainly wouldn't, then this crazy marriage wouldn't last a year, let alone two.

And wasn't that just what she wanted?

So where was the sweet whiff of satisfaction that should have accompanied that thought? Damn, but it was irritating. Just like him parading around in the buff was irritating.

'Don't you have a robe you can put on or something?'

He turned towards her, his lips raised in a smile. 'Does my body bother you?'

'Of course not,' she lied, feeling suddenly too hot and uncomfortable in bed. 'I just thought you might be cold.'

'Do I look cold to you?' He turned fully side on to her so there was no way she could miss his meaning.

Hell, no! Even half erect he looked hot enough to set the sheets ablaze if he came anywhere near them. She blinked and tried—unsuccessfully—to drag her eyes away, fascinated as he pulsed and grew.

'I wouldn't know,' she lied again through a mouth so suddenly dry it was like talking through a layer of ash.

He raised one eyebrow and moved closer to the bed, with a fluid stealth to his steps like a jungle cat closing in on a kill, the look in his eyes dark and turbulent.

This is it, she realised as she pushed herself back against the bed head, her pulse racing as she watched him draw closer, anticipation curling and unfurling in her gut. *At last...*

He leaned over, placing his two hands on to the bedcover either side of her, pinning her down.

'Besides which...' he whispered as he reached one hand up behind her neck, causing her breath to hitch as her world slowed down to a crawl. His fingers caressed her neck, a sensual massage of fingertips and thumb. His lips slow danced a bare millimetre from her own. Already she could taste their welcoming warmth, already she could feel their fluid glide over her own. Then, without warning, his hand dropped to her collar and he tugged on it twice. '...you're wearing my robe.'

It took a moment for his words to register. Especially when she was still too busy looking forward to the meshing of his lips with hers.

But in the space of a blink his eyes had gone from fiery intent to mocking, the sensual slash of his lips now tilted up in amusement, and she realised she'd just been played for a prize fool.

Bile rose in her throat. He'd never intended to make love to her. It had never been on his agenda this morning at all. And yet she'd practically rolled over for him, the man she was supposed to hate. *Did hate.* Especially now. Diablo inspired hate like an art form.

She scooted to the far side of the bed and threw back the covers, collecting the voluminous folds of the robe around her before brushing her hair back from her face.

'Sorry. I won't make the same mistake again. It just seems that nobody thought to pack me any pyjamas or a robe.'

He stood, the look in his eyes inscrutable. 'Maybe because *"nobody"* thought you'd need them.'

'Then nobody was wrong.'

His eyes regarded her coolly. 'There's no need for prudishness now. You are my wife and you have a beautiful body. It's no crime to display it.'

'And if I don't wish to display it?'

After a moment's hesitation he just shrugged. 'Have a shower. I'll get breakfast and coffee organised. I think we'll have it on the terrace. Then I'll take you for a drive. It might relax you.'

'You think? With you along it would have to be one hell of a drive.'

His chest rose on a mighty breath, his nostrils flaring. 'I'll see you on the terrace,' he said at last, as he strode into the adjoining dressing room and slammed the door.

It was relaxing too, Briar thought, or maybe it was just the after-effects of the glass of wine with her bowl of spaghetti marinara. Whatever, it had been hours since they'd left the house, tense and silent, this morning, driving along the coast, streaking along the highway with the top down and the balmy wind in their hair. Together they'd checked out every small town for their galleries and coffee shops until finally they'd found a tiny Italian restaurant with a view out past the string of pine trees that fringed the shoreline to the grey-blue sea and had settled in for a late lunch.

The table had been cleared, their coffee brought and for the first time an easy peace seemed to settle over them. Diablo leaned back in his chair, his white knitted top stretching tight over his broad chest, the colour a bold contrast that only emphasised his olive skin and Spanish good looks.

She regarded his profile as he looked out to sea—the heavy slash of eyebrows, the strong line of nose, the autocratic chin. Not classically handsome by any means but certainly head-turning. In another century Diablo would have been a conquistador, a Spanish adventurer, intent on invasion and conquest. She took a sip of her latte. Funny how some things never changed.

His head swung around, his eyes capturing her frank apprai-sal and narrowing in response.

'You look deep in thought.'

She cradled the warm glass of latte between her hands, feeling suddenly caught out, glad to have something inanimate to suddenly focus her attention on.

'Why did they call you Diablo? Doesn't that mean devil in Spanish? It seems an odd name to give a baby.'

He smiled and leaned forward. 'You don't think it suits me?'

She replaced her coffee cup on its saucer and regarded him levelly. 'I'm just wondering how they got it so right.'

His smile broadened, suddenly taking his features beyond head-turning and into another attention-riveting league entirely.

'*Touché*. It's not a conventional baby name. But my mother was hardly conventional. And hers wasn't an easy pregnancy. I made her suffer so much she took to calling me *el diablo adentro*—the devil inside.' He shrugged. 'The name stuck.'

It was the most he'd ever told her about his family.

'What was your mother like?' she asked, her interest piqued.

He leaned back into his chair, linking his hands over his stomach, looking up at the ceiling. 'She was a strong woman, beautiful and passionate.'

Like mother, like son.

'And your father?'

'I never knew my father. He died before we came to Australia.' His voice was flat, bleak. And, while his eyes were fixed on the ceiling above, it was clear his focus was elsewhere.

'It must have been so difficult for your mother to move from Spain to Australia under such circumstances. Why did she do it?'

'She had no choice. And it wasn't Spain, but Chile.'

'I thought you were Spanish.'

'Yes, Castilian. My parents' families came from a region near Madrid. But my grandparents opposed their marriage—they were both very young and their families were very rich with their own ideas as to their children's future—so they left everything behind and ran away together.'

'But why Chile? Surely at that time it wasn't safe.'

His mouth tightened. 'They knew it wasn't safe, but they were principled. My father had studied medicine and was in demand by the aid agencies, and they saw the chance to work together to help people rather than live in comfort at home but apart. Two years later my father was killed in an attack on their hospital, my mother narrowly escaping, only then realising she was pregnant. She wanted to continue my father's work but I made her too sick to help anyone and then the situation became too dangerous. She fled.'

'She couldn't go home to Spain?'

'Her family had disowned her. She had defied them. They wanted nothing to do with her.'

'Oh, God.' She could barely imagine the suffering his mother had been through, or the pain. And then the bitterness when her family had turned their backs on her in her hour of need— pregnant with their grandchild and still they had wanted nothing more to do with her. It was too horrible. 'How did she ever cope?'

'She worked,' he continued. 'She cleaned, she cooked. She washed and ironed—all her life she battled to bring me up.'

'She must have been so proud of you.'

He looked sharply across at her, a frown drawing his thick dark brows even closer together. Then he lifted his cup to his lips, finishing the rest of his coffee in one swallow. 'It's time we were moving on,' he told her as he stood up to go.

Two and a half hours and a dozen tiny tourist havens later, Diablo turned the car for home.

Briar pushed herself back in the plush leather upholstery. He'd been so different today from the Diablo she was used to.

He'd been charming, the perfect companion as they'd explored shop after shop and she'd surprised herself by actually enjoying his company. And now she knew more about his family than ever before. How that must have shaped him—never knowing his father, being raised by a mother who'd lost everything, including the love of her life, and who had been reduced to refugee status. And, after all that, she'd had to slog her guts out to provide for her son.

Was it any wonder he was driven to succeed? He'd built his mother that house overlooking the sea. He'd given her back something of what she'd lost. Before today, she wouldn't have thought him capable of thinking about anyone but himself.

She slid a glance sideways in his direction, taking in his strong profile. Which one was the real Diablo—the ruthless businessman who undercut the competitor's position until their business collapsed or the charming, flashing-eyed Continental with the heartrending heritage?

He turned his head, capturing her gaze, his dark eyes hidden by his wraparound sunglasses. But they didn't disguise the shift in his brow as he frowned.

'Tired?' he asked, before turning his attention back to the road.

'A little,' she replied honestly.

'Maybe a quiet night is in order.'

His words and his voice stroked her like a caress. But it was the look he followed it with that struck her, melting her bones so that her body sank deeper into the upholstery. 'Or at least,' he added, his look full of meaning, 'an early one.'

His words seemed to smoulder between them. Last night hadn't been quiet, the chemistry between them explosive, the electricity sparking. She swallowed, dry-mouthed, the moisture in her body gravitating south. Was she ready to go another round with Diablo? Her body seemed to think so.

But she'd been ready this morning too, when she'd thought

he was similarly coming on to her, only to have him reject her cold. It hadn't been because he wasn't aroused—there was no way a man that erect wasn't aroused. But after his sensual provocation—his lean, stealthy walk towards her, his pinning her to the bed—after all that, his calculated withdrawal had been like a slap in the face.

Was that what he was doing now—building her up only to smash her down again? Undermining her confidence and her new-found sexuality as effectively as he'd undercut every one of the Davenport business interests, toying with her father's defences until he was ultimately ruined.

She couldn't let that happen to her again. Just as she should never let herself be swayed by his sad stories. This was the same man who had coldly destroyed her father's business. He'd damned near destroyed all of their lives. How could she so easily dismiss what he'd done simply because he knew how to make her feel like a woman?

No, she had to keep what he'd done in the forefront of her mind and ensure she kept a tight lid on her body's reactions. Diablo Barrentes would not possess her. She wouldn't let him.

With a newly reclaimed backbone, she straightened in her seat, directing her attention outside the car.

'Whatever.'

He dragged in a breath and checked the oncoming lane before accelerating in a roar of power past the stream of vehicles ahead, leaving them almost dawdling in their wake.

She wanted him—he could tell. All day long he'd been breaking down the barriers between them, warming her to him, and it had been working. He'd even surprised himself by telling her more about his family than he'd ever told another living soul. And she'd listened, as if she cared, as if it mattered to someone else other than him. But then the golden shutters had come down in her eyes and closed her off to him again.

Damn! His body ached to join with her again. He could have had her this morning too, if he'd wanted. Even huddled behind the covers he had seen she'd just about been begging for it and, *dios*, he'd been more than tempted. But he'd still been too angry—with her for not telling him she'd been a virgin—with himself for making no allowances for it. And he didn't want to take her angry—not next time. He wanted to savour her, to take her slow and not in a heated rush.

Besides, she would enjoy it more when her muscles had time to recover from last night's onslaught. He registered the heated concentration of blood at the memories of entering that glorious body and cursed under his breath. If only he could convince his own body he was prepared to wait that long!

Another vehicle slowed their progress, seguing with his frustration, until the road ahead cleared and the Tuscan's acceleration once again came into its own. He loved how this car handled—its sleek lines, its throaty purr when it idled and its all out roar when he pushed it to the limits. It was almost like handling a woman, putting her through her paces, having her perform at his bidding.

So Briar liked to think she was different? She'd proven with her response to him last night that she wasn't *that* different. It wouldn't take long but she'd come around.

And, when she did, he'd drive her wild. So he would have to wait a bit longer? She would be worth the wait. No question.

The sky was already tinted with a reddish-gold sunset when twenty minutes later he pulled the car up alongside the house. She was out of the door and up the few steps to the porch before he had a chance to round the car and open it for her.

'Briar?'

She pulled off her sunglasses as she wheeled around, tension lining her eyes, her mouth tight as she looked down at him. 'I've got a headache. If you don't mind, I think I might just lie down for a while.'

A headache? The oldest excuse under the sun and she was aiming it at him?

He climbed the steps slowly. Decisively. 'That came on suddenly.' There'd certainly been no sign of it earlier, not until he'd made mention of having an early night. Since then she hadn't said a word, making the rest of their journey in stony silence.

Her eyes followed his ascent up the steps, until she was looking up at him. 'I'm tired. It's been a long couple of days.'

'And dinner?'

She shook her head. 'I don't want anything.'

'Suit yourself,' he said gruffly, reaching past her for the door handle. 'In that case I'll be in my office. I've got plenty of work to do.'

'I can imagine. All those corporate takeovers to manage must take some strategising.'

The snippy edge to her voice irritated him bone-deep and he straightened, pulling his hand away. 'It seems your headache doesn't make you too ill to want to stick your thorns into me.'

She laughed, a harsh, bitter sound. 'You don't even try to deny it.'

'Don't knock it, Briar. I'm a businessman and, without my business, your father wouldn't have the funds now to keep himself and your precious family home afloat. He and your family, yourself included, would have sunk into the gutter without trace.'

'Only because you'd already deposited us there in the first place! You destroyed his business, you stole his clients, you undercut prices till they were unsustainable and drove us into loss!'

'And that's all down to me? And why is it, then, that your father could not defend himself against me, a brash newcomer on the scene, and him a fourth generation businessman? Don't you think it seems unlikely, given his pedigree?'

'You know why. Everybody knows why.'

He tilted his head, moved a step closer, more than satisfied when she backed herself hard against the wall, her hands splayed flat against it. 'Maybe you should fill me in.'

Under the rays from the setting sun her eyes sparked gold fire, her full lips pouting with indignation and he could almost hear the machinations of her mind.

'All right. If you're so desperate to hear what everyone thinks about you. You've only got to where you are because you're ruthless and cruel and think nothing of grinding other people into the dirt beneath your feet. You'll stop at nothing to reach the top, no matter who you hurt along the way, no matter what the cost.'

Her chest was heaving, her colour high, and he was content to drink in her passion and her intensity while she battled to steady her breathing. She was beautiful when she was angry, her eyes alight with challenge, clearly anticipating some kind of fiery response. He smiled. He wasn't about to give her one.

He placed one hand on the wall beside her head and leaned closer, watching her eyes widen when he trailed the fingertips of his other hand down the side of her face.

'And this is a problem because…?'

Her chest rose on a gasp and she turned her head away from him. 'I don't believe you! You're actually proud of your reputation.'

'And you would believe me if I tried to defend myself?'

'Not a chance!'

He shrugged and took her chin between his thumb and forefinger, tilting her face up to his. 'Then why should I bother? You've already made up your mind about me. I'm cruel and ruthless, you say, then so be it. I would hate to disappoint you, my prickly wild rose.'

'I am not your wild rose!' she insisted, trying unsuccessfully to shrug her chin out of his grip. 'I am not your *anything*!'

He tugged her chin higher, leaning in towards her—so close

he could feel her own sweet scent weave its web around him, so close he could taste her heat. 'You are my wife.'

'Only because a lousy piece of paper says so.'

'No! Because you are my woman!'

His mouth cut short her protest, her already parted lips making his quest even easier, giving him access to pillage her mouth, to drink from her sweetness, to feed and build a hunger he felt like a wild animal raging inside him.

One hand tangled in her hair, angling her head closer, releasing the pin at the nape of her head and sending her hair spilling over his forearm like a silken wash.

Dios, but he'd been waiting for this all day.

For an eternity.

She tasted so good. She felt like heaven—her lips, her hair. But it wasn't enough. His hand swept up under her jacket, pulling the fabric of her top away with his thumb. She shuddered as he captured her breast, cupping its fullness, feeling the inviting press of her nipple against his palm. He found that tight bud, rolling it between his fingers, making her moan into his mouth.

And still it wasn't enough. Would it ever be enough? The fleeting thought was irrelevant. He wanted her, and badly. Desperation drove his actions. Anticipation fuelled his every move. He had to have her.

But, dammit, not this way!

It wasn't enough to take her. Not this time. She already thought him little more than an animal. It was time to prove to her there was more to sex than angry rutting. But first she had to want him. She had to be the one who made the first move. He drew his head back, filling his hand with her and squeezing her perfect breast one last time, committing the feel of her in his hand to memory, as he breathed in the heady scent of passion filled air.

She was drowning, battling for oxygen, battling to stay on top of a world that was reeling beneath her, battling to convince herself that she wanted him to stop. So that when he did suddenly, without warning, she felt cheated, embarrassed that it was he who had pulled out of the kiss.

'So what happens now?' She forced the words through choppy breathing and still shakier resolve. 'You throw me to the floor and take me like the caveman you are?'

'If I were going to take you, I wouldn't wait to get you to the floor. I'd take you right here, right now, hard up against this wall.'

A sizzle of sexual excitement coursed through her at the idea, until indignation snuffed it out. 'If I *were* going to take you…' he'd said.

So what was stopping him? She sure as hell hadn't been able to. She hadn't wanted his advances, hadn't gone looking for them, but that hadn't stopped her body embracing every move of his, every thrust of his tongue. If he hadn't stopped, she wasn't entirely sure she could have.

His chest heaving, his eyes guarded with new-found control, he pushed away from the wall—*away from her*—magnifying her frustration with each additional centimetre of distance he placed between them.

Damn him! Hadn't she'd known he'd do exactly this? It was this morning happening all over again. She'd known that he'd take any opportunity to arouse her and then drop her dead, hanging her out to dry.

'Thank heavens you seem to have come to your senses then,' she lied, smoothing her clothing in an attempt to appear blasé. 'I can't say I'd relish either option.'

'No? Then maybe you should tell me what option you would relish.'

'What do you mean?'

'The next time we make love—you will decide when. You will decide how.'

She hesitated, not believing what she'd heard. 'You're saying that you won't make love to me until I give you permission to?'

'No. Not until you *ask* me to.'

She threw her head back and laughed. Maybe she didn't need those contraceptive pills after all. She might be weak when it came to resisting his advances, but there was no way she'd be the one to come on to him. If he remained true to his word and left her alone, she'd already won. 'Then I hope you're a patient man, Diablo, because you're going to have a long wait.'

His eyes narrowed, a muscle twitched in his cheek.

Serves him right, she thought. He'd probably been expecting her to roll over and beg for it right here and now. 'An *awfully* long wait,' she added for good measure.

He loosened his jaw enough to utter just two tight words. 'We'll see.'

'Don't flatter yourself. Do you think you're so irresistible that I'll somehow end up begging you to make love to me?'

He said nothing for a while, just continued to regard her solemnly as they stood framed in the fading evening light, before finally he turned away, pushing open the heavy timber doors. 'I can wait.'

CHAPTER SEVEN

'WHEN are we going back to Sydney?'

On the lounger beside her, she was aware of Diablo stirring and rising up on to one elbow. At their feet the large indoor pool sparkled blue under the clear roof that let the ultraviolet rays in and turned a grey autumn day outside into an indoor summer.

'Don't tell me you're not enjoying our honeymoon?'

'No,' she said, slipping a bookmark into a novel she'd bought during their latest outing. Normally she'd never put down a book by her favourite author, but today everything was wrong, the book not holding her interest, the lounger chair feeling lumpy and uncomfortable, her bikini top straps biting into her shoulders and even the air inside the enormous climate-controlled room feeling too closed in and stuffy. 'It's very…relaxing. But how long are we staying?'

She looked at him, waiting for an answer, and immediately wished she hadn't. *And that was part of her problem.* She wanted to look away but the sight of that broad sweep of satin-smooth skin, packed with rippled muscle tone and corded tautness, wouldn't let her. How could she tear her eyes away from his tightly packed waist and the line of dark hair that led inexorably lower, when it was all she could do to breathe? In a concession to her modesty he was wearing trunks—low black trunks that accentuated more than they hid, low black trunks that had her thinking of—*had her remembering*—what lay below. Even now as she watched the fabric seemed to stir and strain, causing the blood in her own veins to slow to a crawl.

Was that why her pulse kicked up a gear? Was that why it suddenly thundered so loud in her ears—to try to force her sluggish blood from stalling in her veins?

But it wasn't just her blood. Everything, even time itself, seemed to thicken and slow.

'You're bored?'

His words drew her gaze to his face, his dark eyes reflective, brooding, his dark hair loosely tucked behind his ears. Didn't he know? Nobody could ever get bored looking at Diablo. It was like studying some nameless statue carved in marble and wondering at the man who had been so godlike as to have been chosen as the subject. Diablo, with his aristocratic features and powerful shoulders and broad chest, could have been that man, facsimile of the gods and the sculptor's choice.

She unglued her tongue from the roof of her mouth. She'd already swum more laps than she could remember today but it didn't seem nearly enough. 'I think maybe I need to do something a bit more taxing than reading.'

His mouth curved into a knowing smile. 'That could be arranged.'

'I meant—'

'I know what you meant,' he assured her, lifting himself from the lounger with fluid grace. 'There's rain predicted for later today. Why don't we go for a walk along the beach now while we can?'

He didn't have to be so accommodating, she decided, as she shrugged a sweater and track pants over her bikini. He didn't have to appear so at ease with this standoff. It had been three days since he'd told her that making love would be her call. And it had been three very long nights. He'd come to bed so late that she'd been asleep. She knew it had been late because she'd lain awake trying to read till after midnight each night, huddled in an oversized T-shirt she'd found in the walk-in wardrobe. True to his word, he'd left her alone. True to his word, he'd not made so much as a move towards her.

Oh, she'd seen him looking plenty. She'd spied his gaze on her more than a dozen times a day, his hungry eyes unleashing a rabble of butterflies inside her, the unmistakeable signs of his body reacting to hers setting them aflutter. And, more than once, she'd felt his ravenous eyes trapping hers when they'd found her spying on him.

But so what that he caught her looking? She'd never sworn not to look. She was hardly about to do anything more than that. Besides, how would she know how he was holding up unless she did look? Given his past performances, it was more likely he'd crack under the strain than her. Though so far he was making resisting her seem all too easy…

But this wasn't about his powers of resistance. He'd issued her with a challenge and she was up to it. And so far she'd lasted three days. Which meant that so far she was winning the battle.

She grabbed sneakers and slammed her feet into them with a sigh of disgust.

So why did winning feel so much like hell?

Fifteen minutes later there was still no sign of Diablo. She came across the housekeeper dusting in the living room.

'Luisa, have you seen Diablo anywhere? We're supposed to be going for a walk.'

The woman looked up, a broad smile lighting up her kindly features. 'Ah, sí. There was a telephone call. Mr Barrentes took it in the office.'

'Oh. Maybe I'll wait here, then.' She picked up a magazine from the stack of current releases on the coffee table, prepared to wait on one of the armchairs until he emerged.

'No, no, no! Mr Barrentes works too hard. You take him for a walk. It will do him good.'

Her reluctance to interrupt Diablo while at work in his office must have shown on her face.

'You are his wife!' Luisa stressed. 'You come first, not business. Go to him—one look at you will remind him of his duty.'

Briar gave the older woman a grateful smile as she set the magazine back down. Luisa must have known this was no ordinary marriage, but still she'd made Briar feel as welcome to the role of mistress of the house as if it had been a love match.

Still, it was with a nervous tap on his open office door that she announced her presence. He was leaning back in his office chair, both feet on his desk and talking rapid fire into the phone. He looked up at the sound and beckoned her inside, pointing to his watch before holding up five fingers. She let go of a breath she'd been holding. Luisa had been right; she had no need to cower outside his office. She had a right to be here.

Diablo continued with his phone call, speaking nineteen to the dozen in a tone that made Briar glad she wasn't on the receiving end. She did her best to tune out, instead turning her attention to the pictures that lined the walls of the large office. She hadn't been here since that first night and then she'd barely crossed the threshold as Diablo had led her on a tour of the house.

A large painting held pride of place on the wall right behind her, opposite his desk, a painting of a dark-haired woman. Instantly she was struck by the resemblance. The same dark eyes, the same autocratic features, the same strength of character shining out from the dark depths of her eyes—it had to be his mother Camilla. Diablo's good looks were clearly no accident of nature.

She pulled her eyes away from the portrait while the one-sided conversation continued behind her. A collection of at least a dozen black and white photographs had been arranged over a bank of filing cabinets. At first she took them to be old school photographs from Diablo's youth, but as she drew nearer she realised they couldn't be. The crowd of smiling children were arranged in neat rows, and all dressed in the same shorts and shirts with what looked like their teachers standing either end. But they were all Hispanic or South American Indian-looking or a blend of both, the building behind looking like no school she'd ever seen in Australia—and with a name like none she'd ever seen—*La Escuela de Barrentes*.

She blinked and turned to him, to find him watching her even as his short words signalled the end of the call. With a brief, 'See to it,' he replaced the receiver.

'So, you are ready for our walk?' he said, rounding the desk towards her. 'I am sorry to have kept you waiting so long.'

'That's okay,' she answered, refusing to be shepherded from the room. 'Tell me about these pictures. Who are these children?'

He shrugged as if they were of no consequence. 'It is a school in Chile. They take in orphans and children from the surrounding regions and provide them with an education and basic needs.'

'But it has your name on it—La Escuela de Barrentes. Doesn't that mean the Barrentes School?'

'Your Spanish is surprisingly excellent.'

'You *own* a school?'

He shook his head. 'I merely sponsor it.'

Was he kidding? There had to be at least two hundred children lined up in front of that building. 'You're merely a sponsor and yet they named the school after you? That's some sponsorship. However did you get involved in that?'

He lifted a hand to the corner of the nearest photograph, straightening it slightly. 'My mother was lucky,' he answered obliquely. 'She managed to get away from Chile and start a new life. But for those left behind there was no easy escape from those times. Things are changing now but there remains continuing pockets of poverty and lack of facilities. And, had my mother not got away, I could so easily have been one of those children...'

His words trailed off.

'You wanted to give those children a chance at life, just as you had been given.'

He wrapped an arm around her shoulders as they stood there together looking at the smiling faces in the photographs. 'Children represent the future. They are important, more important than anything in the world. Don't you agree? Why do you think I am so keen to start my own family?'

Her mouth went dry. *The future.* He cared about children because he cared about the future?

'You told me you wanted children to ensure you wouldn't be thrown out of Sydney society if our marriage went belly up.'

'And you would have believed me if I'd told you anything different? I think not.'

She looked up at him in surprise. He sure had her pegged. Which was ironic considering all along she'd thought she had him neatly pigeon-holed. *Predatory, cold-hearted businessman who cared for nothing and no one except for himself and his fortune.* But he did care for others—these pictures proved it.

What else might she be wrong about?

She shook her wayward thoughts away as she returned her gaze to the photographs, but she couldn't escape the cloud of guilt that crept over her. Diablo wanted a family, maybe not borne of love, but a family and a future nonetheless. And here she was popping contraceptive pills to ensure he was denied that very chance.

Damn him! She didn't want to feel guilty! She shouldn't have to. She'd never really been consulted about the terms of this marriage. He'd never shared either his love of children or his dreams about the future with her. He'd just assumed she'd fall in with his plans and produce his progeny on demand.

And she couldn't do that or she'd never get away! And wasn't getting away what she wanted?

Confusion swirled inside her mind. Of course she did. She wanted this marriage over as soon as possible. That was her goal—a goal she had to keep fixed in her sights.

'Come,' he said, squeezing her shoulders before dropping his arm to take her hand. 'We should go before the weather deteriorates any more.'

The wind was already up outdoors, toying playfully with the ends of their hair one minute, coming in gusts that threatened to knock them over the next. He led the way down the hill path to the shore under a grey, forbidding sky, the air heavy with the promise of rain and the tiny spray of long ago crashed surf tossed on the wind. It was wild and taxing and invigorating all at the same time.

She jumped down the final two feet to the pebble-strewn beach and stood there, feeling the air refresh her soul. Coming to the beach had been a great idea. It had meant Diablo had had to put on some clothes for a start, not that he didn't know how to best fill out low-slung cut-offs and a black sweater. But at least for a while her tension had dissipated and she could stop thinking about sex and how best to avoid it.

He turned, looking for her, his eyes concerned. 'Too cold?' he yelled over the sound of the surf and the blustering wind.

She shook her head, stray tendrils whipping around her face and unable to keep the laughter from her voice. 'No. I love it.'

His features relaxed and he smiled back. 'Come on, then.'

They walked, barely talking, for what seemed like miles, following the rugged shoreline from the promontory heading towards the tiny bay around which the tiny township nestled, occasionally stopping to pick up a shell along the shore. And somewhere along the way he'd offered her his hand as she'd clambered over a rocky outcrop and somehow it had stayed there, nestled warmly within his own.

How strange, she thought, that she could be walking companionably with Diablo, the man who waited patiently while she discovered each new shell on the sand—the same man she hated most in the world. She slid a glance up at him. But did she? The last three days he'd been the perfect host—polite, thoughtful, considerate. They'd read together, discussed current events, even taken in a movie in a nearby town. And she certainly hadn't picked Diablo for someone who actively cared about the rights and needs of children.

And now they were walking hand in hand. No, just lately it wasn't hatred she felt for him at all—more like a...*fascination*. Because everything about Diablo was fascinating, from the way he moved with stealthy precision, to the way his eyes flamed when they turned on her, and the way they set spot fires burning under her skin.

And he was her first ever lover—leagues better than her few fumbling boyfriends had ever managed to be—why wouldn't she be fascinated by him? No matter how her life evolved after this, he would always remain that. It was no doubt natural she would be intrigued. Especially when he'd made it clear that he intended to make love to her again.

So how long would he wait? A man like Diablo wouldn't be used to waiting, and certainly not for a woman—a woman he believed he had every right to.

How long could he keep that civilised veneer holding up, before it cracked apart under the strain of waiting for her? She shivered. He'd overwhelmed her with his passion on their wedding night. All that power, all that potent virility, and all of it unleashed on her—*inside her*. Would it always be that way between them if she let him?

Between her thighs, her muscles clamped down at the memory of how he'd filled her, how she'd been stretched and had felt so out of control when he'd moved inside her. Which was crazy. A year, a month, a week ago she had hardly been aware of those muscles. Now they seemed determined to make their presence felt, pulsing with a strange ache that lingered even though the initial tenderness had long gone.

Why couldn't she just forget? It should have been easy to resist him, to carry out her promise of making him wait a long, long time before she succumbed. So why did she seem to spend every waking moment thinking about him—thinking about how it would feel to make love with him again—*wanting to make love with him again…*

'Briar?'

The tug on her hand pulled her from her thoughts.

'Are you okay?'

She blinked and came to, her vision filled with dark eyes that one could fall into and never be found. She shivered again and wrapped her arms around herself. 'Sorry, just deep in thought,' she admitted, looking around and taking in her surroundings, praying that he wouldn't ask her exactly what she'd been thinking about.

They'd reached the perfect horseshoe bay that fringed one boundary of the town in a sandy beach that looked today like a white lace edging. Here it was more protected from the wind, the waves still foaming their way up the shore but tamed into a more regular rhythm. It was a week day and only a handful of people dotted the beach.

'There's a café nearby if you'd like coffee.'

The wildness of their walk around the blustery point had been energizing but the relative serenity of this tiny bay was something else, especially now the sun had managed to peep out from behind the clouds. It wouldn't last. Already dark clouds loomed threateningly, a promise of the rains to come. 'I'd like to sit and watch the sea for a while, if that's okay with you, while the sun's still out. Coffee can wait,' she suggested.

He looked out to sea, his hands in his pockets, a frown

tugging at his brow, and for a moment she thought he was going to insist they move on to the café now. But then he shrugged and seemed to relent.

Diablo sat down beside her on a small rise overlooking the narrow strip of beach, leaning back and propped up on his elbows while Briar sat with her chin on her hands, her elbows propped up on her knees and her collection of shells between her feet. If she looked a distance down the coastline towards the large promontory from where they'd come she could still see the occasional burst of spray rising high as the waves beyond the bay pounded at the rock-lined shore, while here the sun felt warm and welcoming on her face.

'It's such a beautiful beach here, so sheltered and peaceful.'

'Deceptively peaceful. There's a strong rip, especially this time of year.'

His blunt words confirmed the signs she'd seen warning swimmers of the treacherous undertow. 'You wouldn't pick it,' she said, feeling lulled by the rhythm of the incoming waves. 'It's so much calmer here compared to on the point. It's hard to believe it's the same day.'

'My mother used to say it's like being in the eye of the storm. She used to walk down here and sit and read for hours.'

She swung her head around, He was talking about his mother and this time she hadn't invited him to.

'She must have loved living here,' Briar said. 'It's so beautiful. Though it must be wild to be up there where the house is when there's a storm. It must feel like being at the very end of the earth.'

His eyes fixed hers in a stare so deep and empty it seemed fathomless. And when his voice came it seemed that too came from the depths of beyond. 'My mother loved the wild weather the best. She used to say that sometimes she could hear my father talking to her on the wind. It made her feel closer to him.'

In spite of the gentle heat from the sun, Briar shivered. She could almost feel Camilla's pain reach out and touch her, the pain of a lonely woman with the hungry wind for company, carrying the cherished voices of the dead.

'That was a portrait of your mother in the study, wasn't it?'

His eyes narrowed as if he was wondering how she knew.

She smiled and hunched her shoulders up. 'The resemblance is unmistakeable. She was a beautiful woman.' She hesitated for a moment before going on. Just because he'd finally admitted he'd had a mother didn't mean he was ready to tell her everything. 'What happened to her?'

He sat up suddenly, blowing out his breath in a rush. 'A stupid accident. Something that never should have happened.'

The heavy silence following his words made it clear he wasn't about to fill her in on the details.

'I'm so sorry,' she simply said. 'My brother died in a car accident two years ago. A truck lost control, crossed the highway and ploughed into the oncoming cars. It was midnight when the police came to tell us the news.' She shivered. 'He was only twenty-six…'

She felt a hand surround hers. 'You miss him still?'

She nodded. 'It's been hardest on my parents, of course…'

She'd been going to add, *especially with the business falling apart*, but she couldn't. Besides, her parents had money now. At least that was one concern they didn't have to deal with any more.

And, no matter what Nat's death had cost her, just as devastating must have been Diablo's loss of his mother. She'd been his only family. She couldn't begin to imagine what that would do to a person.

'Your mother must have missed your father terribly. She never remarried?'

He shook his head as he looked out to the horizon. 'My father was a hero. Nobody else ever came close. Nobody else ever could.'

'They must have loved each other so very much,' she mused, 'to have given up so much and risked everything to be together.'

He swung his body around to face her, surprising her with the intensity of bitterness contained in his eyes. 'But all for what? What was the point of loving like that? What good did it do them?' He picked up a pebble lying half buried in the sand and launched it with a flick of his wrist, spinning it low over the beach. She watched it skip and roll across the sand, only half aware of the seagulls in its path that squawked and rose in a cloud, while his words jarred into focus the conversation they'd had that very first night together.

'I can see what you've got against fairy tales.'

'What are you talking about?' He sounded impatient, irritable, as if he was wishing he'd never agreed to stop and talk.

'You told me you don't put much stock in happy endings. Obviously your parents missed out on their happy ever after, so you prefer to think it doesn't exist at all.'

'Do me a favour. Don't try to psychoanalyse me.'

'Who needs to psychoanalyse when it's written all over you? You feel bitter about what your parents missed out on when their time together was cut so short.'

'And what if I am?'

'Then you must know that for every couple that meets with tragedy, there are those who are happily married, who live and love and who grow old together. Even my own parents have been married for something like thirty years. What about them? Don't their happy ever afters count?'

'All I know is that there was no fairy tale ending for my mother, and if she didn't deserve it, I don't know anyone who does.'

What could she say to that? But at least things were starting to make some kind of bizarre sense, like his high-handed attitude and his lack of consultation with her about their marriage, the honeymoon and all that went with it. All along he hadn't wanted her to be involved—to *get* involved. All along she'd been more of a possession than a partner. Once it would have made her angry—who was she trying to kid?—it *had* made her angry—but now, instead of anger, she felt a kind of aching sadness for him, that his parents' experience had robbed him of a belief in the worth of love and devotion.

It was sad. What Diablo really needed was a woman who would show him how it was possible to love and be loved. He needed a woman who could change his mind about happy endings only ever happening in fairy tales. He needed a woman who could prove it could be so.

Which was ironic really. Because instead he'd been lumbered with Briar, plotting to bail out of this sham of a marriage the first chance she got. That was really going to change his attitude about happy endings—*not*.

But then, what Diablo thought was hardly her lookout anyway. It wasn't her job to change his mind about love and marriage. He'd set up this crazy arrangement. Why should she feel guilty when it all turned to dust?

'Now I understand why you were content to settle for a marriage of convenience—not simply because I provided the right bloodlines, but because you figured there was nothing to lose if it didn't last.'

'There's no reason our marriage can't last. But you're right; you can't lose what you haven't got. My parents loved deeply and lost everything. What's the point?'

She resisted the urge to tell him there was *every* reason why their marriage wouldn't last. 'You're the point!' she said instead. 'Don't you see? They didn't lose everything. Your mother got you! Don't you think that meant something extra special to your mother—to have something of your father to live on, even after she'd lost him?'

'Sure. It meant she had to slog her guts out by herself, working around the clock to provide for me.'

'And you think she did that because you were a liability or because she loved you so much?'

He grunted, showing his displeasure with the question and she sighed. What did it matter what he thought? It wasn't her job to change his view of life, the universe and everything. Instead she watched the seagulls wheeling in circles overhead and thought about the kind of woman his mother must have been; she sounded as if she'd been there for her son twenty-four hours a day. At least that was one thing he couldn't disagree with her about.

He pushed himself up to standing, brushing off the sand from his trousers. 'I'll go and get that coffee.'

She'd made him angry again, but then, what else was new? If he wasn't teasing her, he was angry with something she'd said or done. Still, she bristled as she watched him stride purposefully away across the sand to the grass-lined main street and beyond to the small strip of shops and cafés that lined the esplanade. A table of women were sitting outside and as one their heads turned as he strode past and entered, intent on animated conversation and peering conspiratorially through the front window once he'd disappeared. She shook her head. There was no doubt who they'd be talking about. If they only knew what a hard case he was, maybe they'd know to leave well enough alone. He wasn't worth it. She turned her attention away from the admiring women and wrapped her arms around her knees.

At least now she understood his attraction to an arranged marriage. It was a no risk option. Love was never an issue with Briar—*would never be an issue*—which suited her just fine. *Just fine,* she insisted to herself as once again she contemplated the endless roll of waves lapping at the water's edge.

A few minutes later she was down there, unable to resist the temptation of dipping her toes into the water, her shells jangling in her pockets. The undertow might be dangerous, but the shallows would be safe enough. She could at least get her feet wet. She shrugged off her shoes and rolled up her track pants before strolling along the water's edge, her bare feet splashing in the wash, laughing with the whoosh as the water rushed up around her ankles on the way up the beach and the powerful suction that even in the shallows ripped the sand out from under the soles of her feet when it receded. She stooped down when the vanishing sand revealed another shell under her foot. She picked it up, washed off the sand in the shallows and looked at it, admiring its perfect shape and pastel colours. She screwed her feet into the sands again to search for more.

'What the hell do you think you're doing?'

She looked around in surprise to see Diablo striding across the sand, the look on his face as dark as the storm clouds gathering above.

'What does it look like?' she asked ingenuously. 'I'm swimming to New Zealand.'

He didn't laugh. 'I told you that water was dangerous.'

'Relax,' she soothed, wondering how long it would take him to snap out of this mood as she stepped up the sand towards him. 'The last I heard, paddling wasn't considered an extreme sport.'

She looked at his empty hands. 'Where's the coffee?'

'They're bringing it.'

Of course they were. Behind him she could see a waiter setting up a table for two on the grassy strip overlooking the beach. As she watched, a gingham check tablecloth and a tiny white vase complete with fresh flowers, was added. A waitress followed bearing a tray. Why, when he had mentioned getting coffee, had she ever imagined that he would return bearing two Styrofoam cups?

'You certainly don't do things by halves, do you?' she said as he led her over to the setting.

'And you would have preferred to drink your coffee out of some kind of disposable cup?'

'No,' she agreed as he seated her; he had a point there. She placed her treasure from the sea on the table and lifted her cup up in mock toast. 'Here's to practising safe paddling.'

He had the decency to realise he'd overreacted. He took a deep breath, looking up to the sky before returning his gaze to her, the barest glimmer of a smile turning up his lips. 'Agreed,' he said, touching cups.

'What are you planning on doing with those?' he asked, indicating the shells.

'I don't know,' she answered honestly. 'They're just so pretty; I've never been able to resist shells.'

They drank their coffee watching the storm clouds rolling ominously towards the shore, until Diablo said they should be getting back. They set off along the shore, strolling back along the way they'd come, Diablo staying just above the waterline with her shells jostling noisily in his pocket, Briar splashing her way through the foam. His eyes crinkled, the corners of his mouth turning up, as she skipped through the shallows when the waves broke, her sneakers now tied and still swinging from around her neck. 'You look like a little girl who's never been to the beach before.'

'I feel like it,' she admitted through her smile, enjoying the play of water and sand through her toes. 'I thought it would be colder down at the beach but it's just wonderful.' She squealed as a rogue wave sent a rush of water licking up the shore, intent on catching them both this time.

'Watch out!' she cried, grabbing his arm and urging him up the beach but already too late to save his hand stitched boat shoes from a drenching.

Clear of the water, he stopped to survey the damage. 'You could have warned me,' he accused.

'I did,' she said in between laughter, still holding on to his arm. 'I was just a bit late.'

He lifted his eyes to her face, joining in the laughter until something abruptly shifted between them. His eyes changed in an instant from laughter to something infinitely more dangerous and all of a sudden she was all too conscious of the muscular power of his arm under her hands, of her breasts all but brushing against him, craving contact where there was none, anticipating contact... Heat came off him in waves—sensual, wraparound heat that drew her like a magnet closer to the source, squeezing out what little air remained between them.

His eyes were on her eyes, his gaze darting between them as if reading her, searching for a reason why he couldn't—why he shouldn't—and then they narrowed and dropped to her lips as a hand gathered her in from behind, stroking her neck, its gentle pressure drawing her ever closer, sparking and shorting her circuits. And she knew in an instant what his eyes had been telling her.

He was going to kiss her.

His breathing was fast and shallow. They shared the same air, his lips parted, his mouth already angling over hers.

He was going to kiss her.

Time stood still. The whoosh of the incoming tide, the cry of the seagulls, even the distant movement of traffic in the town all seemed to blur into a single note that sounded out one inevitable truth.

He was going to kiss her.

And she was going to let him.

What harm could come of it? she reasoned with her few remaining functioning brain cells. They were standing on a beach. It could lead nowhere. It was just a kiss, after all.

And then his lips touched hers and her eyelids fell shut on a sigh. How many times had they kissed? A handful, a dozen, two dozen? Surely no more. And yet, as his lips gentled hers, caressing, coaxing, she had the irrational sense of coming home.

Without breaking contact with her mouth, he shrugged off the shoes from around her neck and gathered her in closer, surrounding her with his arms, pulling her bodily against him. From her mouth to her toes, every part of her touched some part of him, she felt every part of her buzzing with contact with him, from the tender sweet passion of his mouth and lips and tongue to the sinewy muscled tone of his calves and the rock-solid core of him that pressed hard against her belly.

Just a kiss? Who had she been trying to kid?

It hadn't been just a kiss. And, just as the sounds had merged around them, the world itself seemed to dissolve and reform. There were just the two of them here, in this moment. His hand edged around her ribcage, his thumb stroking the soft side swell of her breast, sending her senses reeling. Like a drug, she wanted more. She craved more, so that when he cupped her breast fully, his fingertips brushing the electric nub of her nipple, it gave her a momentary high that left her with a desperate thirst for more.

But then it was over. She opened her eyes, confused, feeling the cold rush of his withdrawal where before there had been such delicious heat.

'I'm sorry,' he said, his breath raspy, his forehead touching her own, his hands holding hers out to her sides. 'We should get back.'

She trembled, her mouth trying to find the sounds that would make coherent words that said something other than *why*? while tears of anger and frustration stung her eyes—insane and unnecessary. Because she knew very well why—because he'd told her she'd be the one who would choose the next time they made love. She'd be the one to make the next move.

And while at the time she'd relished the power he'd given her, the power to control his sexuality, right now some primal part of her screamed out that it didn't want it at all. Instead it yearned to be swept away by him, to have both the decision and the responsibility taken away from her.

Why was it so easy for him to stop when it was such hell for her?

A booming sound split the heavens, causing the ground and

even the air around them to shake, as icy-cold needles collided like pinpricks on her heated skin.

He cursed into the sky, taking her by the hand even as the thunderous noise reverberated in her eardrums. 'We have to get back. Come on.'

If it was a race against the rain, the rain won—no question. Before long they were both drenched to the skin, as they jogged along the shore, scrambling over rocks until finally they came to the hill path that led to the house. The wind was higher here and it whipped around them, further chilling her icy skin, the loose tendrils of her hair plastered like ice-cold wire around her face, her sweater and track pants heavy with water. How could it get so cold so quickly? She felt icy to the core.

They made it to the top, soaking and panting, and the clouds sent out a stinging burst of hail to welcome them. They squelched across the lawn and arrived sopping wet on the covered terrace.

She stopped to wrench off her heavy shoes but she was shaking too hard and lost balance.

'*Dios,*' he said, grabbing her before she fell. 'But you are frozen. Forget the shoes. You need to get warm, now.'

Diablo swung her into his arms and carried her through to their bedroom and into the spacious *en suite* bathroom, oblivious to the trail of water sloughing off behind him. 'Bath or shower?' he asked gruffly, setting her down in the middle of the room and keeping an arm around her as if she were suddenly about to keel over.

'Sh…shower,' she managed, even though she wasn't sure she'd last the distance standing up. But neither did she want to wait for the bath to fill. Diablo leaned into the extra large alcove, turning on the taps, running the water until the temperature was perfect.

Then he prised her hands from across her arms and lifted her sodden sweater, pulling it from her shoulders. He raised a foot and relieved her of one sneaker and then the other while she propped her arms, still shaking, against his back and then he eased her track pants down her goosebumped legs.

She stood there, still trembling, in just her bikini, her skin so pale, so icy-cold.

'There,' he growled, dropping his hold on her and already halfway to the door, intent on getting out of there before he did something crazy, 'I'll leave you to it.'

'Thank you.'

Her voice sounded fragile enough to snap, the tight thread running through it reeling him back. He turned. She hadn't budged from where he'd left her, her hair plastered in tendrils over her eyes, her arms crossed over the twin triangles of her bikini top. Clouds of steam billowed from the shower, enveloping her, rendering her almost ethereal, a visitor from another world. Even dripping wet, he couldn't recall having ever seen anyone more beautiful. And, for some bizarre reason, it physically ached to contemplate walking out of here and leaving her.

She was watching him with her large eyes, not moving, clearly waiting for him to go. And, *dios*, he had to get out of there! Before he did something stupid like pulling her into his arms and kissing her senseless. Rendering himself senseless. Just like he had on the shore. *So much for making a deal to wait for her.*

Because she didn't want him—not enough. She was happy to let him take the lead but she'd made clear over the last three days that she would be damned if she'd be the one to make the first move. And he damned himself for the ultimatum he'd given her. Every time he'd caught her eyes on him, all it had done was make him so hard with expectation that he hurt. But she'd pulled back from any opportunity—and there had been plenty—for them to make love.

And the hardest thing of all was to avoid her in the evenings, to wait until he was sure she would be asleep, before he was game to go to bed. It was bad enough trying to rest with her sleeping figure so close, knowing she wouldn't welcome his advances. How could he dare risk her rejection while she was still awake? While he still burned for her?

He dragged in one unsteady breath and took another step towards the door. 'You'd better get in that shower. You need warming up.'

'You need a shower, too. You're as cold as I am.'

'I can wait until you're finished. I'll be right outside if you need me.'

'No!' she protested as he had one hand on the door, her eyes even wider. 'I need you here—to hold me up.'

A gravelly sound issued uninvited from his throat—a growl— as, despite its frigid encasing, his groin kicked into life. 'If I stay here, don't expect me to stop at merely holding you up.'

She lifted her chin. 'I was hoping you might say that.'

Was he hearing her right? Her eyes were wide and glossy, her bottom lip trembling, and he wanted to wrap her up in his arms and warm her, wanted to hold her against him and hear her heart-beat meld with his, feel her body meld with his.

And he wanted those things so badly!

He took a step closer. 'Are you sure?'

'It's my choice, just like you said. I decide when. I decide how.'

She reached behind her back and he saw the strap of her bikini top fly free. Then she peeled away the fabric covering her breasts and pulled it over her head while she held out her other arm to him.

'And that time is now.'

CHAPTER EIGHT

HE swept her into his arms in a heartbeat, capturing her in a tangle of limbs. Immediately he was struck by just how cold she was, like a marble statue, her lips icy, her skin chilled to the touch, and he wanted to breathe life into her, to lend her some of the heat building so rapidly to furnace levels below. Her mouth opened up beneath his on a sigh and she drank in his warmth willingly.

She tasted of salt like the sea spray, she tasted fresh like the teeming icy rain, she tasted of the energy unleashed between the earth and the sky in the height of the storm.

He whirled with her through the steam, spinning her into the shower recess, kicking off no more than his shoes on the way. His clothes were already drenched; it didn't matter where they came off.

He directed her under the stream of warm water, holding her there while she trembled and recovered, letting the warm torrent cascade over her, eradicating the cold chills from her flesh. And before long her trembling subsided and she stretched, reaching up her arms, arching her back under the flow, raising her face into the stream and lifting her breasts up high before him.

He groaned and gave thanks as he contemplated their creamy perfection in the mist. He was only human after all, he would never have lasted another day waiting for her and here she was, offering herself up to him. And somehow thanks didn't seem anywhere near enough.

His fingers trailed down her throat, exploring the sculpted beauty of her shoulders and chest before capturing each breast and feeling their sensual weight. He dipped his mouth to one perfect bud and supped of both her tender flesh and the water that cascaded over her, tasting the very essence of her with it.

She shuddered as he suckled, but this time he knew it wasn't with the cold. This time it was heat, pure carnal heat that set her flesh trembling in his mouth. Her hands grasped for his head, his shoulders as she groaned. But he was already moving, sliding his hands down the concave curves of her waist and over the flare of her hips, his tongue dancing around her navel. His fingers hooked into the sides of her bikini pants, peeling them down, revealing that triangular clutch of curls guarding her most feminine treasures. She held on to his shoulders as he eased her feet out of the tiny garment, running his hands up the long delicious length of her legs while he kissed her belly and pressed her to his mouth.

'You're so beautiful,' he murmured against her flesh, 'so perfect.'

Her hands cradled his head, her fingernails raking through his hair, tangling themselves in its length. He leaned back, watching his hands scoop around her legs and rise up in between.

'Diablo,' she cried out, her fingers stilled and clutching handfuls of hair, as if sensing what he had in mind.

'Are you still cold?' he asked as his fingers gently parted her, exposing her to him.

He was rewarded by her sudden gasp, which turned into a breathy, 'ohmigod' as he pressed his mouth to her, circling that tight pink bud with his tongue.

And the water streamed down as he knelt before her, worshipping her body with his tongue, discovering another taste, another texture to her, another dimension to the complex woman who was his wife.

His woman.

He spread her legs wider with his hands and cupped her sex, holding her to him as she writhed in his mouth, her breathing coming fast and furious. She was hot and ready and so damned tempting and there was no way he could resist temptation now. He slipped one, and then two fingers into her slick, tight space, immediately rewarded by the feeling of her muscles contracting around him.

'Please,' she panted, her voice a desperate cry for release coming to him through the steam and the water. 'I need you.'

She wasn't the only one in need of release. Another part of him ached to occupy that same place and satisfy its own desperate need. He pulled off his sweater and flung it into the corner, where it landed with a wet slap. She wrapped her arms around his neck while he stood and kissed her open-mouthed, unbuttoning his cargo pants, letting the weight of the water drag them down his legs, and suddenly her hand was there, cupping his throbbing length through the fabric of his underwear. Breath hissed through his teeth as she eased the band over, liberating him. *Freedom.* But right now it wasn't freedom he craved. Only in confinement would come release and right now it was the sweet imprisonment of her body he needed more than anything in the world.

'You're playing with fire,' he warned her, removing her hand and placing it back around his neck.

He lifted her high, wrapping her legs around his waist while their lips and tongues danced together. And then he let her down slowly, finding that sweet spot, testing it, letting her absorb his length as he gradually lowered her all the way down.

It was all she needed. In a charge as potent as electricity, muscles clenched and spasmed around him, her head thrown back, legs kicking as she exploded in his arms.

And something inside him burst into life. He wanted to howl

at the moon; he wanted to yell his elation from the mountains of the world. Instead he buried his face in her neck and squeezed her tighter. She was his woman. Unmistakably his.

And he would never let her go.

Her tremors were too much for him and, like a siren's call to a sailor at sea, her climax drew him inexorably closer to his own end. Now that she was quietening, he braced her against the wall, moving inside her tight depths, her unbelievably sweet, tight depths. She matched his movements, angling herself to receive each thrust, encouraging him with her small sighs of pleasure until, with a cry of triumph, he too became shipwrecked on the shore.

Oh, wow! Her senses were reeling, her lungs battling to get her breathing under control and her mind was blank except for that one thought. Oh, wow!

He pressed against her, still inside her, as he let her legs slowly slip to the floor. Amazingly enough, her knees didn't buckle under her. Then he lifted his head and smiled. 'You're beautiful,' he said, kissing her so tenderly that tears formed in her eyes. And then he smiled at her as if she were the most special being in the entire world.

Tenderness. She had never expected it from Diablo. Every time it took her by surprise. And every time it further weakened her resolve.

He wasn't supposed to be gentle.

He wasn't supposed to have a heart.

And she wasn't supposed to want to make love to him.

So much for supposition.

He drew back, pumping some shower gel into his hands.

'What are you doing?' she asked shakily. She'd imagined that now they'd had sex, they would dry off and continue their day.

'What are you supposed to do in a shower?' he asked her. 'I'm washing you.'

Her ideas on what showers were for had just expanded in new and wonderful directions, and washing seemed to be the least interesting of any of them, until he touched her with hands made slippery with the soap, running sensuously up and down her skin with devastating effect. He soaped her body, he glided his hands over her almost as if he were sculpting her, he washed and rinsed her hair and, just as he was about to turn off the taps, she found her voice.

'Oh, no,' she said, before squeezing gel into her own hands. 'I'm not finished yet.'

His pupils dilated and she smiled up at him with more nerve than she felt. 'My call,' she reminded him.

Emboldened by their lovemaking, she set about her task, sliding her hands down each arm and up again, seeking out each indentation, each swell of muscle, each nub of bone, reading him like a blind person read Braille. His shoulders, his chest, his legs—her hands traced the toned perfection of his body; she drank it all in. It was another exercise in discovery, a fascinating journey that taught her more about the male form than she would ever have learned from a thousand books. A fascinating journey that ended in a fascinating place. She skimmed her hands down his sides once more, kissing a trail down the centre of his abdomen and lowered herself to kneel before him.

He groaned as she took him in her hands. He hissed through his teeth when she circled the tip of his erection with her tongue. His knees all but buckled when she took his satin-finished flesh into her mouth and cupped his tight, tight sac in her hand. She heard him utter her name and a feeling like no other coursed through her. She was here with Diablo Barrentes and yet she felt alive, in control and very, very aroused. His hands tangled in her hair, his hips undulating rhythmically with her, unable to remain still as she paid homage to him. She tasted the salt of his juices and he grasped her head, pulling himself away.

'Not like this,' he whispered hoarsely, as he lifted her under her arms and pinned her against the tiled wall, 'when I would rather join with my woman like this…'

My woman.

She shuddered in his arms, opening herself up to him. So how was it that those very words put a sensual thrill down her spine like no other when she'd objected to his use of that expression before?

His woman. She was his woman. And insanely, irrationally, suddenly ecstatic to be so. Because today she'd discovered the flip side of being his woman.

Today she'd discovered that being his woman made him her man.

Her man pushed into her then, forcing the breath from her lungs, and once again she was reminded of his power and his sheer masculinity, delighting in it, embracing it, and then she thought of nothing at all as he withdrew before surging back into her. She did the only thing she could. She clung to him, going with him, feeling the rhythm feeding into her soul and building into something real, something concrete, something magnificent, before he tipped them both over the edge and it was lights showering down on her, splinters of light that twinkled like fireflies dancing around her.

Afterwards he wrapped her, spent and weak, in an enormous bath sheet and carried her to their bed, peeling back the covers and laying her down almost reverentially amidst the pillows and cushions.

Never had she felt more cherished.

Never had she felt more confused.

'How are you feeling?'

Extraordinary. Exquisite. Loved.

Loved?

She stared up at him blankly. Oh, no way! To imagine that would be to let what had happened in the shower go right to her head. *Shell-shocked.* Now there was a better word for what she was feeling. She was simply shell-shocked. At least that much made sense. At least that would explain this strange feeling inside her.

'You're not still cold?'

Heavens, no. Far from it. Luxuriantly warm, infinitely cosseted maybe, but *definitely* not cold. She shook her head, trying to get hold of a world that looked the same as every other day but now felt completely different. 'Shouldn't we be getting ready for dinner?'

'Luisa sent in a tray while we were showering.' He wheeled a trolley over and lifted a plate. 'There's soup and sandwiches. Are you hungry?'

'Not really,' she admitted, knowing that whatever this strange new sensation inside her was, it wasn't hunger driving it.

He climbed into bed alongside her and picked up her hand, kissing the back of it. 'You have to eat,' he said, his eyes glinting up at her suggestively. 'You need to keep up your strength.'

She started to laugh, at first nervously, but he tugged gently on the towel surrounding her, unwinding it from her body, drawing it slowly away, unwrapping her like some precious find, and her laughter changed course—deeper, more sensual and full of meaning. Then, once she was totally uncovered, she stopped laughing and he smiled at her and touched her breast, caressing it, coaxing her nipple into hardness between his thumb and forefinger before dipping his mouth and circling her nipple with his tongue while he glided his hand down her ribcage to her abdomen.

'And you need strength not just for you.' He held his hand still over the surface of her flat belly. 'Is it possible that already my child grows deep within you?'

Oh, God! She turned her head away, a stab of guilt so deep slashing into her that she couldn't face him. Hell, no, it wasn't possible at all that she was already pregnant, not with her popping pills to ensure the exact opposite. But she was hardly about to admit that.

Damn him! Why did he have to be so gentle? Why did he have to be so tender? Why did he have to make it so darned difficult for her? It was the kind of knowledge that deserved to be flung in his arrogant face, not to feel guilty about, and after the way they'd just made love, she was in no rush to spoil the mood.

'It—it doesn't always happen right away,' she faltered, frustrated, still unable to bring her eyes around to meet his. 'Sometimes it takes time—months, even longer. You can't expect…'

His hand hooked under her chin, slowly bringing her around to face him.

'Don't worry,' he soothed, clearly mistaking her hedging for a fear that she wouldn't conceive quickly enough for his liking. 'We have all the time in the world.'

'And if it's not that simple?'

'It's that simple,' he told her. 'You've seen how perfectly we fit together; you have nothing to worry about. And you will make a wonderful mother. Your babies will be beautiful and it is no wonder when I look at how beautiful you are.' He kissed her sweetly on each eyelid as if to reassure her. His dark eyes glinted knowingly as he made a sound like a low growl in the back of his throat. '*Dios*. I thought I was hungry for food, but it is you I hunger for. You left me starving for far too long.'

He dipped his mouth and kissed her lips, the next he directed at her throat and, as he took aim for the third time Briar knew she was down for the count.

Swamped in Diablo's white robe, Briar stood in the dimly lit *en suite* bathroom and stared at herself in the mirror, expecting to find something that would explain this change. Because there had to be something, some physical evidence why she felt so radically different.

What was happening to her?

A week ago, even just a few days ago, she'd been determined, she'd been certain of her path. She'd decided that she was going to be a spectator to this marriage for as long as it lasted and then she was going to get herself the hell out of there, her sense of self intact, her identity preserved.

But, heaven help her, she wasn't just a spectator any more. She was getting drawn in. Deeper and deeper drawn in with the one person with whom she'd sworn she'd never get involved. She was losing her resolve. Losing her determination. Losing herself in a man with flashing dark eyes and powerful arms that cradled her as if she was the most precious thing on earth.

What the hell was wrong with her? Surely she couldn't be starting to have feelings for him?

It couldn't be true. Diablo was great sex—great mind-blowing sex, as it happened—but it was nothing more than lust, a mere temptation of the flesh. And just because in a moment of weakness she'd given in to that temptation didn't mean she could be so easily swayed from her determination—did it? She searched her features in the mirror, looking for some sign, some evidence that she had changed. She delved into the reflection of her eyes, hoping to find the key.

What was happening to her? What had possessed her?

Possession.

Like a kick in the gut, that word shoved her thoughts right back to their love-making, right back to that pivotal moment when he'd called her his woman. And that moment later when she'd been blindsided by a thunderbolt—that Diablo was her man.

His woman. Her man. Even now the concept poured a warm flush of excitement through her veins that frightened her senseless. Surely just a surge of hormones or a moment of insanity. It had to be insanity.

She stared into the mirror, her eyes staring back—wild, unsure, clouded with trepidation.

Because, if it wasn't insanity, it didn't just mean she was starting to have feelings for Diablo. It meant she was in danger of falling in love with him.

In love with Diablo?

Please, no! She gripped the edge of the marble vanity unit to prevent herself from reeling. Diablo was ruthless, an arrogant take-no-prisoners businessman who put the pursuit of wealth above everything else in the world. He'd railroaded her into marriage, he'd cajoled her into his bed.

Except the ruthless businessman had turned one hundred and eighty degrees and shown her he had a softer side, a side that saw him giving thanks for the opportunities he'd been given by supporting the lives of children who otherwise wouldn't have a chance.

And today he hadn't had to cajole her into bed at all. Today she'd invited him to take her. She rolled her eyes heavenwards as with a chill of recognition she realised that was what had changed.

Diablo was no longer merely the jailer of her body for the term of this marriage. Diablo now possessed the keys to her will. He'd unlocked her defences—the defences she'd prided herself upon, the defences she'd relied upon in defying him, in proving she didn't want him.

And if he could do that, then how long would it be before he found the keys to her heart?

Her breath snagged in her throat. It couldn't happen, could it? Surely people couldn't change the way they felt about someone that quickly. Unless…? There was a name for it when people acted illogically towards their captors, sympathising with them, feeling a strange loyalty to them, maybe even falling in love. Stockholm syndrome, that was it. Maybe that was what was happening to her? Whisked away from her own world by her captor to a lonely house, forced to endure hour after hour in his company, was it any wonder that her feelings would soon get scrambled and rearranged? She was a captive bride, held prisoner by a man who wanted to make her his by breaking down her resistance piece by piece.

She gazed at her reflection in the mirror. So it *was* a form of insanity, then. She wasn't really having feelings for Diablo; it was their forced proximity playing on her feelings of entrapment. Things would feel different when they returned to Sydney. Things, and her emotions, would soon get back to normal.

With new resolve, she pulled out the drawer she'd taken for her own and found the small cosmetic bag she'd come in for in the first place. She zipped it open and pulled out the packet of pills, counting them. Five pills left for this month. Five pills. And then what?

For a while there she'd been in two minds as to what to do. Diablo's love of children had taken her by complete surprise, as had his sponsorship of an entire school in Chile. He'd had her feeling strangely sympathetic for his wish for children and suddenly guilty for working against his plans.

She couldn't make any rash decisions. But why should she feel so guilty when she'd been the one pushed and coerced into this marriage from the outset? Why should she feel guilty simply because she had no desire to perform the role of his personal incubator?

He'd never asked her if she wanted children. He'd certainly never asked her if she would mind having his. She'd been told, commanded, bossed into what he thought was submission without a shred of consultation and he'd assumed that once he'd locked her up long enough she'd fall in with his plans.

She popped the tiny bubble and swallowed the pill before stashing the rest away.

To hell with his plans.

He should have been asleep—had almost been asleep—but her sudden departure from the bed had him waiting, his blood quietly thrumming, anticipating her return so he could once again tuck her body in close to his.

Making love with her today had been better than great. He'd known she'd come to him—had only had a moment's doubt that she'd eventually capitulate—and although it had been his own private hell while she'd resisted, in all that time he'd had no idea just how sweet her surrender would be.

It had been heaven to take his time with her, to explore every curve and indentation of her body, to have her explore his. And now there would be time for so much more.

He heard the click of the light switch in the *en suite* bathroom and her quiet footfall across the floor, even though it was clear she was doing her utmost not to disturb him. He sensed the dull swish of his robe as she let it fall from her shoulders, a glimmer of moonlight now the storm had passed turning her skin to pearlescent perfection, before she eased her naked body into the bed.

And he felt her withdrawal from him like a slap in the face as she eased herself gently on to the edge of the mattress and lay down with her back to him.

He suppressed a snarl. After what they'd shared today there was no way he was letting her slide back into some kind of reluctant virgin persona once again.

'Hey,' he said, voicing his protest in the gentlest way he could under the circumstances.

The way her breath hitched short told him he'd surprised her. After a second her head rolled slightly around.

'I thought you were asleep.'

'Come here,' he growled, reaching out for her, intending to draw her close within the circle of his arms. And she came, but instead of melting against him as he'd been anticipating, he gathered an awkward bundle of tangled limbs and reluctant flesh. It seemed to take an eternity to settle her body's suddenly different components in his arms, and even then they felt uncomfortable and stiff, transmitting their discomfort to him in spades.

'What's wrong?' he asked, when for the third time she'd found reason to fidget rather than settle.

'Who said anything was wrong?'

'You're saying everything is all right?'

'I'm just tired. I need to sleep.'

'Then maybe you should try to sleep, rather than fighting with me.'

'I'm not fighting.'

'Good, because you'd be in for a disappointment.'

'You're so sure of yourself, aren't you? You think you know it all.'

I wish, he thought, wondering what the hell was going on in her head. He pulled her tighter in his arms. 'Go to sleep.'

CHAPTER NINE

'I HAVE to get back to Sydney,' Diablo told her the next morning over his *Financial Review* as she joined him for breakfast. 'Something's come up that I need to deal with personally.'

'So soon?' she responded, sitting down opposite him. 'The honeymoon's over, then?'

He arched an eyebrow at her. They'd made love first thing this morning before he'd gone to do some laps and then to his office to catch up with his emails, and he'd assumed from her energetic response to his love-making that she was over her 'tiredness' of last night. Apparently not. But given the reason for this morning's dash back to Sydney, he wasn't exactly in the mood to put up with it either. 'I thought you'd be pleased, seeing you didn't want a honeymoon in the first place.'

She shrugged and poured herself a coffee. 'And still we came. So what I think is hardly going to make a difference anyway.'

He regarded her levelly while she selected a piece of toast and spread it with blackberry jam, her eyes never once making the effort to travel anywhere near his. He carefully folded his newspaper in half and placed it down on the table, every movement calm and quiet while his blood simmered inside. Nobody, but nobody, blew so hot and cold with him like this woman did and got away with it.

Dammit, nobody else had the audacity to even try!

'I thought maybe we could come back here next weekend,' he continued, keeping his voice level despite the provocation, 'seeing you seemed to enjoy it here so much.'

'If you like,' she offered, munching on her toast solemnly before taking a sip of coffee.

'Perhaps we could walk along the beach again if the weather is fine.'

'Perhaps.'

'Or maybe this time you'd prefer to try something different?'

Obviously sick of contemplating her vanishing toast, her eyes slid beachwards. 'Whatever you decide, it's fine with me.'

'Done. I have just the thing in mind. I'm going to throw you down on this table in the middle of breakfast, rip your clothes from your body and make passionate love to you.'

She was halfway to a nod when her head swung around, her eyes opening wide. They collided with his, amber guns ablaze, colour flaming her cheeks.

Got you, he thought.

'What the hell are you trying to prove?'

'Sex on toast,' he taunted, feeling suddenly jauntier than he had any time since she'd sat down. 'Sure beats bacon and eggs. Then again, I'm still a bit peckish; maybe we needn't wait till next weekend.' He pushed himself out of his chair and paused for a moment, doing his damnedest to look predatory. 'I'm willing… What's to stop us going for it right now?'

Her chin jerked up, the slash across her cheeks brighter still.

'Maybe you might think to ask first.'

He smiled. 'You already acquiesced, I seem to recall. Whatever I decide is fine with you—or words to that effect.'

She glared at him for a moment before her own chair scraped back across the terrazzo-tiled floor and she stood, her stance showing she was ready for flight. 'What time do we have to leave? I have to pack.'

'You've hardly touched your breakfast.'

She threw her napkin down on her half-eaten toast. 'I've had enough.'

And so had he. 'What the hell's wrong with you?' he demanded, catching up with her as she turned and wheeled away, giving up all pretence of staying cool. 'Yesterday you couldn't wait to get me into that shower. Today you're acting like some prickly virgin.'

This time she did look him in the eyes and he took the full brunt of the topaz fire she turned on him. 'I apologise for my inexperience. Obviously, if sexual experience had been part of your selection criteria, you might have chosen a woman who satisfied your requirements one hell of a lot more closely.'

'I wasn't looking for experience.'

'No, you're absolutely right. You were looking for someone who wasn't in a position to say no. Lucky me,' she said, the irony dripping from her words while her eyebrows rose to accentuate her words, 'I drew the short straw.'

They made the journey back to Sydney in stony silence, Diablo's mood getting blacker with each passing kilometre.

He'd had her. For twelve hours yesterday she'd been his, body and soul. She'd mirrored his wavelength, she'd moved like an extension of him. She'd been his for the taking and he'd devoured what she'd offered like a starving man.

He'd always believed she was perfect for his needs, and on their wedding night he'd had an inkling of just how perfect. But yesterday she'd blown away all his expectations. She was better than perfect. She was a goddess and, wherever that goddess had gone, he wanted her back.

He thought back over the hours she'd almost seemed part of him. There was nothing he could think of that had made her angry. On the contrary, she'd seemed as blown away by the sheer impact of their love-making as he'd been himself. Then, without warning, she'd locked herself into the bathroom, only to return a changed woman, the goddess vanquished, replaced with a sassy-mouthed she-cat who was happier sparring than making love.

He thumped the heel of his hand against the steering wheel. The amber-eyed she-cat alongside him barely acknowledged the sound, still resolutely gazing out the windows.

The sports car negotiated its way through the building traffic with a throaty roar. He took the freeway heading for the city and, as they passed the turn-off for Mosman, finally she found her voice.

'Where are we going?'

'To my apartment.'

'But I thought you might drop me off...' Her words trailed off and he allowed himself a smile.

'You thought I might drop you off at your parents' house? But why? You're my wife now. You live with me.'

'I thought you had to work. What will I do?'

'Get acquainted with your new home.'

'I don't even know where you live.'

'Then you'll soon find out.'

She turned her head to look out the window so he couldn't read her face and take satisfaction from her disappointment. Truth was, she could have found out about where Diablo lived, plenty of times, if she'd bothered. But she'd never bothered. She'd never even broached the subject. She'd never wanted to know anything about the man or his private life, had never sought the information, even after she'd learned of their engagement, preferring to avoid thinking about her future as much as possible. Now she wished she hadn't been quite so blinkered. She might feel more prepared.

'What about all my things?' she asked, swinging her head around to look at him. 'And my car?'

'Packed, delivered and waiting for you. All efficiently taken care of while we were away.'

'You certainly didn't waste any time.'

'Wasting time is not the way I work.'

She rolled her eyes. 'I hadn't noticed,' she muttered, before turning her attention out of the window to the looming outline of Sydney CBD.

She descended back into silence, her hopes for a return to sanity and clear-thinking taking a sharp dive. She'd been crazy to imagine he'd let her out at Blaxlea before he went to work. It was hope that had blinkered her thoughts, hope that when they were back in Sydney life might take on some sort of normality once again. But how could life return to anything approximating normal when she would still be imprisoned in Diablo's world? All he was doing in moving her from El Paradiso to his own home was merely replacing one gilded prison cell with another.

She drew in a deep breath and let it out slowly. Okay, so she had to get used to new digs. At least it was in Sydney and not halfway up the coast. He'd still be working most of each day—and she'd have her car. So she might be in prison, but not necessarily in isolation. She would cope. And she'd soon rationalise those bizarre feelings she'd been having about this man she'd married.

They crossed the Sydney Harbour Bridge and took an off ramp for the city centre. A few minutes later Diablo steered the car into an underground car park at the base of a multi-storey office block.

'I thought you were going home first.'

'This is home.' He pulled the car into a secure garaged area. 'And there is your car,' he said, indicating the neat Honda coupé beside them, 'just as I told you.'

He led her to the private lift, pressed a button for the penthouse and stood silently next to her as the lift carried them the forty-plus floors to the top. The doors slid open to a plush entrance lobby, complete with marble floor and massive timber doors curving in an arc around the lobby. He unlocked the doors and regarded her for a few moments, a hint of amusement curving his lips. 'Isn't it traditional at this point that I carry you over the threshold?'

'I am impressed,' she blistered, her eyebrows raised in mock salute. 'I didn't realise cavemen had traditions—beyond clubbing women over the head and dragging them back to their cave, that is.

'And, just in case you're tempted,' she added for good measure, 'you've already done that.'

His amusement dissolved into a scowl as she swept past him into the spacious apartment and she wondered if she hadn't overplayed her hand. It was one thing to make sure she didn't fall for his charms, it was another entirely to antagonise him into something much more dangerous. And she knew exactly how dangerous he could be when provoked. So when the hell would she ever learn to bite her tongue and not provoke him? It was a line she had to be careful not to cross.

She came to a halt inside the spacious living area, pretending to take an interest in her elegant surroundings. She knew she'd been less than pleasant company since this morning. Waspish, snippy and downright rude—and that was when she hadn't been sulking in silence. As a defence against her wayward feelings it wasn't going to earn her any friends, but she wasn't looking to be friends, not with a man who treated her like his latest corporate acquisition, more interested in the return she'd pay rather than her inherent value.

But what alternative did she have? She had to do something to shore up her defences against this man, defences that had all but tumbled down as easily he'd tumbled her once more under his warm body this morning.

How quickly he'd aroused her, his hands weaving their magic on her skin, his sculpted body fitting with hers. How skilfully he'd made her cry out with release before he'd followed her with his own guttural cry of triumph. *How ashamed she'd felt that he could reduce her to a combination of irrational nerve-endings and pulsating flesh.*

Thank goodness he'd left to go swimming before he'd seen her own eyes swimming—behind the tears of frustration that he'd left her to deal with. Because how could she hate him when he made her feel so good? And how could she *not* hate him when to him she was just a body, just a wife, just a potential incubator for his children?

'The living room,' he indicated with a sweep of his arm as if he'd taken her silence for interest in her surroundings. He then gestured with three decisive strokes of his hand. 'The kitchen, dining room and that's the study through there. There's also a full bathroom downstairs in addition to a powder room. Bedrooms are upstairs.'

She battled to look interested when all that struck her was how different it was to the house they'd just left that morning. Where El Paradiso was a rambling hacienda, full of colour and different levels and a surprise around every corner, this apartment was a statement to executive neutrality. Cool blonde timbers, caramel-coloured furniture and beige rugs adorning a light marble floor. Almost every horizontal surface was polished—and practically bare.

She wandered through to the dining room, where beige upholstered chairs sat rigid like tombstones. How appropriate, she thought, half expecting to see a dining table in the shape of a coffin. A feature wall behind the dining table proudly boasted fawn paint instead of taupe. *Some feature.*

'This looks homely,' she said, with just a touch of irony as she ran her fingertips along a white oak buffet unit, wondering if her duty statement as wife extended as far as redecorating.

'It's home,' he said flatly. 'Make yourself comfortable. I have some affairs to attend to.'

He wandered back towards the front doors and this time his words earned a reaction. 'You're leaving? Leaving me here? What do you expect me to do?'

He shrugged. 'Become familiar with the apartment. It's your home now, too.'

He picked up his keys from the side table by the front door where he'd left them. 'I shouldn't be too late.'

'And if I want to go out?'

'Where do you need to go?'

'I don't know.' She threw her arms out wide. 'Is there a clause in my contract that says I'm to be kept in solitary confinement?'

'Don't be ridiculous,' he snapped back. 'I was just asking what you had in mind.'

'Who knows?' she insisted. 'Lunch, visiting my mother, shopping?' She seized on the last word as if it was a lifesaver. 'I'm betting the fridge is as overcrowded as the rest of this apartment.'

His eyes revealed more surprise than rebellion at that comment. 'You intend to go grocery shopping?'

'What else do you plan on eating tonight?'

He sent one dark eyebrow skywards. 'You never told me you had such a keen interest in the kitchen.'

Her own eyebrow arched in response. 'You never asked.'

He wasn't about to admit it. He merely pulled out a tiny drawer in the hall table, holding out a card. 'Here's a key. That will get you into the private lift and the entrance doors. Your car has already been fitted with a remote for the garage.' He hesitated for just a moment as he looked at her. 'Maybe going out is a good idea. At least then you might be able to summon up a smile on my return.'

She sighed and looked at the floor, feeling like a child who'd been rebuked for whingeing too long, knowing that she had, and wondering just what the hell she could have done instead.

'I'm just tired,' she said. Tired of being on alert, tired of playing cat and mouse with her emotions.

'Still tired?' he asked. 'Or maybe suffering PMT? If it's the latter, then the sooner we get you pregnant the better.'

She glared at him. 'And maybe I just don't like you. Ever consider that?'

He merely scowled and looked at his watch. 'I have to go. I'll see you later.'

'Apparently,' she said.

He paused, one hand on the door, looking over his shoulder at her. 'You wouldn't go doing anything stupid, would you?'

'Define "stupid",' she responded, crossing her arms.

He made a sound like a dull roar and abandoned the door, letting it swing closed as he swept her up in his arms. '*This* is stupid,' he growled, as his lips clamped down on hers. Shock held her rigid. Until his heat melted it clean away. Dark velvet heat filled her mouth, capturing her senses, liquefying her bones. She unwound her arms and clung to him desperately, knowing that if he let go she'd fall without that solid anchor of muscle and bone to hold her up. They exchanged lips and breath and tongues, all of it the taste of longing, the texture of desire. They exchanged the thumping pulse of blood everywhere their bodies touched, their blood dancing to the beat of the most primitive of drums.

And when finally he withdrew from the kiss, his breathing ragged, his eyes wild, it was like a punch to her gut.

'*Dios*,' he said, setting her upright, letting her go. 'I must be crazy,' he said, before turning to let himself out of the apartment.

The door closed with a hushed click. Beyond its thick sound-proofing the bing of the lift doors was but a shadow of a sound. But she heard it. Just as she was sure she heard the lift doors sliding shut. And just as she was sure she heard the ragged beat of his heart echoing hers all the way to his office somewhere below.

* * *

He must be going mad. Diablo fastened a tie around his thrumming throat and waved a passing hello to his PA as he headed for his office. She nodded a greeting and mouthed 'he's waiting inside' before returning to her typing.

He must be going mad. There could be no other explanation for the fact he wanted the very woman who was driving him crazy. She was driving him mad. She was like quicksilver, first rolling one way and then the other and just when he thought he had her she would roll away again, totally unable to be either controlled or contained.

But that kiss… If he hadn't had this meeting that kiss would never have stopped there. Dammit all—why did she have to make this so difficult?

The private investigator stood as Diablo entered. 'Paul—' he nodded, shaking hands briefly, while turning his mind to the present crisis '—has it been confirmed?'

The heavy-set man nodded, his square ex-cop jaw resolute. 'I'm sorry, Diablo. But your friend is up to his old tricks again. And we've got the evidence this time, plenty of it.'

'Damn! It wasn't just a one-off, then?'

'Not according to last night's pictures.'

'Show me.'

The investigator handed over the manila envelope, waiting in silence until his employer had had time to digest the first few pictures at least.

'And there's more.'

'Tell me,' said Diablo, sliding the photographs into a folder on his desk.

'He was heard saying he wouldn't stop until he'd got it all back—with interest. Starting tonight.'

With a crunch Diablo slammed his fist into the desk.

'He has to be stopped, once and for all.'

Paul nodded. 'Agreed.'

'And tonight. This has to end.'

'I'll take care of it,' said the investigator.

'No,' said Diablo, dismissing him. 'Fill me in on the details. I'll take care of this myself.'

CHAPTER TEN

THE apartment felt as welcoming as it was colourful. Briar wandered from room to room, checking out her new home, trying to get a handle on what it told her about Diablo. But it was odd. Where Diablo was hot, passionate and driven, this penthouse seemed cold and impersonal. Beautiful but bland. And, while Diablo had a regal kind of Spanish beauty, nobody would describe him as bland.

She strolled through the master suite upstairs, unsurprised to see that neutral had been the decorator's catchword even here. She glanced into the enormous *en suite* bathroom, hoping that at least here there would be something that might tell her about the man she'd married, but even his toiletries had been hidden away beneath the wide vanity that ran the entire length of one wall. She opened one cupboard door and, with a start, came face to face with her own belongings. He hadn't been joking when he'd said all her stuff had already been moved. He'd omitted to tell her they'd been moved by the neat police.

Two doors along she found Diablo's toiletries. Not a huge collection. But then he didn't look like a man who fussed and preened over his appearance. He didn't need to. One lonely bottle of aftershave. She popped the top and took a whiff. She recognised it. Diablo had worn it at the engagement party and at the wedding. But not since then. He seemed to prefer his own particular brand of testosterone for his signature scent.

She returned to the master suite and threw open the shuttered wardrobe doors. Just as Diablo had promised, her clothes occupied half the width of the wardrobes, all hanging more neatly than she'd ever seen them.

She shivered. It was odd. All her things were here and yet she felt like an intruder, as if she didn't belong. Suddenly it was all too much. It was all too forced. She slammed shut the doors and raced down the stairs.

Thank goodness he'd agreed to give her a key. She couldn't stay here, not in this house with no soul. He had to let her make changes—lots of them—if he expected her to live here.

On the way out she checked the refrigerator. Just as she'd suspected, it boasted little more than a tub of butter, a wedge of Camembert and a handful of beers. She picked up her bag and the key Diablo had left and let herself out. She'd soon fix that.

Her mother was home. Good. Briar snapped shut her mobile phone and stashed it in her bag, before steering her car from the underground car park into the flow of traffic.

It was good to be home, back in Sydney and at the wheel of her car. A vehicle behind tooted its horn, protesting her opportunistic change of lanes and for the first time that day she let herself smile. The busy Sydney streets felt alive and full of energy after the soundproofed neutrality of the penthouse. She didn't care that it was cool with a light drizzle starting up; she pressed a button, letting her window slide down, inviting the hum of the city to surround her. She breathed deeply. She felt alive again, almost back to normal.

Almost. She was still married to Diablo.

And what had she learned of her husband today? Only that he must spend more time in his office than the penthouse, more time eating out, more time living.

The penthouse was obviously little more than his dormitory, a glorified hotel room within easy reach of his desk. Just another of his long list of possessions. *Just like her.*

As she neared the house she still considered her home, the road wound through suburbs lined with small shops, outside which were parked every model of BMW and Mercedes imaginable. Tables covered with umbrellas or protected with blinds spilled on to the pavement and the smell of good coffee, toasted foccacia and wood-fired pizza drifted out to her. Her stomach rumbled. It had been hours since breakfast—what little breakfast she'd eaten. As soon as she arrived home she'd raid the pantry. Now the staff were back, she might even be able to wangle Mavis into making her a sandwich.

The rain came harder now and she closed her window against it. Minutes later, she pulled into the long semicircular driveway and saw her mother waving to her from the garden. 'Whatever are you doing?' asked Briar, getting out of the car as her mother pulled off her gloves to give her a hug. 'You'll get drenched.'

'Just some dead-heading and neatening up. I've got the bridge club here tomorrow and I want everything looking nice for them.' She looked at her daughter for a moment. 'Oh Briar, it's so lovely to see you. Come inside.'

'It's great to see you too,' Briar said, smiling as she waited for her mother to remove her wide-brimmed hat and boots. 'Surely Charlie should be doing the tidying up, though? That's what he's paid for.'

Her mother smoothed her silvery-blonde bob back behind her ears and shrugged. 'We had to let him go—at least on a daily basis. He'll still come every month to do the lawns for us. Now, come and sit down and we'll have a nice chat. I've got all the papers for you—there are some wonderful photographs—it was such a lovely wedding—my bridge girls haven't been able to stop talking about it.'

She took Briar's arm and led the way through the house.

'You let Charlie go?' Briar asked, stunned. 'But why? You're supposed to have the money for all the staff now. We'd only just managed to get him back.'

'I know, and I was disappointed, but your father thinks it's a good idea to keep economising after our close call. Seeing we were getting the hang of it. Cameron wants to invest what we'd otherwise spend so we build up a nest egg in case we need it. Don't you think that's wise?'

Briar raised her eyebrows. She guessed it was, though it didn't sound like her father at all. 'So long as you don't end up doing all the work yourself.'

'Don't worry, Cameron's assured me of that.' She entered the kitchen. 'Now, what can I get you? Coffee or tea? I'm just about to have a cup of tea myself. And have you had lunch?'

'Tea would be great, thanks. And I could certainly do with a sandwich. Is Mavis around?'

Her mother pressed her lips together and sighed. 'Not till dinner time. We've cut her hours, too.'

'So who gets the meals?' Briar asked as her mother filled the kettle and turned it on. 'Not you, surely? You hate cooking. You always have.'

Carolyn rested a hand on her daughter's arm. 'I know, but I can make toast and cut a sandwich and it just seemed an extravagance we could do without.'

'And the shopping? And the washing? And the cleaning? Mavis was more than just a cook. She was the housekeeper.'

'I've been getting groceries delivered!' her mother exclaimed with a brightness that seemed less than sincere. 'Do you realise how convenient that is?'

Briar opened a canister and spooned some tea into a pot as her mother put together a couple of sandwiches while they waited for the kettle to boil.

'I think I'd better have a word with Dad. It's one thing to economise, but I know how stressful it was before. Is he around?'

'No, he's out somewhere, I forget the details.'

Briar picked up on a frown her mother probably hadn't
realised she'd given. 'Is everything all right? With Dad, I mean?'

'I think so. He's just out such a lot lately. Trying to re-estab-
lish connections or network or some such. I don't know. Anyway,
I don't know if it will do you any good at all to talk to him. He
seems very determined to keep a tight rein on the money this
time. He talks about it constantly. Anyway, how about we head
for the conservatory where it's warm and bright and catch up with
all your news? You must have so much to tell!'

That was one way of putting it, thought Briar as she carried
a tray with the tea things through. But how much would her
mother really want to hear? And wherever would she start?

'So,' her mother said, 'how was the honeymoon? I must say,
I'm surprised to see you back quite so quickly. I had an idea
Diablo was planning on staying away longer.'

Briar raised her eyebrows. Clearly Diablo had filled her
parents in on their travel arrangements. She must have been the
only one kept in the dark. 'He had to return suddenly for business.
I'll write the phone number down for you.'

'Such a shame,' her mother said, sipping her tea. 'And did you
have a good time? You looked awfully pale at your wedding.
Everyone said so. So it's good to see you've got some colour in
your cheeks again.'

'Weddings are supposed to be stressful, aren't they? I was
bound to be pale.'

The older woman smiled and picked up a sandwich before
leaning back in her cane chair, where the fronds of patted palms
danced upon her shoulders. 'I seem to remember feeling that
way, yes. Still, it doesn't take long to settle into married life and
then you can't imagine not being married.'

'I don't know,' Briar confessed, studying the sandwich in her own hands as if it held all the answers. 'There's still so much I don't know about Diablo. I think it might take me some time to settle into this marriage, if I ever do.'

'Of course you will! And, if it helps, I didn't know your father very well when we married either. And here we are, thirty-five years later, still married.'

Briar looked up. 'I thought you two had known each other for years.'

'Well, we did, in passing. Our parents moved in the same circles of course, so we would often attend the same functions, but it was actually our fathers who thought we'd be a good match and brought us together.'

'What? You told me you met Dad at a party.'

'We did, but it was our fathers' doing.'

'They arranged your marriage?'

She laughed. 'Oh, that makes it sound so medieval. It wasn't like that at all. Although my parents thought it made sense, me being the only child and heir. Of course, they wanted me to marry well.'

'I don't believe it! And you went along with it?'

'I didn't even realise what was happening for a while—neither of us did. I just thought it was a coincidence that Cameron and I kept bumping into each other. I didn't realise that our fathers were pulling all the strings. And, I have to tell you, Cameron was a very good-looking young man. It was no hardship at all being with him. In no time at all they'd announced our engagement and that was that.'

That was that.

Briar could sympathise. She'd gone from single to married in what felt like sixty seconds. But her mother had never acted like a woman who'd been dragged kicking and screaming against her will into the marriage bed.

'But you love him,' she argued. 'You've always loved Dad.'

Her mother's eyes glistened with moisture. 'That grew. It wasn't love at first sight or anything. That took time. And I know it doesn't work for everyone, but having you and Nathaniel helped tremendously to bond us together.'

Her mother's eyes misted over and Briar reached out a hand to hers.

'Diablo wants us to have a baby. As soon as possible.'

She was rewarded with a wide smile. 'How wonderful! I'm so pleased.'

'Don't get too excited. I don't really know if I'm ready to have children yet.' *Let alone with Diablo.*

'Nonsense,' her mother retorted. 'You've always wanted to have children at some stage. And it's wise not to put it off for too long. Have them while you're young and energetic to run around after them, I think.' She sipped her tea and contemplated her daughter thoughtfully over the rim. 'Do you think Diablo will make a good father?'

Briar sighed. It wasn't something she'd wanted to think about, not given their circumstances, and yet it was a question she seemed to have more than enough material already to confuse her stance. 'I don't know. I mean, I'm not sure—it seems a huge step. We hardly know each other and it seems just silly to bring a baby into the equation when we've still so much to learn. But children seem to mean a lot to him and he is kinder than I ever thought possible—and generous. Did you have any idea he supports an entire school in Chile?'

'Well—' her mother leaned forward and replaced her now empty cup on her saucer '—it seems to me you're already softening your ideas towards Diablo. I know how rushed your wedding plans must have seemed, but do you see how quickly these feelings develop? I think you might already be falling for your new husband.'

Briar shook her head. 'Oh, no. I don't think so. I just think we were stuck together in the same house for a few days and I started to see his point of view on a few things. It's exactly the same as when hijackers take hostages who over time start to sympathise with their captors. That's all. We have nothing in common. Nothing.'

Her mother laughed. 'You should listen to yourself. You sound so melodramatic! You have nothing in common? So things aren't working out, say, in the bedroom department? If Diablo's thinking children, they'd want to be.'

The younger woman blinked at her mother, feeling herself flush. 'Um, that all…seems fine.'

Her mother sighed. 'Good. You know, when this marriage proposal scheme first came up, I was so worried for you. Diablo seemed, well, so mysterious and determined, and I know how these Mediterranean men can be quite…demanding, if you know what I mean.'

Briar cleared her throat. How did one tell one's mother that the sex with one's husband was mind-blowingly good? 'It's fine,' she repeated instead.

Her mother hardly seemed to notice. 'Mind you,' she continued, 'I felt a lot better when I saw the way he looks at you. It's quite clear he's besotted with you.'

It was Briar's turn to laugh. 'I don't think so. If there's one thing I know about Diablo, he doesn't do besotted. I suspect that when he looks at me he merely sees just one more possession in his ever-expanding portfolio.'

Her mother raised an eyebrow pointedly. 'You think so? Then, in that case, it's up to you to change that perception. Let him get to know you better, talk to him. You'll soon have him falling in love with you, just like you're beginning to fall in love with him.'

'You have to stop saying that! Don't you remember what he did to Dad? What he did to all of us? We were almost ruined and all because of him. How could anyone think I could ever love someone who was so ruthless?'

'He's a businessman—'

'That doesn't excuse what he did!'

'Maybe not, but he didn't have to help us get us back on our feet either.'

'Hardly out of the generosity of his heart.'

'Besides which, who we fall in love with isn't always within our control, however much we'd like to think it is.'

Briar had no comeback for that one but she still didn't believe it. Falling in love had never been on her agenda. Having Diablo's babies, likewise. If that suddenly changed, then how would she ever extricate herself from this mess of a marriage?

Falling in love with Diablo would ruin all her plans. How could she leave him if she loved him? And yet how could she stay when she knew she'd never be more than one more of his precious possessions?

'Look, if I was falling in love with Diablo,' she reasoned, immediately wondering why she was even bothering to pose the question, 'then wouldn't I know it? But all I feel lately is confused. I don't even know my own mind any more.'

Her mother picked up Briar's hands between her own. 'And what do you think falling in love feels like? It's like losing yourself, feeling alternately confused, excited, happy, never knowing whether to laugh or cry with happiness and frequently doing both. But you never really lose yourself. Sure, you abandon being a free agent, but what you gain from being in love is worth so much more.'

'But it's too soon! We've been married no time at all. It can't happen that quickly. Not when you don't even like the person!'

Her mother arched an eyebrow. 'But is that true? You really don't like Diablo?'

Of course! she wanted to shout. I don't like Diablo—I hate

him. But the words wouldn't come. Even though she wanted them to. Even though they had indeed been true once. She had detested the man, despised him, hated him with a passion.

But now the truth had changed. She didn't hate him at all—not really. She couldn't even say she disliked him. Hatred, dislike, had been replaced by another force. Her mind wandered back to his goodbye kiss at the door—that one soul-shattering kiss that had seemed to rip her soul from her and take it with him when he left. There was no way she could pretend she hated him after that. No. Loathing had been flushed out by another more potent force. She *wanted* him, plain and simple. And right now that was all she was prepared to admit to.

'It doesn't make sense,' Briar protested, disbelieving, the foundations of her life seeming to quake beneath her.

'We're talking about love,' her mother said, patting her on the hands. 'It's not supposed to make sense. Now, would you like some more tea? You look like you could use it.'

Briar let herself into the apartment, worried that Diablo would be angry she'd stayed out so late. She hadn't meant to, but by the time she'd finished talking to her mother and helped her dead-head the rest of the garden once the rain had eased, she was much later than she'd planned getting to the supermarket, which meant she'd hit the peak hour traffic on the way home. The fact most of it was going in the opposite direction was the only salvation.

But it had given her plenty of thinking time, which was what she'd needed—time to digest her mother's words and time to apply them to her own beleaguered thoughts.

When she'd gone into this marriage she'd expected she'd feel the same way about Diablo at the end of it as at the beginning. And yet, even after just a few days, her feelings towards her new husband were changing. And if she'd gone from out-and-out hatred to wanting him in that short space of time, what more could happen in a year or two?

'I'm home!' she called out, to nothing but the answering hum of a hungry refrigerator.

So he wasn't back yet. For once, a stroke of luck. She shrugged her overflowing bags of groceries down in the kitchen and dashed off to shower and get changed. Ten minutes later she was back, having changed her jeans and boots for a flirty layered skirt and fitted off-the-shoulder top. She'd pulled back the top section of her hair into a clip, leaving the rest to float around her shoulders. It was a style that made her feel feminine without impeding her in the kitchen.

She sorted the groceries, arranged the ingredients she'd need for dinner and set about organising a venue. The tombstone-filled dining room wouldn't do at all, but the tiny breakfast setting on one wall of the kitchen would be nicely intimate. She adorned it with a new chequered tablecloth, bold in blue and gold, set two new candle-holders with honey-coloured candles in the midst and set two places. She'd suspected his flatware would be expensive, white and unadorned and she'd been right, so she was glad she'd picked up napkins to complement the tablecloth and add more colour.

She stood back, surveying her work. It looked good. Cheerful. Inviting. Although it still lacked something...

With a spike of inspiration, she dashed up the stairs and found the bag of shells she'd tucked away in her case that morning. They were perfect. A perfect reminder of that day they'd really connected, a perfect reminder of how that day had ended. Maybe he might forgive her a little for her snippiness if he understood how much that day had meant to her?

She set them down between the candles and a raffia-covered bottle of Chianti she'd bought and uncorked in preparation, and set about preparing a simple dinner of spaghetti marinara with salad and garlic bread. Mussel soup and an Italian grocery shop-bought cassata would complete the meal. It wasn't a Spanish menu, but she knew he loved Italian food and, with any luck, she'd have it all ready by the time he came back.

Maybe tonight they could talk. Maybe she could explain to him how confused she'd been feeling. Maybe she'd have a chance to let him know that she'd like to become more than just a possession to him.

By eight o'clock she had everything ready, an inch away from simmering, a few moments away from serving. Breathing a sigh of relief, she checked her make-up, removed her apron and allowed herself half a glass of Chianti. After all, if she was going to tell Diablo half the things she expected to tonight, she could do with a dollop of intestinal fortitude along the way.

By nine o'clock she'd drained her glass and had resorted to reading a magazine she'd found in the living room.

By ten o'clock she'd exhausted the magazine and flipped through every cable channel going, still finding nothing to hold her interest—not when one question dominated her thoughts. Where was he? He'd told her he wouldn't be too late. Was this Diablo's idea of not late? Or did he simply not care?

Which gave way to the ugliest thought of them all. Maybe the important meeting he'd rushed back for was nothing to do with business after all? Maybe he'd needed time with a lover to atone for the time spent with his irrational wife?

And just because he'd never been photographed with the same woman twice didn't mean a man like Diablo wouldn't have a lover stashed away somewhere discreet. He'd obviously had plenty of lovers before her appearance on the scene—why should that change now, simply because he was married? He probably couldn't wait to rekindle old flames.

But then he'd kissed her when he'd left the apartment. Was he that cruel, to go straight from her arms to a lover's?

And how could she really blame him if he *had* sought sanctuary in another's arms?

No. She couldn't blame him. But that didn't stop her wanting to strangle whoever he was with!

At eleven, she flipped through the phone book, looking for Diablo's office number, annoyed she hadn't yet loaded his phone numbers into her mobile. No rush, she'd thought—when was she ever likely to want to call him? She dialled the number for his office and unsurprisingly received an after hours message. 'Leave your message after the beep,' the machine instructed. *Where are you?* she was tempted to ask. But he should be here long before he ever got such a message. And what would he make of a message like that? Would he think his distant wife had suddenly turned into a clinging vine?

She circled the kitchen, checking out a soup that was past its best and putting a lid on the tomato sauce she had already prepared, waiting for Diablo to walk through the door so she could add the seafood. The fresh pasta sat ready next to its pot, waiting for him to come so she could boil the water. Waiting. Everything pointlessly waiting. She checked the time once more and decided that, even if he came home now, he would have already eaten.

Almost midnight. Diablo clearly wasn't coming home this side of tomorrow. And the irony of the situation almost made her laugh out loud. That on the very day she'd started admitting to herself that she wanted her husband, and that she'd seriously started entertaining ideas that maybe she was falling in love with him, she'd already lost him. He didn't even care enough to come home so she could tell him!

She wanted to be angry. She wanted to rail against the sheer injustice of it all. She wanted to leave and find herself a bed in some anonymous hotel—somewhere where Diablo wouldn't find her.

But what was the point? If he didn't come home, he'd never

appreciate her token gesture. And, instead of anger, all she felt was a bone weariness that sapped her of all energy.

She took one last look around the kitchen before she snapped off the lights and headed upstairs to bed. She wasn't hungry anyway.

It had been a bitch of a night. Diablo let himself into the darkened apartment hours later than he'd intended, looking forward to nothing more than drinking a beer and going to bed. And if Briar had any sense, she was already tucked up, fast asleep. Given her mood lately, it was probably just as well. He wasn't in the mood for little Miss Snippy right now and, with what he had to tell her, it was better she had a full night's sleep first. He rolled his neck from side to side. *Dios*, he was tired.

Enough light filtered through the blinds that he could make his way to the refrigerator without turning on a light. Besides, the tempting smell of garlic coming from that direction was enough to lure him. Briar must have organised herself a pizza. With any luck there might be a piece or two left over. His stomach growled at the prospect.

He pulled open the fridge door and blinked at overflowing shelves of smallgoods and vegetables, a covered salad and what looked like a plate of uncooked seafood.

He stepped back, the light from the fridge illuminating more than the usual empty benchtops. With a frown he let the door go and snapped on the down lights, taking in the pans on the hot-plates and the pasta still in its bag nearby. But it was the table, set for an intimate dinner for two, that stopped him in his tracks.

'What the…?' He wandered over, looking at the table, the Chianti, a tablecloth he didn't recognise and candles. He picked up one of the shells, curling his fingers around it, weighing it lightly in his hands. Briar had cooked him dinner? He'd half thought she'd merely been being contrary. He sure hadn't expected this. But she'd obviously been expecting him.

He flipped the shell over in his hand, and then he flipped it again. He'd meant to call. And then he'd got caught up and suddenly it had been too late. Not that he'd thought she'd give a damn anyway. She hadn't seemed too thrilled to be with him at all today. *Yesterday*, he corrected himself.

He looked around the kitchen. Obviously she had given a damn if she'd gone to this much trouble. Who knew?

He climbed the stairs to the bedroom, surprised to find the light in the *en suite* bathroom still on. Had she left it on for him or had it been for her own benefit, her first night in a new home? The light spilled across her face and her hair that ribboned across the pillow. He frowned and looked closer. A shadow marred her pillow where there should be none. He looked closer, touching the pads of his fingertips lightly to the area. Moisture? Had she cried herself to sleep? Something inside him yawned open and, for the first time since his mother died, he felt himself wanting something he couldn't have.

If only he could get a handle on what it was.

He stood there for a long time, looking down at the sleeping form of his wife—his beautiful wife, his complex wife.

What was tonight's dinner meant to represent? A peace offering? Or merely the latest tactic in her hot and cold war?

He doubted she even knew herself.

One thing was for sure—after going to that much trouble she wasn't likely to be in a good mood when she woke up. Which made what he had to tell her even more difficult.

He unbuttoned his shirt as he made for the *en suite* bathroom. *Dios*, what a mess.

The unfamiliar sound of a telephone ringing wrenched her from her dreams. Strange dreams. Uncomfortable dreams. Dreams filled of loss and sadness and yet the sensation of heat and strong arms around her. But, just the same as she'd gone to sleep, she woke up alone.

Maybe not so alone, she suddenly realised, her scratchy eyes registering the indentation in the pillow beside her, her ears registering the play of water and muted hum of the exhaust fan from the *en suite* bathroom in between the ring tones.

What time had Diablo come back?

She blinked and made a stab for the phone, lifting it from its cradle. 'Hello?'

Through the sobs she recognised her mother's voice. 'Oh, Briar, I'm so glad it's you. We've had such dreadful news and I don't know what to do.'

CHAPTER ELEVEN

ADRENALINE powering her senses to red alert, Briar sat bolt upright in bed. 'What's wrong? What's happened?'

'Your father had a meeting with Diablo last night. He's cut us off totally. No more allowance. No more money. We've still got the house for now but I don't know how we're going to manage.'

'But why?' Briar asked, trying to form a picture of whatever had transpired last night. Diablo had met her father? Was that where he'd been all that time? With her father and not with a woman? Nothing made sense. 'I don't understand.'

'Neither do I. I thought we were managing so well. And I'm worried about your father—he only came home a few hours ago and he seems so agitated and, well, frankly I'm worried about him.'

'There has to be a mistake. Diablo can't do that. The agreement…'

'Cameron said the agreement was off.'

Air hissed through Briar's teeth. 'And did Dad say why?'

'Oh dear, Cameron was very upset. I don't think—'

'Tell me,' she insisted, her fingers tightening around the phone.

Her mother sobbed again. 'Cameron said Diablo didn't need him any more. That he'd got what he wanted.'

Her eyes turned in the direction of the *en suite* bathroom.

Bastard, she told him in a mental blast that should have melted a path clear through the walls. *You total bastard*!

'Do you think you can talk to him? Do you think you can do any good?'

Briar was already out of bed, scrabbling for clothes, determined to get dressed before Diablo emerged from the bathroom. 'He's not going to get away with this. Don't worry. I'll sort something out. I'll be right over, okay?'

Briar pulled on jeans and a sweater, each item donned to the accompaniment of a curse, all of them directed squarely at Diablo. She was just pulling her hair into a rough ponytail when the subject of her cursing appeared, one low-slung towel casually knotted at hip level, while he dried off his hair with another, his satiny skin still glistening from the steam.

He stopped in the open doorway, the hand rubbing his hair slowing to a halt. 'You're awake, then.'

She turned her head away, raising an eyebrow as she plonked herself down on the bed to pull on her boots. 'Your powers of observation astonish me.'

Out of her peripheral vision she saw him walk to the wardrobe, pulling open one door. 'So you are angry with me. I thought you might be.'

'Of course I'm bloody angry with you! What the hell did you expect?'

'I didn't realise it was so important.'

'You broke your word. You lied to me.'

He groaned and turned. 'Don't you think you're overreacting just a little? I was prepared to apologise, but now I see that would merely be pointless.'

'You think an apology would make up for what you've done? You've got some nerve.'

'Then what do you want?'

'To get the hell out of here.'

'You're leaving because I didn't call?'

'What the hell are you talking about?' she demanded, facing up to him.

'I had no idea you'd go to so much trouble.' He continued to look at her as if she were mad. 'Dinner. Candles. A table set for two.'

She waved his words away with a slash of her hand.

'I'm not talking about last night.'

His chest expanded on a deep breath. 'Then, to use your own eloquent words—what the hell *are* you talking about?'

'My mother just called. She told me you're reneging on the agreement. No more funds, no more cash.'

He dumped the towel he was holding on to the floor. 'Ah. Then you've heard.'

'Oh, yes, I've heard it all. I've heard how you gave my father the happy news, telling him the "gravy-train" was over now that you've got your polite society wife in the bag.'

His eyes glistened, suddenly merciless. 'Well, that's a blatant lie for a start. Nobody would ever make the mistake of calling you a polite society wife—least of all me.'

Briar squeezed her hands into fists. If that comment was supposed to support his defence, he was way off base. She pulled open the wardrobe door, yanking out the bag she'd unpacked just last night and slamming it down with a thump on the wide bed.

'So don't I at least get the chance to defend myself?'

'Sure.' She unzipped the bag and looked at him. 'Did you or did you not tell my father you were cutting off their funds—the funds you promised when you married me?'

His eyes narrowed, hardened, glistening like stone. 'I did.'

She flipped the bag open. 'Then that's all the confirmation I need. If your deal with him is off, then your deal with me is off, too. I no longer am required to be your wife. I guess we'll all breathe a sigh of relief about that.'

She made a move towards the wardrobe but he stepped in front of her, his legs planted wide, his arms crossed over that bare chest and with the towel lashed around his hips looking like an ancient Egyptian god painted on a wall—tall, proud and disapproving. Except this man was far from being some two dimensional painting. Even now she could feel the heat coming from him, the air crisp and crackling with electricity around him.

'You don't get out of being my wife that easily.'

'Maybe you should have thought of that,' she said, glaring up at him, 'before you pulled the pin on this agreement. You can hardly expect me to stay married to you after this. I can't believe that even you could be so callous, especially after everything my father was doing to make a new start. You probably don't have any idea how hard he's been working—trying to find ways of saving money—economising.'

The statue in front of her frowned. 'Economising—how?'

'I knew you wouldn't realise,' she said dismissively. 'Dad thought it a good idea to save some money. He figured they'd managed for so long without every convenience that they could get by with less household help. He was saving the rest for a nest egg. And now that you've pulled the pin, it's just as well he's set something aside to invest.'

Diablo snarled, his lip curling. 'Oh, he "invested" it, I have no doubt. What I do doubt is that there is any such "nest egg" to fall back on, given the type of investments your father prefers are generally the "double or nothing" variety.'

'What are you saying?'

'Just that if he's been running to form, he's probably already gambled it away.'

'You're insane! You don't know when to give up.'

She sidestepped around him and opened the wardrobe door, reaching in for the few items she'd unpacked only last night.

'And where do you think this meeting I had with your father took place last night? At the local church hall?'

'You tell me. You're the one making the accusations here.'

'At a very private, very select gaming club. In fact, the fourth I'd tracked him down to…'

She shrugged. She hadn't known her father ever went to such places, but what of it? 'He's over eighteen; it's hardly illegal. So what were you doing there?'

'Trying to stop him.'

That pulled her head around. 'From what?'

'From gambling all that was left of the money I had transferred to his account on our wedding day.'

'I don't believe you. You want to renege on the deal you made with my parents and now you're trying to find a way to pin it on my father.'

'Your father is a gambler. He promised me when we made this deal that he'd stay out of the gambling dens.'

'Why should I believe you?'

'Think about it. Why else do you think his interests made for such easy pickings? Because he'd already gambled away their cash flow.'

'Because you stole it out from under him!'

'No—because, no matter what his status, your father is not the world's sharpest businessman.' He cut off her protest before she could put voice to it. 'Competent, sure, but Cameron Davenport is no world-beater in the business stakes. He'd been losing money for years. It didn't matter for a long time—there was plenty to lose. But when it did start to matter, he found himself a way of replacing what he'd lost. Or that was the plan.'

'I don't know why I'm even listening to this.'

'Because it's the truth and you need to hear it! But, God knows I didn't want to be the one to tell you.'

'Don't give me that. You're enjoying this. You've always wanted what my father had—the place in society he occupied, his moneyed connections. And now you've got all that—and me—it's still not enough. You have to pull him down to rock bottom.'

'I didn't want this!'

'I don't believe you.' She zipped up the only half-filled bag and jerked it off the bed. 'This is exactly the way I expected you to behave, given your reputation. I don't know why I ever trusted you.'

'And just where do you think you're going with that bag?'

'Somewhere I should have gone last night. I'm going home. *My home.*'

'And what do you think that will achieve?'

'It will get me away from you, for a start. Besides, my parents need me now.'

'So you're going back to dear old Dad?'

'At least he loves me!'

His eyes narrowed, one dark eyebrow arched pointedly. 'Are you sure this has nothing to do with last night? A prepared meal—a table set for two? What were you hoping to achieve— some kind of declaration of love eternal?'

'From you? Hardly!' she exclaimed, and at least that much was the truth. 'I couldn't give a damn about last night!' She pulled up the handle on her bag and started for the door, the prick of tears stinging her eyes. 'It's about being there for people— people who love you. You wouldn't understand.'

'Oh, yeah,' he said, a cruel tilt sullying his perfect mouth, 'I understand perfectly. Like the daddy who loves his sweet daughter so much he gambled her away in a hand of blackjack.'

Her head snapped around and she took one final look at the man she'd been married to for little more than ten minutes and yet which felt emotionally like ten lifetimes. 'And that's your last desperate attempt to justify what you've done?' She shook her head slowly from side to side. Was there no end to the ways he could twist the truth to his own purposes? Did he forget she'd been there that night in her father's study when this deal had been put together?

And to think she'd felt stirrings of jealousy that he might

have been with another woman. To think that she'd even imagined she was starting to fall in love with him! She'd even been dreaming of having his babies! Thank God they'd never had that chance to talk last night. That she'd never revealed how she felt. How much more stupid would she feel today if she had?

Because she couldn't love him. There was no chance of that—especially not now. This empty ache she felt inside was merely a cold gaping slash of betrayal, growing ever larger when she realised how close she'd come to laying down her heart for him.

'I hate you,' she spat at him. 'I never realised how much until now. I never want to see you again.'

'And when you discover I'm telling the truth, what happens then? Don't expect to come crawling back.'

'Not a chance,' she said. *'On both counts.'*

'So you're leaving me.'

'What was I just saying about those powers of observation?'

'In spite of our contract?'

'I'd say that particular pile of trash doesn't count for much right now, wouldn't you?'

'And if you're pregnant?' he called out behind her.

She stopped, breathed in deep and twisted around. 'Look Diablo—'

'And don't tell me about how unlikely it is. There's still a chance.'

If only you knew, she thought, thanking the heavens there was no risk of that happening to further complicate matters.

'How about we just cross that bridge *if* we come to it?'

Normally the drive out of the city relaxed him—leaving the city behind, heading for the seclusion of the coast and the fresh sea air. Not today.

Today his stomach was tied in knots, his mind tangled with unfinished business.

And that annoyed the hell out of him.

Because she'd gone. The woman who'd driven him crazy with not knowing what she wanted had made her choice and walked out of his life. The fact it was the wrong choice was her problem. But, instead of feeling as if a weight had been lifted from his shoulders, he felt as if an anvil had been implanted inside his chest.

She'd walked out on him. And at the time he'd been happy to let her go. He didn't need the endless sparring. He wouldn't miss the aggravation. And, if she wanted to believe her father over him, then what could he do? Even when—*if*—she pressed Cameron for the truth, would he tell her? Or would he be satisfied to let Diablo take the rap for everything that had gone wrong—just like before?

How he could have looked Diablo in the face last night and deny he had a problem when he'd all but gambled his life down the toilet, he didn't know.

All he did know was that it had been pointless trying to work in the office. It had been worse in the apartment. The cleaner had been thorough, eradicating all trace of food from last night's aborted dinner attempt, but still the cloth remained on the table, the candles and shells gaily adorning the chequered fabric, the fridge full of food she'd never cook.

Briar had made him dinner. Just like a real wife. A thin smile forced its way to his lips. A *real* wife. How about that?

The smile dissolved as he accelerated through a bend. No doubt she'd be stuck with making meals for her parents now. Because with their funds exhausted, the cook would be certain to go, and the cleaner and all the other assorted household help. Briar would no doubt end up doing the lion's share, a poor little Cinderella. Only this Cinderella would have neither a fairy godmother nor the happy ending she'd been so keen to advocate.

So be it. Maybe then she'd believe what he'd been telling her. He steered the car on to the road leading to El Paradiso.

No happy ending. That was no surprise. He'd never expected one. It was just a waste that it had had to finish this way.

She found her mother in tears, slumped on a stool at the kitchen bench. 'Briar!' she cried, falling into her arms like a bag of bones. 'Your father locked himself in the study after he came home and he refuses to come out. I'm so worried about him.'

Oh, God, Briar prayed, *please don't let him do anything crazy.* She massaged her mother's back, trying to soothe her before she went in search of her father, while inwardly she churned with fear for all of them. How desperate must her father be feeling right now?

'I'll go to him. He'll talk to me. He has to.' And if he didn't she'd call someone—an ambulance, the police, even the fire brigade—anyone who could knock the door down.

Her mother looked up suddenly, her features pinched and her voice desperate. 'Did you talk to Diablo? What did he say?'

How could she tell her? A spike of anger lanced her fears. *Damn Diablo and his broken promises. Damn him for his callous accusations.*

'I've left him, Mum. I'm not going back.'

Her mother let her go, her red-rimmed eyes wide with shock. Then she cradled her daughter's face with her hands.

'Oh, Briar, no.'

She covered her mother's hands with her own and pulled them slowly away between her own. 'I had no choice. I couldn't stay with him, not after this.'

'But there must be some explanation, something we can do. You can't throw what you've got away.'

'No. I've decided. And right now I have more important things to worry about, like seeing if Dad's okay. Now, maybe you could knock up a couple of sandwiches? I bet Dad hasn't eaten for ages.'

Bare minutes later, she knocked on the study door. 'Dad, it's me.' She waited a few seconds, then tested the handle. Locked, just as her mother had told her.

'Dad, are you okay?'

'I don't want to see anyone.'

Relief flooded through her at his voice. She leaned her forehead against the timber. 'Please let me in. I need to talk to you.'

Seconds passed—long, silent seconds that seemed to stretch for ever, and then she heard it, the metallic click of the key grating in the lock.

She held her breath just a few seconds longer before trying the handle again. This time it turned and she let herself into the room. It was dark, the blinds drawn, no lights on and at first it was difficult to see anything. Her nostrils twitched. The air was heavy with the combined aroma of stale cigar smoke and malt whiskey, overlaid with a blanket of absolute despair. Even the ticking of the grandfather clock seemed oppressive. But it wasn't the room, she realised, it was her father's desperation colouring the air, as his body slumped into the chair behind his desk, his forehead resting on his hands.

'Dad,' she said, 'I've been so worried about you.'

He lifted his head and, even in the dimness, she could see the haggard lines that marred his features and the red-lipped rims pulling down from his eyes.

'Briar.' His voice came as a croak. 'What are we to do?'

She tried to smile. 'We'll work something out. We always do.'

He sighed and held out a hand to her. 'What would we all do without you?'

She circled the desk and took his hand, squeezing it, before kissing him on the cheek and sitting down at his feet, resting her arm on his knee just as she'd done when she was a little girl and had just wanted to be with him. 'I bet I could still get that job at the gallery if I wanted it.'

He touched her chin, lifting it around. 'You shouldn't have to do that.'

'I don't mind helping. We have to do something.'

'I don't deserve you. And you certainly deserve a better father than me.'

'Rubbish.'

He shook his head. 'You shouldn't be thinking about getting a job. You have your own future to think about. You have another life—a married life.'

She shook her head, praying it wouldn't shake loose the tears that were suddenly so close to falling.

'Not any more. I've left him.'

'My God. I've ruined everything.'

'No, you didn't ruin anything. Diablo did that when he reneged on the contract. I hate him for what he's done. And I hate myself more for ever trusting him. I should have seen this coming. Maybe I could have stopped him. Maybe I could have done something…'

'Briar—'

'…but at least things can get back to normal, even if we might be a bit broke. It's just so good to be home with you both. We'll manage. I know we will.'

'Briar,' her father said more strongly this time, 'you have to listen to me.'

She looked up at him. 'What is it?'

'You can't leave Diablo.'

'Of course I can. He reneged on the deal. He broke the contract. I'll make an appointment with our lawyers. They'll find some way out of this.'

'Diablo didn't break the terms of the contract.'

His words silenced her, fear gripping her heart as Diablo's accusations leached back into her mind. But Diablo had been lying—hadn't he? 'What do you mean?'

'*I* broke the contract. Diablo was only doing what he'd promised me he would. I was too stupid to believe he wouldn't.

And I was stupid enough to think I'd get away with it. I thought you were still up on the North Coast. I thought he'd never find out. One decent winning streak, I thought...'

'Oh, Dad. No...'

'And I was winning, for a while,' he whispered, his eyes staring blindly ahead in the gloomy study. 'Just one more bet, I told myself, just one more and really clean up and show Carolyn and you that I wasn't worthless, that I didn't have to rely on Diablo's handouts. But I lost. And then I had to have one more bet to get back what I'd lost. And then another. But I kept losing. And that's when Diablo found me.'

Her thoughts in turmoil, her emotions in tatters, Briar battled to make sense of her father's admission, the crippling realisation that Diablo had been right.

'Mum told me you'd cut back on home help to economise—but you were using the money for their wages to gamble, weren't you?'

Her father fixed his desperate gaze on to her. 'It's true. And do you know what the worst thing was? I was too stupid, even then, to admit that I had a problem.'

'Oh, Dad.' She squeezed his hand as the first tears squeezed from her eyes and she knew that the worst thing had been calling Diablo a liar. She'd told him she hated him because of it. Given that she loved him, *what did that make her?*

'I've been sitting here all morning,' her father continued, 'blaming Diablo for everything. I came in here to work out how I was going to get back at him, but the longer I thought about it, the more I realised it wasn't Diablo's fault at all. I'm the one to blame. I'm the one responsible. I've wagered away an entire fortune and a half and I was willing to let Diablo take the blame for everything.'

'It's not all your fault. If he hadn't pursued the takeover so ruthlessly...'

'He did what he had to do. He saw a weakness and he took

advantage. Of course I hung it all on him, badmouthing him to everyone who would listen. It was easier than admitting that I was a failure.'

'You're not a failure!'

'I've lost a fortune along with my own and my wife's sizeable inheritances. What should I call myself?' He set his bloodshot eyes on hers. 'I tried to tell you, on your wedding day. I wanted you to know it was all my fault, that I was sorry.'

She blinked, thinking back to that day, when her father had seemed the one who needed calming, the one who needed reassurance.

'You did try,' she said, nodding. 'I remember. But tell me, what happens now?'

'I'm going to get help this time. I promised Diablo weeks ago that I would and I never followed up on it. I should have. Today I'm going to do it.'

'Then I'll come with you,' she said.

'No,' he said firmly. 'Your place is with your husband.'

She turned her head away, not wanting to think about the mess she'd left behind this morning and the man at the centre of it. He'd said such horrible things—inexcusable things. Even if he'd had to reveal her father's gambling, he hadn't had to twist the knife by suggesting he could gamble his own daughter away. 'I don't think I have a husband any more.'

He tilted her face around until she was looking up at him. 'You should go to him. Don't let your marriage fall apart because of my weakness. I have enough on my conscience without that, too.'

'I want to stay with you—help you.'

'And don't think I don't appreciate it, child. But I'm the last person in the world who deserves your support.'

'That's not true! You're my father.'

'It's more than true. I know you were railroaded into this

marriage, but I knew Diablo would make you a good husband. I would never have let you go to someone I didn't respect.'

'I thought you hated him.'

'I did, for his skills and his business acumen and because he's one hundred times the businessman I am—in fact, all the very reasons I respect him.

'But then he proved himself beyond that. He knew you would hardly be overjoyed at your marriage, whatever the reason, so he let everyone think he was to blame for our circumstances, saving you and Carolyn from discovering my sad secret. And then he let you believe he had paid for you, to protect you from the ugliest secret of them all.'

She rose to her knees, her hands on his arm, imploring. 'What do you mean?'

'Our arrangement, for Diablo to marry you in return for money and this property, wasn't quite as it seemed.'

Chills radiated from her core to her extremities, like tiny icicles needling their way through her. 'No. You didn't. Please, God, tell me you didn't…'

He squeezed his eyes shut. 'Briar, I'm so sorry. You were the only thing I had left, the only thing worth something. Diablo told me to stop, that I'd lost enough, but still I didn't listen. He already had the house; he already had everything. But my luck had to change so I ignored him. I told him I still had you—winner takes all—and he told me I was a monster and that I was mad, but still I played. And lost. I gambled with my daughter and I lost and I'll never be able to forgive myself for it.'

'You wagered me away.'

She bit down on her lip, trying to staunch the tears, the tears that found an echo in her father's eyes. They tracked a ragged path down his stubble-covered cheeks as the clock chimes sounded out the hour.

He sniffed and wiped his face with a handkerchief. 'Diablo

came up with the plan to say he'd take you in settlement for the house. He didn't have to. He'd already won everything we had. I know he wanted a good marriage, but I suspect he felt sorry for me, and even more sorry for you.'

'I don't know what to say.'

'You don't have to say anything. It's me who has to make amends. The one good thing to come out of all this is that you married a good, strong man. He'll never make the mistakes I did. Can't you see? Your place is not with me, the man who gambled you away—your place is with Diablo. He's a good man. Go to him.'

Briar squeezed her father's hand. If only it were as simple as that. He'd asked her what she'd do when she found out he was telling the truth. He'd told her not to come crawling back. And her response came back in horrible wide screen detail. *'Not a chance,'* she'd asserted. *'On both counts.'*

And Diablo *had* been telling the truth.

And, if she wanted him back, she had no choice.

She was going to have to go crawling right back.

Just as soon as she worked out how...

CHAPTER TWELVE

BREATHING time. Briar needed breathing time to work out what she was going to do. An apology was the very least she owed him, but would he accept it from her, the way she'd stormed out on him? And beyond that... Beyond that was hope. If he would talk to her, maybe she could admit her mistakes, tell him how wrong she'd been. Tell him how she was willing to try again.

Tell him she loved him...

But until she worked out how, it was a good distraction to have her father's well-being to focus on, and making sure he carried out his commitment to change. Her mother took the news of her husband's addiction like a diagnosis that finally gave her a long-awaited answer. "It explains quite a lot," she said. "At least now we know what we're dealing with."

Then she'd located a counsellor they were all happy with and by the end of the day they'd all met and talked and mapped out a course of action. It wasn't going to be easy but with support her father could overcome his addiction.

It was late by the time they came home from the counsellor's and Briar could see her mother was exhausted. While half of her was desperate to see Diablo, the other half knew that her parents needed her more. Maybe by tomorrow, she told herself, Diablo would have had a chance to cool down and might be more receptive to her words. She could only hope.

So she fixed dinner for them all and spent the evening with them, sleeping that night in her old bed. It felt so strange to be back and yet it was barely a week before that she'd left to become a married woman. A married woman who now had an enormous problem. How to save her marriage when she'd been the one to so thoroughly assign it to the garbage bin.

She thought about calling, but what she had to say had to be said in person, so after a sleepless night she left early despite a foggy, aching head, determined to surprise Diablo before he left for work. But the apartment was empty and as cold as a grave, the dining room chairs chillingly taunting her in their two rigid lines. She rang his office only for his PA to tell her that Diablo was not available and wouldn't be for some time.

'Didn't I meet you at the wedding?' Briar cried desperately, recognising the PA's voice. 'Can't you tell me where he's gone? You have to tell me.'

The PA's tones softened and Briar felt pity coursing down the line; she was sorry, she said, but she couldn't reveal where he'd gone, least of all over the phone.

'I'll come down to his office,' Briar offered.

'I'm sorry,' answered the PA, before hanging up.

Briar flopped down in the kitchen at the tiny table where she'd planned to show Diablo that he hadn't made a mistake marrying her, feeling beaten, utterly defeated. Her hand drifted to the shells still lying there and she smiled as she remembered finding them. She picked one up and held it close, moving it, watching its pink lustre dance in the light.

They'd been happy for such a short time, just a few hours, but the memory of that one very special day made her heart swell. Those hours she'd been in Diablo's arms had been so magical, until she'd scared herself stupid with the realisation she might be falling in love with him. And then everything had gone pear-shaped. She'd sent them pear-shaped.

If only she had the chance to go back and make things better! She curled her hand around the shell as the random thought struck her.

Maybe…

On a hunch she raced to the phone and redialled Diablo's office. 'El Paradiso!' she cried, as soon as his PA answered. 'Is that where he's gone? Is that what you can't tell me?'

The PA hesitated. Then her voice softened. 'Please understand, I'm not telling you anything. But drive safely, Mrs Barrentes.'

Briar nervously pulled up at the security gates outside the house early in the afternoon and pressed the intercom button. Luisa answered, delighted to hear her voice, delighted to let her in.

She was under no misapprehension Diablo would share the same sentiments as she parked her car beside the entrance and with shaky knees made her way to the door. Halfway there it swung open and for a moment she smiled, expecting to see Luisa's broad face beaming a welcome. But it was someone much taller, much more daunting, who stared down at her now and shrank her smile right away, as the niggling headache that had been building behind her eyes all day turned suddenly blinding.

Diablo stood in the open doorway, looking every bit as dark and imposing as he had that first night at her house. How strange, she thought, that back then he'd been the one on the outside, the one seeking entry.

How the tables had turned.

'For someone who never wanted to see me again, you've driven a long way to do exactly the opposite.'

She swallowed, hard. 'I have to talk to you.'

'Why do you think I'd be interested in anything you have to say?'

She stole a breath, trying to unravel the speech she'd been rehearsing the entire journey from the roof of her mouth. But the speech was stuck fast there along with her tongue while blood pumped louder and angrier in her temples.

Diablo leaned into the doorway in his signature style, crossing his arms and legs. Even with his dark hair swinging loose around his face and dressed in a casual shirt and shorts the action carried with it an air of superiority. 'Well?'

The words of her planned speech dissolved in a feeling of overwhelming inferiority.

'I spoke to my father,' she blurted out instead. 'You were right—about everything. I'm sorry.'

A muscle twitched in his jaw.

'Is that it?'

'Diablo…' She took a step closer but he uncrossed his legs, suddenly growing taller and looking down at her so imperiously that she stopped. 'I know you must be disappointed with me. I'm sorry I didn't believe you, but how could I? It was just too horrible.'

'So you preferred to believe that it was me who could make up anything so horrible.'

She lifted both her hands. 'Of course I did. Why should that be such a surprise? You have to understand—'

'I understand! I knew what you thought about me when we married. I knew you weren't happy. But I thought that with time you might get to know me, and see that I am not such a monster as you believed. But you chose to paint me in the worst possible light every chance you got.'

'Then maybe if you'd been straight with me from the start things might have been different! But what was I supposed to believe when nobody told me the truth, treating me like some child who had to be protected from the truth? You cultivated my beliefs about you. You supported them. What hope did we have?'

'Obviously, none at all,' he said, flicking off her grievances like some annoying insect. He stared down at her, his eyes temporarily softening. 'It is my turn to apologise. I didn't think you needed to know all the sordid details of your father's deal.'

She gritted her teeth, hissing air between them before huffing it out. 'I know you were trying to protect us all from the truth, but I was bound to find out some time. And, when I did, how could I not feel bad about the whole deal? Don't you see that? What else was I supposed to think?'

He swiped a hand back through his hair, his eyes looking at a point somewhere over her head.

'I have no idea. Now, if that's all…?'

Panic seized her thoughts. He was trying to send her away?

'No, it's not all!' she protested. 'Dammit, but I will not be dismissed like some nameless messenger! I'm still your wife, after all.'

His eyebrows reacted to her words with a lazy hitch. 'A title you seemed to have major objections to only recently.'

She forced her shoulders back. 'I acted hastily. I don't deny it. But there were, you'll agree, extenuating circumstances. So I've decided I should give our marriage another go.'

His lip curled. *she'd decided.* She had some nerve. 'How do I know you won't change your mind again? You've been running hot and cold on me ever since our engagement.'

She looked up at him, her amber eyes marred with shadows. 'Because, in addition to learning the truth about my father and the dealings that brought us together, I've just discovered something that means I can't just walk away from this marriage.'

For just one instant his heart jumped in his chest—but just as quickly he damped down on the thought. There was no chance she was delivering the news he most wanted to hear from a wife.

'And that is?' he asked, already losing interest.

'I love you,' she blurted. 'I came to tell you that I love you.'

He laughed at his own folly. He'd been right in assuming it was nothing that really mattered.

'You love me?' he mocked, as she seemed to shrink before him. 'What is this? A last-ditch attempt to mount a rescue mission for your broke family—you're offering to sell yourself to me again? I warn you, the price would be nowhere near as generous as the first time around.'

'No! This has nothing to do with my family! This has to do with you and me. My parents don't even know I'm here. My father's getting himself sorted out. We spent yesterday finding him a counsellor and getting him some real help. He's determined to beat his addiction this time.'

'So you're not here for the money?'

'Why won't you listen to me? I'm here because I love you! God only knows it was the last thing I wanted to happen, but it did.'

'This from the woman who told me in no uncertain terms little more than a day ago that she hated me? And yet now who professes to love me?'

Her amber eyes flared and she crossed her arms over her chest. 'So I was angry.'

His eyes followed the movement, in spite of himself enjoying the swell of breasts outlined beneath her scoop-necked top and, even more, the sliver of stomach revealed as the hem hitched up. Last night he'd smelt her hair on his pillow, her scent on his sheets, and he'd ached long and hard, trying to get her out of his mind, without success. How much harder was it going to be tonight when he could imagine himself sliding his hand up that top and capturing those lush breasts? How much harder was *he* going to be?

'You get angry a lot,' he muttered, without returning his eyes to her face.

'So do you,' she rejoined, 'but I still love you in spite of it.'

Touché. He blinked, slowly, and slid his eyes back to her face. 'Nevertheless…a pointless endeavour.'

'Which means what exactly?'

'Which means I can't help you. I thought I'd already told you,

I believed we could make this marriage work but don't expect me to love you. Now I'm not even sure our marriage can work at all and so if you think you're going to put pressure on me to expect me to love you...'

She shook her head. *Too eagerly?* 'No,' she said, 'I can't change the way you feel, any more than I can change the way I do. But I'll take whatever you're offering—' She hesitated, looking suddenly unsure despite her earlier bravado. 'If you're still offering, that is.'

'Don't you remember?' he argued menacingly. 'You turned me down flat. You were the one who walked away.'

'I know.' She held out her hands to him. 'But I was wrong. Which is why I'm here now. Don't you understand what it took to come here?'

He let her stand there, waiting for his response. She'd walked out on him because she'd thought he'd lied to her, when in fact it was truth he'd actively hidden from the start. Could he really hold her accountable for walking out on him like she had, when he'd engineered the circumstances? Besides, he still burned for her. And she was right here, right now...

'So what exactly is it you want?'

'I want to be with you,' she whispered. 'I want to wake up with you every morning. I want to make love with you every night and every day. I want to be the mother of your children. I want the whole damn package.

'Don't you get it?' she implored when he didn't make any attempt to respond. 'It's not just about loving you—I *want* you. I don't want to live without you, and if you want me too, even if you don't love me, then that's enough for me.'

Something larger than a mere heart had to be pumping in his chest, the thumping like the boom of a drum beating louder, faster, rising to a crescendo, heralding a decision that ultimately he had no choice but to make.

He opened his arms to her and said simply, 'Come here.'

* * *

Briar collapsed into his arms, sobbing with relief, sobbing with happiness, and he kissed her tears away with the warmth of his lips, kissed her heartbreak away with one warm velvet mouth. She felt his tension radiating from his muscled flesh. She felt his need in the air they shared.

He lifted her into his arms and carried her through to the bedroom, undressing her slowly, reverentially, and shucking each garment away with a flick of his wrist while she scrabbled for his buttons and gave thanks to whatever force had shone over them and brought them back together.

And then, when they were both naked, he worshipped her body with his mouth, his hands and every part of him, travelling with her to that one blissful place that only they could share.

'Never leave me again,' he told her gruffly in the minutes afterwards while he stroked her hair as she lay nestled into him.

'I'm not planning on going anywhere,' she said.

'Now that would be a shame. I was about to suggest we might move this reconciliation to the shower.'

She smiled up at him. 'You have a real way with words, Mr Barrentes. Last one in is a rotten egg.'

He kissed her on her sassy mouth before she scooted out of the bed. He watched her go, enjoying the sway of her hips as she walked naked across the clothes littered floor, every lush curve of her, every movement a temptation to sin. *And he was just the man for the job.*

He was so glad she was back. He'd been mad to think he could ever live without her. He would never get enough of her. And he wanted more. So what was he still doing in bed? It was time to join her in the shower. And maybe time to give her the news that her father doing something active about his addiction was just what he'd been wanting to hear all along. It was good news and, if it were true, it was his intention to reintroduce funding, albeit with a few more controls in place from the start.

Briar washed her hands and splashed water on her face, catching sight of her reflection in the mirror. Were they really her eyes shining back at her? She looked so different already, just an hour after arriving, despite the persistent headache behind her eyes. But, even so, her skin was flushed, her eyes sparkling and her lips plump and pink.

She looked—*loved*. And why shouldn't she? She sure felt loved, whatever Diablo maintained about it not being on his agenda. Would she feel any better if he did profess to love her? Not likely.

She felt a familiar cramp down low, making more sense of the lingering headache, and placed a hand to her belly until the twinge eased. Soon she'd have her period and next month, when they made love, there'd be a chance she would give Diablo the baby he craved. Only this time it would be a baby both of them wanted.

Her fingers spread wide over her abdomen. Diablo's baby, growing inside her. How that prospect now seemed exciting where once she had been so fearful.

She reached down to the second drawer for a painkiller, only remembering that she'd cleared out her supplies when they'd left for the city. Had she brought any with her? She wrapped a towel around her, meeting Diablo on the way in. 'Leaving already?'

'I need my handbag,' she said. 'I think I left it in the car.'

'What's wrong?'

'Just some cramping. But I think I brought some pain relievers.'

He put his hands to her shoulders. 'Are you all right?'

'It's just my period coming. It's not serious.'

The moment she'd said the words she wanted to pull them right back. His mouth turned into a grim line. 'Your period.'

She touched his arm. 'Please don't be disappointed, Diablo. It's only the first month. It's no time at all. And it's not like we've been together every night. We have to have a better chance if we at least sleep together, right?'

He smiled. 'Of course, you're right. But be warned, next month I won't let you out of my sight.' He reached for his robe. 'I'll get it; you stay here.'

'I can do it,' she said, wishing she'd never said anything, but he was already gone.

She put a hand to her head as her headache kicked up a notch and a sick feeling fizzed dangerously in her gut.

The seconds turned into minutes but then he was back and handing over the bag along with a glass of water. Briar breathed a sigh of relief. So that was what had taken him so long.

'Th…thankyou,' she said, accepting the bag while moving a few steps away as nonchalantly as she could. 'Maybe you should get started in the shower?' she asked, wishing he would disappear.

'I can wait,' he said, his tone unreadable. She shivered as she unclipped the inner pocket and found her strip of pain relievers and was just removing them when that sick feeling in her stomach roiled again. *Because there was nothing else there.* She looked again. Not a thing. Yet there should have been the last couple of pills for this month and a brand-new strip besides—a strip she'd been intending to throw away. She frowned as she contemplated the painkillers in her hand.

'Something wrong?'

'No,' she said much too quickly while her mind did cartwheels trying to work out where she might have left them. At the apartment? At her parents' house?

'So you're not looking for these?'

She looked up, to see him brandishing the two damning strips, and felt her world slide away.

'I can explain…'

CHAPTER THIRTEEN

'DIABLO,' she pleaded, shaking her head as he waved the pills damningly in the air, 'it's not how it seems.'

'You're telling me you're not on the pill?'

'Yes! I mean no. I mean—'

'So you are on the pill.'

'Well, yes, but I was going off it—'

'Of course you were, which is why you have another packet, all ready to go. How many more do you have that you keep locked away somewhere else? Enough for six months? Twelve?'

'No, stop this. You have to listen to me.'

'Why the hell should I listen to you any longer? You've just promised me all kinds of love and devotion and life together, including professing a desire to be the mother of my children, and then I find you slipping a pill to ensure that never happens.'

'I wasn't! I wanted a painkiller for my headache—that's all. Nothing more than that.'

'You weren't going to take today's pill?'

She turned away and when she looked back she could see the executioner all ready to make the blow. 'I was just going to finish the course, that's all. Next month I wasn't going to take them. I'd already decided.'

He threw the strips rattling down on to the bed. 'No wonder

you didn't think you might be pregnant. No wonder you told me it was too early. All that time you were mocking me, because you knew there was no way you could be pregnant. It's *unlikely*, you said. *"It doesn't always happen"*. But you were laughing behind my back. You had no intention of having my children.'

'It wasn't like that. You don't have any idea how guilty I've felt.'

'You've felt *nothing*! Not if you could break our agreement so coldly like that.'

'What agreement?'

'You know damned well—the one you signed when you agreed to become my wife. The one where you agreed to have my children.'

'Maybe I did sign it,' she slammed right back at him. 'I had no other choice if I was to try to save my family. But I never agreed to have your children. Because you never damned well asked me!'

'It was part of the contract!'

'Don't you think it was enough to expect me to marry you? How could you pin children on me as well? You knew I hated you then. What the hell were you thinking?'

'I was thinking you were *au fait* with the basic requirements of signing a contract and living with the conditions you'd agreed to with your signature. Obviously not. You had your own idea of what this marriage entailed.'

'Okay, so I objected to your assumption I'd have your children, but how else could I fight what I'd been corralled into? What do you think your mother would have thought about your plan to simply "produce" children?'

'What's my mother got to do with this?'

'Your mother was a woman who obviously loved deeply. You were the product of that love. Don't you think she'd be disappointed if she knew you wanted to create a child under contract, rather than it being the natural progression of a loving relationship?"

Silence, as heavy and dank as a storm cloud met her words.

'You don't know the first thing about my mother.'

'From what you've told me, I know she was a woman in love, a woman who loved her child because he was the product of that loving relationship, rather than because of what opportunities it might afford her in business.'

'And what's that got to do with you?'

She breathed out on a long sigh. 'You never gave me a chance. And yet I'm the one who came back today saying I want to make this marriage work. I'm the one who has decided to have your children, despite your heavy-handedness, because I want to, not because you've told me to.'

'Which is why you're on the pill, no doubt, because you're so keen to have those very children.'

She threw her hands up in the air. 'I don't believe you, Diablo. You should just listen to yourself some time. Maybe staying on the pill isn't such a bad idea after all. I'm not sure the world is ready for any more Diablos. One is no doubt more than enough.'

His eyes glistened, as slick and cold as black ice, his features darkening. 'Don't bother changing your practices on my account. Because it won't matter one iota. I was wrong to ever think you'd make a suitable mother for my children. I was wrong to ever think this could work.'

'Diablo,' she pleaded, suddenly aware of how close she was to losing him. She couldn't let that happen. She couldn't lose him again. 'But of course it can work. It will work—you'll see.'

'What I see,' he said, brushing her aside, 'is that it would have been better if you'd never come out here today.'

She reached out to him, crushed when he moved away in response. 'But I love you. You can't send me away. What do I have to do to prove I love you and want your children?'

He regarded her for a moment—so damningly that she knew she'd been judged and found wanting before he delivered his sentence. 'All I wanted was a wife who would bear my children. I never asked for her love. I never asked for it and I certainly never wanted it.'

Any hope she'd harboured for their future was snuffed out in his cold, analytical dismissal. She drew back.

'Then damn you, Diablo, you won't have either. At least not from me.'

She dragged on her clothes.

'So you're leaving me, once again?'

'I thought you were throwing me out,' she said, pulling on her boots. 'But don't worry, this time I won't be back.'

'So go,' he called after her. 'I won't stop you.'

She hurled herself from the house and left in a crunch of gears and a screech of tyres, cursing herself for her stupidity, cursing herself for deciding to finish the month's course rather than throw the damned pills away. She punched the wheel as the tears began to fall. 'No,' she protested, swiping at her eyes, not wanting to cry now, not when she needed to drive. But the tears became a deluge, flooding her vision, so instead of taking the turn for the highway, she turned down towards the town, finally pulling to a stop in the car park near the beach where she'd once shared coffee with Diablo.

Like the last time she'd been here, the beach was nearly deserted, the weekend visitors gone home. A walker strolled along the water's edge while a family group halfway between her and the water—a mother with three young sons—built a sand-castle to the enthusiastic encouragement of their yapping puppy.

She swallowed down on some ragged breaths and moved from the car's interior to the strip of lawn overlooking the beach. The sea breeze played with her hair and she turned her face into it, letting it cool her heated skin. She jammed her hands in her back pockets as she watched the matching pair of snowy-haired toddlers give up on building the sandcastle and run up and down the beach with the puppy instead, whooping into the wind as they threw a stick for the dog to fetch, their mother calling for them not to wander too far.

Diablo would have liked boys. And they would have been beautiful. Small, dark-haired boys with flashing dark eyes and long limbs. And an attitude. She smiled in spite of her grief. Oh, yes, *definitely* an attitude.

As sandcastles built by small children went, it was impressive, she could see, with turrets made out of upturned buckets of sand and the beginnings of a decent moat. One of the twins had returned to help dig and had bobbed down too close to his brother, with ensuing howls of protest and flailing of arms. Someone ended up with sand in his eyes and the howls intensified while their mother battled unsuccessfully to settle things down.

Briar smiled sadly and turned her attention to the sea once more. A movement caught her eye; something—a stick—flying low through the air, landing in the foaming wash. She sat up higher as the puppy bounded into the receding wash, eager to retrieve the prize for its young owner, even as the back wash carried the stick further out. The boy stood at the water's edge, calling for the puppy to come back, his little voice carried away by the wind as the dog paddled on, disappearing behind a wave.

Surely he wouldn't?

Already she was up on her feet, an uneasy feeling crawling through her bones even while she tried to tell herself not to panic. The walker had long ago disappeared into the distance, leaving the beach all but deserted. She watched as the boy turned and took a step towards his family, where the action and the shouts had escalated, before he obviously decided there was no help coming from that quarter and took off into an outgoing wave to rescue his puppy.

'*No!*' Briar yelled, wrenching off her boots and taking off across the beach, wishing she'd done something earlier. She should have alerted the mother, called out a warning—*anything*.

The mother looked up, surprised to see someone hurtling past even as she held her two fighting children apart.

'Your boy!' Briar called as she surged towards the shore, catching the mother's startled cry.

But the waves beat her, knocking the boy off his feet and spilling him into the water. She heard the mother scream behind her, spurring her on. She could still see the boy, his limbs flailing—she mustn't lose sight—before another wave crashed over him and he disappeared into the foaming water.

She scanned the water frantically where he'd disappeared, but the water was already pulling back and there was no sign of him. How could he vanish so quickly?

She raced through the shallows and plunged into the water, the icy temperature shorting her system, stunning her momentarily while she battled to get her bearings. Something scraped her arm—the puppy, the stick in its mouth, returning to shore. It was little consolation. Where was the boy? Already she could feel the undertow sucking at her, wanting to pull her down, wanting to fill her lungs with the sandy wash.

She dived under the next wave. If she went with the current, if she didn't try to fight it, she'd have more of a chance. She surfaced again, scanning the water around her, before ducking under, spinning around where the tossing tide let her, searching for a flash of colour, anything that would tell her where he was.

The rip had her again when she thought she saw it—the faintest hint of something light in the sand-tossed depths. Could it be the boy?

Her lungs bursting, she hit the surface, striking out, going where the current would take whatever it was she'd seen before she dived again, searching frantically for another glimpse of anything to give her hope. And then her hand brushed against something slippery—skin—and she grabbed hold as best she could and burst through the surface, gasping, dragging the boy's limp body with her.

Two things hit her simultaneously. Already they were metres out from shore, but, more critically, the boy didn't appear to be breathing. Already the adrenaline rush of diving into the water was seeping away, leaving her suddenly exhausted, his slack weight a heavy burden on her shoulder. How would she make it back to the beach in time for him—if she could make it back to the beach at all? But right now she had no choice. She had to try.

She cradled him under his chin, keeping him tucked close to her, and struck out towards the side of the bay where she knew the undertow wouldn't fight her so much, the muscles in her arms burning, the weight of water in her jeans a cold weight dragging her down.

Something churned the water nearby and her blood froze. Not sharks, not now! She tugged the boy closer, stroked harder despite her burning muscles.

'Briar!'

Diablo! She didn't know what he was doing there, but never had she been so happy to see anyone.

'The boy,' she gasped, still desperately stroking with her free arm while she battled to keep her face above the roll of the sea. 'He's not breathing. I don't know if I can make it.'

'*Dios*! I'll take him,' he said, relieving her of her precious burden. 'Can you make it by yourself?'

She nodded, already peeling off her jeans underwater and letting their unhelpful weight sink into the depths. 'Go,' she said, spitting out a mouthful of salt water. 'Get him to shore. I'll follow.'

'I'll be back,' he called, but already he was surging away. It was a struggle after that, but no longer the desperately urgent race to get to shore. She took her time, not trying to fight against the current, to eke out her energy. When she heard the roar of an outboard engine and saw the rubber dinghy heading towards her she knew she was saved.

'The boy?' she gasped as Diablo and a lifeguard dragged her on board and wrapped towels around her. 'How is he?'

'He'll make it. The paramedics revived him. He's on his way to hospital now.'

'Oh, thank God,' she said, giving in to the cold as violent shivers racked her body.

'You could have been killed,' Diablo told her, pulling her close to his side as the dinghy made for shore. 'I told you this beach had a bad rip.'

'Maybe you should have told the boy that!' She shivered again and pressed herself closer to his body, seeking his warmth despite his seething anger. Why should he be so angry? She knew she'd taken a risk but what choice had she had? The boy wouldn't have stood a chance otherwise. What was his problem?

'You should have called for the lifeguards.'

'There was no time! He would have drowned in a heartbeat.'

'*You* could have drowned in a heartbeat,' he said. 'You're lucky you survived.'

'I'm sorry I did, given all you seem to want is to tell me off.'

They hit the beach before he could respond and it seemed as if a dozen welcoming hands were waiting to haul her from the boat, which suited her just fine as her knees buckled beneath her. They carried her to a second ambulance waiting to check her out. A cuff was slapped on her arm and questions fired at her from all directions while Diablo stood brooding, drying himself off nearby.

A policeman took the details once the paramedics had finished their assessment. 'You're a lucky woman,' he told her, 'but that young Norton boy and his family have even more reason to be grateful. You saved his life. I'm sure the mother will want to thank you personally in a day or so.'

'We're both lucky my husband was there,' she admitted, nodding in Diablo's direction. 'I don't think I could have managed to bring him in on my own.'

The policeman closed his notebook. 'I was surprised to see Mr Barrantes in the water. It must have been difficult for him.'

She shook her head. 'I don't know what you mean.'

'You didn't know? His mother drowned on this beach five years ago. Two teenage girls got themselves into difficulties and she tried to help them. All three of them were swept out to sea. The girls washed up within a few days. It was three weeks before his mother's body was recovered.'

Ohmigod! She was vaguely aware of the policeman still talking but all her attention was now fixed on Diablo, standing with his hands on his hips, looking out over the choppy sea. He'd told her she'd died in a senseless accident. Now she understood. She'd drowned trying to save someone else's life. No wonder he'd chewed her out.

The policeman touched her gently on the shoulder. 'You should get warm. Are you going to the hospital for observation or have you decided to go home?'

She looked at the solitary figure of Diablo standing nearby. 'Home,' she said, though wondering where exactly that was now.

She stood up, testing her land legs. Why had Diablo been here? Was it purely coincidence he'd turned up at the beach when he had or had he followed her here? The barest glimmer of hope sparked inside her.

She walked to his side, still clutching the blanket tightly around her. 'Diablo?'

His eyes turned down towards hers although Briar had the distinct impression that he was still focusing on the sea.

'Diablo, thank you for what you did. I couldn't have managed without you.'

His mouth pulled tight as her words registered. She had brought his mother's death back, in unholy graphic horror. But the twisting in his gut right now wasn't entirely to do with remembering what had happened back then. Something else was gnawing away at him, something else that had clamped a hold on his organs when he'd seen her running full pelt for the water and had driven him to follow her—the thought that he could lose her for ever when he'd only just recognised the truth himself.

He had to say something—anything—but this thing grabbing hold of his gut was squeezing down tight.

'I shouldn't have been so angry with you,' he managed at last. He tried to make it sound like an apology but his voice still came out gruff and disapproving. 'But what you did was still crazy.'

'I understand. And I'm sorry to do that to you. I only just heard how your mother died.' She touched his arm. 'But in that split second that child's life was the most important thing in the world. I'd watched him playing with his puppy. I'd seen how close he was to the water's edge and I'd done nothing. I could have alerted his mother, I could have done something. *I should have done something.* So, when I couldn't get to him fast enough, when I saw him sucked under those waves, I knew that if something happened to him I could never live with myself. But you saved us. You rescued both of us.'

He shook his head. '*You* saved the boy. I didn't even know there was a child in the water until I reached you. I thought...'

He raised a hand to his forehead. Oh, God, what he'd thought when he'd found her empty car and seen her plunging fully clothed into the waves! *Dios.* He hadn't stopped to think. He hadn't even registered that the woman screaming on the shore for help had been screaming for her own child. He'd thrown her his phone and told her to call emergency and he'd kicked off his shoes and dived in after Briar.

'You didn't realise there was a child?'

'No. I came after you.'

She must have sensed something in his voice; her lips were slightly parted, her amber eyes swirling with questions.

'Why were you at the beach?' she asked. 'How did you find me?'

'I watched you from the house. As soon as you'd cleared the gates I knew I'd made the biggest mistake of my life. I hadn't listened to you. I'd never given you a chance. I knew without a shadow of a doubt that this time you wouldn't come back—and I had to get you back. When I saw your car take the road into the town I knew I had a chance to catch you.'

Her lips turned into a tremulous smile. 'You came after me.'

He reached down and took her hands in his. 'I couldn't believe I'd been stupid enough to let you go again. So when I saw you diving into that surf I knew I had to find you so I could tell you…'

'Tell me what?' she whispered.

He sighed. 'This isn't easy for me to say, but when I watched you drive away back then it felt like my heart ripped in two.'

Her eyes shone up at him, bright and uncertain.

'I love you, Briar. I had to follow you and let you know. There was no way I was not going to find you in that water. There was no way I was going to lose you again.'

'You love me?' she questioned. 'You always said—'

'I know what I said. I was wrong.'

'I don't believe it,' she cried, tears filling her eyes. 'You love me. You really love me. And you're never going to lose me.'

'I thought I already had,' he told her. 'When I took you so savagely on our wedding night and you cried and ran from the bed. Already I feared I'd lost you.'

His words revealed another side of him she'd never suspected. 'But I wasn't crying because of what you'd—we'd—done. Don't you know, I was crying because you'd broken through my defences so completely? I wanted you, even when I told myself I shouldn't.'

'I didn't hurt you?'

'I loved what you did to me, the way you moved, the way you made me feel when you made love to me. I'd never felt so alive and that's what scared me so much. That's why I cried.' She raised a hand to his face, her eyes widening. 'So is that why you didn't want to make love to me after that?'

He clasped her hand, brought it to his mouth and kissed it. 'Oh, I did. Believe me. But I knew I'd been so rough with you—too rough. I wanted you to have time to recover and to find you did want to make love with me. But I couldn't believe it when you took so long.'

She laughed, remembering. 'You certainly didn't make it easy for me.' Her smile widened. 'I love you so much, Diablo.'

'And I love you.' His lips dipped lower, sweeping over hers in the gentlest of passes that promised so much more. 'But tell me—there's something I must know.'

Her eyes moved from his lips to his eyes, a tiny frown creasing her brow. 'What's that?'

'It occurs to me that in our arrangements before I omitted to ask you something important.' He suddenly dropped to one knee before her. 'Briar, will you marry me?'

She beamed down at him, salt water once again filling her eyes, only this time it was tears. 'Oh, Diablo, I'd say yes in a heartbeat. You know that. But I can't, I'm already married.'

He looked up at her amber eyes and her lush mouth, already mentally preparing for his next assault on that and all points south just as soon as he got her home.

'Then do you promise to stay married, forgoing all others, and to share your husband's home and his future and his love, for ever and ever?'

She cocked her head suspiciously. 'I'm assuming there's no obeying involved in this arrangement?'

He gave a low chuckle that hummed right through her. 'Mr Barrentes wouldn't be so foolish as to ask.'

'In that case,' she told him, pulling him up and wrapping her arms around his neck, 'I do.'

And then Diablo kissed his bride.

EPILOGUE

Twelve months later

THEY arrived two weeks early in a flurry of excitement—two dark-haired babies, one brandishing the flashing dark eyes of his father, the other with the misty blue that would make way to a lighter colour over time.

Now, barely twenty-four hours later in their private hospital suite, Diablo watched as they lay supported on pillows, suckling at their mother's breasts.

'Dios,' he said, cupping each baby's soft downy head in the palm of his hand, 'I have never seen anything more beautiful. You have made me the happiest man in the world.'

Briar beamed up at him. 'Aren't they both perfect?'

'It is no wonder,' he said, pressing his lips to her forehead, 'when they have such a perfect mother. You were magnificent during the birth. I wanted to at once weep with joy and yet cry at the pain you were going through. I have never before felt so helpless.'

'Thank you,' she said, 'for just being there and squeezing my hand.'

Diablo helped her ease the sleepy babies into a burp and then into their cribs beside the bed.

'And now all we need for them are the perfect names,' she

said. 'Have you thought any more about naming them after your parents?'

'Cosmo and Camilla?' He smiled. 'I like it very much. Our boy should be Cosmo Nathaniel, don't you think?'

'Oh, Diablo,' she said over the lump in her throat, one hand over her mouth while the other reached for her husband's. 'To name him after my brother, it would mean so much to my parents—to all of us.'

He nodded. 'I know. And if it was, as the counsellors believe, your brother's death that drove your father to the desperation that led to his gambling, then maybe this child can help keep him well. Cosmo Nathaniel Barrentes it is. And, as for Camilla...' He reached over and touched the pads of his fingers to the soft newborn down of her temples. 'Her name should be Amber. Amber Camilla.' He turned to his wife. 'Do you like it?'

'I do. But I don't understand. Why Amber?'

He moved his hand from his child's temple to his wife's. 'The answer is here, in the colour of your eyes. I love how the colour changes and throws sparks when you are angry, or shines like gold when you are happy, like you are now, or turns molten when we make love. I want to name our child after your beautiful eyes—the eyes of the woman I love.'

He tipped up her chin with his fingers. 'And I *do* love you, Briar, with all my heart and soul.'

And the man she loved kissed her so tenderly, so sweetly, that she could feel his love reaching out, enveloping her in its thick, warm folds, and she smiled to herself as he deepened the kiss. Her husband might never have believed in fairy tales, but she knew their happy ever after was only just beginning.

millsandboon.co.uk Community

Join Us!

The Community is the perfect place to meet and chat to kindred spirits who love books and reading as much as you do, but it's also the place to:

- **Get the inside scoop from authors about their latest books**
- **Learn how to write a romance book with advice from our editors**
- **Help us to continue publishing the best in women's fiction**
- **Share your thoughts on the books we publish**
- **Befriend other users**

Forums: Interact with each other as well as authors, editors and a whole host of other users worldwide.

Blogs: Every registered community member has their own blog to tell the world what they're up to and what's on their mind.

Book Challenge: We're aiming to read 5,000 books and have joined forces with The Reading Agency in our inaugural Book Challenge.

Profile Page: Showcase yourself and keep a record of your recent community activity.

Social Networking: We've added buttons at the end of every post to share via digg, Facebook, Google, Yahoo, technorati and de.licio.us.

www.millsandboon.co.uk